THE CHOSEN
AND THE DAMNED

In a Northwestern city . . . a man leaps to his death, saving his last breath to warn a stranger of evil things.

In a small public park . . . a priest pours gasoline on himself, then lights a flame to save his own soul.

In the town of Oldenburg . . . the sprawling house called Gestern Hall stands silent and alone. Waiting for those to feed its nameless hunger. And watching with . . .

Golden Eyes

A novel of vampiric passion and terror by

JOHN GIDEON

Author of *Greely's Cove*

Also by John Gideon

GREELY'S COVE

GOLDEN EYES

JOHN GIDEON

BERKLEY BOOKS, NEW YORK

If you purchased this book without a cover, you should be aware that this book is stolen property. It was reported as "unsold and destroyed" to the publisher, and neither the author nor the publisher has received any payment for this "stripped book."

GOLDEN EYES

A Berkley Book / published by arrangement with
the author

PRINTING HISTORY
Berkley edition / December 1994

All rights reserved.
Copyright © 1994 by John Gideon.
This book may not be reproduced in whole or in part,
by mimeograph or any other means, without permission.
For information address: The Berkley Publishing Group,
200 Madison Avenue, New York, New York 10016.

ISBN: 0-425-14287-6

BERKLEY®
Berkley Books are published by The Berkley Publishing Group,
200 Madison Avenue, New York, New York 10016.
BERKLEY and the "B" design
are trademarks belonging to Berkley Publishing Corporation.

PRINTED IN THE UNITED STATES OF AMERICA

10 9 8 7 6 5 4 3 2 1

INTRODUCTION

~

Poverty Ike's Halloween Tale

Poverty Ike and his riverfront saloon were more than fixtures in the little town of Oldenburg, Oregon—they were institutions. Like the mighty Columbia River that lazed past the town's doorstep, they seemed ageless.

For many years the townspeople observed a tradition that seemed older than anyone in Oldenburg except Poverty Ike himself. Just after sundown on Halloween, they brought their young children to the saloon to hear him tell a story, an honest-to-goodness spook tale guaranteed to put the kids in the mood for trick-or-treating. The stories came right out of local history, Poverty Ike claimed.

The adults listened as raptly to the tales as their children did, maybe because something about them rang true, although none admitted to believing them. Or maybe they listened because the stories belonged exclusively to Oldenburg, as Poverty Ike did, a fact that made them feel somehow privileged.

To get ready for the event, Poverty Ike always gave the saloon a good cleaning. He threw out the barflies and hung a blanket over the oil painting of a nude woman behind the bar. He set out garish little Halloween decorations on the tables, cardboard goblins and witches that he bought at the five-and-dime in nearby Astoria, and strung orange-and-black crepe-paper streamers across the high ceiling. Finally he placed a barrel of floating apples in the center of the barroom, so the kids could bob for them before going trick-or-treating—a holdover from the old days before people became obsessed with communicable germs.

Poverty Ike told his tales in a way he'd apparently learned from his father, or maybe from his grandfather (no one knew just where he'd learned it), using language that didn't fit the image of a crusty old barkeep. During the short time the telling took, he actually sounded like a man of learning, as if he'd studied at Harvard or Cornell or some highfalutin' university in Europe. He told the tales with feeling, with passion, with dramatic gestures and inflections that wove a spell thick enough to put in a bottle. He told them so well that people returned with their children every Halloween, year after year, decade after decade.

On Halloween of 1966, however, he told a tale that some townspeople found disturbing, if not outright offensive. Others complained (though not to Poverty Ike's face) that it contained stuff not suitable for kids. Still others felt that it was incomplete, that it didn't wind up with a satisfying climax in which good wins over evil.

When he caught wind of the grumbling sometime later, Poverty Ike merely smiled in his quiet, wrinkled way. "That's how it can be with history," he said. "History sometimes isn't all that satisfying."

Halloween of '66 turned out to be the last time he held his annual event. The following year a few townspeople straggled into the bar as usual with their kids in tow, only to hear the old man say that he'd retired from the storytelling business. The people of Oldenburg, he declared, had lost their taste for his kind of tale. The town had changed, as little towns do, having suffered the closing of nearby sawmills and canneries, having watched so many of its people move away to Portland and other big cities. His kind of stories belonged to the past, he said, to an age when people still had time for childishness.

Nobody ever succeeded in persuading Poverty Ike to resume his storytelling. Other old-timers retold the tale of '66 now and then, but mostly they just talked about the way it had entertained some and offended others. No one could tell it the way Poverty Ike had told it, no matter how hard they tried.

The tale started like this.

PART I

That which we call the world is the result of a
host of errors and fantasies. . . .

—Friedrich Wilhelm Nietzsche

PART 1

1

Mark Lansen

It's September 15, in the year 1846, and the town of Oldenburg hasn't even been born yet.

Queen Molly rises from her fireside and pokes her gray head around the deerskin curtain in the doorway of her lodge. Someone's coming, she feels—not yet near enough to be heard, smelled, or seen; but someone's coming, just the same. Cathlamet Village is quiet but for a stray cough or snore. The neighboring lodges are dark but for slivers of firelight gleaming through cracks in the cedar planks.

She glances up at the stars through rips in the clouds. Dominating all others is the one the ancients called the Blood Star, a piercing red disk that has grown ever brighter over the past seven nights. The seers among the Fish People believe that changes in the Blood Star warn of war, plagues, hard winters, and all other kinds of evil.

Queen Molly's heart grows cold, like her hands.

She backs away from the doorway, and the deerskin curtain moves aside suddenly, startling her, but when she sees her visitor's face, she sighs with relief. Elspeth Carey hovers on the threshold, waiting for an invitation, which Queen Molly gives with a wave of a crooked hand. . . .

—from Poverty Ike's Tale
Halloween of '66

i

Later, with his sanity in tatters, Professor Mark Lansen would look back and tell himself that the horror started on the final day of the spring term, on Friday, June 3, 1988. In reality it started long before that, and he knew it. But a man needs to draw the line somewhere, to find beginnings and endings, to separate the knowable from the unthinkable. So Mark Lansen drew the line, and it served his purpose.

ii

While passing out the graded term papers on that day, he joked lightheartedly with the students, most of whom were graduating seniors. His willingness to cut up in class was one reason he was among the most popular teachers at Portland State University, despite the legendary toughness of his courses in medieval history.

"I'm sure you're all anxious to get started on your summer reading," he quipped, "so I've asked the bookstore to lay in a supply of Lynn White's *Medieval Technology and Social Change.* Buy two and get a ten percent discount. Offer good while supply lasts."

The students really got a charge out of that one.

He kept them only long enough to pass out the papers and wish them a good summer. A few bona fide history majors hung back to say good-bye and thank him for his relentless pounding of knowledge into their skulls, which always made Mark Lansen feel good.

While en route to his office in Cramer Hall, he ran into his department head, Liz Schatzmann, a graying whippet of a woman with lively black eyes and thick horn-rims. Her friends and fellow faculty members called her Skeezix.

"A word, Dr. Lansen? I know you're anxious to get out of here, but—"

"Forget it, Skeezix. I'm *not* teaching any summer classes. I don't care who's bailed out on you at the last minute. My contract says I'm exempt from summer work every fourth year, and this is a fourth year. You're looking at a liberated serf!"

"Lighten up, will you? I filled the summer teaching slots back in February. I'm just after some small assurance that you won't fritter away the whole vacation, that's all."

Skeezix, God love her, believed that Mark was capable of world-class scholarship. Several years earlier he'd penned a monograph on French urbanization during the Hundred Years' War, and the American Historical Association had hailed it as a sure precursor to an important book-length work. Since then

Skeezix had hounded him mercilessly to write that book. She'd even offered to arrange a sabbatical so he could travel to Europe in order to examine primary sources.

Now he assured her that he would spend the entire summer writing his ass off. In fact, he planned to hole up in his parents' house in Oldenburg, where nothing could distract him—just Mark and the computer. Oldenburg was the village he'd grown up in, scarcely an hour's drive west of Portland on the banks of the mighty Columbia.

"Not good enough, Lansen," said Skeezix. "I need to know what I can expect from you next fall. And I want more than vague promises this time. You have what it takes to be a star in this business, but, Christ, you're no spring chicken anymore. You need to start writing and publishing, or you'll be a JAT all your life." JAT stood for *Just a Teacher*. Skeezix loved to contrive acronyms and abbreviations.

"Skeezix, I'm barely out of rubber pants," Mark protested. He was thirty-four. "I *like* being a JAT. You'll never convince me it's any worse than being a JAB." This stood for *Just a Bureaucrat*, which is what department heads were, he often kidded her.

Skeezix wasn't about to let him off the hook. She demanded a detailed outline of a book and a supporting bibliographical essay by the start of the fall term. "If it's up to snuff, I'll use it to pitch a grant proposal to AHA and the Council for the Humanities," she declared. "We'll get you some cash, a ticket to Paris, and some time to write. Sounds pretty good, doesn't it?"

Mark grimaced and muttered something about no promises set in concrete. "Tell you what, though: Come fall, I'll drop a manuscript on your desk that'll knock your socks off. It'll bring tears to your eyes, it'll be so good."

"I'm holding you to it. If I don't get tears, you're DM. Tell your wife and brat hi for me, and have a great summer." DM stood for *Dead Meat*.

iii

Mark had not been totally truthful with Dr. Schatzmann. Though he did intend to spend the summer writing in the quiet little town of his boyhood, the book on medieval urbanization figured nowhere in his plans.

What he really meant to do was write a short history of Oldenburg. He'd planned for years to take on this task, but had only recently decided to put it off no longer.

Mark Lansen thought of his hometown as a graveyard of dreams—dreams that pioneer families planted in the soil, dug from the ground, or built with rough-hewn logs. He felt a historian's need to write about those dreams, to tell the world why most of them had failed. In so doing, he hoped to contribute in some small way to society's understanding of the American frontier, and maybe even achieve some understanding of it himself.

He'd assembled the reams of notes he'd made over the years, stuffed them into cardboard boxes, and called his mother to tell her he would need his old room for the summer. Oh, and by the way, could he bring Thaddeus? Tad, his son, was nine going on thirty, a devotee of heavy metal, Rollerblades, and mountain bikes. No problem, his mom had said. Mark explained not very convincingly that Deidre, his wife, could not tear herself away from her lucrative architectural practice at the height of the building season, so she would spend the summer here in Portland, not Oldenburg. She would visit on most weekends, of course. Mark's mother had answered this with a polite *I see.*

The idea of writing about Oldenburg excited him far more than the gargantuan challenge of turning out a major tome on organization in medieval France. Though Oregon history was not his official field, having grown up in Oldenburg gave him an intimate perspective that would serve the project well. The regional press with its parochial interests was bound to love such a book, and teachers of Oregon history would surely assign it to their classes in colleges and universities throughout the state. Mark relished the notion that he might actually earn some decent money on his own. No reason why Deidre should be the only tycoon in the family.

Skeezix, of course, would be furious with him for diverting his precious creative energy from medieval urbanization. But ultimately she would forgive him, he hoped, especially if he convinced her that this small book was merely a tune-up for the big one.

iv

Lugging three briefcases bulging with things he'd told himself he would need over the summer, he locked his cluttered office and left it, hoping not to darken its welcome mat again until fall. As the glass doors in the main entrance of Cramer Hall closed behind him, he tasted that peculiar joy known mainly to teachers and students, the exhilaration of stepping over the finish line of another academic year. Summer lay before him like a promised land, a place where no nerve-jangling buzzers chopped your day into fifty-minute segments, where no academic deans lurked to ambush you and blackmail you into chairing this or that committee.

The common area between Cramer Hall and the Smith Memorial Center swarmed with activity. Students bustled around with knapsacks on their backs and suitcases in their hands, most headed home for well-deserved vacations. Others weaved through the throng on bicycles, and still others sat in knots on the wooden benches in the shade of the skybridge that connected the two buildings.

Mark headed across campus toward the West Hall parking garage. The afternoon sun warmed his shoulders like a mild liniment, making him wish he'd not worn his tweed sport coat. He stopped a moment for one last glance at Cramer Hall, which had long vertical windows in its blond facade that made it look vaguely bunkerlike.

"Good-bye, Yellow Brick Sweatshop," he said almost aloud, grinning. *"You won't have Mark Lansen to kick around for the next three months."*

His eyes landed on a solitary figure standing next to a brick planter at the front corner of the building—a woman, tattered and bedraggled, obviously a street person. Mark blinked, shook his head, and told himself that she was not staring at him. Then he felt the feather touch of her gaze, her eyes met his, and he shuddered. He felt himself go weak.

She seemed old, ninety at least, maybe even older. Dressed in a toilworn overcoat of gray wool and laden with baskets and bags, she was a creature from a child's nightmare. Her hair was wild and hoary where it poked out from a furry winter hat. Her face was the color of neglected wood, scored with years of suffering. On her feet were oversized logging boots worn white, out of which sprouted her twiggy legs. Slung by a strap from one shoulder and partially covered by a threadbare shawl was an antique spinning wheel, which by itself should have been too heavy for a woman of her age. Yet she stood strong and still under her load, hunched but not broken, staring at Mark Lansen like a hungry, old she-wolf.

He saw something familiar in her face, some feature so obfuscated by age that he couldn't identify it. He *knew* her. She was a stranger, but he knew her. And she knew him, he felt.

He forced himself to turn and walk in the direction he'd been heading. Oddly, the day no longer seemed so warm, or the sun so bright. The afterimage of the hag hung in his mind like a threatening cloud.

He halted beside the fountain on the main campus thoroughfare to collect himself, setting down his heavy briefcases. He stared a moment at the bronze Rubenesque nude that reclined amid anemic jets of water in the center of the fountain. Pigeons waddled and muttered on all sides, and the traffic noise of Portland seemed to fade.

Street people weren't exactly unknown on this campus. Located on the southern fringe of Portland's downtown business district, PSU was an urban institution. Occasionally some of the city's estimated five thousand homeless made their way south from the Burnside Bridge area to panhandle among the students at PSU, or merely to rest in the shade of the spreading elms and oaks that grew along the campus thoroughfares. If they became troublesome, the campus police rousted them.

Like most mainstream citizens, Mark Lansen usually ignored street people. They made him feel strangely guilty, as if he did wrong by passing them by and carrying on with his own mundane life. He consciously avoided making eye contact with them, thus ensuring no exchange of emotion, no sharing of their tragedy. But he *had* made eye contact with the hag near Cramer Hall, and something had definitely passed between them.

A threat or a warning? he wondered. He imagined that he could feel her stare burning a spot between his shoulder blades. He shook the feeling off and picked up his briefcases, telling himself he'd been working too hard. Summer was arriving not a nanosecond too soon.

V

He felt the first inkling of a headache as he passed by a portable camper that housed a Mexican food concession on the corner of Park Avenue and Montgomery Street, and he briefly considered stopping to buy a cold drink. Then he remembered the tiny pharmacy in the ground floor of Ione Plaza, only a dozen steps farther. What he really needed was a couple of Excedrin.

Ione Plaza was one of the tallest buildings on campus, a looming, twelve-story monolith of ugly gray cement. The Corner Drug Store was a cranny from which the proprietor dispensed junk food, magazines, and incidentals to the tenants who lived in the apartments above. Mark bought a small tin of Excedrin and a can of orange Diet Slice, or "Diet Slime," as his son Tad would have called it.

He parked his briefcases near the magazine rack and swallowed a couple of tablets, washing them down with soda. Three more long swigs, and the can was empty. He tossed it into a garbage bin, retrieved his briefcases, and stepped out into the afternoon sunshine.

He headed for the busy sidewalk, already feeling better but still strangely aware of the old woman he'd seen outside Cramer Hall. He'd taken scarcely five strides from the Corner Drug Store when he heard a woman's shriek that caused the hair on his neck to bristle. A jogger with a large white poodle on a leash stopped suddenly in front of him, raised his eyes skyward, and shouted something. Mark looked up, and his blood turned to ice.

A dark spot grew ever larger against the blue sky, as if some prehistoric flying reptile was sweeping down on him. It hurtled toward the ground with its limbs spread wide. Creation seemed to slow, and fractions of seconds ticked by as though the world lay submerged in molasses. Sunlight glinted off something shiny gripped in the falling man's hand. Diet Slime rose in Mark's throat as the realization hit him: A man had jumped from the roof of Ione Plaza. The man was screeching now, filling the afternoon with his horror. Unless Mark moved off this spot, the man would land on him.

Mark leapt to one side, whether under his own power or pulled by the jogger with the poodle, he never knew. One of his briefcases slipped from his grasp and burst open, pouring out a blizzard of papers, pens, and half-eaten rolls of Breath Savers. The falling man hit the ground with a sound that reminded Mark of someone shattering a watermelon with a baseball bat.

A geyser of gore rose from the concrete, showering Mark, the jogger, and the poodle. The surrounding pedestrians gasped collectively and shrank away from the mess on the sidewalk. Women screamed, men shouted, and the blood-spattered poodle barked excitedly. Someone fainted.

Mark found himself on his knees beside the victim, staring in shock at the blank, middle-aged face that ended just above the eyebrows. The top third of the man's head had disintegrated with the impact. The brain lay in an irregular mass that extended several yards onto the green grass. An eye had popped from its socket and hung grotesquely on its stalk. Internal organs had exploded from the abdomen and now oozed up under the blood-soaked army jacket.

"Are you okay?" asked the jogger, crouching next to Mark, gagging.

"I think so. I think I-I'm . . ." Mark inhaled deeply to control his own gut. "I'm fine."

"Okay, okay. I'll go call nine-one-one." The jogger jerked wildly on the leash to haul the poodle away from the steaming body, and they bounded away into the roiling crowd.

Mark could not tear his eyes from the dead man's face, which had a long, uneven beard the color of tungsten wire. The cheeks bore the scars of years in the streets and a pinkish network of tiny broken blood vessels that betrayed decades of hard drinking. His clothing was ragged and verminous, suggesting that he'd lived under a bridge or beneath a loading dock.

Mark's stomach lurched when he saw the long switchblade knife still clutched in the man's right hand, the sunlight glaring off its long blade. Incredibly, the impact after a twelve-story plunge had not dislodged it.

An absurd notion flitted through Mark's mind—that this homeless man had meant to kill him, perhaps to punish him for all the times he'd turned away from street people. Reflexively he laid his hand on the dead man's shoulder, mindless of the filth and blood that covered the old army jacket. "I'm not turning away now," he whispered.

The dead man's one intact eye rotated in its socket and stared at him. The mouth, though burbling with blood, moved. *"Root it out, Dr. Lansen."* He said this as casually as a passerby might comment on the weather.

Mark's heart nearly stopped. This was a dream, surely. People who've just fallen twelve stories onto a cement sidewalk don't start talking to you.

"No dream, Dr. Lansen," gurgled the man. *"If you know what's good for you, root it out. Take it from someone who knows."*

That was when Mark Lansen lost control of himself and started screaming.

2

Charred Sticks

i

The Personal Journal of Father Charles Briggs

"January 17, 1988: Back in the Middle Ages many priests and monks claimed to have been visited by the Devil, just as Christ was. Surviving such a visit, and fending off the temptations that came with it, were deemed proof of spiritual strength. Until fairly recently I was skeptical of such things. In my more humanistic moments I've even wondered whether the Church actually invented the Devil in order to assure mere humans that they're incapable of dreaming up *pure evil*. This might be the Church's greatest contribution, I'd told myself—assuring men that they are above certain things.

"Now I'm about to do something I've solemnly vowed never to do. I'm about to break the seal of the Sacrament. Everyone knows that a priest must never divulge what he hears in the confessional, but here I am, about to do it anyway.

"These days I'm certain that the Church didn't invent the Devil. And I'm not so certain that the Devil doesn't visit priests. On top of that, I doubt that there's any evil a mere man can't dream up. . . ."

ii

Nearly five months after penning those lines, Father Charles Briggs scribbled the *final* entry in his journal with a shaking hand. He leaned back from the antique rolltop desk that had served him for more than a quarter century, rubbed his watering eyes, and forced them to focus on the grandfather clock that stood in the near corner of his study. Eleven fifty-four. Only six minutes left in the third day of June 1988.

The final entry.

He closed the heavy book, which had a leather strap that could be inserted into a brass lock on the front cover, and took an ornate key from his pocket. He locked the strap into place, and dropped the key into a stamped envelope that held the letter he'd written earlier to his friend, Tressa Downey. He put the envelope into the breast pocket of his suit coat, then jotted a quick note to his housekeeper, Mrs. Lidderdale, instructing her to deliver the locked journal to Tressa at the earliest opportunity.

There. The book was closed on the life of Father Charles Briggs.

As he got to his feet, he heard something outside the window of the study, a rustling in the shrubbery, a wheezing cough. One of the Pellagrinis, no doubt. Perhaps both. Bernie and Fran had visited him several times during the past week, sent by the gentleman who Father Briggs could only believe was evil incarnate.

Bernie and Fran Pellagrini had been dead since March.

Father Briggs gripped the edge of the desk to steady himself, fighting down a wave of nausea. He went to the door of his study and stopped a moment to listen, to think, to mouth a short prayer. The rectory was silent as a sepulcher.

He staggered against the doorjamb, so weak with fear and doubt that he could barely stand. He'd planned to put on his vestments before doing what he must do this night, hoping that by wrapping himself in the holy cloth of the Church he might somehow find the grace to absolve him of the mortal sin he was about to commit. Now he worried that wearing his vestments might actually compound that sin.

He made his way to the cabinet in the hall outside the study, opened it, and pulled out a dusty bottle of Jameson's that he kept for special occasions. Father Briggs seldom drank hard liquor, but if this wasn't a special occasion, nothing was. He tipped the bottle to his lips and grimaced as the Irish whiskey burned his throat. The alcohol affected him immediately, blunting the bright edge of fear. His mind became clear again. He took another long pull from the bottle and thought of the whiskey priest in Graham Greene's *The Power and the Glory*. Charlie Briggs had yielded to sundry cravings from time to time, but booze, thank God, was one he'd always been able to control.

He heard another noise from the study, a clumsy thumping that suggested the Pellagrinis were trying to get in through the window. Hastily he replaced the bottle and headed down the hallway to the rear porch of the rectory. A left turn took him through a door into the garage, where his old Chevy Vega waited.

Before climbing into the car, he opened the gardener's chest and hauled out two one-gallon cans filled with gasoline, which he loaded into the rear seat. He was in a hurry, because he wanted to leave before Bernie and Fran made their way to the garage. He didn't want to see their faces. Not again, not ever.

iii

The night was a velvet curtain, blinding and muffling. As he pulled out of the drive, he glanced back at the rectory, the home he'd known and loved for so long. It stood dismal in the moonlight, as if already in mourning. Next to the rectory loomed St. Pius X Roman Catholic Church, the center of his universe these past twenty-five years, the gathering place of his ever-dwindling flock. Blinking away tears, Father Briggs said a soundless goodbye.

He drove down Church Avenue and turned right on Main Street, which climbed a steep, wooded hill into the heart of Oldenburg. He halted at the post office, got out, and dropped his letter to Tressa Downey into the mailbox that stood on the corner.

Lingering a moment in the feeble glow of the streetlight, he glanced both up and down the block. Not a soul stirred on Main Street. The humble storefronts and offices seemed like hollow fixtures in a deserted movie set. The silence of Oldenburg nearly overpowered him. Not that he'd expected a crowd at midnight, even on Friday—but *some* sign of life would have been a blessing, some small signal that among Oldenburg's 2,491 souls was one yet untouched by the evil that now prowled after sundown.

Night was no longer good in this town.

He drove up Main Street to Kalapuya Avenue, turned right, and continued up the hill past City Hall to the main entrance of Kalapuya County Park. After parking in the graveled drive, he opened the Vega's hatch and hoisted out the cans of gasoline. Another fifty steps took him to a clearing where a pillar of dark metal rose from a stone pedestal, a bronze statue of the legendary Indian medicine woman, Queen Molly. She stood like a squat sentry in the night, robed in ceremonial beaver skin and resplendent in beads, her left arm folded across her stomach. She held her right hand high, as if to bestow a benediction upon anyone who took the time to visit.

Father Briggs set down the cans and stared up at the statue, wishing the stars were bright enough to show him Queen Molly's face clearly. He'd always loved that face. In her eyes was a look of saintly compassion, on her lips a sad smile of forgiveness. Her expression seemed to say, *It's all right, whatever you've done, whatever you've suffered. You'll have your peace, I'll see to that. I'll take care of you.*

Perhaps this was the real reason he'd chosen this spot—to meet his end under the comforting gaze of an old Indian woman whose bronze eyes surely held the secret of absolution. To him this was as important now as the need for an open area where the fire could not spread and do unintended harm.

iv

He sank to his knees, wondering whether the archdiocese in Portland would follow the old Church tradition and bury him face down in his casket, as with other suicides, whether it would allow him a final resting place in hallowed ground, where suicides were not normally allowed.

Such questions were probably pointless, he told himself: There'll hardly be enough left to bury.

How stupid he'd been, how sublimely arrogant, to think that he could face up to a creature like the gentleman on the hill and win. His chief problem had been *faith*. To accept the reality of the gentleman's evil was one thing. To fight it was another matter entirely. Fighting it required more faith than Charlie Briggs could muster.

The visits by Bernie and Fran Pellagrini had proved that mere death was no refuge. The gentleman on the hill possessed the power to roust corpses from their graves, a hideous truth that shook Charlie Briggs's theology to its very foundation. In order to escape him, Father Charlie needed not only to die, but also to destroy his remains so completely that the gentleman would have nothing to work with.

Hence the gasoline.

He blessed himself, prayed the words of the sacrament of extreme unction, and begged the Holy Mother's intercession. He prayed that God would see this not as a suicide, but rather as a step taken by a desperate servant to save his soul.

What had become of the souls of Bernie and Fran, he couldn't even guess, but he prayed for them, too. He doused himself with gasoline, first from one can and then from the other. The noxious fumes blinded him and burned his lungs and throat, causing him nearly to faint.

"Hail Mary, full of grace," he sobbed, digging for the Bic butane lighter he'd bought earlier today, "the Lord is with Thee. Blessed art Thou amongst women. Blessed is the Fruit of Thy Womb, Jesus . . ."

He flicked the lighter, and life ended in an explosion of agony that lasted only a few seconds, mercifully. The light of the human torch danced against the face of Queen Molly as the priest expired, as his body twitched and writhed. Soon, little remained on the ground near the pedestal but a skeletal bundle of charred sticks among glowing orange coals.

Father Charlie Briggs was safe. For the time being.

3

Aftermath

Elspeth Carey is a fair young woman who wears a gray dress and a shawl of coarse wool. On the third finger of her right hand is a large ring of silver, a casting of a lion with a horribly fanged snake draped around its head. Under one arm she carries a basket, and under the other a spinning wheel. Inside her belly is the child whom Queen Molly, in her wisdom of such things, has declared overdue.

"I should have known it would be you," says the old woman. "Who else could slip into the village at night without waking all the dogs?"

"I need your help, Molly," says Elspeth in perfect Kalapuya, the language of the Fish People. "A bad time has come, and I can't face it alone." Her pale lips tremble, and her eyes dart around nervously.

"I will help you if I can," answers the medicine woman. "You are the daughter I prayed for, but was never given."

Elspeth's husband is Jordan Carey, an English mercantile agent in the employ of the Hudson's Bay Company, the most powerful enterprise in the vast Oregon Country. The Company has sent him from Ottawa to its outpost at Fort Vancouver, near the juncture of the Willamette River and the Columbia—a full day's passage from Cathlamet by canoe. Out of concern for Elspeth, Jordan built a log house in the forest near Cathlamet Village. Here his pretty wife escapes the insults and petty injuries she would suffer in Fort Vancouver, the kind she's endured most of her life. With only her husband and the good-natured Cathlamets for company, Elspeth pursues her strange calling unmolested. . . .

—from Poverty Ike's Tale
Halloween of '66 (continued)

i

The first thing Mark Lansen saw when he awoke was a beautiful Asian face, and behind it, morning sunlight slanting through venetian blinds. A full thirty seconds dragged by before he remembered that he'd spent the night in northwest Portland's Good Samaritan Hospital.

"So how are we doing this morning, Dr. Lansen?" the face asked sweetly. "Any aches, itches, or evil humors?"

Mark rubbed his crusty eyes and narrowed them on the nameplate pinned to the woman's baggy white jacket: BESS WONG, M.D. A stethoscope was draped over her neck. "Couldn't be better, Bess," he answered, grinning through a yawn. "Except I'm hungry enough to eat a live chicken."

"Would you settle for eggs Benedict and some stewed prunes? Specialty of the house."

Mark said he would, and Dr. Wong jotted a note on her clipboard.

The catastrophe of yesterday afternoon was still vivid in Mark's memory, but it seemed as though it had happened to someone else, as if he'd seen it in a movie. The paramedics had taken a hysterical man to the emergency room, and Mark had witnessed the scene through that man's eyes. The doctors had examined him, sedated him, and insisted on keeping him overnight for observation. Deidre and Tad had come to sit with him awhile, and they'd all watched television. Then, sleep, thanks to the drug, and after that, morning.

"So what's the verdict?" he asked. "Do I need a phone call from the governor to get out of here?"

"Your chart says you were checked over from stem to stern, and nobody can find anything wrong with you, so I guess you're free to go as soon as you've had breakfast. How did you sleep?"

"Like a dead man."

"Has anything like this ever happened to you before?"

"You mean, has anyone ever jumped off a building and almost killed me?"

"I *mean*, have you ever experienced things that you know couldn't have happened? Heard any voices, say, when no one was around? Bells, music, stuff like that?"

"Not that I can remember. This was a new first. I hope it was also a last."

"Then you do understand that the man who fell off that building couldn't have spoken to you."

Mark looked away and swallowed before answering. "Yeah, I guess I do. Things like that don't really happen, do they? Unless, of course, the guy lived for a minute or two after landing—"

"No way. I saw the DOA file on him. Most of his brain ejected upon impact, and his spine was broken in three places. There's absolutely no question that he died instantly. And none of the other witnesses saw anything that looked like a dead man talking to you. In short, dead people don't talk, Dr. Lansen."

Mark smiled weakly.

"By the way," said Dr. Wong, changing the subject, "your wife was here earlier this morning, but you weren't awake yet. She'll come by a little later. She tells me you've been seeing a therapist."

Good old Deidre, thought Mark. Leave it to her to get all the facts out on the table where everyone can riffle through them. "Not very often," he answered in an apologetic tone. "Deidre— uh, my wife and I—were having a few problems a while back, and we started going to a shrink—I mean a clinical psychologist—for some counseling. After we got things straightened out, I kept on going. Not on a regular basis, mind you. Just now and then."

Naturally Dr. Wong wanted to know why.

Some bad dreams that recurred from time to time, Mark answered, and a phobia for garden slugs, of all things. Nothing very heavy-duty, in other words. Talking to the shrink was really just an outlet, a way to vent day-to-day pressures.

"I see," said Dr. Wong. "Well, I'm no shrink, but inasmuch as you've never experienced any severe psychological or emotional symptoms in the past, I'm going to sign you out of here." She then ventured the off-the-cuff opinion that Mark had suffered a minor hallucinatory "event" brought on by the severe shock of seeing someone die violently only a few feet away. Probably nothing to get excited over, she further opined. She did suggest, however, that he see his therapist sometime soon, just to talk things over.

ii

Home again, after what seemed a decade instead of a mere overnighter.

Deidre behaved positively solicitously toward him, which was totally out of character, but Mark didn't point this out to her. She led him to the rear deck of the house and deposited him in a padded lounge chair. She brought him a tall glass of iced tea and rounded up magazines for him to read. She even fetched his slippers and put them on his feet. She pampered him as though he was recuperating from triple-bypass surgery. Mark loved it.

The special treatment didn't last long, unfortunately. "Sweetie, I've got to go back to the office for a while," Deidre said, touching his arm. "I have a meeting with a developer first thing Monday, and I need to get some things ready for him. Stephanie's coming in to clean later today, and I've asked her to fix some lunch for you and Thaddeus. You'll be okay, won't you?"

Of course he would be. It wasn't as if they'd planned to spend the weekend together, after all. If someone hadn't jumped off a roof yesterday and nearly killed him, he and Tad would have left early this morning for Oldenburg. As it was, this would be a normal weekend in the Lansen-Garland household—Daddy Bear and Baby Bear at home, dreaming up things to keep themselves occupied, while Momma Bear's at the office, making money.

Mark didn't say this, naturally. He just smiled and waved good-bye.

iii

From where he sat on the sunny deck, he had a clear view of the building where his wife worked—the U.S. Bank tower, the tallest in town, known to Portlanders as Big Pink. The offices of Burnham, Lazlo, and Garland occupied much of the twenty-ninth floor. Mark sometimes fantasized that if not for the mirrorlike windows of Big Pink, he could borrow Tad's telescope and peer into Deidre's office, perhaps catching Clay Burnham, the senior partner, in the act of porking her.

At least she hadn't porked her way into a full partnership, he told himself, as though this was something he could take comfort in. Deidre Garland (she'd kept her family name after marrying Mark) was a hugely talented residential architect who had reached the top through hard work and raw ability. She'd found her niche early in her career, specializing in turning out updated versions of the early "Portland house," a squat, heavy-timbered bungalow found mainly in the city's old neighborhoods. Her designs proved popular among yuppies who wanted an alternative to the prosaic "country" houses that abounded in the suburban housing tracts around Portland, and soon she had more clients than she could handle. Long before Clay Burnham ever lured her into bed, he made her a full partner and created a separate residential design department for her to manage.

Deidre had designed the house in which the Lansen-Garland family lived. It stood on a lushly vegetated hillside in Portland's exclusive Washington Park neighborhood, overlooking the Willamette River and the gleaming towers of downtown. It boasted all the amenities, including a spa, central air-conditioning, three studies (one for each member of the family, even Tad), and an expansive rear deck with a magnificent view.

Mark hated the house, but he pretended to love it. He would have preferred an older, less lavish home in a middle-class neighborhood, something more suited to a lowly professor of history. Deidre, of course, could not be expected to live like a plebeian, so Mark kept his mouth shut and made the best of things. This, he was loathe to admit, had become the story of his domestic life.

iv

Tad joined him on the deck, wearing a Bugle Boy tank top, acid-washed denims, and expensive Nike athletic shoes. Atop his head was a set of earphones attached to a Sony Mega Bass Dolby Walkman. He looked like an adman's vision of the Ultra-Now Kid.

"See this?" he asked, handing Mark the latest *Oregonian.* On the front page was a color photograph of the previous afternoon's scene outside Ione Plaza on the PSU campus, showing the ambulance, paramedics, the grim-faced crowd. A white sheet covered a shapeless mass on the sidewalk.

"Man Plunges to Death at PSU," read the headline.

"You're a celebrity," said Tad, beaming. "It says you tried to help the guy, but you were overcome with shock and taken to the hospital. It's neat. I'm putting it in my scrapbook."

Mark shook his head and mussed his son's chestnut hair. "That's what we call 'reportorial license,' Tad Bear. I didn't try to help the guy. I knew he was . . ." He cleared his throat. "I knew he was dead, I guess. At least I was pretty sure."

"Was the guy really gooshed? I mean, was he like splattered all over the place?"

Mark fought a sudden urge to spit up. "What do you say we talk about something a little more uplifting?"

"Okay." The boy plunked himself into the deck chair next to his father's, not the least put off. "Are we still goin' to Gram's and Gramp's?"

"Like I told you on the way home from the hospital, we're still going. We're just leaving a couple of days later than planned, that's all."

"Can we still bring our mountain bikes?"

"You bet."

"And can I still bring my telescope?"

"I've told you twenty times, you can bring your telescope, your dinosaur books, your Rollerblades and your Walkman. You can bring anything that fits in the car, except your Nintendo out-fit."

"Aw, come on. I can't believe you're going to make me leave the Nintendo here. I promise I'll only play it in my room at Gram's and Gramp's. You won't even hear—"

"No way," said Mark firmly. "We're going to have just one blessed season free of beeps and boings and explosions. We're going to do active, healthful things, you and I, like biking and hiking and fishing with Gramp. There won't be time for sitting in front of a video this summer. You won't miss the Super Mario Brothers, believe me."

Tad lowered his face and pouted a moment, but this was just for show. Mark smiled in spite of himself and felt a rush of love for the boy. Unquestionably, this kid was the best thing Deidre and he had ever accomplished together.

Tad had Mark's long limbs, piercing hazel eyes, and perfect white teeth. He also had his father's to-hell-with-it sense of humor, Mark liked to think. Deidre's genetic contribution included the high forehead, a button-nose, a smattering of freckles, and a love of mathematics and science, apparently.

The kid got mostly A's at Catlin Gabel, one of Portland's best private schools. Notwithstanding his addiction to heavy metal rock and Nintendo games, he regularly immersed himself in higher pursuits, some of which, like astronomy, endured. His latest fancy was dinosaurs, and he'd used his allowance to buy half a dozen heavily illustrated books on paleontology (a word he'd only recently learned to pronounce properly). The shelves of his room sagged with volumes on past obsessions, including whales, space exploration, and caves. Most of the books were beyond the reading level of average nine-year-olds, Mark had lately noted with pride. To his mild disappointment, Tad had expressed no real interest in human history.

Looking at his son now, Mark felt lucky to be alive. He pulled Tad close and kissed him on the forehead, incurring a surprised giggle. He knew again that he would suffer any torment to stay close to this kid. He would even endure Deidre's little outrages, her subtle put-downs, her infidelity. Tad was entitled to two on-site parents, even if one of them was so full of herself that she had little room in her life for the things that really counted.

V

Tad decided to put in some serious Nintendo time, since he would be forced to quit cold turkey come Monday. Mark settled down with the latest issue of *Road and Track* and occupied himself with a road test of the Porsche 944 Turbo.

The doorbell chimed, and a moment later, Stephanie, the young woman who cooked and cleaned for the Lansen-Garlands three times a week, walked onto the deck through a set of French doors. Two men were out front, she told him, claiming to be police and asking for Dr. Lansen. Should she let them in?

Mark tossed aside his magazine and padded to the front door, his slippers slapping his heels. One of the men was tall and black, immaculately dressed in a blue blazer and a crisp button-down shirt. His partner, blond and overweight, wore a double-knit sport coat that looked like it came from K Mart circa the Ford administration. The black man showed Mark his badge packet, which identified him as Detective Sergeant Douglas Noel, Portland Police Bureau, Homicide. The white guy was Detective Ted Clack. Could Mark spare them a few minutes?

"We have something we think you should know about," said Sergeant Noel with gravity.

Mark led them into the house and out onto the deck, where he offered them chairs and iced tea. They accepted both, and Detective Clack commented on the magnificent view. The morning haze had burned off, and the panorama looked like a picture from *National Geographic*. On the northern horizon Mount Saint Helens reared in all her snowy glory, quiescent after her murderous eruption of eight years earlier. In the east loomed Mount Hood, also a volcano, but one that had yet to pull her sister's violent stunt.

"So, what can I do for you guys?" Mark asked. "I told the police everything I knew about the accident yesterday, although I'll admit I wasn't all that coherent. They probably couldn't make heads or tails of anything I said, right?"

"Your statement was just fine," replied Sergeant Noel. "You were very coherent, given the circumstances." He took a sip of iced tea and added, "This isn't exactly an official visit, Dr. Lansen."

"As a matter of fact, Dr. Lansen, we're here on our own time," put in Detective Clack.

"Please—you guys don't have to call me *Doctor*. I don't take out tonsils. I don't even play golf. I'm just your ordinary history professor out of Sears Roebuck. Call me Mark."

"Yeah—well, here's the situation, Mark," said Sergeant Noel, opening the manila folder he'd brought with him. "We've done some routine digging on the man who jumped off the roof yesterday. His name was Leo Fobbs, as you probably read in the paper—homeless guy, not exactly one of the city's leading citizens. You told the investigating officers that you'd never seen the man before, is that right?"

"Right. I didn't know him from a fire hydrant."

"Well, he was apparently familiar with *you*." Noel spread a pile of photocopies on the glass-top wicker table in front of him. "These came from a duffel bag he'd left with a buddy at Baloney Joe's over on East Burnside. Know the place?"

Mark did. Baloney Joe's Junction was a haven for street people run by a private relief organization. Noel explained that Leo Fobbs had a meal voucher from the establishment in the pocket of his jacket when he died. The police had visited Baloney Joe's and located a man named Sam Darkenwald, the friend with whom Fobbs had left the duffel bag.

"Looks like Mr. Fobbs was keeping some kind of file on you," said Noel, pushing the photocopies across the table. Mark picked one up, stared at it, and felt a chill. It was a copy of an old campus newspaper article announcing an addition to the PSU history faculty, Dr. Mark Lansen, accompanied by a bad photograph. The next was a 1987 issue of the *Oregon Humanities Newsletter*, with a bold headline: "Lansen to Offer Seminar on Medieval Criminal Justice." Again, a photograph.

"This is unbelievable," he managed to say. "I don't understand it. I don't understand it at all."

There was another article from the campus paper, with a headline announcing the appointment of Dr. Mark Lansen as faculty advisor to Phi Alpha Theta, a national history honorary society. Next to it was a photograph of Mark shaking hands with the outgoing faculty advisor. Someone had drawn a circle round Mark's head with a felt-tipped pen.

Sergeant Noel sipped his iced tea, never taking his eyes from Mark's worried face. "Your office is in Cramer Hall, right?" he asked.

"Yes. Third floor."

"We have some statements from people who saw Fobbs on campus yesterday morning—one of them is a janitor in your building. He says he threw Fobbs out after catching him in the stairwell between the second and third floors."

Mark swallowed and said nothing. He picked up another copy from the wicker table and studied it. This one was a History Department faculty roster, which gave the office locations and telephone numbers of all the history teachers at PSU. His name was underlined, possibly with the same felt-tipped pen.

"Another person saw Fobbs in the West Hall parking garage on campus," continued Noel. "He was on level two, hanging around an old green BMW. I checked the DMV files and found out you own a seventy-five BMW 2002. It's green, isn't it?"

"Lime-skin metallic, original paint. Runs like a clock. And my assigned parking space is on level two, which you probably already know."

"Dr. Lan—I mean, Mark," said the black cop, "officially we have absolutely no reason to think this thing was anything other than a suicide. But Ted, here, and I both thought we should notify you of what we found out concerning Leo Fobbs—that he was apparently stalking you for some reason."

"*Stalking* me?" Mark coughed after sucking some iced tea down the wrong pipe. "That doesn't make any sense. I didn't even know the guy."

"But maybe he knew someone who knows you," suggested Detective Clack. "The fact is, he kept quite a little jacket on you." He nodded at the copies on the table. "Fobbs apparently kept track of your comings and goings. He knew where your office was, where you parked your car. He obviously had some reason for going to the trouble of rounding up all this information on you."

"And you think," said Mark, still sputtering, "that someone put him up to it—that he was maybe working for somebody?"

"We don't know what to think," confessed Sergeant Noel. "But we can't discount the possibility that he meant you harm. We just thought you should know about it."

"Oh, come *on*, guys! I hope you're not suggesting that Fobbs was trying to kill me. Couldn't he have dreamed up a better way to do it than taking a kamikaze dive off a twelve-story building? If you ask me, that's a pretty iffy method of offing somebody!"

"Like I said, we don't know what to think," reiterated Sergeant Noel. "All we know is that some poor old drunk jumped off a roof and almost killed the man he'd been collecting information on for God-only-knows how long. Chances are slim we'll ever find out the whys and wherefores. We don't have the manpower or the budget to throw at little mysteries like this one, so we've already closed the book on it."

"You've closed the book on it," repeated Mark, staring at Big Pink in the distance. High overhead a V-shaped formation of Canada geese lazed northward, honking noisily. He listened a moment, thinking. "So, what do you suggest I do, now that you've shared all this with me?"

"I'm afraid we can't offer much in the way of advice," said Detective Clack apologetically. "But if I were you, I'd watch my ass for a while. I'd try to think of something, *anything*, that might explain why all this happened. And if I came up with something"— he pulled a business card from his frumpy double-knit sport coat and handed it to Mark—"I'd give us a call."

vi

Mark got little peace and quiet after the detectives left, thanks to the telephone.

The first call came from his parents, John and Marta Lansen in Oldenburg. Like nearly everyone else in town they subscribed to the *Oregonian*, and today's front-page coverage of Mark's bout with the grim reaper had given them a hellish fright. Was he *really* okay? Was there anything they could do? Would he and Tad still be coming to spend the summer with them?

Yes, no, and yes, he answered, in that order. The rest of their questions he put off with a promise to give them all the gory details when he arrived on Monday. He withheld any mention of what the detectives had told him earlier that morning.

Then he asked if *they* were okay. He thought they sounded stressed out. He asked whether Kristen, his twenty-year-old sister, was giving them any trouble. She was a junior at the University of Oregon in Eugene and was home for the summer.

Nothing like that, his father answered. The problem was—and this was a bombshell—an old friend of the family, Father Charlie Briggs, had taken his own life late last night. The town was in a state of shock. The Lansens weren't Catholics, but Charlie Briggs and John Lansen were golfing buddies from way back. For the past two decades the priest had come to dinner with John and Marta at least once a month. Charlie had loved Marta's hearty Scandinavian cooking as much as he'd loved talking about law and politics with John, who was one of Oldenburg's two resident lawyers.

Mark had known Father Briggs, of course—short but well-muscled, a shiny bald head, bifocals, and twinkling Irish eyes. He remembered a kind, sensitive man who always had time to share a joke with a kid.

"You'll probably read about it in tomorrow's paper or see it on the news," volunteered John, "so I might as well tell you now. He burned himself to death, Mark. Poured two gallons of gasoline on himself, then touched himself off with a cigarette lighter—just like those Buddhist monks used to do in Saigon during the Vietnam war." John's normally big voice became small and a little quivery. "Did it in the park, right next to that old statue of the Indian woman. Didn't leave a note, as far as anyone knows."

Jesus Christ, thought Mark, *what's happening to my world?* He managed to wrap up the conversation with his parents, using mainly monosyllables, and hoped they didn't detect his agitation.

He felt as if creation was unraveling. Since yesterday's encounter with the hag outside Cramer Hall, he'd suffered a steady assault on his sanity, starting with Leo Fobbs's death plunge off Ione Plaza. Moments later he'd hallucinated a conversation with the dead man. Next came the detectives' revelation that Fobbs had been gathering information on him, and had probably been stalking him for some unknown reason.

Now *this*: An old friend of the family had burned himself to death.

For the next hour the telephone bleeped steadily with calls from acquaintances who had read the morning paper and wanted to make sure Mark was all right. Colleagues on the PSU faculty. Neighbors. Beer-drinking chums. Mark appreciated their concern, but he was in no shape emotionally to handle this much happy talk. After the eighth call, he recorded a message on the answering machine: *"Hi, you've reached the Lansen-Garland residence. All's well here, even with Mark, who's soaking in the hot tub right now. If you want to leave a message, do it when you hear the ear-splitting beep. If you don't want to, that's okay. We'll understand. 'Bye, now!"*

vii

When Deidre called around seven to say that she would be putting in a late-nighter at the office, Mark switched off the machine and took the call. He pretended to understand her explanation perfectly and even feigned sympathy.

He and Tad drove to the Pizza Oasis on Burnside for some dinner, then returned home to watch a Seattle Mariners game on cable. Tad fell asleep during the bottom of the eighth inning, so Mark guided him to his room, pulled him out of acid-washed denims, and tucked him in.

Deidre came home just as the late news was ending. She looked a little tired, which was certainly understandable, given the workday she'd just put in. Mark pretended to be asleep as he watched her slip into her pajamas. Her blond hair was long and luxuriant, her body lean and tanned, her blue eyes bright. She'd approached her mid-thirties gracefully and had yet to embark on that rapid aging trip taken by many blond women who soak up too much sun on golf courses and tennis courts.

Suddenly Mark wanted her, and he felt himself hardening. Her heavy breasts jiggled tantalizingly under her satin pajama top as she padded around the bedroom to finish the myriad little chores women must do before hitting the sack. Satin flowed deliciously over the mounds of her bottom, making him yearn to slip his hand beneath her waistband. In his mind he saw himself bounding playfully out of bed to "attack" her, as he'd often done when their marriage was new, wrestling her to the mattress, stifling her giggles with a deep kiss, pressing his groin into hers and running his tongue over the pebbles of her nipples.

He ached for her but made no move and faked sleep whenever she turned in his direction. Her face had the relaxed glow of a woman already satisfied. Mark groaned and turned onto his side, as if stirring in sleep, hating Clay Burnham with every fiber. Deidre killed the lights and climbed lightly into bed. She was snoring softly long before Mark managed to drop off.

4

Dead Giveaway

Elspeth reaches around the licks of the fire and touches Queen Molly's brown hand. "How long have we been friends, Molly—five years?" she asks. "I've told you much about myself in those five years, but I've kept some things back. I didn't want to place you in danger. That's the way it is with some things—even knowing about them can be dangerous."

Queen Molly understands this and nods.

"I've not told you about a dreadful task that I must perform, one for which I've prepared since long ago. And I've not told you about my Enemy." Elspeth's voice wavers, and she swallows before going on. "He's come for me, Molly. He wants my unborn daughter. Even at this moment he's near." She glances at the deerskin curtain and draws her shawl more tightly about her.

"Cannot your man, Jordan, protect you?" asks Queen Molly. "Is this enemy stronger than he?"

"Jordie's in Oregon City, trading with the American settlers," says Elspeth. "But even if he were here, he would be no match for—"

The wind interrupts her, whistling through gaps in the cedar planks, rattling the skins that hang on the inner walls of the lodge. Elspeth reaches into the basket she's brought with her and rummages through a hoard of bottles, vials, and pouches until finding a hinged block of dark, glossy wood. She opens it and holds it out for Queen Molly to see.

Mounted inside in a ring of pewter is a disk of shiny obsidian, the breadth of a woman's fist, black and lustrous. A scrying mirror, Elspeth calls it. By uttering the right words a witch can gaze into it and see truth beyond the reach of ordinary mortals' eyes. In this way she's learned of the Enemy's journey from his lair on the Tualatin Plain, which lies several days' walk south of here. Elspeth has looked into his eyes and read his hellish intentions.

"He hungers for my child," she says in a husky voice, causing

*Queen Molly's scalp to tingle. "He means to kill me in order to
have her. I am prepared to fight him, but I must have your help."*

"You need only to tell me what I must do."

*So Elspeth tells her, and Molly's face goes slack with
dread....*

—from Poverty Ike's Tale
Halloween of '66 (continued)

i

You awaken.

The warm night presses in, and you can no longer tolerate the
sheets against your skin. You need air; you crave freedom of
movement. Your wife's slow, rhythmic breathing tells you she's
safely asleep.

You swing out of bed and dress, taking care not to let your
keys jingle in your pants. On the way out you pause before the
closed door of Tad's room, and somehow you can hear his met-
ronomical heartbeat, as if your sense of hearing has acquired the
sharpness of a dog's. He too is asleep, which is good, because
now you're free to do what you must do.

Except you don't know exactly what that is, do you?

You must go somewhere, meet someone. You're sure this isn't
a dream, because dreams don't deliver the clarity of sensation
you're experiencing: the perfume of blossoming rhododendrons
in the yard, for example; the heat of exertion in your shoulders
and arms as you roll your old BMW out of the garage and down
the drive; the hardness of the paving stones under your feet.

You roll-start the Beemer in order to avoid waking anyone
with the winding of the starter, and leave the headlights off until
you're a block from the house. The road curves down the hillside, and between the fashionable homes you catch glimpses of
the jewellike lights of the city below. It's very late, and the
streets are deserted. You feel as if you're the lone surviving soul
in this sprawling metropolitan anthill, a man singled out and
saved for some secret purpose.

ii

You skirt Washington Park and cross Vista Avenue into the heart of downtown Portland, then head south for the campus of PSU. Before you know it, you're out of your car, walking up Park toward the intersection with Montgomery, where looms the dark, lifeless bulk of Ione Plaza.

The campus of Portland State University is blacker than the commercial blocks north of here, thanks to the leafy canopy that filters the light of moon and stars. For some reason the street-lights are out, which gives you a twinge of anxiety. Despite the darkness you can clearly see the familiar details of this region where you ply your chosen trade—the vine-covered walls of the buildings where you hold forth in lecture; the tan bricks of Cramer Hall, where you read and write and give audiences to your students; the gurgling fountain where lies the lonely bronze nude, whom even the pigeons have forsaken with the coming of the dark.

You see that you're no longer alone. The hag stands twenty paces ahead, staring at you as she did on Friday afternoon, be-draggled and stooped. She turns and walks a few steps to her spinning wheel, bends to it and sets it into motion, never taking her shining eyes off you. As the windy whine of the wheel reaches your ears, you again feel that her face looks familiar. *She's here because of you,* whispers a silken voice deep inside your brainpan, and terror stutters along your spine. *You know her.*

She beckons to you, motions you toward the intersection of Montgomery and Park, where Ione Plaza casts a black moon-shadow over the walk. You don't want to go, but you know there's no avoiding this. You follow the walk in a curve to the right and detect a red glow spilling from a window in the Corner Drug Store—a neon Pepsi sign. On the sidewalk near the en-trance lies an irregular mass covered with a sheet, and you don't need to ask what it is.

iii

Something soft squishes under your foot, and you bite your tongue to avoid jabbering with panic. The cement walk is littered with slugs, their bodies elongated and shiny with slime. They leave wet trails of mucus as they squirm toward the sheeted mound ahead. *So, that's it!*

The hag hunkers with her spinning wheel next to the trunk of a huge oak on your left, and you're close enough to appreciate the stony glare in her eyes, the reek of her body. You catch a glint of silver from her right hand as it describes a circle over the spokes of the wheel—a huge ring. The windy song of the wheel grows louder as she urges it faster, faster.

I know what this is now, you tell her. *It's just another cheap slug-dream, the kind I've been having since I was a kid. Some people are scared of spiders, others are scared of snakes. My phobia is slugs, okay? I get variations on this nightmare two or three times a year. . . .*

But this one has a new twist, doesn't it?

I'm not buying any of this. It's just a dream. The slugs are a dead giveaway.

Your bravado doesn't move her.

iv

Okay, I'll play your silly fucking game. You want me to go over and pull the sheet off that body, right? And you want me to be scared shitless when old Leo Fobbs looks at me and says something really bloodcurdling. Am I right? You've been seeing too many horror movies, old woman!

You resolve to get this over with, and you move forward gingerly, stepping with precision between the odious little creatures who populate the sidewalk. Now and then you misstep, which is easy to do, because the slugs become thicker as you move nearer Leo Fobbs's sheeted remains. You suffer a thrill of revulsion each time you crush one under your heel, and you wish to God you were safe in your bed with Deidre, cold and unloving though she is. Anything would be better than this.

You reach the sheeted mound and crouch, praying that you don't lose your balance, which would force you to put a hand to the ground in order to steady yourself. The slugs are a slimy carpet here, and you'd surely touch one with your bare hand, which you know would be unbearable right now. You glance back to where the hag stood, and you gasp when you see that she's no longer there, even though you can still hear the whirring of her spinning wheel. Beyond the red aura of the Pepsi sign hangs a wall of black that curves around you like the inner surface of a septic tank.

You're truly alone now, except for the company of a dead man and tens of thousands of slugs whose eyestalks distend hideously from their heads, waving slowly back and forth as if urging you on. *My kingdom for a flamethrower,* you think, and you chuckle inanely as you imagine Andy Rooney beginning his weekly installment on "60 Minutes" with *"Why is it that every time you really need a flamethrower, you can never find one . . . ?"*

You pull the sheet away from Leo Fobbs's head, expecting the worst. But all you see is the face of a dead man with the top third of his head missing. This is old news.

"I saw the DOA file on him," you recall Dr. Wong saying this morning at the hospital. *"Most of his brain ejected upon impact, and his spine was broken in three places. There's absolutely no question that he died instantly."*

You're almost disappointed. Old Leo's expression is as blank as a puddle of milk. You touch his stubbly face, and it feels like a pork roast that someone has forgotten to put in the refrigerator. You whip the sheet away, exposing the rest of the body.

Nothing new. Blood-drenched field jacket, verminous blue jeans, sneakers encrusted with grime. The body lies twisted and misshapen, just as it had on Friday. But wait. Something *is* different. You remember that Leo's brain had lain in an irregular mass extending away from the skull, having exploded outward over the cement and the grass boundary. Now you can find no trace of that brain.

Maybe the slugs have eaten it, you say to yourself.

Or—

You tilt Leo Fobbs's head forward and stare into the awful cavity, which proves a stupid thing to do, because the slug that's curled up inside seizes this opportunity to launch itself at your face. It's the size of a large house cat. It has the mouth and teeth of a badger, the slitted, golden eyes of a cobra. It engulfs your face, stifling your scream, and presses its warm, wet mouth to your ear: *"Root it out, Dr. Lansen. . . ."*

God help you, the voice belongs to Tad, your son.

"If you know what's good for you, root it out."

5

Baloney Joe's and Beyond

As they pick their way over the path that leads to the river's shore, Queen Molly feels as if someone is watching. She often reaches behind to touch Elspeth, needing the warmth of human contact. At the river's edge they mount a cedar canoe and paddle beyond the forested mound the whites call Puget Island. Helped by a waning moon, they land on the southern shore without even getting their feet wet. They set out with their cargoes through a stand of rustling aspen, trudging up the mountain with Queen Molly in the lead. Elspeth begins to breathe loudly from the exertion, and Queen Molly worries about her and the child she carries. They stop often to rest against mossy fallen logs, their eyes wide against the dark.

Several times Queen Molly hears noises around them—the rustle of sword fern, the squelch of spongy ground under a heavy foot, the snap of a twig. Her heart welters, for she knows well the warnings of the holy men against violating this ground. The foolish few who have come this way (and lived to brag of their foolishness) tell of weird lights that float among the trees, of animals who whisper with human voices, of potent magic that swirls in the air. . . .

—from Poverty Ike's Tale
Halloween of '66 (continued)

i

Mark Lansen joined his wife at the wicker dinette on the deck. Overhead a blazing morning sun hung against a crystalline sky, while fog blanketed the city below.

"That was some nightmare you had last night, sweetie," said Deidre over scones and freshly brewed decaf, not even looking up from the Sunday paper. "Do you remember it?"

"No, not really," Mark lied a little shakily. The nightmare lay on his mood like a fresh bruise. "Hope I didn't scare you. I must've screamed, huh?" He poured coffee into a mug.

"Like a banshee—not to mention kicking and throwing your arms around. It's been a long time since you've had a slug dream, so I figured you were dreaming about the accident on Friday." She then informed him that Thaddeus was at a neighbor's house, playing Nintendo and watching videos with his best friend, Josh.

She's going through the motions, thought Mark. *Won't even look up from the fucking paper. Should I tell her about the cops' visit?*

He did, and the tale snatched her interest away from the *Oregonian's* coverage of George Bush's and Michael Dukakis's respective drives toward their parties' presidential nominations. The fact that she actually rested her chin on a fist and watched him as he talked made him feel hopeful and warm. The center of her attention was a sunny spot that he couldn't occupy very often these days.

"So, what do you make of it?" she wanted to know when he'd finished. "Can you think of any possible connection between this Leo Fobbs person and yourself?"

"Are you kidding? Before Friday I didn't even know the guy existed."

"But there's got to be a connection," she insisted, blue eyes flashing. "I mean, why would some low-grade derelict who lives under a bridge suddenly take an interest in an obscure history professor he's never met—enough interest to go out and procure old press clippings about him, for the love of God?"

Obscure history professor. Mark's hopeful feeling vanished. He agreed that nothing the cops had told him made sense, not in the sane world of cause and effect. At least not yet.

"Yet?"

"I'm going down to Baloney Joe's and find this guy Darkenwald—the friend Leo left his duffel bag with. If he can't tell me anything enlightening, he might be able to point out some of Leo's other acquaintances, and maybe one of them will know something."

Deidre thought that was a bad idea and said so. Wading around among the bottom-feeders at Baloney Joe's wasn't a healthy thing to do, surely. Mark felt thankful for this show of concern over his well-being and was about to give up the idea when Deidre said, "But if you actually go, can you be back by three? I need to put in some office time this afternoon, and that's when Thaddeus is due back from Josh's house."

Once again Mark came to earth hard.

ii

Downtown Portland teemed with Sunday morning churchgoers and brunchers. Mark waited in the queue at the west entrance of the Burnside Bridge while a tall-masted sailboat motored beneath it toward the posh marina at River Place a dozen blocks upstream on the languid Willamette. At last a horn blared, the bridge lowered, and he drove across into the "other" Portland—a clutter of old industrial and commercial neighborhoods that had yet to feel the touch of gentrification and probably never would.

Baloney Joe's Junction was a low, decrepit building less than a block from the river. Mark parked off Burnside and walked up to the front entrance, where a score of street-weary men waited for a free breakfast. Some leaned against the dirty glass-brick walls on either side of the door, smoking and trading quiet talk, soaking up the newly arrived sunshine. Others sat on the curb, chatting over a bottle wrapped in a brown paper sack. Mark felt their stares as he moved past them, and wished he'd not worn the costly suede jacket Deidre had given him several Christmases ago. He stood out like a peacock among a scatter of starving crows.

He hesitated before entering and debated with himself over whether he should go through with this. At best he was an intruder here, a freshly shaved and well-dressed interloper from the affluent world west of the river. At worst he was a prey animal, a soft target who carried his cash in an eel-skin wallet.

What was so damned important about seeking an explanation of something that might well be inexplicable? he asked himself. After all, Leo Fobbs was dead and well beyond harming anyone, wasn't he?

Mark had rehearsed answers to those questions earlier, expecting Deidre to ask them over breakfast, but she hadn't. So he answered them now—to himself.

For starters, this was more than itchy curiosity. Detective Ted

Clack had suggested that Leo Fobbs might have known someone who knew Mark, and that Fobbs had stalked him on that person's behalf—which sounded absurd, yes, but no less absurd than what had actually happened. That someone, presumably, was still alive, meaning that the danger might not have passed.

Stronger in Mark's mind was the likelihood that Fobbs had acted on his own. If this was so, he wanted to know why. Maybe Mark had known Fobbs in an earlier decade, conceivably under a different name, before Fobbs's life belly flopped onto the mean streets. Maybe they'd even been classmates at the U. of O. in Eugene, where Mark had done his undergraduate work, or at Washington University in St. Louis, where he had taken his doctorate. Had he somehow wronged the man without knowing it, causing him to want revenge? Mark needed to know.

More urgent was the simple need to *act*, to exert some control over his life. Since his encounter two days earlier with the bedraggled woman outside Cramer Hall, he'd felt as if some black influence was perturbing his orbit, manipulating events, terrorizing his sleep. He needed to prove that he was still in charge of himself, that he could steer his life wherever he damn well pleased.

He pushed through the front door of Baloney Joe's Junction.

iii

Nearly an hour later a Baloney Joe's staff member pointed toward the front entrance and said, "That's him—the guy with the red-plaid jacket and sunglasses."

Mark had volunteered to be a server in the chow line, feeling a need to make himself useful while waiting for Sam Darkenwald to show up. This seemed the least he could do to repay the Baloney Joe's staff for their good humor and willingness to help him.

"Be careful with him," added the staff member, "and whatever you do, don't let him think you're from the FBI. He thinks government agents are shooting some kind of waves at him."

Mark handed her the tongs he'd used to dispense link sausages to the seemingly endless procession of homeless men who trooped through the chow line. He thanked her and promised to become a regular volunteer—next fall, after summer vacation.

Then he made his way between the long, crowded tables to the edge of the hall. Here the line crawled along the wall toward the counter where eggs, sausages, and hotcakes awaited hungry bellies.

Feeling self-conscious, he introduced himself to Sam Darkenwald, who turned out to be an amiable man in his early fifties, and looked fit, considering his circumstances. Gray hair that had probably been red once upon a time poked out in greasy tufts from the band of his battered cowboy hat. He stood at least an inch taller than Mark and was wider in the shoulders, possibly because of the half-dozen shirts and sweaters he wore under his dirty red jacket. In stark contrast to his distressed clothing, he wore expensive-looking sunglasses.

"Would you believe I was once a Schedule C presidential appointee?" Sam Darkenwald asked Mark, pumping his hand. "Well, I *was*—Department of Health, Education, and Welfare. HEW, we called it back then. I was one of your big dogs, honest to God."

Mark had no problem believing this.

He accompanied Sam through the chow line, explaining in a low voice why he'd come, emphasizing that he was *not* with the FBI or any other government agency. After Sam had filled his plate, they sat in squeaky metal chairs near the end of a long table covered with butcher paper. On the opposite wall was a colorful but inappropriately idyllic mural depicting street life among recognizable Portland landmarks, probably painted by someone who had never tasted personally the rudeness of the streets.

Sam said that news of the death of his old pal hadn't surprised him much, when he'd heard it from the cops. He'd always expected something horrible to befall Fobbs.

"The man was certifiable," he declared, gesturing emphatically with his fork. "Not like me, you understand. *My* brain's not totally burned out on booze, like Leo's was. I'm a legitimate psychotic—I didn't *drink* myself crazy. Working for the feds made me this way, after they started zapping me with electromagnetic waves."

"Had you known Leo long?"

"Five years, give or take. We roomed together down in Sullivan's Gulch. . . ." This was a makeshift camp for the homeless beneath the west terminal of Portland's Banfield Freeway.

Mark had read that the site had been a "Hooverville" during the Great Depression.

Sam related how he'd often shepherded Leo through the day, leading him across the bridge to the Blanchet House in Old Town for a free breakfast, then across Burnside to the Rescue Mission for lunch. From there they often headed back across the bridge to Baloney Joe's, where they could spend the night if they were early enough to beat the rush. Otherwise they slept in Sullivan's Gulch or under Interstate 5.

Mark asked whether Sam knew anything about Leo's background.

"Damn right I know. He trusted me, just like *everybody* trusts me. People know I won't do 'em wrong, know what I mean? Would you believe I'm a published novelist? *Dead Man's Circle*, Ballantine Books, nineteen sixty-eight, by Samuel L. Darkenwald. Look it up."

This too Mark was ready to believe. Sort of. He politely reminded Sam that he'd been speaking of Leo Fobbs's past, then listened intently to the account of Fobbs's unfortunate life, mindless of the clatter of silverware, the background din of voices, or the thick smells of street people and oily cooking that hung in the air. Sam Darkenwald told the story directly and succinctly, seeming to embellish nothing and frankly admitting any gaps in his knowledge.

Leo Fobbs went to college somewhere in Texas and became a petroleum engineer in the Panhandle oil patch. He married, fathered at least two children, then divorced. He drank. He lost jobs, and drank some more. When the big oil bust hit during the last decade, he lost his mind along with his job.

He hit skid row and landed in a West Texas mental hospital, where he existed safely and comfortably for a time. Not long after the start of Ronald Reagan's presidency, money to care for people like Leo dried up, and the institution had no choice but to show him the door.

"I ended up on the street myself, right about that time," explained Sam. "Got myself ejected from a silly bin back in Maryland."

He'd met Leo in Minneapolis. "Great city, Minneapolis. Generous people, nice cops, good social services. A man can score a real good free dinner in that town. Only trouble is, they get a winter there that'll freeze your piss while it's still in your bladder. I could feel that killer winter coming on, so I said to Leo, 'Hey, man, we've got to get our asses down south, or maybe out west. . . .' "

The upshot was that Leo Fobbs and Sam Darkenwald ended up in Portland, Oregon, where they'd stayed for about five years.

Was there any possibility, Mark asked, that Leo Fobbs had ever gone to school in Eugene, Oregon, or in St. Louis? Or even in Oldenburg, for that matter? Had Leo ever lived in Oregon before coming here with Sam?

"Not unless he lied his ass off all those years I knew him," answered Sam. "I think I can say unequivocally that Leo never lived in St. Louis or anywhere in Oregon before he went crackers. By the way, did I mention that I'm a periodontist? You can tell by the condition of my gums." He parted his upper and lower lips with his dirty fingers, exposing savaged gums and decaying teeth. Mark winced, but said nothing. His heart sank. "Got my D.D.S. at the University of Maryland School of Dentistry, nineteen sixty-four," said Sam. "I'll give you a free checkup when you have time." He drank deeply of his coffee, and Mark wondered how much of what Sam had told him was believable. *Periodontist—my God.*

"Like I said before, I'm trying to find out if I've ever come into contact with Leo," said Mark. "He must've had some reason for gathering information about me. He was watching me, Sam. He'd collected a bunch of press clippings from the PSU newspaper—"

"Yeah, yeah, I know all that. He started carrying that stuff around with him about the time he went completely off his axle. 'Bout six months ago, near as I can recall, back when he totally lost touch with reality."

"Why *me?*" pressed Mark. "Had we known each other sometime in the past? Or had he read something about me that really pissed him off? Try to help me on this, Sam."

"Well, I can't say for sure," said Sam, looking thoughtful, "but it seems to me all this started about the time Leo started seeing that woman. . . ." His voice trailed off.

"What woman? Are you saying Leo was romantically involved with someone?" This seemed an outlandish possibility, but Mark didn't smile.

"She visited us one time in Sullivan's Gulch—walked right across the exit ramp and found us under the freeway, like she knew where we were ahead of time. I say 'we,' but it was Leo she was after."

"Who was she?"

"Never found that out. She called to Leo by name, though, and he got up off his cardboard and went down to the pavement where she was waiting. He staggered, I remember, 'cause he really had a load on that day. He'd been sleeping. Right around New Year's, come to think of it, and I was too cold to sleep, even though I was trying to. Anyway, this woman called out to Leo, and he went to her. They talked for a while. She gave him something, and he put it in his pocket. Never would tell me what it was."

Sam had his suspicions, though. He figured she'd given Leo a switchblade knife. A little something to break the ice. Sam had later caught glimpses of it.

"Who was this woman, and what did she want with Leo?" Mark suddenly had a hunch that it involved a nightmare-figure laden with baskets, bags, and an antique spinning wheel. He described the hag he'd encountered on campus just before Leo jumped off Ione Plaza. Was *this* the woman? he asked, pressing.

"Nah, she was nothing like that—much younger. And she wasn't any street lady, either. I never really got a clear look at her, but later, after Leo started seeing her on a regular basis, I saw her car—one of those expensive foreign jobs, a red one. What are they called—Mercy-Bentleys, something like that?"

"Something like that," Mark answered. Sam's voice had started to modulate freakishly, making Mark edgy.

"Anyway, Leo started seeing her once a week or so, usually on Couch Street over in Old Town, but sometimes on this side of the river, like down on Ankeny. I used to worry when he went over to Old Town, 'cause you've got some real bad actors over there—tar heroin retailers, junkies, folks like that. I followed Leo now and then, just to be on hand in case some cracked-out punk tried to stick a blade in him. . . ."

Despite the dark lenses on Sam's sunglasses, Mark could sense the hurt in his eyes. Sam's voice grew louder as he talked, and people began to look up from their plates. Any cracked-out punk would be wise, Mark decided, not to cross Sam Darkenwald on the street.

"Usually she'd park in an alley, or sometimes in a parking lot. Old Leo would just sit in the car with her, and they'd talk. Then he'd get out after a while, and she'd drive away in her Mercy-Bentley. I figure she gave him those newspaper clips about you, and the pictures, and the phone list. I figure it was because of *her*—"

Sam Darkenwald suddenly broke down, burying his face in the frayed sleeve of his red jacket. He sobbed hugely, drawing the stares of men around him. Mark put a hand on his shoulder and tried to imagine how valuable a true friend must be if you're living on the streets.

"It was because of *her* that Leo went off his axle, Mr. Hansen," Leo blubbered, taking off his glasses to blot his tears. "She made him crazier'n he already was. It was on her account that he started chasin' you all over the place—at least that's how I've got it figured. Leo didn't give a rat's ass about you, Mr. Larsen. He was only doing what she told him to." He paused to lean away from the table. He pressed a finger against one nostril and blew a wad of snot onto the floor. Then he did the same with the other nostril.

Fighting his rising gorge, Mark said, "Sam, you've got to tell me everything you remember about this woman. It's very important. I'm sure you can understand—"

"Of course, I understand. But I can't tell you anything more, because Leo would never tell me anything about her. It was like they had some deep, dark secret between them. And whatever it was, it ate Leo up. It ate up what little of himself he had left. In the last six months he hardly said two words to me, except to ask me to keep his duffel bag when he was off—" Another flood of weeping swept over him. "She gave him money, and that let him drink. She gave him enough to suck down four, five bottles of Night Train a day. A man can't drink like that and live very long, Mr. Hansen . . ."

To which Mark agreed, shaking his head.

". . . so if he hadn't've taken a swan dive off that building, sooner or later he would've barfed his guts out on some curb and choked to death. And I guess it would've been sooner rather than later." Sam put his glasses on again. "By the way, did I mention that I used to breed championship mules? It's true, I swear to God, before the FBI started following me. I had the biggest mule herd in upstate New York, one of the five biggest in the country. I've been in shows on four continents—"

Mark got to his feet slowly, tiredly, then reached down to shake Sam Darkenwald's hand before leaving.

6

The Voice of Reason

They draw close to the place the Cathlamets call Mesatchie Illihee, the haunt of evil spirits, which Queen Molly told Elspeth about years earlier. Tonight Elspeth has asked Queen Molly to guide her here, for in this place is great power, surely. She means to draw upon that power to fuel her own magic, to use it against the Enemy who at this very moment prowls nearby.

The white woman cries out, dropping her spinning wheel and basket. She clutches her abdomen and staggers. Queen Molly lets go of her own burden and grasps the girl around the shoulders.

"The water has broken," Elspeth gasps. "The pains are coming!"

"Easy now, my girl. Mesatchie Illihee is only a few steps away. We'll go there, you and I, and you will rest."

"My basket, Molly! Find it for me!"

Queen Molly finds the basket and holds it up. Elspeth pulls from it a tiny amulet on a string of gold and presses it into Molly's hand. "When the baby comes, place this around her neck!" she whispers. "You must do it the moment she is born. Promise me you'll do it, Molly!"

"Yes, I will do it. But you must come now. You cannot give birth here."

They pass alongside a storm-warped pole that men had carved with totems and erected hundreds of summers ago. At its top roosts the winged head of Sahalee Tyee, the god who rules the world of the Fish People.

The wind dies abruptly. The moon is barely high enough now to daub the crowns of the tallest trees with silver. In the center of the clearing is a low knoll covered with grass, where Elspeth lies down, clutching her belly. "We'll need a fire," she whispers. . . .

—from Poverty Ike's Tale
Halloween of '66 (continued)

i

"You're sure you have everything?" asked Deidre, leaning through the passenger window of the old BMW to kiss her son good-bye. She was dressed for work in a white cotton piqué suit, which sported a fitted skirt and a double-breasted coat with brass buttons. Mark caught a whiff of her perfume and wished she would kiss *him*, too.

"Everything except Nintendo," answered Tad with a hint of rebuke aimed at Mark. He hugged his mother hard.

"Thaddeus, I happen to agree with your father on that point," said Deidre. "A break from the video screen will do you good." She glanced up at Mark, but showed no inclination to lean in his direction. "Take care of my baby, okay?"

"Count on it. We'll look forward to your first visit."

"Not next weekend, but maybe the one after that. We're in the teeth of the building season, you know. . . ." Mark nodded and smiled thinly. They'd been over all this. Touching Tad's cheek, Deidre said, "Miss you. I'll call you tomorrow." She then headed toward the garage and her yellow Cadillac Allante. Mark watched her as she got into the car, admiring the smoothness of her walk, her simple elegance, the way her body moved beneath her clothing.

"Let's go!" urged Tad, yanking him back to reality. "It's already seven-thirty!"

Mark started the engine and backed out of the drive. "Listen, Tad Bear, we have to make one short stop before hitting the road—downtown. You can stay in the car and listen to your tapes, or you can tag along. I won't be more than half an hour, I promise."

"Aw, Dad—we're *never* going to get to Gram's and Gramp's!"

"We'll get there, believe me. I just need to talk to someone for a few minutes—"

"Your shrink, right?"

Mark's mouth fell open. He couldn't recall ever talking about his therapist in Tad's presence. Had the boy overheard his call to Dr. LeBreaux last night, when he should have been asleep in bed?

"Well, yeah," Mark answered. "I just want to . . . oh, I don't know . . . *talk* to her for a few minutes."

"No sweat. You probably need to talk after everything that's happened in the last couple days."

Mark appreciated the grown-up response and said so.

ii

Dr. Kyleen LeBreaux was five years Mark's senior, a striking, ivory-skinned woman whose raven hair hung straight to the base of her slender neck. With her enormous dark eyes she would have made a good hypnotist, Mark often kidded her—getting lost in them was so easy. She practiced in a plush condominium apartment at River Place, which fronted the marina on the Willamette River.

Mark gazed through the window of her study at the naked masts of sailboats and told her about the Leo Fobbs catastrophe. He told her about suffering the hallucination in which Fobbs, who was clearly dead, spoke to him. (*"If you know what's good for you, root it out."*)

He related his encounters with the hag, both in the real world and the nightmare world. He told her about Father Charlie Briggs's ghastly suicide, the revelations of the Portland cops and his conversation with the bizarre Sam Darkenwald at Baloney Joey's Junction. He wrapped up with a description of the vague fear gnawing his guts—that some dark invader was steering his course with an invisible hand.

"And that's everything?" she asked.

"The whole jar of pickles, and I've only used sixteen minutes. Must be some kind of record, huh?"

"Mark, I've got another patient due in less than half an hour. Would it piss you off terribly if I dispensed with the psychobabble and cut to the chase?"

"Not at all. I appreciate your squeezing me in like this. Besides, my son will probably hot-wire my car and drive it to Oldenburg if I'm gone much longer."

"There's nothing wrong with you. Go in peace."

"That's *it?* That's all you have to tell me?"

"It's all you need, Mark." She leaned back in her chair, and Mark couldn't help but let his eyes wander over her lithe legs. She wore a bright red jacket-dress over a black skirt and a white blouse—chic, yet very professional. He had noticed over the years that she had a thing for red, and the reason was obvious: She looked great in it.

"The fact is," she continued, "you've had a spurt of bad luck—the incident with Leo Fobbs and the suicide of your friend, the priest, either of which would've taxed a person's emotions. You're entitled to be upset, even a little unhinged, given the circumstances. In view of the trauma you've had, the hallucination is nothing to get worked up over, unless you start suffering more of them, and you won't. You're not nuts. I should know."

"What about the woman with the spinning wheel?"

"What *about* her? You met a bag lady, and you thought she looked familiar. You dreamed about her—happens to everybody."

"But it was a *slug*-dream, Kyleen. Doesn't that mean anything?"

"You have a simple phobia, which doesn't exactly set you apart from the rest of humanity, Mark. Like I've told you a hundred times, you're lucky, because your particular phobia isn't debilitating. It's not even particularly rare. It doesn't keep you from working, or going out into the open air or driving or flying. You've learned to handle it well. Still, you have to expect harmless little phobic nightmares from time to time."

"The dream itself isn't what's scaring me."

"Oh? Then what is?"

"How about the fact that Fobbs was stalking me? How about the mysterious woman with the Mercy-Bentley . . . ?"

Kyleen LeBreaux snickered at this, which set Mark to giggling. Soon they were laughing loudly together, more at each other's attempts to stop laughing than at Sam Darkenwald's butchered name for an expensive European car.

"Mark, I'm sorry—this isn't professional. The fact that Leo Fobbs kept a file on you is worth being uneasy about, certainly. But consider this: The guy was a drunk, an addict. Living like he was, drinking heavily in all likelihood, he was undoubtedly psychotic. My professional opinion is that anyone who'd jump off a twelve-story building is very sick."

"Meaning?"

"Meaning that his obsession with you must have a simple, real-world explanation."

"Such as?"

"Such as, he was rooting around one day in somebody's Dumpster, somebody who subscribed to PSU's campus newspaper, somebody who kept back issues of the *Humanities Newslet-*

ter and whatever other periodicals that Leo kept clippings from. The guy throws all this stuff away, and Leo finds it in the Dumpster. He sees your picture, and in his sick mind he thinks you're the one who stole his first girlfriend away. Or maybe he thinks you're the drill instructor he hated when he was in the Marines. Or maybe you're the villain who existed nowhere except in his psychotic nightmares—who knows?"

"*We* never will, will we?"

"That's right, because he's dead. He can't hurt you or anybody else. You shouldn't waste valuable energy worrying about whatever might've motivated him, because those motives died with him. Suffice it to say that Leo Fobbs was in the grip of a psychopathic obsession that lacked any rational basis. It would be a mistake to make any more of it than that."

"And what about Sam Darkenwald's story?"

"Oh, give me a break! Didn't you say Darkenwald thinks he's a dentist?"

"A periodontist. He offered me a free checkup."

"And a published writer?"

"A novelist."

"And what else—a horse trader, didn't you say?"

"A breeder of championship mules. His mules have been in shows on four continents. He was also a presidential appointee, worked in the old Department of Health, Education, and Welfare. Also, the FBI is after him, shooting him with some kind of radiation."

"*Please*—*!*" Dr. LeBreaux smothered another laugh by pressing her long fingers to her lips. Mark noticed that her nails matched her lipstick and jacket-dress. "Mark, listen to yourself. You're talking about a derelict who admits to having been an institutionalized psychotic. He's clearly still suffering delusions. You can't believe a word he says, even though he himself may fervently believe everything he's told you. A *periodontist* . . . !" Giggles squirted through her pursed lips.

"So the woman with the big European car was just a figment of Sam's imagination?"

"Either that, or she actually did exist somewhere in his past. He might've encountered her somewhere and kept her memory alive until he could use it in a good fantasy. That's typical of schizophrenia, Mark—the delusions feature things of the real world. One thing I'll guarantee, though, is that Sam's story about

the woman and her relationship with Leo Fobbs was either made
up for your benefit or a full-blown schizophrenic delusion."

"So I have nothing to worry about," said Mark, staring
through the window toward the marina. "I'm just your regular
happy, healthy guy who . . ."

His throat constricted as his eyes focused on a smear across
the window glass. He took a deep breath to quell the revolt in his
stomach. The smear was a trail of mucus left by a slug that was
easily five inches long when fully stretched. Its cinnamon-
colored body glistened wetly in the cool morning sun as it inched
upward from lower right to upper left. Mark wanted to scream,
but he bit his tongue to keep from doing so.

Kyleen LeBreaux saw the revulsion in his face and rose out of
her chair. Reflexively she turned her eyes to see what had captured
his stare, and whispered, "My God!" when she saw the slug.

"Mark, it's all right," she said, taking both his hands in hers.
"It's on the outside of the glass. It must've crawled out of the
flower pots on my deck. I know your fear is real, but try to remember that it's just a harmless little animal. It can't hurt anyone, Mark—tell yourself that, and then believe it."

Mark swallowed hard and forced his eyes away from the
abomination on the windowpane. He felt queasy, chilly. He felt
the sting of sweat on his forehead and upper lip. "I-I'll be okay,"
he managed. "I should probably go."

"Mark, I'm so sorry this happened."

"You're not to blame, Kyleen."

"I know, but still, I'm so sorry. Please don't let it ruin your
day. Go to your son now, and go to Oldenburg, and write your
book, and do all the other things you said you wanted to do. And
don't make so much of what's happened to you since Friday.
You're *okay*, Mark. You're a good man and a good history professor, and you deserve to be happy. Now go."

She herded him toward the door, and he went compliantly. Before closing the door after him, she caught his sleeve and said,
"Remember, Mark—there's no unseen force that's rearranging
your destiny. Your life is in your own hands. *You're* the one
who's calling the shots, okay?"

"Okay," he answered, trying hard to believe her.

7

Tressa

i

After parking, Tressa Downey stood in the drive and stared a moment at the rectory, which appeared unchanged physically. The old brick walls rose dark and straight as ever. The window-panes glistened as one would expect, given the legendary compe-tence of Father Briggs's housekeeper, Amy Lidderdale, and the surrounding shrubbery bristled green, as it did every spring. Though her rational brain insisted that the place was unchanged, Tressa's heart said otherwise: Father Charlie's death had left a sadness that hung about the eaves like a chilly mist.

Mrs. Lidderdale, a hawk-nosed woman in her mid-sixties who wore her frizzy gray hair in a French roll, answered when Tressa rang. She thrust open the storm door and pulled the younger woman inside.

"Tressa, Tressa, thank you for coming," she said in a voice thinned by two days spent weeping. "I shouldn't've called so early in the morning, but I really did need to catch you. There are people here from Portland, from the archdiocese, and they're poking through all of Father Charlie's things. I didn't want them to see—" She stopped herself and glanced over her shoulder. "Let's talk in the parlor," she whispered.

She led Tressa into the parlor and offered coffee, still whis-pering as if the rectory was full of spies. Tressa declined the coffee, saying she needed to go home and change for work, which should have been obvious from the sweaty running gear she still wore. "Mother gave me your message when I got in from jogging," she explained, "and I drove right over. I really don't have much time, Mrs. Lidderdale." The workday at the courthouse started promptly at 8:30 A.M., only twenty minutes from now.

"I understand, dear, so I'll make this short. Wait here, and do make yourself comfortable. I'll be right back." Mrs. Lidderdale ducked into the hallway, leaving Tressa alone in the dim parlor with its fading wallpaper, heavy-limbed furniture, and lighted painting of the Blessed Mother.

From somewhere down the hall, perhaps from Father Charlie's study, issued men's low voices. Priests from the archdiocese, Tressa figured, sent to Oldenburg to arrange the funeral, to gather up the reins of the parish and sort through the business left unfinished by their fallen brother. She hoped not to encounter any of them.

Her mother had raised her in Father Charlie's parish, but Tressa wasn't keen on most priests. In college she'd worshiped at the altar of humanism and had fallen away from the Church. Priests were walking, talking anachronisms, in her view—educated men who clung to superstition and represented it as truth to the ignorant. Priests made her uncomfortable, and she steered clear of them when she could.

The one exception, of course, had been Charlie Briggs, whom she'd numbered among her closest friends since her early childhood, even after college. More than anyone else, he had helped her piece together the fragments of her life in the wake of drug addiction, the loss of a child and a marriage, the demolition of a bright career in theater. Never once had he patronized her. Fencing with him over the meaning of human existence had lately become one of the chief joys of her life.

Since learning of Father Charlie's gruesome suicide two days ago, she'd lived in a fog, too numb to eat, sleep, or even shed tears. She knew that the numbness would soon wear off, however, and her bruised heart would ache from the loss. Already, standing in this familiar old parlor, she felt a sob thickening in her chest.

Mrs. Lidderdale returned, carrying a heavy-looking book that was locked with a stout leather strap. She unloaded it into Tressa's arms. "He left his last instructions to me in a note," she said, tears forming behind her glasses. "I'm to make sure you get this. It's locked, as you can see, and I have no idea where the key is. Unless, of course, *you* have it."

"You're sure? No, I don't have any key. I can't imagine . . ." Tressa studied the brown cover of the tome. It had a sturdy brass lock that held the strap in place. Elaborate gold-tone script said simply *Journal*, and in the lower right corner, *Fr. Charles Francis Briggs.*

"He locked it to keep me from reading it, no doubt," sniffed Mrs. Lidderdale. "He once told me that the sin of gossip stained my soul, and he was right. I *am* an incurable gossip, and I'm nosy. I would've sneaked a peek or two at what he'd written, and I would've blabbed it all over town, sure as the moon rises and the tide comes in."

"Don't be so hard on yourself, Mrs. Lidderdale. Father Charlie loved you like a sister. He often told me so."

"Thank you, Tressa. I just want to say that—" She pulled a much-used handkerchief from her frock and pressed it to her mouth, as though holding back words that she herself didn't want to hear.

"What is it?"

"I can't help but think that the journal tells why he did this horrible thing to himself. Maybe I'm a blithering old fool, but I suspect there's a good reason why it's locked. Father Charlie may have felt no good could come from anyone reading it, and this is why there's no key. He might've hidden it or thrown it away. Anyway, I haven't told the folks from the archdiocese about the journal, and I don't want them to see it. I'm sure they would insist on taking it, and I'd end up having an awful row with them. Father Charlie wanted *you* to have it, after all, and I intend to see his wishes carried out."

"I appreciate this, Mrs. Lidderdale. You're doing the right thing, I'm sure." Tressa moved toward the door.

"I suppose a person could cut the strap off," continued the housekeeper in a conspiratorial whisper, following close on Tressa's heels, "but a lock is a lock, isn't it?—meant to keep things out of sight. Please remember that if you're ever able to get the book open, Tressa. It may contain secrets you'd rather not know."

ii

The Kalapuya County Courthouse stood on the corner of Park Street and Chinook Avenue, surrounded by tall cedars and Douglas firs. Built in 1878 of gray granite, it had a magisterial dome and Georgian columns painted to look like marble.

Tressa Downey parked her Honda Accord in the paved lot that served both the courthouse and the Kalapuya County Library next door. Because her visit to the rectory had put her behind schedule, she'd driven the four blocks to work this morning rather than walk as she normally did.

She trotted up the front steps and negotiated an obstacle course of scaffolding in the rotunda, where workmen were busy restoring the gilded filigree on the interior of the small dome. She sidled through the door of the Board of County Commissioners' Office, glancing at the clock in the reception area. She was eight minutes late.

Her formal title was Executive Assistant to the Commissioners, meaning that she supervised two secretaries and a receptionist, but her authority was more nominal than real. Both secretaries had worked here far longer than she, and neither really considered Tressa the boss. Only the receptionist, Ginger Truax, seemed genuinely deferential toward her. Ginger was a bouncy blond girl of twenty-one, one of those delightful creatures who never stopped smiling.

Tressa had inquired about the job six months earlier, after reading about the vacancy in the *Oldenburg Clarion*. During the initial job interview, the chairman of the commission, Ed Nyberg, painted quite an alluring picture of the position, promising research, speech-writing and news media relations— responsibilities suited to a thirty-four-year-old woman with Tressa's background and high energy level. At her mother's urging, Tressa took the job, feeling ready for real work again after a full year of rest and recovery.

"Ed needs to see you, Tress," wheezed one of the secretaries without looking up from her word processor. She was Penny Gwynn, a woman too wrinkled for her forty years. Smoking all her adult life had roughened her voice. "He was looking for you at eight-thirty and told me to send you in when you finally got here."

Tressa thanked her with overdone civility and darted into her cramped office to grab a pen and pad. So armed, she strode to the end of a short corridor and tapped on a door with stenciling that identified the office as that of the Honorable Edwin Nyberg, Chairman, Kalapuya County Commission.

"Come in," said a voice on the other side.

Tress found the commissioner leaning against the edge of his

desk, chatting with the county attorney, Don Gravely, who sat on
a fake-leather sofa. Nyberg was as round and ruddy as Gravely
was slight and pale. He had thinning sandy hair, while Gravely,
a much younger man, sported a toupee styled in an oily pompa-
dour, which bespoke his admiration of Ronald Reagan.

Tressa apologized for being late and took the offered seat next
to the county attorney, who stared unabashedly at her legs. Her
skin crawled.

Nyberg waved off her apology. "How would you like to take
a little drive up Nehalem Mountain this morning?" he asked. He
handed over a sheet of paper from his desk. "Remember this?
You'll recall that the new leading citizen of our county plans to
donate a rather princely sum to the county for the repair and restoration of the band shell in Kalapuya Park—up to ten thousand
dollars, as a matter of fact."

Tressa had seen the offer when it arrived several weeks earlier.
The letterhead sported a four-color picture of Gestern Hall, a
Gothic relic that was home to one of the community's oldest
families. A year earlier the sole surviving Gestern heir, Clovis,
had returned from living overseas, or so the local story went, and
had converted the house into a bed-and-breakfast establishment.
He'd renamed it the Nehalem Mountain Inn, as the letterhead
confirmed. His signature carried a noble flourish suggestive of
good breeding and expensive schools.

Nyberg handed her another sheet. "This," he said, "is an official estimate from a building contractor in Astoria . . ."

Tressa scanned the estimate, which was $9,675, including ma-
terials and labor for rebuilding the stage, shoring up the rear
wall, and rewiring the lighting system of the band shell.

". . . and so we've naturally decided to take him up on his offer," concluded Nyberg, his broad face beaming. "That old band
shell is next to useless in its present sorry condition, but it could
be a real asset to the community again."

Gravely spoke for the first time. "Did you know that Mr.
Gestern contributed five thousand dollars back in February to
buy uniforms for the high school band? And that a month later
he gave fifty thousand to the Courthouse Restoration Fund?"
Tressa nodded. "This man has become very important to our
community, Tressa, and we need to make sure we handle him
right." Gravely had a way of telling people things they already
knew.

"If we get our ducks in a row and finish this project, we can have concerts in the park this summer, just like in the old days," added Nyberg. "God knows this town could use a little music." His tone implied that Oldenburg was languishing in the grip of the Black Death.

"So here's the deal, Tressa," said Gravely, using an important-man tone that mocked his unimportant appearance. "We need to clear this estimate with Gestern and arrange for transfer of the money as soon as possible. He called this morning and asked us to come up to Nehalem Mountain around nine o'clock. Unfortunately the commissioners and I are tied up with zoning variances for the rest of the day, and we don't want to ask a man like Clovis Gestern to reschedule. So we thought, 'Why not send Tressa?' You're certainly better-looking than we are, and Mr. Gestern's a red-blooded American boy. I'm sure he'd much rather see you than us. What do you say?"

Tressa let the sexism go by and said yes, as if she actually had a choice.

iii

The morning smelled sweetly of spring. As she walked to her car, she told herself that Father Charlie would have loved a morning like this—a day for golf, or a walk in the park, or a quiet chat with a friend on a sunny sidewalk. With thoughts like these she distracted herself from a burning curiosity about the locked journal that Father Charlie had bequeathed to her.

She turned right onto Main and drove through cross streets with names that attested to Oldenburg's Indian heritage: Clatskanie, Wahkiakum, and Klickitat. The main drag climbed a steep hill past the Bonneville Power Administration district office and the dignified, old law office of John Lansen.

Main Street narrowed as the town petered out. Beyond the city water tower, where the forest grew to the edge of the asphalt, it became Benson Creek Road. Tressa crossed the bridge over noisy Benson Creek, which tumbled through a cemetery in a sunlit meadow, where crumbling headstones cast crooked shadows across the green. She rounded a curve, and the forest broke yet again. A splintery wooden arrow on the left identified Queen

Molly Road, which looked recently graveled. A newer sign
pointed the way to the Nehalem Mountain Inn.

The road mounted the gentle grade and eventually took her to
a clearing on the mountainside with a postcard view of the town
nestled in its valley. A thin haze blanketed the Columbia River.
A supertanker crawled upstream toward Portland, and a pair of
hawks drifted in lazy circles overhead.

In the center of the clearing, Gestern Hall stood cold to the
sky, a Gothic marvel with a steep gable roof, a tall tower, a
porte cochere, and arched doors of dark wood. Elaborate tracery adorned the pointed windows, rendering quatrefoils against
stained glass. Juniper shrubs and Oregon grapes grew ragged
along the stone walls, which themselves were chaotic with
vines.

The house seemed impossibly old in Tressa's estimation—*too*
old for Oregon. She remembered one of the many local legends
about this place: back in the 1850s, the Gestern family had transported the ancestral house from Europe to this spot on the American frontier, stone by stone, timber by timber—all at colossal
expense. If the legend was true, Gestern Hall could be the genuine article, an artifact of a long-dead age.

She parked under the porte cochere and entered the house
through the heavy front door, to which someone had affixed a
brass PLEASE COME IN sign. A short foyer opened onto an entrance
hall that boasted two suits of authentic-looking armor, crossed
battle-axes on the walls, and a dark Oriental carpet. A newly
built registration desk flanked an ornate staircase.

Tressa inhaled the heavy silence and felt strangely vulnerable.
All her life she'd known Gestern Hall as a landmark on the face
of Nehalem Mountain. It was familiar and everlasting, like the
moon or a favorite planet, but it had also seemed far off, un-
touchable, almost mythical. Now, standing inside its maw, she
remembered . . .

iv

. . . One afternoon during her fourteenth summer, she and a
friend, Gina Pellagrini, are riding horseback up Queen Molly
Road, past Gestern Hall to the timbered summit of Nehalem
Mountain. Gina's father, Bernie, is one of Oldenburg's few gen-

uinely rich men, the owner of Pellagrini's Appliance Mart on the corner of First Street and Church Avenue. Bernie has given his daughter a pair of colts for her birthday, and Gina has asked Tressa to ride with her.

Seeing Gestern Hall up close for the first time is a shock. Tressa and Gina halt their horses and stare at the bleak old house from Queen Molly Road, their eyes wide. The place that has inspired so much local myth verges on dilapidation. Bear grass and wildflowers grow man-high in the yard, and the windows yawn forlornly.

Tressa feels something wriggle in her innards as she stares at the house, some intuitive alarm, maybe, that has survived countless millennia of mammalian evolution, a device that warned her early ancestors against ambush by saber-toothed tigers and cave bears—something that whispers, *Go no closer.*

How stupid, she thinks after she and Gina are galloping toward the summit again. A case of teenaged willies, certainly. There was absolutely nothing to be scared of. . . .

V

How stupid, she thought at this very moment, two decades later, standing for the first time within the stone walls of Gestern Hall. A shadowy old house couldn't scare her these days—not after the cruelties she'd suffered in the real world beyond the shadow of Nehalem Mountain. She would sooner meet a ghost or a goblin than face losing a child. She would readily wrestle with a werewolf rather than endure even one minute of withdrawal from cocaine addiction.

"Good morning, Miss Downey," breathed someone behind her, and she whirled crazily, adrenaline pumping. The voice belonged to a doughy woman of late middle age, who wore a long, drab dress and a shawl. The costume looked vaguely medieval, which Tressa supposed was part of the inn's ambiance. "You're a few minutes early, but Mr. Gestern will gladly see you." Her mouth was full of crooked, rotten-looking teeth that turned her S-sounds into faint whistles. Her color was bilious, as if she had liver problems. "If you'd care to follow me. . . ."

Tressa felt silly for nearly jumping out of her skin and stammered an apology. She followed the woman down a dusky hallway to a pair of massive double doors.

"Miss Downey is here to see you, sir," whistled the woman after rapping on the aged wood. Tressa noticed that she had dark, urgent eyes.

"Ah, yes," said a melodic male voice from within. The doors opened inward, pulled by a tall, straight man in his early thirties who wore expensive-looking tennis togs. His eyes were hazel, his face angular, his brown hair cropped fashionably short. "Ms. Tressa Downey, the emissary from the County of Kalapuya," he said, as if announcing a visiting dignitary to a royal court. "Welcome to the Nehalem Mountain Inn. I've been expecting you." He ushered her into a walnut-paneled study with tall leaded-glass windows facing east and south, through which sunlight flowed amber, green, and scarlet. From a vaulted ceiling hung an iron chandelier that held gnarled, melted candles.

"I'm Skip Gestern, owner and operator of this humble establishment," he said, offering his hand. "And this dear lady is Mrs. Bellona Drumgule, whose family has been closely associated with my own for many generations." Tressa shook the doughy woman's hand and saw that the look of urgency had not left her eyes.

Mrs. Drumgule asked whether she should bring anything from the kitchen, and Gestern suggested coffee and croissants. He shepherded Tressa to a brocaded settee near the window and seated her.

"I hope you'll forgive the informal gear, Ms. Downey—I used to play a lot of tennis, and these are great for knocking around the house. Someday I plan to put in some courts and do more than just knock around—providing I can find someone who plays, that is. Do you by chance play?"

"Using the term loosely, yes. Mostly I chase the balls I knock over the fence."

Gestern laughed. "I think we'd be well matched. I dress for the game much better than I play it. By the way, do you mind if I call you Tressa? You can call me Skip. Clovis doesn't really fit anyone under a thousand years old, it seems to me."

Tressa smiled and gave her permission for using first names. "I've brought the paperwork that Commissioner Nyberg discussed with you on the phone," she said, opening her attaché case. "If you'd care to take a look at the estimate for the remodeling of the band shell, I'll—"

"Oh, hell, let's dispense with the official folderol! It's too early in the day for such dreary stuff, don't you think?" He strode to an antique writing table near the window and took a checkbook from the top drawer. He scribbled a check, tore it out, and handed it to her. "If there's a balance, give it to the welfare fund with my compliments."

She examined the check with eyebrows raised and wondered how it felt to drop ten thousand dollars so casually. "Would you mind signing this memorandum of understanding?" she asked, offering him a sheet of paper from her attaché case. "It merely confirms that you're giving a gift to the county without having it reduce your taxes, and that you expect no—"

"Sure—same as the last time, I assume." He knew the bureaucratic drill, having recently given many thousands for school band uniforms and the restoration of the court house.

"Well," said Tressa, "that was quick. I suppose I should thank you on behalf of Kalapuya County, but that seems a little lame. You probably deserve a parade in your honor or at least a ceremony of some kind."

"Not at all. I'm only doing what's right, and no one deserves special treatment for that. The Gestern family has been part of this community for nearly a century and a half, and we've profited handsomely from it. The time has come to give something back, that's all."

Gestern's accent took Tressa back to a summer she'd spent in Cambridge, Massachusetts, where she'd worked in the Brattle Theater Company. It had that slightly adenoidal quality she'd always associated with New England's snooty upper crust. Still, Skip Gestern was charming in a preppy sort of way, not at all as she'd imagined him.

Mrs. Drumgule arrived with the coffee and croissants. Tressa accepted a cup but declined the pastry in the interest of slimness. Mrs. Drumgule glided silently away.

"I understand you're a theater person," said Gestern, surprising her. "A professional actor and director, I hear." Tressa set her cup down, and stared at him for several long seconds. Who had told him this? That Clovis Gestern could have talked about her with someone seemed nigh unbelievable.

She wondered what else he'd heard. "I *was* a theater person," she replied finally, using a tone more fulsome than she'd intended. "I'm a regular working stiff now."

"I was hoping that you would organize a production someday, and put it on in the band shell—share your gift, as it were. I'll bet the folks of this town would appreciate a little light comedy on a hot summer's night, especially if the cast was local."

"No Henrik Ibsen or Eugene O'Neill?"

"Oh, hell no," laughed Gestern. "Something light and farcical, I'd think."

"I'm afraid my theater days are gone forever," answered Tressa with a smile that she feared was a sad one, and it was.

Skip Gestern's acute hazel eyes registered the meaning, and he smoothly changed the subject. "Well, what do you think of our little establishment, now that the restoration is nearly done? Since you're a local girl, I assume you know what it looked like before."

"Only from the outside. I have to say I'm impressed, though— it's like walking into a medieval fantasy."

"I'll give you the short tour, starting in this room." He rose from the sofa, leaving his own coffee untouched, and beckoned her to the tallest of the stained-glass windows. Heavy brocaded drapes swooped downward from the arched top. Woven into the fabric was a tapestry of medieval ships with square sails and blank-faced oarsmen. Flowers, birds, and fantastic creatures surrounded the ships. Gestern explained that these were seventeenth-century copies of actual tapestries from the era of the Hundred Years' War, executed during a neo-Gothic revival.

"The house itself dates from the same period," he went on, while Tressa got lost in the incredible play of color in the threads. "Hardly anyone in the Middle Ages actually built anything like this, since real Gothic architecture was mainly cathedrals and castles—seldom anything so prosaic as mere houses."

Tressa touched the brocade lightly and said, "So it's true about your family having brought this house over from Europe."

"Oh, true indeed. Stone by stone, stick by stick. From Burgundy in France, around Cape Horn to San Francisco, and then on to Astoria via the Northwest Steam Navigation Company. Quite a feat in eighteen fifty-eight, no doubt. It took a dozen shiploads, if you can believe the family records, and nearly three years to reassemble the old barn when they finally got it here."

He chuckled irreverently and steered her toward a row of paintings.

The nearest was a framed diptych that looked very medieval. Its left panel showed Christ wearing a gilded halo in the Garden of Gethsemane, talking secretively with a tall man dressed entirely in black. The right panel showed Christ carrying the cross up the tortuous trail to Golgotha, and at the side of the trail stood the same man in black, his face triumphant, as if he knew a great secret.

Something about the scenes disturbed Tressa. She barely heard Gestern talking about how many of the furnishings in the house were genuine medieval artifacts, even though the house itself was a mere three centuries old. The paintings had that flat, staged quality so characteristic of art in the Middle Ages, but they seemed alive with meaning, vital with dark secrets that Tressa felt a curious urgency to know.

Another painting depicted the Annunciation, with the Virgin dressed in medieval black. And yet another, which a small plaque identified as the work of someone called the Master of Wittengau, showed the entombed body of an emaciated Christ, with Mother Mary holding his wounded hand. The same dark-clad man lurked in the shadowy background of both paintings.

Tressa gasped audibly when she felt a breath of cold kiss her ankles and calves. Skip Gestern's pleasant voice droned on in her ears, detailing the long and expensive process of restoring Gestern Hall, while the coldness shot up past the hem of her sensible business suit, skimming her thighs like a zombie's fingers. She would have screamed if she could have found her voice, but it was all she could do to find her next breath. The room spun.

Suddenly someone was shaking her, spitting her name. It was Skip, his hazel eyes brimming with concern. "Tressa, are you all right? Are you ill?"

The coldness sliced through her panty hose and touched her groin, sending a lightning-bolt up her spine. Her breath froze in her lungs. She felt herself slipping toward the floor, but Skip's strong hands caught her and guided her into a Windsor armchair.

"Mrs. Drumgule! Bring some cold water! Quickly!"

Within seconds Tressa had her wits about her again. An avalanche of suspicions rumbled through her mind, but she dismissed each of them instantly as ludicrous.

No, the coffee had not been drugged.

No, she'd not been mildly poisoned by a gas leak.

And no, Clovis Gestern had *not* hypnotized her in order to cop a feel.

She sipped the water that Mrs. Drumgule brought and politely turned down the offer of a room for a brief rest. No, she didn't need a doctor, and, yes, she felt well enough to drive back to town. She wanted nothing more than to get out of this place.

"You're sure you won't let me drive you?" asked Gestern, following her out of the study.

"I'll be fine. I just need some air."

Gestern effused apologies as he trotted on her heels, begged her to visit again, perhaps for dinner and an evening of good conversation. Tressa promised that she would, but in her heart she vowed never again to darken the door of this house.

When she reached the foyer, she regained her sense of the appropriate, having remembered that she represented the County of Kalapuya and that she carried Clovis Gestern's ten-thousand-dollar check in her attaché case. She turned to him, intending to thank him a final time, maybe even to promise a play in the band shell, as he'd suggested.

She started when she saw his face, dark with anguish, his mouth working to form words but issuing nothing. For a terrible moment Tressa felt a deep pity, and she verged on throwing her arms around him.

Then she saw movement on the staircase near the registration desk, behind the backs of Skip Gestern and Bellona Drumgule, and her sanity returned. A young girl stood on the stairs, darkly handsome despite a milk-white scar at the corner of her mouth. She had lustrous black hair done in a hip rat's nest, deep brown eyes, and severe cheekbones. She wore a bulky medieval peasant's costume that could not hide a tired stoop.

The girl stared at Tressa for a full five seconds, pleading silently with tragic eyes for something Tressa could not begin to know. Then she dashed up the stairs, as if running away to hide. Fear knotted Tressa's stomach—fear of whatever had frightened the dark young girl, of whatever had touched her so intimately in Gestern's study just moments ago. She stammered something about the county's gratitude, something else about being sorry. Then she turned and walked as steadily as she could through the dusky foyer to the double doors that led to the porte cochere. Mrs. Drumgule stayed close at her elbow, talking, her S's whistling. Skip Gestern stayed behind, silhouetted against the meager light of the entrance hall, standing silent as though stricken with grief. Tressa threw a final glance back at him as Mrs. Drumgule muscled open the heavy doors, but saw only his retreating shadow on the Oriental carpet—a shadow grossly misshapen, as if its owner was not quite a man.

8

Fish Hawk Ridge

Queen Molly gathers sticks and dry leaves from the sheltered edges of the clearing. When she turns back to the knoll, her mouth drops open in shock: Elspeth has loosened her long hair and peeled off her clothing. She stands naked, her arms outstretched, her sweating face turned skyward, her breasts and belly pink with the light of the Blood Star.

She chants in a language that's gibberish to Cathlamet ears, in a melody as mournful as a night wind. Queen Molly works while Elspeth chants, beating down the wet grass to make a place for the fire. Only when the fire sizzles and pops does Elspeth crouch to the warmth.

She sets to work with things from her basket, mixing together foul-smelling liquids in a shallow bowl, adding powders and spices from earthen jars. At times she mutters low words or holds the bowl over the fire to heat the mixture. Then, to Queen Molly's astonishment, she tips the bowl up and guzzles the potion, chewing the bits of offal afloat in it.

The fire flares, throwing a swarm of sparks into the night, and silence falls over Mesatchie Illihee. Elspeth cries out from a stab of pain and topples onto her back beside the fire. Queen Molly tears off her beaver robe and lays it over Elspeth's naked body, cradling her head and stroking her brow. The baby comes, a girl, as Elspeth knew it would be.

Queen Molly receives the baby from her mother's body and wipes her clean with a doeskin cloth that she herself has chewed to feathery softness. Remembering her promise, she takes out the amulet, which the crackling firelight shows to be a smaller version of the silver ring Elspeth wears, and slips it over the child's head. She wraps the bawling infant in Elspeth's woolen shawl and lays her at Elspeth's breast. . . .

—from Poverty Ike's Tale
Halloween of '66 (continued)

i

"God, we must look like Okies," Mark Lansen quipped as he turned onto the Oldenburg exit from U.S. 30, referring to the fact that the car was loaded floor to ceiling with stuff (most of it Tad's).

"What're Okies?" Tad wanted to know. He'd just finished a giant-size blueberry Slurpee from the 7-Eleven in Rainier, where they'd made a pit stop on the drive from Portland, and his lips were a ghastly blue.

Mark explained that during the thirties "Okies" were poor migrants who piled their ragtag household goods into their Model T's and set out for the Golden West, seeking a better life. The term derived from Oklahoma, where many of them originally lived.

Mark had enjoyed the drive from Portland. The world had started to seem good again. Under a sky of roaring blue they'd motored west from Portland through a lush river valley carpeted with evergreen, past farms and mills and refineries and a giant nuclear power station called Trojan. They'd rolled through quiet little burgs nestled in the green hills—the towns of Columbia City, Clatskanie, and Scappoose. With every passing mile Mark's anticipation sharpened over settling down to write the little book he'd put off for so long, a history of the town in which he'd grown to manhood, of the people and events that constituted the roots of his own life. Like many historians who had gone before him—notably, the Emperor Claudius of first-century Rome, who was more a scholar than a politician—Mark deemed the writing of history a way of *living* it. Writing the book about Oldenburg would be his vehicle into the past, a means of experiencing a world denied him by the accident of being born at the wrong time. He would know life on the American frontier, its excitement and expectations, its perils. He would witness the settling of the lower Columbia, the building of Oregon. He would find—

What?

What was he *really* looking for? he asked himself.

He let the questions lie and signaled a turn onto the Oldenburg exit.

ii

The exit ramp ended at an intersection with Main Street, and Mark turned left into Oldenburg, Oregon, population 2,491, according to a welcome sign posted by the local Chamber of Commerce. Quaint storefronts and frame houses squatted on both sides of the twisty, hilly street. A trio of church steeples poked high through the treetops, as if vying with each other in the proclamation of rural godliness. To the east, where the town was newer, loomed signs for Chevron, Texaco, and McDonald's, proclaiming something else entirely.

Thomas Wolfe was wrong, thought Mark: You *can* go home again. Oldenburg always made him feel welcome, and sometimes he wished he'd never left. He loved this little old town for its simple purity. He loved its sense of history, the unhurried tempo and the quiet.

From the very beginning, the people of Oldenburg had earned their eats through honest toil on the land or water, and for this Mark respected their memory enormously. They'd cut timber and floated the logs to the German Point mill on the banks of the Columbia. They'd fished the river and the ocean beyond its mouth. They'd sweated for pennies an hour in the once-thriving Hilde cannery that now huddled in ruin on the river's edge. Most of the surviving families, the ones who had hung on after an onslaught of decades and tough times, still worked hard for their living, mostly with their hands. This wasn't a yuppie bedroom community, but a real town with a real past.

The Lansen family house stood in a peaceful neighborhood on the timbered hillside of Fish Hawk Ridge, overlooking Kalapuya Park and the campus of the county high school. It was a comfortable old Tudor surrounded by sturdy hemlocks, oaks, and maples. Neither the biggest nor the grandest house in Oldenburg, it bespoke the reputation that John Lansen, Mark's father, had fashioned as a lawyer and businessman. It was an *honorable* house.

Mark followed the curving driveway around to the rear, where stood the four-car garage. He pointed to a tall oak, and said, "The neighbor kids and I used to climb that tree and hang old tires from it. Tires make great swings, you know. Then we'd have jousting matches and try to knock each other out of our swings with padded broomsticks."

"Cool," said Tad. "Can we make one, Dad Bear? I bet Gramp

knows where we could get an old tire." He eagerly offered to climb the tree to tie the ropes on, or better still, *two* ropes, if they could find two tires. He and Dad Bear could have jousting matches, just like in the "olden days." Mark promised to ask Gramp about a tire, a length of rope, and a ladder.

They parked next to a new Saab sedan that Mark had never seen before and entered the house through the rear porch. They heard low voices coming from the neighboring sitting room, which fronted a glassed-in area crowded with potted plants—Marta's beloved solarium.

"She's resting now, and I gave her some flurazepam, which will help her sleep," said a competent-sounding male voice. "Make sure she has a good dinner tonight, lots of fruit juice and water but no alcohol or coffee. She should be fine tomorrow, but if she has any more trouble, call me at the Medical Center."

"Thanks for coming, Nat," said a female voice, which Mark instantly recognized as that of Kristen, his sister. "I appreciate your making a house call. I didn't think doctors did that anymore."

When Mark and Tad stepped into the sitting room from the kitchen, Kristen's face broke into a grin. "Mark, Tad! You made it!" She rushed over, hugged and kissed them both, made them lay their luggage down.

At twenty she was tall, blond and willowy, every inch a fresh-faced coed. Mark saw that she'd gotten her hair cut in a style he hated, one popular among his wife's friends in the country club set: It looked as if someone had placed a bowl on her skull and shaved the lower part of her head right up to the rim.

"Guys, meet Nathaniel Schell," she said, pulling them into the room. "He's Oldenburg's answer to St. Elsewhere, and he makes house calls."

Mark extended his hand to a wiry, well-tanned man in his late thirties, who looked as if he ran marathons, who looked suited to the Saab in the drive. Nat Schell wore a blue seersucker sport coat, faded Levi's with pressed-in creases, and a pair of shiny new penny loafers.

"Is Gram sick?" Tad wanted to know, beating his dad to the punch.

"Your grandmother's feeling a little under the weather," answered the doctor, smiling at the boy. "Nothing serious—

probably just nervous exhaustion. She should be her old self by
tomorrow morning."

Kristen then explained that Marta Lansen had neither slept nor
eaten since hearing the news of Father Charlie Briggs's suicide
more than two days ago. She'd become weak and dehydrated.

"Well, I'd best get moving," said Nat, glancing at his watch.
"Velma Selvig is due at the Center for her hay fever shot in five
minutes. Nice to meet you, Mark, and you, too, Tad." He headed
for the door, then turned to face them again. His eyes shifted between Mark and Kristen as he studied one, then the other. "You
know, the family resemblance between you two is really remark-
able."

"That's what everybody says," said Kristen, chuckling. "Peas
from the same pod, I guess."

The rear porch door slammed, signaling that the doctor was
out of earshot, upon which Mark and Kristen erupted into giggles. When Tad asked what was so funny, Mark took him by the
hand and led him into the front parlor, where a bank of old family photographs occupied an entire wall. Kristen brought up the
rear.

"I think you're old enough to hear the truth about your old
man," said Mark with mock solemnity. "You're no little kid anymore, right?"

Tad nodded.

The uppermost cluster of photos showed Mark at various
stages of his life, beginning with one snapped on the day John
and Marta rescued him from foster childhood in Portland. It
showed him in the driveway of this very house, a skinny twelve-
year-old leaning against the front fender of a shiny 1966 Buick
Electra, his face nervous, his dark hair shaggy like the Beatles'.
Later shots showed him in his high school years—debate competition, Key Club, a school play (he'd portrayed Tully Bascom in
The Mouse That Roared). His senior prom picture showed him in
a powder blue dinner jacket with black piping, smiling grandly
with his perfect teeth. On his arm was the clear-eyed beauty he'd
dated throughout his high school years, the one he'd been dead-
certain he would someday marry—Tressa Downey, the smartest
girl at Kalapuya County High.

Mark showed his son the pictures and briefly explained the
significance of each one. "The bottom line, Tad Bear, is that I
was adopted," he concluded. "I never knew my real parents. As

you can see, there aren't any pictures of me as a baby or a first-grader, or even when I was a fairly big kid like you."

"Who were your real mom and dad?" the boy asked, looking concerned.

"The only thing I know for sure is that my mother lived around here somewhere, and that she left me with an outfit called the Methodist Guardians in Portland. Gram and Gramp came and got me when I was twelve—picked me from thousands of other kids, and brought me to live here. It was the best thing that ever happened to me. I don't know anything at all about my father."

Tad studied the photos intently, occasionally squinting to make out some detail. His face was serious, and his hazel eyes brimmed with unspoken questions. Mark hoped that Tad had not sensed the incompleteness of the story he'd just told, that he wouldn't ask what had become of his real grandmother.

Mark directed his son's attention to the middle bank of photos, which featured Kristen, the Lansens' only child by blood. In one shot she was a slobbering baby in a frilly crib (the smile was due to gas, Mark had often teased her). In another she was a toddler cavorting on the lawn with Helga, the cocker spaniel puppy she'd gotten from Mark on her third birthday. Here she was on a bicycle, there in a sandbox with the little Pellagrini girl from next door. Other pictures recorded her steady growth from contrary tomboy into woman, capturing the blue gleam in her eyes, her brilliant grin.

"Want to know what's really weird?" asked Kristen. "Gram and Gramp had been trying to have kids for years before they adopted Mark, your dad. They'd gone to practically all the doctors between here and Portland, but no luck. Then—bingo—Gram turns up pregnant with me after they'd given up and adopted a boy!" A little practical joke played by nature, Mark offered. Kristen and he had often snickered and traded cross-eyed glances whenever someone remarked how much alike they looked, since he was unrelated to Kristen by blood.

True, though, they *did* look alike, despite the differences in their coloring and ages. Their faces were similarly long and narrow, their eyes deep-set and large. Both had squarish jaws and perfect white teeth. "All just coincidence," Mark said.

Tad looked troubled. Mark hoped he hadn't overestimated a nine-year-old's capacity to understand and accept such things.

"I don't know about you guys, but I'm getting hungry," said Kristen, changing the subject. "Why don't you haul your things up to your rooms, and I'll start some lunch. But be quiet, okay? Mom needs her sleep."

Mark hoped that Tad's silence signified nothing more than consideration for his sleeping Gram.

9

Dumpsters

i

Sam Darkenwald scored big in the Dumpster behind the Truong Wah Vietnamese restaurant on Portland's East Burnside: almost half an order of clear noodles with chicken sauce and water chestnuts, still warm in a cardboard take-home tub. Garnished with the usual thrown-out sprouts and shoots, the noodles would make a decent lunch, his first meal today.

Sam tucked the cardboard tub into his jacket and put on his prized Serengeti sunglasses. Then he darted out of the alley and headed for his favorite resting spot on this side of the Willamette River—the garbage rack behind the East Side Masonic Temple.

By the time he got there he was hot and sweaty, so he shed his heavy red-plaid jacket and his sweaters, which still left him wearing three shirts. The cool shade of the building was a blessing for which he was thankful, even though he'd vowed long ago never to complain of the heat. To a homeless man, heat is far preferable to cold.

He took off his sunglasses and ate the noodles with his fingers, sitting cross-legged on the asphalt with his back against a Dumpster that buzzed with flies, his battered cowboy hat resting on a knee. Too soon he was finished, having licked the container and his fingers clean. Already his mind turned to the question of where to look for his next meal.

But his thoughts wandered. He became aware of a rare, almost forgotten feeling from another life—something that had crept over him again and again in the three days since his only real friend jumped from a high-rise apartment building: loneliness. Sam missed Leo. He worried about the weirdness that had gripped his friend in those last six months. Some instinct warned that the trouble wasn't over yet, that Leo's death hadn't really *cured* anything. Despite the warmth of the spring day and the three shirts he wore, a chill rattled through him.

ii

He dozed, then bolted awake. He'd heard something he couldn't define, and he knew he was no longer alone in the alley. Layered over the background rush of city traffic was a windy whirring like nothing he'd ever heard. He leaned away from the Dumpster to glance up and down the alley, but he saw no one.

The sound was very close.

He got to his feet, coiling himself to fight, if need be. He reached behind him and took the lid from an aluminum garbage can, a serviceable shield against a switchblade or a crowbar. As he edged around the Dumpster, the whirring rose in pitch and became stronger. His heart started pounding so hard he worried that it might burst.

What he saw on the other side of the Dumpster raised the hairs on his neck and caused his balls to shrink. She was the oldest, ugliest woman Sam Darkenwald had ever seen. She sat amid a collection of dirty bundles and baskets like a pack rat in her nest. A gray overcoat hung from her misshapen body like a worn-out hide. Her gauzy hair stood out in bunches beneath a mangy fur hat. Her eyes chilled him, and her twiggy fingers made him think of dead trees. A stink rose from her like steam from a sweaty racehorse.

She labored over an antique spinning wheel, urging it faster, faster, until its whine filled Sam's head like a squadron of hornets. Sunlight leapt off a huge silver ring on a finger of her right hand, inscribing hypnotic circles in the air as she turned the wheel.

"Don't be scared of me, lad," she said through a near-toothless grin. "Count yourself lucky if I'm the worst you've ever seen."

She was without a doubt the worst Sam had ever seen. He tried to count himself lucky, tried to answer, but his vocal cords wouldn't cooperate.

"I see you're havin' trouble breathing. It'll pass, if you take a nip of this." With her free hand she handed him a small green bottle from a leather pouch. Sam held it to his nose and grimaced. Its contents smelled vaguely like Vick's VapoRub.

Against his better judgment he put it to his lips and drank, having no idea what to expect. The herb potion produced a quick shower of sparks behind his eyes and made his innards instantly cool. Within seconds he felt utterly calm.

"I sought you out, Sam Darkenwald, because you're already touched. The things you'll see in the days ahead would break the reason of any sane man, but *you*—well, let's say you're beyond that kind of harm."

"How do you know my name?"

"I know all about you, lad. I know enough about you to have chosen you for a special service. I know you've got the fortitude and the honesty to do all that needs doing. Are you willing?"

No one had called Sam "lad" for probably forty years. "Can't say, ma'am," he answered. "You haven't said what you want me to do."

She spoke to him quickly and with economy of words, as if time was critical: Go to unit 214 of the Town Center Motel on Sandy Boulevard, scarcely half an hour's walk east of here. Find a man named Bob Gammage. Tell him that the girl he's seeking, one named Skye Padilla, is in a place called Gestern Hall, near a town called Oldenburg.

Could Sam remember this—especially the names? The names were very important.

"No problem, ma'am," he answered. "I used to be a certified public accountant and a junior partner in one of the Big Eight firms. I'm a hell of a lot smarter than I look."

"I'm sure you are."

"And that's all you want me to do? Just tell this Bob Gammage character about the girl—what did you say her name was?"

"Her name is Skye Padilla. Bob Gammage will know who you mean. By the way, he may look ferocious, but he'll not harm you. Remember that he is no one to fear. And yes, this is your only errand for now."

Minutes later Sam Darkenwald was headed up Burnside toward its junction with Sandy, where the neighborhood seemed slightly more respectable. His mind was full of his errand, full of wonder over the old woman he'd just met. He said the names over and over to himself—Skye Padilla, Gestern Hall, Oldenburg, to make sure that he wouldn't forget them.

iii

The knock on the door of unit 214 jarred Bob Gammage out of exhausted sleep. He'd spent the night in Old Town, loitering among the addicts and the throwaways of urban America, searching for a face he'd seen only in photos, asking questions while trying to remain unobtrusive—all to no avail. Dawn had broken by the time he made his way back to the Town Center Motel on Sandy Boulevard, and the whores were checking out and going to wherever whores go when the sun comes up.

Bob Gammage's bones ached. His mind ached. His *soul* ached. He'd slept like a hibernating snake—coldly, dreamlessly. Now he groped under the mattress for his well-oiled Sig Sauer nine-millimeter. He snapped off the safety and padded to the door, holding the weapon close to his side.

Who the fuck could *this* be? he wondered. He'd told no one other than the Portland cops where he was staying. He opened the door only as far as the security chain allowed, and peeked around the edge. A derelict stood on the other side—a fairly big guy in a shapeless, moth-eaten cowboy hat and a heavy plaid hunting jacket that must have been unreal in the noontide heat. Unbelievably, he wore a pair of hundred-dollar shades.

"You've got the wrong fuckin' room, Speed," Gammage growled. "Get outta my face, okay?" He leaned against the door, but the derelict jammed a boot into the opening, keeping it from slamming. Gammage's anger level ratcheted up a notch. "I *said* you've got the wrong room. Now beat it."

"I don't have the wrong room, Mr. Gammage. I have something you want—some information. I hear you're looking for a girl named Skye Padilla."

"And just who the hell are you?"

"Samuel L. Darkenwald, Colonel, U.S. Marine Corps, Retired."

"Tell me how you know Skye."

"I don't know her myself, but I ran into someone who does. I know where she is. You interested?"

Bob Gammage was interested. He unhooked the security chain and motioned Sam Darkenwald inside.

iv

The hag had said that Bob Gammage was not someone to be feared, but Sam couldn't help feeling some misgivings. Gammage was a short and blocky man, the kind you could hit with a haymaker, only to watch him come back at you with homicide in his eyes. He had a knife scar across the left side of his forehead and shoulder-length hair streaked with gray. On one sinewy forearm he had a tattoo of a Mandarin dragon and on the other a screaming eagle.

"Sit in this chair, and don't move," he commanded Sam. "Do anything weird, and I swear to God I'll put a cap in you."

Sam sat in a threadbare armchair that smelled vaguely of baby poop, while Gammage dressed. He studied the room's trappings—the cigarette-scarred carpet, the cheap TV bolted to the wall, the dust-encrusted window sills. Long ago Sam would not have deigned to sleep in such a room. Long ago Sam had rented only suites in which the help left mints on your pillow.

Gammage sat on the bed when he'd finished dressing and smoked a cigarette, eyeing Sam with blank, unfeeling eyes. "Talk to me, Speed. And spare me any bullshit about life in the Marines."

Sam repeated what the hag had told him, almost word for word. Gammage stared at him silently for a full thirty seconds, as if to detect any sign of a liar's twitch.

"That's *it?* The girl is in Oldenburg? Where the fuck is Oldenburg, anyway?"

"Little town out toward the ocean. I rode through it once in a freight car."

"Tell me about this Gestern Hall or whatever it's called."

"That's what it's called, I guess—Gestern Hall. And that's about all I know about it. My—uh—*friend* didn't say any more than that."

Gammage rose from the bed and swung into motion. He stashed his gun into a small canvas bag. He gathered up his shaving gear, a few pieces of dirty laundry, and some magazines, then stashed those, too, all in the space of thirty seconds. Thus packed, he turned to Sam.

"I don't know why I believe you, Speed. I get the definite feeling you're not telling me everything."

"I wouldn't lie to you, Mr. Gammage, and I wouldn't hold

anything back. I'm a former federal circuit judge. If I lied to you, I'd be violating the canons of judicial ethics. My word is gospel, you can be sure of that."

"I thought you were a career Marine," Gammage chuckled, shaking his head.

"Mr. Gammage, I'm a lawyer and a jurist. Went to Yale Law School, Class of 'Fifty-nine, tenth in my class, Law Review. I served—"

"When's the last time you ate?"

"Oh, about an hour ago, I guess."

"You got a place to sleep?"

"Half a dozen of 'em."

"Any with a roof?"

"Not so you'd notice, except for the Rescue Mission. Oh, and Baloney Joe's has a roof, I guess. I stay there when I can beat the rush."

"You want to run with me for a few days? I'll feed you, put you up, as long as you stay out of my hair and do everything I say. Cause me any problems, and I'll shoot your fucking knee-caps off."

"I'd be delighted, Mr. Gammage. But I can't figure why you'd want to take someone like me along with you. I'm a psycho, in case you hadn't guessed, an honest-to-goodness paranoid schizo-phrenic. My illness can get fairly bizarre at times."

Gammage paused a long time, looking thoughtful. "Let's say I have this feeling you might come in handy. It's my gut talking, and my gut only lies to me about half the time." He picked up a towel from the filthy carpet and tossed it over. "Get yourself a shower. I'm not letting you into my car, smelling like that. We'll buy you a clean shirt and a pair of pants at the Goodwill."

While Sam showered, Bob Gammage spread an Oregon road map across his knees and telephoned New York. With a father who had nearly lost hope of ever seeing his daughter again, he shared the news of this latest, unsubstantiated lead. Studying the map, he said, "Oldenburg's only a couple hours west of here, so I'll be there tonight. I'll start looking for Gestern Hall first thing in the morning. This could be another false alarm, Mr. Padilla, so don't get your hopes up, okay? I'll call you soon as I know any-thing, same as always."

10

A Big, Square-Headed Norsky

By the time the child nurses to sleep, the fire is nearly dead.
Queen Molly sits rigid as a fossil, staring at him who waits at
the woods' edge.

"My magic will keep him away for a time, yet," whispers
Elspeth. "Here, take the child. I have work to do."

The old woman cradles the baby while Elspeth digs in the
ground with a pewter bowl. Queen Molly senses a new presence
in the thicket, a powerful animal-spirit hunkering unseen in the
deep shadow. Her tingling senses tell her of something feline,
bigger than any animal native to this forest, a great cat summoned by Elspeth's magic. Is this the beast whose face is on
Elspeth's silver ring? she wonders, shivering.

Elspeth toils with dreadful urgency, scooping bowlsful of
dirt into a mound beside the hole, never pausing, never slow-
ing. When at last she ceases to dig, tears stream down her
face. She reaches for her basket and takes from it a bag woven from strips of pale skin, a kind Queen Molly has never
seen. She kisses it reverently. Pulling it to her chest, she
sings:

> "Ye stirrings of old darkling Pow'rs below—
> Having bless'd my mother's skin,
> Lovingly from her flesh to spindle spun
> To preserve my breath therein—
> Bless it once more, to complete deeds begun,
> To let a little babe grow.
>
> "From maggots, foul worms, from filth of the ground
> Guard her and hold fast her life . . . !"

She finishes the song and turns her glistening eyes to Queen

Molly. "Give her to me," she whispers hoarsely. "The time has come."

—from Poverty Ike's Tale
Halloween of '66 (continued)

i

John Lansen styled himself a "big, square-headed Norsky," and sometimes bragged that before he went to law school he could chop as much wood as any paid logger in Oldenburg. Tonight he made a promise to his grandson over dinner: The day after tomorrow the three of them—Tad, Mark, and Gramp himself—would visit McCullen's Texaco near the U.S. 30 on-ramp and badger old man McCullen into selling them a pair of used tires cheap. Then they would string the tires from the tall oak behind the Lansen house, and the jousting matches could begin, just like in the "olden days" when Mark was a boy.

"Cool!" exclaimed Tad, beaming.

Mark laughed around a bite of halibut. "I hope you're not committing *me* to a jousting match! I've got a book to write. Besides, I'm getting a little old for that sort of thing."

"Aw, come on, Dad Bear," said Tad. "You said we were gonna do healthy things with Gramp this summer, remember? Wouldn't this be healthy?"

"Healthy for *you*, maybe." Everyone around the supper table laughed, except Gram, who merely smiled. She seemed subdued and tired. She'd lost a little weight in the several months since Mark had seen her, and wrinkles had deepened at the corners of her eyes. But despite the fact that she was pushing sixty, Marta Lansen was every inch the comely woman he'd first met in the reception room of the Methodist Guardians twenty-two years earlier, still rosy-cheeked and honey-blond except for some silver near the roots.

The effect of the drug that Dr. Schell had given Marta earlier today hadn't quite worn off, Mark assumed. Neither had the trauma of losing an old friend, Father Briggs.

"Come on, everybody, eat up!" ordered Kristen. "Fish doesn't keep well, and I'll only have to throw it out." She'd cooked a fine halibut dinner with boiled potatoes, steamed asparagus, and a mountain of green pasta salad. She'd become a low-fat fanatic

at the University of Oregon, an avowed crusader against cholesterol. "More juice, Tad Bear?"

The boy took a refill. "Why can't we get the tires tomorrow,
Gramp?" he asked. "Why do we have to wait until the day *after*
tomorrow?"

"Because tomorrow's kind of a special day, Tad," the big man
answered, his ruddy brows knitting. "We've lost someone—a
close friend. Tomorrow's the day of his funeral. We'll want to
spend time thinking of him, and being thankful for having
known him. You can understand that, can't you?"

Tad seemed to understand.

ii

After dinner, Marta went straight to bed. Kristen drafted Tad
and Mark to help with the dishes, which they were glad to do,
even though they griped about it. With the chores done, the three
of them joined Gramp on the screened front porch, where he sat
in a wicker swing, smoking his favorite pipe and gazing across
the valley toward the river. The lights of the little town of
Cathlamet, Washington, glistened on the dusky opposite shore.
Crickets chirruped in the azaleas that hugged the porch.

After talking awhile, they all went back to the garage, where
Gramp proudly showed off his recent acquisition, a scandalously
black Alfa Romeo roadster. "I finally got my yuppie car," he
joked. "Trouble is, I'm too damn old to qualify for yuppiedom."

"Who'd want a yuppie for a dad anyhow?" laughed Kristen,
hugging the big man and digging a knuckle into his ribs to tickle
him.

Next to the Alfa squatted an MGB of indeterminate vintage,
since it was in various stages of disassembly—John Lansen's latest restoration project. "This one I'm going to keep," he announced. "I'm through restoring cars and selling them to rich old
farts who don't know a crankshaft from Cornwallis."

One of the bays of the four-car garage had always functioned
as a workshop, and still did. A workbench ran along the back
wall, above which hung ranks of tools. A heavy-duty block and
tackle hung from steel members in the ceiling, useful for pulling
engines from cars.

Mark had inherited his adoptive father's passion for automobiles. In this very garage, he told Tad, he and Gramp had spent countless happy hours, tinkering over go-kart engines built by the likes of McCulloch or Briggs & Stratton. And later, struggling with interior sheet-metal screws from a 1958 Olds that Mark had naïvely planned to race as a stock car. And later still, trying to rebuild various English carburetors. Here they'd coped with and cussed the various U-bolts, clamps, studs, and cap nuts from a parade of rust-buckets, including a Sprite, a TR-3, two VWs, and a Porsche. Bits and pieces of those wonderful old wrecks could still be found somewhere in this garage, Mark was willing to bet.

The evening air cooled rapidly. A breeze whispered along Fish Hawk Ridge, rustling the hemlocks that grew along the property lines. Gramp suggested they retire to the house and catch the Dodgers-Mets game on satellite—a showdown between Hershiser and Gooden. He seemed anxious to go inside, as if the night was chillier than it was. He glanced once or twice toward Nehalem Mountain.

Tad, being a Seattle Mariners fan, fell asleep before the fifth inning, and Mark herded him up to bed. "Some baseball fan you are," he muttered under his breath. "Didn't even make it to the seventh-inning stretch."

iii

When Mark came back downstairs, he found that Kristen had trundled off to her room to read, and John had retired from the parlor to his study, where he'd organized a pair of Scotches on the rocks. He handed one to Mark as he came in, then closed the door for privacy.

The study smelled deliciously of oiled wood and seasoned leather. Behind John's huge desk stood a mahogany shotgun case, flanked by bookcases. Mark's eyes wandered over the brass lamps, the books, and the winged leather chairs, and he thought of the countless fine arguments he'd had with John in this room. They'd debated the Vietnam War (John for, Mark against), the Equal Rights Amendment (Mark for, John against), and Watergate (John thought Nixon got a raw deal). Later, when Mark was grown and teaching history in college, they'd spent many more evenings here, sipping brandy or beer and trading theories about the way the world operates.

John clinked his glass against Mark's. "Sorry we couldn't have arranged a happier scene for your homecoming, son. This thing about Charlie Briggs has thrown your mother and me into one hell of a funk. Anyway, here's to a happy summer, and life getting back to normal."

They drank. Mark said that his parents had nothing to apologize for. That Father Briggs had killed himself certainly wasn't *their* fault.

They sat across from one another in the old winged chairs, as they had so many times, and John asked how things were with Mark and Deidre. Mark answered with a long, eloquent silence.

"That's what I thought," said John. "Does she want a divorce?"

Mark had long ago shared with his father the troubles of the Lansen-Garland household, even the fact that Deidre was sleeping with Clay Burnham. Mark had always been able to talk about anything with John, no matter how sensitive, no matter how vile. "Not bloody likely," he answered. "She knows I'd fight her tooth and nail for Tad, and besides that, the guy she's sleeping with is *happily* married."

"And since Burnham would never agree to divorce his wife, Deidre's content to have stolen moments with him, is that it?"

That was about the size of it, confirmed Mark. He was determined to hang onto the marriage for Tad's sake, even if it meant merely going through the motions. "I want him to have the kind of thing with me that I had with you when I was growing up," Mark added. "I want him to have two parents. Besides, Deidre's a good enough mother, when she makes time for it. Tad doesn't need to know that his mom and dad never touch each other anymore."

John wagged his head in sympathy.

"But what about *you?*" Mark wanted to know. "Are you holding up okay? I can't put my finger on it, but something's telling me that Charlie Briggs's suicide isn't the only thing wrong around here."

John took a slow pull from his Scotch and studied the ice cubes floating in it. "I have the same feeling," he said finally. "I've had it ever since Bernie and Fran Pellagrini died back in March."

Mark winced. He'd known about the Pellagrini tragedy, of course, but had forgotten about it in the crush of his own troubles. A mere three months ago, John and Marta's neighbor, Bernie Pellagrini, took a nine-iron from his golf bag and beat his wife to death with it. He then loaded his deer rifle and wedged its muzzle under his chin. The Lansens heard the shot in the dead of night and called the Kalapuya County Sheriff's Office. Deputy Sheriff Will Settergren answered the call and found Bernie in the garage, missing a chunk of his head. Fran lay across the huge bed in the master suite, beaten bloody and lifeless.

"Neither of them ever let on that anything was wrong," said John, still incredulous over the tragedy. "Bernie was getting ready to sell his appliance store and retire—had a ton of money saved up. You remember Gina and Sarah, their little girls? Sarah had just gotten married and moved to Portland. She was expecting a baby. Bernie and Fran were ecstatic about becoming grandparents. Life seemed good." He sipped again from his Scotch and grimaced. "And yet . . ."

"Yet what?"

"There was *something*. I can't say what it was. Maybe I haven't figured it out yet. You haven't heard the worst, though." In a shaky voice that Mark didn't like at all, his father explained that two weeks ago the caretaker of Benson Creek Cemetery discovered that some sicko had violated the Pellagrinis' graves. The caskets lay open and empty. The bodies were still missing.

Mark's stomach did a slow flop, like a dying fish in the bottom of a bucket.

"Tell me what kind of sick bastard would do something like that," whispered John hoarsely. "Bernie and Fran were two of the finest people you'd ever want to meet. Hard-working. Honest. They came from good immigrant stock, and they cared about their neighbors. Back before I made any money, Bernie lent me enough to get my law practice started. He never would've asked me for it if I hadn't paid him back on my own. That's the kind of people they were, Mark."

He drained his Scotch and rose from his chair to fetch another. "You can imagine how folks around here felt about the thing with the graves. It was like taking another Sunday punch on top of the first. And then—just when everybody's starting to recover from *that*—Charlie Briggs pours two cans of gas on himself and burns himself to death." John leaned forward in his chair and stared hard at his son. "You don't think I'm crazy for saying there's something wrong in this town, do you?"

Mark had never seen this vulnerable side of his father. He'd always assumed that nothing could shake John Lansen's hard Norwegian bearing, that no catastrophe was beyond the big man's ability to cope. He supposed, though, that all sons eventually must face the unwelcome reality that their fathers are not supermen.

"I'm glad I came back," he said, needing to fill the silence. "Maybe I can help you and Mom get through this."

"Maybe so," said John. "We can use all the help we can get, believe me."

11

Poverty Ike's

i

Darkness was falling by the time Bob Gammage hit the Oldenburg off-ramp. He'd underestimated the driving time from Portland to Oldenburg, thanks to a paving project that the state highway department undertook this afternoon on a stretch west of the town of Rainier.

Sam Darkenwald sprawled in the passenger's seat of Gammage's old Dodge Charger, snoring loudly despite the heat and the sticky vinyl. Shaved and showered, wearing a clean shirt and jeans that Gammage had bought for him at the Goodwill in downtown Portland, he looked almost mainstream. To Gammage's chagrin, though, he'd insisted on keeping the smelly old sweaters and the heavy jacket he'd worn earlier—something about needing the layers of cloth as shielding against the electro-magnetic radiation the FBI was beaming at him. Gammage had convinced him that the FBI probably would not follow him to Oldenburg, but Sam had balled up the clothing and stashed it in the rear seat, just to keep it handy.

During the drive from Portland, they'd chatted amicably, even becoming guardedly friendly. Sam had recounted one of his many life stories—this one about having served a stint as conductor of the Bowling Green Symphony in Bowling Green, Kentucky.

Gammage halted at a stop sign and stared at the snoring derelict, asking himself for the umpteenth time if taking a paranoid schizo in tow was really such a good idea. His gut answered yes. Sam either knew something about the missing Skye Padilla, or he knew someone who did. Gammage wanted to keep him within easy reach, in case Oldenburg turned out to be a dead end. If this happened, he meant to spirit Sam back to Portland and convince him to produce the mysterious "friend" who had sent him Gammage's way.

Oldenburg turned out to be one sorry excuse for a town. Its twisty, hilly streets were deserted, a fact that made Gammage vaguely uneasy. A quick tour revealed only two hotels still in operating condition, and only one of these had a vacancy—the Luxor on the corner of Floral Avenue and First Street, near the center of the business district. Gammage rented two rooms and installed Sam in one, himself in the other. Too late he discovered that his room was the one with the leaky faucet.

ii

Bob Gammage was not your ordinary, garden-variety private investigator. His specialty was runaway kids, and his success record was extraordinarily good. He didn't merely *find* the runaways—he brought them back, even if doing so required breaking the arm of the kid's pimp, drug dealer, or boyfriend. The wishes of the runaway child were of even less concern to him than her constitutional rights.

His services were expensive, not because he made much money on his cases, but because serious searching involved much mileage and many hotel rooms, numerous long-distance calls, and occasional bribes. Most of his clients were affluent types from respectable suburban neighborhoods. He regretted that poor people couldn't afford him.

In searching for a lost child, he readily dived into the filth of urban street life, where most of his clients' kids ended up. Thanks to his background as an undercover detective with the New York Police Department, he knew how to blend in with the pimps, druggies, and social predators who peopled that dark world. He talked their language, knew how to wangle information from them. He knew their moves.

In order to look the part, he kept his graying hair ragged and long. In warm weather (like today's) he wore a red fishnet tank top and grungy white pants. To reinforce his "legend" as an ex-con, he'd littered his hands with ballpoint tattoos—a crude dagger, a pair of Nazi swastikas, and the words "Death-Dealer" on the underside of his left wrist.

He'd searched for seventeen-year-old Skye Padilla for the past four months, tracking her from fashionable Scarsdale, New York, where her parents lived, to Portland, Oregon, on the opposite coast. Gammage had confirmed that she'd made stops in Pittsburgh, Oklahoma City, Denver, and Salt Lake City. Along the way she'd lived on the streets and in cheap motels, turning tricks and working odd jobs to eat. Maddeningly, she'd stayed a step ahead of him, as if she somehow sensed that he was on her trail.

Since arriving in Portland, Gammage had found only a handful who could remember meeting Skye, and none who claimed to know her. One who did remember her was a pale teenager who hung out in Pioneer Courthouse Square, a spidery punkster who called himself Slade. He claimed to have seen Skye talking to a "creaky old geezer" in Waterfront Park, and had naturally assumed the old guy was asking her for a "date," since this wasn't the first time Slade or his pals had seen this man approach teen-aged girls. Skye had walked away with the man and had gotten into his car. Unfortunately Slade remembered nothing about the car—not its color or make, whether it was old or new, or whether it was even a car at all, and not a pickup or a van. His description of the old man was generic enough to be useless.

Skye's father, Umberto Padilla, was a building contractor who had made himself rich by buying and remodeling old apartment houses in marginal Brooklyn neighborhoods, then renting the apartments to yuppies for $3,000 a month and up. After his daughter disappeared, he sought out Bob Gammage, having heard his reputation.

"Find my daughter, Mr. Gammage, and bring her home to us," he'd wept, clutching the investigator's sleeve with his manicured fingers. "I don't care how much it costs or how long it takes. I don't care what you have to do. Just find her, and bring her home."

Bob Gammage had nodded solemnly, had agreed to do all he could. He understood well how Mr. Padilla felt. Gammage, too, had lost a daughter to the streets, a fact that made a personal matter of every case he took.

iii

The desk clerk at the Luxor was a fat woman of sixty, whose name was Clara. She claimed never to have heard of Gestern Hall and immediately lowered her eyes, which Gammage took for a sure sign of lying. He asked her to recommend a place to eat, and she gave him a list of five. Without being asked, she included a warning about a sixth.

First on the list was Katie's Restaurant—down the block on the corner of Church Avenue and First Street, but it was closed. The Dairy Queen across the street, the second of Clara's recommendations, was open, but its lot was empty. Same story with the Burger King on the corner of Church and Main. Nobody in town was in the mood for fast food this evening, apparently.

Directly opposite the Burger King was a clean-looking place called Baldridge's Family Eatery, which had the look of a chain. Like the others, its lot held not a single car.

Sam wanted to stop at Baldridge's, but Gammage nixed it: "Too respectable. I want a place where the local yokels drink beer and talk loud, somewhere we can ask questions without looking too fucking obvious."

They didn't bother with the McDonald's near the highway, which Clara had said was a good bet. Sam griped that if they didn't stop somewhere soon, he wanted Gammage to let him off near the Dumpsters behind Baldridge's.

They crossed the tracks, heading toward the river, where loomed a massive old ruin that looked like a cannery. On their right was an abandoned railroad depot that had a skinny brick tower. Next to it stood a hulking derelict that a faded sign identified as the Brownsmeade Hotel. Further on was Dunwoody's Mercantile, which had a sagging front porch and ancient signs hawking Chesterfields and Roi Tans from behind hazy windowpanes. Incredibly, the place seemed to be open for business, but no customers were in sight.

And finally, Poverty Ike's—the last and least on Clara's list. It was a rickety-looking, two-story building with bat-wing saloon doors and a flickering neon sign that attracted legions of flying bugs.

"Only eat at Poverty Ike's if you're really hard up and you don't mind grease," Clara had warned. "No telling what you might catch in *that* place."

iv

With Sam on his heels Bob Gammage pushed through the
swinging doors into a high-ceilinged barroom that reeked of stale
beer and sawdust. An old Willie Nelson tune thumped out of an
ancient jukebox, grating on Gammage's nerves. Beyond a pair of
well-worn pool tables stood an ornate back-bar of dark mahogany, carved with caryatids at either end and crammed with bottles.

Gammage caught sight of himself in the tall mirror behind the
bar, and was glad he'd put on clean slacks and a decent shirt. He
wasn't playing the street wolf here, and he'd taken pains to look
half-assed respectable, which was about the best he could do
these days.

At the bar sat Poverty Ike's only patrons for the moment, a
trio of stringy old men with walnut faces and watery eyes—
regulars, no doubt. Drinkers of Jim Beam by the shot with short
chasers of Pabst Blue Ribbon. Smokers of Pall Malls or Lucky
Strikes.

"What's it gonna be, young fella?" asked the barkeep, a tall,
silvered man with thick bifocals and a week's growth of gun-
metal stubble. This had to be Poverty Ike, said Gammage to
himself. The old guy looked like someone who remembered Oldenburg's boom time, whenever that might have been. He
probably remembered the three old sots at the bar when they
were strapping young fishermen or cannery workers or millmen,
back when this saloon was the center of social life for the local
hard hats.

Gammage ordered a beer and a burger for himself, a Pepsi and
a chicken-in-a-basket for Sam Darkenwald. Poverty Ike yelled
their orders in some kind of code to the cook in the rear, who repeated them for accuracy. Gammage and Darkenwald took their
drinks to a nearby table, sat, and waited for their food.

v

"Learn anything?" asked Sam after Bob Gammage returned to
the table more than two hours later. Gammage had bought four
rounds of drinks for the old codgers at the bar. Sam had watched
as the investigator engaged them in small talk, told dirty jokes,

passed out smokes, and nursed a single beer. Now he was back, looking tired and disgruntled as hell.

"Nobody wants to talk about Gestern Hall," muttered Gammage, lighting a cigarette. "I told them I'd read about the place a long time ago, and I was just curious enough about it to swing by this neck of the woods, hoping to see it. Best I could do was to get one of them to confirm that there actually is such a place, and it's somewhere near here."

"Hell, I'd already told you that, Mr. Gammage."

"So you did, Speed, so you did. But I gotta *go* there and scope it out, right? I need to drive by a couple of times, maybe eyeball the place for a day or two."

"Why can't you just ask somebody if they've seen Skye Padilla? Tell them you heard she was at Gestern Hall, and you need to talk to her."

Gammage rolled his eyes and tried to explain that this wasn't Portland, that you had to watch your step when tracking a runaway kid through a wide spot in the road like Oldenburg. If Skye was in town, she might have hooked up with some solid citizen, trading lovey-dovey favors for meals and shelter. Such a citizen might make big trouble for an outsider who started poking around and asking embarrassing questions. Best to get the lay of the land before tipping your hand, Gammage said. Best to do it subtly, quietly.

Sam nodded as if he agreed, and now pondered more serious matters. So far this evening, he'd pounded down two orders of chicken-in-a-basket and four Pepsis. Now he thought about hitting Gammage up for another of each. Eating was a great way to combat boredom, he'd found. Eating was something a homeless man never got tired of doing.

Then his eyes met those of the bartender, the wiry old man who called himself Poverty Ike. Sam suddenly felt dizzy and not at all hungry. Poverty Ike carried a tray to their table, set a beer in front of Gammage and a Pepsi in front of Sam.

"Fellas at the bar want to return your generosity," he said to Gammage over the twang of steel guitars. "It's always nice to get new blood in here, 'specially if he's willing to buy the house a round or two."

Gammage thanked him, then held up his glass to show his appreciation to the old farts at the bar. Curiously, none of them was looking in his direction. To Poverty Ike he said, "You don't exactly have a rush hour on your hands, so why don't you join us?"

Ike tugged a gold pocket watch from beneath his apron, popped it open, and looked at it. "I'd like to, son, but it's almost midnight, and I got a regular customer coming in—young buck named Bayliss, runs the ThriftyKwik grocery over on Commerce Way. You might've seen the sign on your way in."

Gammage nodded.

"Gary Bayliss comes in every night after he closes down, right about now. We always shake the dice for beer, and he always loses. With the way things are these days, business being so slow and all, you've got to keep your regulars coming in, know what I mean? You've got to keep 'em happy." Poverty Ike winked a watery eye at Gammage. "But keep your offer open, and maybe I'll take you up on it sometime."

On his way back to the bar, Poverty Ike glanced back at Sam, and their eyes locked again. Something stirred the hair on the nape of Sam's neck, as if a demon had breathed on him.

Just then the bat-wing doors swung open. A bull-shouldered man in his early forties entered the saloon and bellowed a loud hello to all present. He parked himself on a bar stool and started shaking a leather cup with dice in it, bantering with Poverty Ike. This must be the "young buck," thought Sam, the one known as Gary Bayliss.

Sam's chest tightened, and he fought for breath. Deep inside his skull he felt the invasion of a thing he couldn't name. He'd suffered a similar sensation earlier today, in the alley behind the Masonic Temple in Portland, as he'd gazed into the incredible face of the hag who'd sent him to Bob Gammage. Sam had seen *power* in that face, a power that sent invisible tendrils through the orifices of his skull, searching, probing, manipulating. It hadn't frightened him then, strangely. It frightened him now.

He started to shiver and quake. He spilled his Pepsi down the front of the shirt Bob Gammage had bought for him. The room tilted crazily, as if he'd just stepped off a carnival ride, and the glass slipped through his fingers and shattered on the floor. He looked to Gammage, who had just swallowed the last of his beer. Gammage would help him, he hoped.

Trouble was, Gammage looked very drunk, as if he'd just sucked down three bottles of Ripple. His eyes were glazed, his eyelids heavy, and his head bobbed slowly.

Then everything became clear to Sam. The guy who had just

entered the saloon, the one called Bayliss, was FBI—no doubt
about it. The storm inside Sam's head was the effect of electro-
magnetic radiation, which probably came from a generator in
Bayliss's car out on the street. The Bureau had tracked him from
Portland and had now moved in for the kill. Bayliss was playing
his role flawlessly, pretending to be occupied with a game of
dice, shaking for beers with Poverty Ike. Sam could feel his side-
long glances, as if he were merely waiting for the radiation to
take effect and render Sam totally helpless.

Best to strike first, Sam reasoned. Best to get the first licks in,
and throw the bastards off balance. Bob Gammage would be no
help, drunk as he was, so Sam Darkenwald was on his own,
which was nothing new.

He bolted to his feet, swaying like a great tree ready to fall.
He pushed aside the table, sending plates and glasses to the floor.
Heads turned in his direction, and mouths fell open. He picked
up his chair and gave a war whoop that cut through the din of
steel guitars and nasal harmony like a Klaxon. He charged the
bar with the chair held high, huffing like a Cape buffalo, his eyes
round and white.

He meant to brain the man called Bayliss.

vi

Deputy Sheriff Will Settergren answered the call from the dis-
patcher, since the only other deputy on shift was across town on
a barking dog complaint. *"Fist fight and brawl at Poverty Ike's,
man with a gun. . . ."*

Settergren cringed, for this was serious shit. In the three years
he'd carried a badge for the County of Kalapuya, he'd never
once confronted someone with a gun. He'd given out his share of
speeding tickets on U.S. 30, answered the rare domestic-dispute
calls, and even foiled a burglary about a year ago. But a man
with a gun—this was *serious* shit, worse than answering the call
to the Pellagrini house back in March and finding the Pellagrinis
hideously dead; worse even than driving around in the dark
streets of Oldenburg for seven hours at a stint, *alone.*

Will Settergren swallowed hard and unsnapped his holster. *"Man
with a gun"* was the kind of thing that could get a cop killed, if he
wasn't careful. He switched off the radar gun on the dashboard of

the old Ford cruiser and started the engine. With blue lights ablaze he burned rubber away from his favorite speed trap on U.S. 30 westbound, half a mile east of the Oldenburg exit.

Two minutes later he screeched to a halt outside Poverty Ike's. Parked at the curb were a '73 Charger with New York plates and a customized '81 Chevy pickup that he recognized as Gary Bayliss's. Bayliss had a bumper sticker on the tailgate that said, "How's My Driving? Call (503) EAT–SHIT."

With his Ruger revolver in one hand and his two-handled baton in the other, Will peered over the swinging doors and witnessed a scene that could have come out of a John Wayne movie. Gary Bayliss and another man—a big dude with wild eyes and shaggy gray hair and a pair of broken sunglasses dangling absurdly from one ear—were clubbing each other with chairs. Shards of bottles and shattered crockery littered the floor. They'd obviously traded some pretty nasty blows, because Bayliss had an angry gash over one ear, flowing red, and the wild-eyed guy had a bad bruise on one cheek.

As Will charged through the swinging doors, he became aware of a third man who was struggling to his feet behind an upended table, an ugly man with a boxer's stony build and elaborate tattoos on his hands and forearms. The man looked as if he'd taken a punch and ended up on his ass. Now he staggered crazily against the bar, fighting for his balance.

Will saw that he had a gun in his hand, and felt his bones go cold. He heard himself scream, "*Police!* Hold it right there!" He saw his right hand come up to shoulder height, saw the red-painted muzzle-sight on his Ruger settle on the man with the gun, almost as if his hands and arms had minds of their own.

The man wheeled and lurched, obviously very drunk, perhaps even drugged. "I'm just trying to break this up, Officer. I'm a—" Suddenly Gary Bayliss let fly with his chair, and the man whirled. The pistol in his hand went off, shattering the huge mirror in Poverty Ike's back-bar.

Will Settergren's muscles tightened reflexively, and his Ruger barked. He hadn't meant to fire, but adrenaline had surged through his piano-wire nerves. A more seasoned cop might have held his fire a few seconds more, maybe long enough to give Bob Gammage a chance to throw down his gun and surrender.

No such luck for Gammage, though. The steel-jacketed .38 hit him hard, and he went down like a ton of bricks.

12

Under an Evil Star

Queen Molly quails with revulsion. Her stomach lurches as understanding bursts like a thunderclap in her brain. She tightens her hold on the sleeping baby. "No, my girl," she says in her weak English, "not this. We find another way, yes?"

"There is no other way, Molly," sobs Elspeth. "Now, please. Give her to me."

Queen Molly lowers her face and holds the bundle away, knowing the uselessness of resisting. Her flesh crawls as she visualizes the tiny child enclosed in a bag of human skin and buried alive in the cold earth.

Alive, yes. For Elspeth does not kill her, but kisses her and holds her close before slipping her into the bag, naked except for the amulet, sleeping the perfect sleep of newborns. Elspeth lays the bundle gently into the hole and mutters songful words as she carefully places bowlful after bowlful of dirt on and around it. . . .

> —from Poverty Ike's Tale
> Halloween of '66 (continued)

i

You breathe in the moist air of the Oregon night.

You recognize separate scents as if each has whispered its own name—the tartness of cedars and hemlocks, the sweet perfume of wild roses growing on the slopes of Fish Hawk Ridge, the spicy aroma of hazelnuts wafting up from the orchards in the valley below.

And something *else*, too, warm and coppery, pervading the night like the strains of an unholy hymn. You hear its name in your nostrils, but your mind repels it. Still it calls to you, as hunger calls a starving snake, rhythmically, rhythmically.

This can only be a dream, right?

You climb out of your bed, and the sweaty sheets fall away. You see the details of your boyhood room clearly, even though the only illumination is a shaft of moonlight slanting through the latticed window.

On the walls hang framed posters of dragsters, Indy racers, and classic roadsters with swoopy fenders and chromed radiator caps—cherished artifacts from your teens. Your thirty-two-ounce Louisville Slugger leans in a corner with your Rawlings catcher's mitt slung on the handle. Here and there lie beloved old books—histories and historical fiction, most of them, the books that captured your heart and launched you on a career of looking ever backward through time: Viking sagas and Arthurian tales, accounts of William's conquest of the Saxons, epic stories of the Knights Templar and the Hospitalers.

Years ago, after you'd left the nest, your mother packed all this stuff into cardboard boxes and relegated it to the attic, where nearly everyone's childhood eventually ends up. Your old bedroom became a respectable "guest room." Has someone carted all these trappings of your childhood down from the attic, then crept in and planted them in the room while you slept?

Suddenly you understand that time has done a perfect one-eighty, that you've realized every historian's unspoken craving: You've entered the past. How or why, you haven't a clue, because dreams don't need *how* or *why*. Dreams need only *you*.

ii

You pad into the hallway and down the stairs. Doors open before you under their own power. You pass through the covered porch into the rear yard, feeling as if some force is guiding you toward a rendezvous with someone or something you can't even guess about.

Night lies heavy upon the verdant landscape. High in the sky hangs a piercing red gem so bright that you almost mistake it for a distant airplane with its landing lights on. You stare at it stupidly and blink once, twice, before realizing that it's Mars. Never have you seen the planet this bright.

The hunger calls to you again—rhythmically, rhythmically—and you let it guide your steps, because you don't know what else to do. As a powerless dreamer, you really don't have any choice but to let this thing play itself out. You enter the flagstone walk that leads to your mother's garden, and endure a sudden jolt: The flagstones are cold and moist against the bare soles of your feet. Your mind screams, *This is no dream!*

You raise your gaze again to the lucid sky. Mars shines so brightly that even the moon wears a pinkish veil. You say to yourself, *This is all part of it, isn't it?*—the redness in the sky, the hunger in your gullet, the jaunt back through time into the lost region of your boyhood. All this has a purpose ... just as Leo Fobbs had a purpose in taking a swan dive off Ione Plaza (*"Root it out, Dr. Lansen"*). Just as Father Briggs had a purpose in drenching himself with gasoline and ending his life in a storm of fire. You've told yourself that you've come back to Oldenburg to write a history of the town, but your *real* purpose goes much deeper than that, doesn't it? *It's all coming together now. . . .*

The sharp odor of ammonia stings your nose. You've reached the edge of the garden, where your mother's prize-winning roses grow. You focus on the figure that squats on its haunches a few paces ahead, a young girl blond and luminously blue-eyed, a freckled tomboy of seven or eight. She holds a red plastic spray-bottle in her tiny fist.

Kristen grins a killer's grin when she sees you, then bends again to her task. The flagstones around her are black with slugs, and she's taking delight in spraying them with ammonia. The hellish little creatures squirm and writhe when the deadly mist hits them, then quickly shrink and die.

Your stomach revolts. You'd vomit if you could, but whoever heard of vomiting in a dream? You don't really know whether it's the spectacle of gleeful murder that sickens you, or merely your old phobic revulsion to slugs.

Your little sister is resolute in her work, but she glances up to smile at you occasionally. Her trigger finger seems never to tire. Insane as it is, you can hear her heartbeat and breathing, and they serve as perfect counterpoint to the rhythm of your hunger. How can you possibly be hungry, you wonder, when you're so nauseous you can hardly stand?

Ah, the irrationality of the dreamworld, you say.

Except this is no dream.

iii

You vividly remember one hot day from real life, from the waking world, when you found your little sister doing exactly what she's doing now. You were about twenty, home for summer break after your sophomore year of college, and Kristen was about the age she seems at this moment. You had come outside to sip a cold beer, to hear the birds sing and feel the sunshine on your shoulders. You found Kristen with her red spray-bottle of ammonia, patrolling the border of the garden, killing slugs wherever she found them.

I just can't handle the groaty old things, you heard her say, and you chuckled. *They kill Mom's plants. The world's a better place without them. I wish I could kill them all.*

You edged away from the garden then, your stomach boiling, needing distance between yourself and the slugs. You'd like to do that now, but your feet won't cooperate, and you feel like a cartoon figure, moving and breathing at the behest of some lunatic animator.

Kristen bolts upright, and you see the reason: The slugs, incredibly, have besieged her. Their heads all point toward her. Their multitudes form a radial pattern all around her. The creatures' eyestalks stretch toward her, waving to the rhythm of your hunger. They move ever closer to Kristen, whose trigger finger works furiously.

The red spray-bottle has gone dry.

Kristen looks up at you, her eyes round and pleading, but the very sight of you contorts her face in terror. You gag as your vision blurs, as the hunger sets your muscles to quivering. The slugs' onslaught grows more furious. They stream out of the garden in slimy rivulets, out from the shadows of your mother's flowering wisterias, the clumps of camellias and irises and ornamental allium, apparently bent on one objective: Kristen.

How much time elapses before they finally reach her, you don't know, but they *do* reach her. She beats at them wildly as they climb her bare legs and worm their way under the cuffs of her baggy shorts. She can't dislodge them, can't turn them back. Her cries cut you to the quick, but you can't move. You stand like a petrified block of bone.

They're at her eyes now, at her nostrils and ears and mouth. They worm their way in, seeking any warm opening, leaving her skin glistening with mucus. You see that they have metamorphosed beyond the common shell-less snails you know them to be: They've become huge, the size of squirrels and rats. Their eyes are golden bulbs at the tips of their stalks.

You hear a rustling in a nearby stand of azaleas, something bulky and wet, at least the size of a man. Your scalp tingles, and your bladder lets go. This can only be the granddaddy of all slugs, the commander-in-chief of the horde that's devouring your little sister as you watch. You wonder if it has teeth and claws, whether it will follow its soldiers toward Kristen, or whether it will come for *you.*

Kristen's thrashing slows, as if her body is submerged in honey. Slugs cover every square inch of her now, and you can barely make out her form in the light of the moon. Your rage builds as her squeals die. You hear only the homely song of frogs in the pond at the center of the garden, the beating of your own heart, the rustling in the bushes a mere arm's length away.

Now you hear an intrusion from the *real* world, the one in which slugs are not predators but only annoying pests—the world of credit cards and presidential elections and office workers who discuss the latest installment of "L.A. Law" during their coffee breaks. You embrace the sound and cling to it, because *this* sound is your vehicle back to sanity.

A muffled sob. A whimper against a pillow.

It cuts through the madness and takes over your heart.

It comes from the throat of your son. Instinct tells you that he needs you, and that's more than enough.

iv

The spell breaks, and you lope toward the house, scarcely feeling the humid air against your skin or the damp grass beneath your toes. You don't know how you do it, but you skitter up the outside wall of the old Tudor house to the second-floor window, behind which Tad lies in bed. Somehow your fingers and toes stick to the aged stucco and the exposed timbers, as if your skin has suction cups.

Tad needs you.

You press your face against the glass, wondering whether you should force your way through the latticed window, when . . .

V

. . . Tad screamed, jarring his father fully awake. Mark Lansen gasped when he realized that he was sitting at Tad's bedside, holding the boy close to his chest. If the scream hadn't died in the fabric of Mark's damp T-shirt, it surely would have woken everyone in the house.

"It's okay, Tad Bear, I'm here. There's nothing to be afraid of." Mark was amazed that his own voice sounded so calm, so strong. He switched on a table lamp.

"I-I heard something," Tad managed, clinging to his father. "Something was trying to get in through the window. I thought it would go away, but it didn't. It might still be there." His cheeks were shiny with tears.

"You've had a nightmare, Tad Bear. We all have them now and then." Mark felt his flesh crawling. He consciously avoided looking toward the window, choosing instead to bury his face in his son's soft brown hair. "I'll stay here until you feel better, all right?"

"But what if—?" A sob shook the boy, and he threw a frightened glance around the room.

"Like I said, it was only a dream. You don't see anything scary around here, do you?"

Tad collected himself and wiped his eyes. Reluctantly he surveyed his surroundings, more thoroughly this time. "I'm sorry, Dad Bear," he whispered finally, his embarrassment showing. At nine he was approaching the age where boys conclude that tears aren't manly. "I guess I shouldn't be such a baby, huh?"

Mark took a deep breath to control his own stuttering heart. "Hey, you're not a baby just because you had a bad dream. I get them myself." If the kid only knew. "The nice thing about dreams—even bad ones—is that they're over when you wake up. Nothing in a dream can hurt you, Tad Bear. Always remember that."

"Okay, I'll try to remember. But—"

"But what?"

"You won't tell Gramp that I woke up crying like a little kid, will you? Or Kristen, either?"

Mark smiled. "We'll keep it between us, if that's what you want."

He suppressed a sudden yearning to see Kristen, to ensure that she was alive and breathing, which was nonsensical in the extreme. Of *course* she was alive and breathing, merely sleeping peacefully in her room down the hall. *Nothing in a dream can hurt you,* right? "You'd better go back to sleep now," said Mark. "Tomorrow's going to be a busy day, the first real day of your summer vacation. You'll want to be bright-eyed and bushy-tailed in the morning."

"Okay."

Mark bent low and kissed his son's cheek, but as he started to straighten up, Tad caught his hand. "Dad Bear, can I ask a question?"

"Sure you can—anytime you want. I'm always here to field questions."

"You'll tell me the truth, won't you?"

Mark's stomach churned. That his son would ask this assurance was scarier in its own way than the nightmare he himself had just endured. Like all dads, he wanted his boy to think of him as incapable of a lie. "You know I will. I always tell you the truth, don't I?"

"I-I guess so."

"So ask away."

"Dad, I'm not adopted, am I?"

Mark's mouth went dry, and he had to work hard for a good swallow. Was *this* at the root of his son's fears, the misapprehension that he didn't really belong to Mark and Deidre? Had the boy gone to bed worrying that the awful truth would pop out someday, that he would discover some hideous secret about his own origin? Mark damned himself for treating the subject of his own adoption so flippantly. He should have shown more sensitivity toward his son, should have spent more time preparing him for a revelation this large.

Mark enfolded Tad in his arms again. "No, Tad Bear, you're *not* adopted. Remember when I explained the sperm and egg, and—"

"And how a woman can get pregnant if you boink her without using a rubber?"

"Uh—yeah, except we call it sexual intercourse."

"That's not what we call it at school."

"I suppose not. At any rate, your mother became pregnant with my sperm, and you're the result of that."

"Of you boinking her, huh?"

Mark gulped. "You're *our* kid and nobody else's. You'll always be our kid, even when you're all grown with kids of your own. You might become the director of Mount Palomar Observatory, but Mom and I will be there to make you pick up your room and eat your vegetables."

The relief in the boy's hazel eyes was like a ray of sunshine. "Thanks, Dad. I guess I'll go back to sleep now."

"Good. Sleep well."

Mark switched off the table lamp and tucked his son in. He stood a moment at the bedside, gazing down at the boy lying in the moon glow. Involuntarily his eyes went to the window. What he saw nearly made him swallow his tongue: On the outer surface of the glass was a smear of slime about the diameter of a grown man's face.

13

Prayers for the Dead

i

The archbishop himself drove in from Portland early on Tuesday, June 7, 1988, to say the Requiem Mass for Father Charlie Briggs. Tressa Downey sat with her mother in the rear of the sweltering church and listened hard to the singsongy liturgy, trying to glean even a scrap of comfort from it. She failed.

She envied the pious around her for the peace the Mass seemed to give them, and wished she could share in it. But she'd shed her faith years ago. Myth and superstition could no longer comfort her.

During the homily, she discovered that she had taken a brass key from her pocket and was clutching it tightly in her fist, as though it would fly away if she relaxed her grip. It had arrived in yesterday's mail, addressed to her, enclosed with a letter from Father Charlie. He'd apparently mailed it the evening he killed himself. According to the letter, the key would unlock the heavy book that the rectory housekeeper had presented her yesterday, the journal of Father Charles Francis Briggs.

Tressa was unable to sleep Monday night. Neither was she able to do what Father Charlie had admonished her to do: Read the journal.

At least not yet.

After the homily came the eulogies, and after these the Eucharist. Father Charlie got the full treatment, which his parishioners took as a signal of his high standing among the learned Catholic clergy in Portland. The service shifted from St. Pius X Roman Catholic Church to Benson Creek Cemetery, where the archbishop concluded his lugubrious office with a flourish of crucifix-waving and the sprinkling of holy water. Thus he committed Father Charlie's charred remains to the earth, having apparently decided that the priest's self-inflicted death was the result of mental illness and not a true suicide. Therefore the church's prohibition against the final resting place in consecrated ground did not apply.

Though she struggled not to, Tressa wept stinging tears as the casket sank into the ground. The numbness she'd felt since learning of his death three days ago faded away. In its place were raw pain, the hollowness of loss, the excruciating certainty that she would never see her friend again.

The word *never* had such a bitter taste, but it was one to which she was no stranger. Less than two years earlier she'd attended another funeral, that of a little girl not four years old. As she watched the archbishop toss a handful of dirt into Father Charlie's grave, Tressa's mouth reflexively whispered the name *Desdi*.

ii

She and her mother rode home with Velma Selvig, who had become Tressa's best friend, next to Father Charlie, since she'd moved back to Oldenburg. Velma owned and operated the Royal Kokanee Inn, a hulking old bed-and-breakfast hotel that stood near the Columbia shore in the forested outskirts of Oldenburg. She'd lost more than seventy pounds during the past year— thanks in part to joining Tressa for a daily jog—but she was still pleasingly plump at thirty-seven and happily unmarried. She had short, rust-colored hair and snapping green eyes that often itched with hay fever in the late spring.

"I could drop you at the courthouse, Tress," said Velma, halting her Toyota in the driveway of the Downeys' small house on Second Street. "I have to go by the *Clarion*, so it'd be on my way." In addition to running the Royal Kokanee, Velma wrote a column for the weekly *Oldenburg Clarion*, which gave her a way to use her English degree. The newspaper office was just up the block from the courthouse.

"Thanks, Velma, but Ed Nyberg gave me the day off. The commissioners figured that the courthouse wouldn't be very busy today."

"There isn't a soul in this town who won't be mourning Father Charlie today," said Tressa's mother, Cynthia Downey, an angular woman of fifty-five who spoke with a Southern lilt that betrayed her Georgia upbringing. "He was a man beloved of Catholic, Protestant, and Jew alike. Even the Chinese cannery workers loved him, I hear tell—before the Hilde cannery closed, naturally."

Cynthia's accent came and went, depending on her mood, which in turn depended on how much of her daily ration of Southern Comfort she'd nipped. It was thicker than usual today.

"Surely you'll come in for a cup of coffee and a smidgen of my peach cobbler, won't you, Velma?" offered Cynthia. "I trust that Tressa would welcome the company of a friend at a time like this."

"I'll take you up on the coffee, but not the cobbler, unfortunately," said Velma, patting her stomach. She switched off the engine.

Four-twenty-nine Second Street, the house Tressa had grown up in, was a modest frame bungalow with a stone porch. Lilacs grew along the edges of the porch, and a huge butterfly of colorful plastic hung near the front door. Tressa and Velma sat in the living room, which her mother had crammed with frilly Early American furniture over the past three decades. Porcelain knick-knacks occupied every available surface. On the walls hung lurid still lifes, which Cynthia thought beautiful beyond words.

"What do you say we sit out back?" suggested Tressa, once her mother had administered coffee. "Seems like a shame to waste all this sunshine." Her real purpose was to get away from Cynthia, who would monopolize any conversation if given half a chance. Besides, Tressa had things to say that she didn't want her mother to hear.

They sat at a round table under the full force of the noonday sun. Cynthia stayed inside to "listen to her story," which meant watching "All My Children" on TV.

"I hope you'll forgive this, kiddo," said Velma after sipping her coffee, "but you don't look so good. Maybe you ought to take a little vacation. Why don't you head down to Lincoln City for a few days, and get yourself a room on the beach? Take along a good book, and listen to the surf. It's guaranteed to cure anything short of leprosy."

"I need to work another six months before I have any time coming," said Tressa with a weak smile. "My problem is that I haven't been sleeping very well."

Velma could understand that, and said so. She knew how close

Tressa and Father Charlie had been. In a sense, he had been the father she'd lacked since her real father abandoned his family when Tressa was a toddler.

Tressa listened to this and wondered whether to tell Velma about the journal, the letter, the key. Or even more important, about that *other* thing. After all, she'd told Velma damn-near everything else about herself in the year since they'd met, including the whole sad saga of cocaine addiction, divorce, and rehab. She'd held back only one morsel of tragedy from Velma, and that was the story of Desdi. She'd revealed to no one in town that she'd ever had a child, except to her mother and Father Charlie. Tressa doubted she would ever tell Velma or anyone else about *that*.

"It's not just Father Charlie's death," Tressa said now, and she saw Velma pause with her cup halfway to her mouth. "Something happened yesterday, something I don't quite understand. When you add it to everything else that's happened in the last three days . . ." Her mouth stopped working, and she stared at the tall sugar pine that grew in the center of the yard. It sighed in the light breeze.

Velma set her cup on the table and leaned forward in her chair. "What is it, Tress? If you need to talk about it, I'm here."

"I—I think . . ." The words seemed impossible to utter. She reached across the table and gripped Velma's hand, as if to draw the needed strength from her friend. "I think someone tried to rape me yesterday."

iii

After hearing Tressa's account of yesterday's trip to Gestern Hall, Velma sat speechless, her coffee growing cold, her mouth hanging open. Tressa worried about how it had sounded:

A fugue brought on by staring at medieval paintings that hung in Clovis Gestern's study. *Right.*

Something crawling up her skirt to touch her crotch, though she couldn't see what it was. *Uh-huh.*

The appearance of the dark young girl on the staircase of the Nehalem Mountain Inn. *I see.*

Her insane urge to throw herself in Clovis Gestern's arms, just before leaving. *Ah, and now the truth comes out . . . !*

"I wouldn't blame you if you started involuntary-commitment proceedings on me," she declared finally, needing to fill the silence. "It all sounds perfectly crazy, doesn't it?"

"I think it sounds—" Velma grabbed through the pockets of her green blazer for a Kleenex, which she just managed to press to her face before the sneeze came. "Damn this hay fever! I was going to say that it sounds perfectly sinister. What happened is that someone molested you, girl. I think you ought to take this right to the police. No telling what else is going on in that house. What do you suppose Clovis Gestern is doing to that frightened young girl you saw?"

"But I didn't actually *see* him do anything," Tressa reminded Velma. Both of Gestern's hands had been in full view.

"I hope you're not trying to say that you imagined the whole scene. I know you better than that. You're not the kind to hallucinate getting felt up."

"Aren't I? You believe that, and I believe that, but would the sheriff believe it? Or the district attorney, for that matter? Look, Velma, I wouldn't even be able to testify against Gestern, because I don't have any reason to think he did anything wrong. All I know is what I felt."

Velma mulled this reality, scowling as if it smelled bad. "Are you cast-in-concrete certain you didn't see Clovis Gestern put his hand up your dress?"

"I'm afraid so. If I'd seen him or anyone else do it, I'd tell you. And I'd certainly tell the cops about it, you can be sure of that."

So, what in God's name did Tressa think had happened? Velma wanted to know. Had another man sneaked into the room? Had someone drugged her somehow? Had the grotesque Mrs. Drumgule been the culprit?

Speculating, Tressa threw out the possibility that the stress of Father Charlie's passing might have built up inside her and caused her to snap momentarily. She was, after all, a recovering cocaine addict. No one could say how much damage the addiction had done to her brain. Hallucinations weren't exactly unknown among people in her shoes.

"I'll never believe that," said Velma flatly. "You're one of the healthiest, most stable people I know. You've even been a good influence on *me*, for God's sake. You got me running, exercising, caring about myself, and even gave me the encouragement I needed to lose serious weight for the first time in my life. I'm literally a shadow of my old self, and I've got you to thank for it."

Tressa brushed aside the flattery. "No one can take credit for the new you except *you*, Velma."

"The point I'm trying to make is that something really did happen to you at Gestern Hall. I'll not sit here and listen to you doubt your own sanity. The only question you face is what to do about it."

Tressa rose from the table and wandered to the edge of the patio, her face turned up to the bright sky. Then she glanced back toward her friend. "What should I do, Velma?"

"Let me think on it. You think on it, too. In the meantime, stay active, stay involved. Spend your time with people you know well, people you trust." She got up and moved close. "Listen, I've just been appointed chairperson of the Dukakis campaign for Kalapuya County. I'm throwing an organizational get-together this Friday at the Royal Kokanee. Why don't you show up? It'll be your chance to join the ranks of the politically correct."

Tressa grimaced. "I'm not sure our Republican county commissioners would look with favor on my backing a Democrat for president."

"Fuck 'em. You're entitled to your own beliefs. Tell 'em you'll sue the county for trampling your First Amendment rights, if they try to fire you. That'll get old Ed Nyberg's goat, believe me."

"Okay, you've talked me into it. What time?"

"Six o'clock sharp. If everything goes well, you'll be home before dark."

14

The Shark Circles

A strange mechanical whirring comes to Queen Molly's ears. She glances up and gasps when she sees the source—Elspeth's spinning wheel, standing in its spot near the fire, turning as though driven by a spirit's hand. The louder Elspeth sings, the faster the wheel turns.

As Elspeth tamps the final bowlful of dirt into place, a peal of rough laughter erupts, raising the hairs on Queen Molly's neck, a man's laughter that batters the night like an angry storm. He's ventured forward as the fire dimmed, and now stands at the base of the knoll. He's tall and lean, dressed in a dark coat and a collar of snowy white. His eyes and teeth gleam.

He speaks in English to Elspeth, who cowers over the living grave of her child. "This is not the end of it, you know. I'll have her yet, when the time is right." His body turns, and he moves toward the thicket again, so much like a man, yet unmanlike somehow.

At the edge of the clearing he faces the knoll and gives a short, final laugh. "I'll simply wait, little Elspeth. Simply watch and wait. I have all the time in the world, you know. All the time in the world!"

Then he's gone, a shadow fading through the forest.

—from Poverty Ike's Tale
Halloween of '66 (continued)

i

Like most human beings, Mark Lansen possessed an incredible ability to suppress unpleasant realities. By the afternoon of Tuesday, June 7, he did indeed suspect that during the past four days something had gone horribly wrong with his life, but he'd pushed that suspicion deep into the cellar of his mind. As some fat men choose to ignore chronic chest pain and continue to smoke three packs of Camels a day, he chose to carry on with the chores and rituals of his life, telling himself that all was well.

Just below the surface of his subconscious, however, swam the truth in slow, lazy circles, like a man-eating shark in orbit around a sinking boat.

ii

The argument in John Lansen's study grew loud enough to be heard in the upstairs bedroom, where Mark was sorting the notes he planned to use in writing his history of Oldenburg. He'd tackled this small job to occupy his mind and to keep his imagination from running wild. Last night's nightmare, far and away the worst slug-dream he'd ever suffered, had rattled him thoroughly, leaving him anxious and shaky throughout the whole morning.

The voices of his mother, his father, his sister, poured through the heating vent in the bedroom, but Mark couldn't hear actual words. What he could hear was the anger.

He went downstairs and found the door to his father's study closed. Marta opened it when he knocked, and smiled at him through angry, fearful tears. For the first time since he'd arrived from Portland, she looked more her old self. Anger was a tonic, maybe. She hugged him immediately and apologized if the shouting had disturbed him.

"Now that you're here, maybe you can talk some sense into your sister," said Marta, still wearing the black outfit she'd donned for Father Briggs's funeral. Affixed to her bosom was an heirloom brooch of silver and copper, the kind Norwegian women wear mostly to weddings and funerals and nowhere else. "She's about to do something very, very stupid, something her father and I don't approve of at all."

Kristen stood at the window with her arms folded across her chest, staring out and pouting. The afternoon sun shone gold in her hair. "Nobody has explained why it's so stupid, or why everyone is so upset about it. If someone did that, maybe then we could have a rational discussion like grown-ups."

John stood next to his shotgun case, his cold pipe clenched in his teeth. "The reason your mother and I disapprove of your working for Clovis Gestern is that neither you nor anyone else in this town really knows the man. We've already told you that."

"The guy comes from one of the oldest, most respected families in town," said Kristen, turning from the window. "He's a regular philanthropist, for Christ sake. Hasn't he donated band uniforms to the school? Hasn't he bankrolled the restoration of the courthouse? What else do you want him to do—shit turkey sandwiches?"

"You will *not* use that kind of language in this house, young lady!" shouted Marta, her cheeks aflame. "And you'd do well to remember the Fourth Commandment while you're at it, assuming you can recall anything at all from your Small Catechism!"

"I don't think I'd be dishonoring you and Dad by taking a summer job that sounds like something I'd order out of a catalog, Mom. But if I've offended you, puh-*leez* forgive me!"

Mark jumped in, hoping to play the mediator. "Can we dispense with the Sturm und Drang long enough for someone to tell me what this is all about?"

It was about an offer of a job that a young man named Clovis Gestern had extended to her, Kristen explained. She'd met him in Kalapuya Park early this morning while the rest of the family was at Father Charlie's funeral. She'd gone to hit a tennis ball against the backboard. Gestern had come to practice his serve in the adjacent court. They'd introduced themselves, chatted. Kristen had mentioned that she was studying commercial art and advertising at the University of Oregon. Mr. Gestern (he'd asked her to call him "Skip") had said that he was about to launch an advertising campaign for the Nehalem Mountain Inn, which he owned. Was Kristen by any chance knowledgeable about desktop publishing, about Apple Macintosh systems in particular? If so, he might be interested in hiring her to help with the campaign. He'd just taken delivery of the necessary computer equipment, but when it came to data processing, Skip was a total novice. He could use help from a trained professional.

"I almost fainted!" exclaimed Kristen. "I've just finished two courses in page layout, graphics, and editing on the Macintosh. This would be the perfect chance to try out some of my stuff in the real world." She'd soaked up the academics of art, editing, and advertising, she added, and she knew a lot of theory, but she'd yet to hold down a real job—which all her professors said is the best possible classroom. Gestern's offer was like a gift from heaven.

Mark said he didn't see anything especially egregious in the idea of Kristen taking on summer work of this kind. After all, wasn't this what she'd trained for in college?

"You haven't heard the kicker yet," said John, firing up his pipe. "Gestern wants her to live up there in the mansion all summer—wants her to move in with him, bag and baggage."

"It's not like I'm signing on to be his concubine," Kristen said with a sneer. "The man has just bought twenty thousand dollars' worth of computer equipment and software. He's converted one of the main-floor rooms into a desktop publishing studio. He's obviously serious about running an in-house advertising and public relations show. He needs help getting started, that's all. You'll never convince me he bought all that state-of-the-art stuff just to lure some young thing into his mansion. If that's his idea of trolling, somebody ought to sit down with him and give him a few pointers."

"You're talking as if you've actually seen all this equipment," said Mark.

Which Kristen had. She and Skip Gestern had driven up to the mansion for a quick tour. "And believe it or not, I'm still in one piece—didn't even get a hickey. By the way, he's really done wonders with that place—it looks like something out of Prince Valiant. You'd like it, Mark, your being a medieval historian and all. It's full of stuff from the Middle Ages."

"There's absolutely no good reason why this Clovis Gestern character should expect you to live in that house," declared Marta, standing ramrod straight. "Gestern Hall isn't more than twenty minutes from here. You could easily drive to work in the morning. For heaven's sake, I'd think even *you* could see through his intentions, Kristen."

Kristen turned back to the window and planted her fists on her hips. "Mom, I've told you. Skip wants his advertising person to live at the inn for a few months, to soak up its ambience and charm, learn its history. That person needs to absorb the spirit of the place in order to write compelling ads and promo materials. If you knew anything at all about advertising, you'd know that this isn't an outrageous idea. It actually makes very good sense."

"And if you knew anything about life and living, you'd know what a crock that is," said John, close to losing his composure.

"A serious, bona fide businessman doesn't hire an undergrad to run his advertising and PR. There's more to this than meets the eye, little girl, and you'd be wise to listen to your decrepit old parents, for once. Tell her, Mark! Tell her what a horrendous mistake it would be to move in with someone she knows nothing about."

Mark wasn't quite ready to be put on the spot. He could certainly understand John and Marta's apprehensions. On the other hand, Kristen wasn't a little girl anymore. She was, in fact, on the threshold of legal adulthood—only a few months shy of twenty-one. He was about to offer that Kristen, as a grown-up, was entitled to choose her own course with respect to her career, but she beat him to the punch.

"I don't need to be told anything," she said evenly, "not by Mark or anyone else. The issue is settled. I'm sorry we couldn't reach an agreement like civilized adults." She moved toward the door, her shoulders squared, her chin thrust out. On reaching it she whirled around and said, "I'm moving out today. Under the circumstances, I think it's best if I don't spend another night in this house."

iii

Mark wandered upstairs to check on Tad and found him in his room, sprawled on the bed. He wore his Sony Mega Bass Dolby Walkman on his head, and seemed totally absorbed in a book on astronomy. Strangely, he'd drawn the curtains and was using the bedside lamp to read. He didn't even see his father at the door, and Mark ducked out again, rather than interrupt healthy intellectual recreation.

Kristen met him in the hall, laden with books and bags. He took part of her cargo from her and followed her downstairs, then out to the drive. They loaded the stuff into her VW, speaking only minimally.

"That's the last of it," said Kristen at last, slamming the rear hatch. "I'm sorry you had to get mixed up in this, Mark. I just hope you can see my point of view."

"Don't tell Mom and Dad, but I think I'm on your side. Even so, I wish you weren't leaving so soon. Couldn't you wait a cou-

ple days, until they've had a chance to recover from all this madness with Father Briggs? If you gave them a little time—"

"Wouldn't do any good, Mark. If I give them more time, they'll
just use it to try to change my mind. Mom and Dad need to realize
that I'm my own person, that I have my own life to live. Anyway,
they'll get over this. I'm not making a permanent break." She came
to Mark and put her arms around his neck. She kissed him in a
way that he found slightly unsettling, and he pulled back, embarrassed. "Let's not be strangers, okay?" she said, showing no trace
of self-consciousness. "We may not be living under the same roof,
but we're still in the same town. No reason why we shouldn't get
together for a few giggles now and then."

He surveyed her with brotherly approval. Kristen had indeed
grown into a beautiful young woman, despite her mixing-bowl
hairdo. "Are you sure you'll have any time? Sounds like you'll be
pretty busy with the ad campaign and all. Plus, you'll probably
have an army of horny young dudes hitting on you all summer."

"For you, big brother, I'll *make* time. Good luck with your
book, by the way. And feel free to drop by the inn anytime you
want—I'm sure Skip won't mind. Be sure to bring Tad."

John and Marta appeared on the back porch, their faces long,
their shoulders rounded in defeat. Kristen went to them, pecked
each on the cheek, and said low parting words that Mark
couldn't hear. Then she bounded down the flagstone walk and
got into her VW. She backed out of the drive and sped off on Tillamook Way, headed for Nehalem Mountain.

Mark approached his parents, who had descended from the
porch to stand arm in arm in the hot afternoon sun, to watch their
little girl go. "Tell you what," he said, placing a hand on John's
shoulder. "I'll make a point of driving up to Gestern Hall every
other day or so, just to say hi. I'll scope out the situation, kind
of keep an eye on things. Would that make you feel better?"

What he saw in their faces he didn't like. Something told him
that this was more than the simple despair parents endure when
their youngest child takes her first purposeful steps away from
hearth and home. What he saw was *fear*, pure and potent.

John fixed him with a cobalt stare and said, "Why don't you
come down to my office tomorrow morning, Mark? I have some
things I think you should see."

With that, he and Marta turned and walked slowly back to the
house.

15

The Lockup

i

Bob Gammage craved a cigarette during the short drive from the Astoria Community Hospital to Oldenburg, but Deputy Will Settergren wouldn't let him have one. The other deputy, a baby-faced kid named Fanning, offered him a stick of gum. Gammage thanked him but declined, because his tongue was badly swollen and tender. He'd bitten it when the bullet hit him—when was it? Two nights ago already?

"I read that statement you gave to the state police yesterday after you woke up from your surgery," Fanning said. "That's no bullshit—you used to be a cop?"

"No bullshit. Twenty years. Retired in 'eighty-four and got into the private investigation biz. Specialize in missing kids. I'm on a case right now, as a matter of fact."

"Well, it looks like you're going to be out of commission for a while," said Settergren, signaling a turn onto the Oldenburg exit. "Assaulting a peace officer with a gun can get you twenty years in Oregon, maybe more."

ii

The Kalapuya County Jail occupied a corner of the basement of the Kalapuya County Courthouse. It consisted of four tiny cells, a padded drunk tank, and an inmate common area with a black-and-white TV set bolted to the ceiling. Outside the main steel door was a cramped receiving room with a long counter, file cabinets, a desk and a Compaq computer. The whole complex smelled vaguely of urine, antiseptic, and damp earth.

"I like what you've done with the place," said Gammage as Deputy Settergren led him to his cell. "Aren't you going to take my picture and fingerprints, or does that cost extra?"

"We'll wait till Sheriff Conrad gets here," answered Settergren. "He likes to take the pictures and do the finger-printing himself. By the way, you'll be getting a visit from Dr. Nat Schell twice a day until you make bail. If he prescribes any painkillers or other medication—"

"Which I hope to God he does."

"—we'll dispense it to you according to the doctor's directions. You'll be glad to know that the county's paying for your medical care until your court case is over. You also get three meals a day from Katie's Restaurant while you're in here, whatever's on special."

From the reception area came a shout that echoed around the cell block, along with the thumping of someone's fist on the counter: "Anybody home?"

"Sounds like your lawyer's here," said Settergren, locking Gammage's cell. "Don't go away."

iii

Bob Gammage and his lawyer held their consultation in the common area of the cell block, since the county had no other inmates in custody. Settergren supplied a pot of lukewarm coffee and an ashtray.

"I hear you're the best lawyer in town," said Gammage, eyeing the expensive camel-hair sport coat that John Lansen wore. "You look the part, I'll say that for you."

"I'm the *only* lawyer in town who's in full-time private practice, and I normally don't handle criminal matters. When you asked for the best, that's what you got. You also got the *worst*."

Gammage chuckled and explained that his only other alternative was to wait for court-appointed counsel, which the state police in Astoria informed him could take a week to arrange. He didn't have a week to hang around.

"Then I'm afraid you're in for a little disappointment, Mr. Gammage," said John, lighting his pipe. "The prosecutor intends to charge you with assault, drunk and disorderly, and unlawful discharge of a firearm within the city limits of an incorporated community. He'll settle for a combined sentence of six months in the county slam, with all but thirty days suspended. It's a done deal, if you say the word."

Gammage's ugly face whitened a shade. "I don't understand this: I didn't assault anybody! I tried to break up a fight—right?—and this guy named Bayliss clubbed me with a bar stool. I took out my piece and waved it in his face, hoping he'd back off, but just then the deputy blew in. Bayliss pitched a chair at me, and my piece went off, that's all. The round didn't even come near anybody. And for your information, I *wasn't* drunk! I think someone might've dropped a bomb in my beer. That's what it felt like—some kind of heavy-duty sedative."

John Lansen explained that he couldn't do any better than the deal he'd just described. If Sheriff Conrad had gotten his way, the charges would have included assaulting a peace officer, assault with a deadly weapon, and resisting arrest. Convictions on those charges could have sent Gammage to Oregon State Prison for many moons.

"Hey, I've got a permit for the gun," protested Gammage. "I'm a duly licensed private investigator, which I'm sure the county mounties have checked out by now. If that's not enough, I'm a former cop! I may *look* like unmitigated scum, but I'm a solid citizen, for Christ's sake, and I've got the papers to prove it."

The prosecutor had noted all this, said John, and for that very reason had reduced the charges. The fact remained that Gammage had waved a pistol at a peace officer and had fired it.

"If you want to take the D.A. to the mat, that's your business," said John, "but if you do, you'll need a full-blown criminal lawyer, which I'm not. My strong recommendation is that you take this deal. Otherwise I'll go ahead and arrange bail." He paused, staring his client straight in the eye. "If you don't take the deal, you'll probably end up in OSP for God only knows how long, instead of here in the county lockup for a month, eating nice meals from Katie's."

Gammage ran his good hand through his tangle of gray hair. "Counselor, I'm working for a man who's lost his little girl," he said wearily, which brought an empathetic look from John Lansen. "I've been after her for the last four months. All I want is to find her and bring her home to her family. I tracked her to Portland, but the trail went cold. I got a lead that says she's around here somewhere. She's supposed to be in a place called Gestern Hall—"

John Lansen's eyes widened suddenly, and his broad face flushed. "You're sure about that? She's at Gestern Hall?"

"That's what my source says. Anyway, I drove over here from Port—"

"Hold it right there," commanded Lansen. "I want you to start from the beginning. I want you to tell me the whole story, right from the get-go. But before you start, let me get Settergren down here with some decent coffee."

16

Revelations

The night weakens as the Blood Star wanes, and the eastern sky brightens. Elspeth puts a hand on Queen Molly's arm, waking her. The old woman has not lain down, but has sat upright beside the smoking embers, guarding, praying, finally dozing off.

"You must go now, Molly. You must leave this place and never return."

"What about you, my girl? Who will care for you, keep you safe?"

"Don't trouble yourself over me. I'll be provided for."

Queen Molly gets stiffly to her feet and collects her things, knowing that little more needs saying. In the waxing dawn her skin looks like smoke-stained hickory, her eyes like lumps of wet coal. She pauses a moment and listens to the morning, seeking any impression of the great cat who guarded them from the Enemy. She feels nothing but the soft warmth of dawn.

"If you see Jordie," says Elspeth, "tell him—tell him I—" She stammers, lost in a storm of grief. "No, don't tell him anything. That would be best, I think."

"If you wish it, so be it. This secret will be yours and mine alone."

Elspeth throws her arms around her friend and weeps, burying her face in the nap of the beaver-skin robe. "Thank you for helping me," she says through salty tears.

"A mother does for her child what she must do. Though you did not come out of me, you will always be my daughter." Queen Molly touches Elspeth's head, then trudges down the knoll. After a few steps she turns and says, "Abide with Sahalee Tyee, my Elspeth."

Queen Molly never again visits Mesatchie Illihee, and neither does she ever again lay eyes on Elspeth Carey. Sixteen years later, on the tenth of January 1863, she breathes her last, at the

estimated age of ninety-one. Her lodge is scarcely any quieter af-
ter she's gone.

—from Poverty Ike's Tale
Halloween of '66 (continued)

i

Mark Lansen slept late and ate an old-fashioned breakfast that
his mother lovingly prepared, the kind Kristen would have
pitched a fit over, true-believing foe of cholesterol that she was:
two eggs fried in butter, four strips of crisp country bacon, and
toast smothered with Marta's homemade blueberry preserves. He
washed it down with scalding coffee brewed Norwegian style
(strong enough to grow hair on a golf ball, his father sometimes
joked).

"The old-timers around here say we're in for drouth," said
Marta, taking the chair across the breakfast nook from him. Mark
figured that his mother was the only person in America who still
said "drouth" instead of "drought."

"Might happen in eastern Oregon, but not here," he opined
around a bite of bacon. "We're too close to the coast. We'll get
our share of rain, no matter what."

"I hope you're right. I've just planted a whole new batch of
allium, and the bulbs need moisture."

The faraway tone of her voice caused Mark to look up from
his breakfast. "You're still worried about Kristen, aren't you?"

Marta smiled sweetly, yet anxiously. Hers was perhaps the
sweetest face he'd ever known. "Is it that apparent? I thought I
was doing a pretty good job of disguising it."

"Mom, it's not like she's run off to join the Hell's Angels.
She's taken a summer job, that's all. She's still your daughter,
and she loves you. You haven't lost her. Things will work out
beautifully—you'll see."

Silence ensued, during which Marta studied the hardwood tabletop. "It's not just the job at Gestern Hall," she said finally.
"Your father and I have been worried about her for the past six
months or so."

"Oh? Why?"

During the past two college terms in Eugene, Kristen had had
no fewer than three roommates, Marta explained. One of those

roommates, a music major named Andrea, who had been Kristen's close friend since their freshman year, had telephoned John and Marta several months earlier to suggest that they urge Kristen to get some therapy.

The problem was her *dreams*. Wild, violent dreams, from which she awoke screaming and shaking.

Dreams during which she sometimes got out of bed and thrashed around the apartment, breaking things, shrieking, and scaring the living daylights out of whoever her current roommate happened to be. Understandably, each of her roommates had moved out on short notice.

In all other aspects, Kristen's life seemed normal. Her grades were good. She was dating and participating in extracurricular activities at school. Rather than try to force her to see a therapist, John and Marta had decided to increase her housing allowance, which enabled her to live alone until summer vacation. They'd planned to watch her closely through the summer and talk her into seeking psychological help, if this seemed appropriate.

But that wasn't possible now, Marta lamented. Kristen had flown off to live in that horrible old Gothic house for the summer, out of her parents' sight. That house, in Marta's view, could give a perfectly balanced person nightmares, much less . . .

"Are you suggesting that Kristen's unbalanced?" asked Mark, trying not to look as apprehensive as he felt.

Marta shook her head. What worried her was Kristen's long history of bad dreams, which had afflicted her since she was a toddler. The dreams had come and gone throughout her childhood. Extended periods often went by, occasionally whole years, without a single nightmare, and then—here Marta snapped her fingers—they always came back. The cycle of trouble sometimes lasted six months before it abated.

Mark was no longer hungry, and he pushed his plate aside. Now that his mother had mentioned it, he did recall that his little sister had been the victim of dreams and night scares throughout her girlhood. He'd forgotten how serious the trouble had been.

ii

Mark sat at the desk in his old bedroom for more than an hour and pored over his notes, but concentration was nigh impossible. An irksome question buzzed in his mind: *Does she dream about slugs?*

A noise from his boyhood reverberated through the rear wing of the house—the slamming of the back porch door, which in another life would have drawn an angry holler from John Lansen, if he'd been home to hear it. Mark intercepted his son on the staircase. Tad had three chocolate-chip cookies in one fist, a glass of milk in the other. Marta worked fast.

"Come on, Tad Bear, I have something to show you."

"Is it gonna take long? Can I go to the whizzer first?"

"No, it won't take long. And it's the bathroom, not the whizzer."

"But *you* always call it—"

"I know, I know. I want *you* to call it the bathroom. Now hurry up."

Tad put on his patented I'm-only-trying-to-be-like-you look, then scurried into the bathroom, leaving his cookies and milk on the banister post. When he returned, Mark led him up the narrow rear staircase to the attic.

The air up here was musty and close. It smelled smartly of mothballs. Mark reached overhead and pulled a string, switching on a bare bulb that dangled on a cord.

Boxes and crates lay everywhere, crammed into corners and piled high. Old coats, old sweaters, old suits—all covered with clear plastic—hung on clothing racks. Bicycles, tricycles, and boxes of forgotten toys lined a sloping wall, hemmed in by trunks full of disused knickknacks and pieces of dusty furniture that had outlived their usefulness.

"Wow, there's a lot of bitchin' stuff up here," said Tad, pushing the last of a chocolate-chip cookie into his mouth. He put down his glass of milk and knelt before a huge chest, which stood open. Inside it were an ancient Royal typewriter, an equally ancient adding machine with a long chrome handle, and sundry artifacts from an office, all from the early days of Gramp's law practice. Outdated law books lay in tall stacks behind the chest, the topmost covered with dust and festooned with cobwebs. Tad pulled the handle of the adding machine, and the contraption issued a satisfying *thuk-chunk*.

"Is this what they used instead of calculators in the olden days?" he asked excitedly.

"It wasn't that long ago, Tad Bear. I've even used one myself, believe it or not." Mark surveyed the wealth of junk that lay on all sides. "What I wanted to show you is over here, I think."

He crouched into a corner under the slanting roof and opened a trunk, incurring a creak from rusty hinges. He started taking things out, a battered catcher's mitt, a pair of cleated baseball shoes caked with long-dried dirt, books with torn dustcovers, a faded Dodgers cap, which he put on his head. Finally he found what he was looking for, pulled it out, and set it on the floor between his knees.

It was a mildewed canvas bag that looked older than he was. It, along with its lowly contents, had belonged to his birth mother. On the day of his adoption by the Lansens twenty-two years ago, an officer of the Methodist Guardians Foundation had gone to a vault, returned with this bag, and handed it to Mark. As far as anyone knew, it was all that his real mother had left him. She'd left written instructions to send these items along with Mark, if a family ever adopted him permanently.

He'd kept the bag all these years and had occasionally dragged it out of some dark storage place and opened it. In this bag, he now told Tad, who hovered wide-eyed over his shoulder, were his only real memories of her.

He tugged the bag open, forcing the zipper when it balked, and took out a photograph, frayed around the edges and dim. He held it up so his son could study it.

"Her name was Rita," he said. "Rita Crowe. She was my real mother."

"Then *your* last name would've been Crowe," observed Tad, looking reverent, "if Gram and Gramp hadn't adopted you. And so would mine."

"Maybe so," said Mark. He didn't know whether his real mother and father shared the same name, or whether they'd even been married. As he'd said before, he knew nothing at all about his father.

"She's neat," breathed the boy, running a finger along the edge of the photo. Had this been her high school graduation portrait? Mark had often wondered. Probably not. Her face seemed too salted with experience to be that young. It was the face of a comely woman who could have been twenty-five, or thirty-five, or any age in between. On anyone else her early-1950s hairdo would have looked frumpy, but on Rita Crowe it was lovely. A curious little trinket hung from a glittering chain around her neck.

Her gaze conveyed feelings and messages that Mark was certain existed only in his imagination—sadness, regret, apology. In the depths of those magical eyes he sensed a willingness to take responsibility for the chaos that had been his early childhood. She could have done better by him, the expression seemed to say. She was sorry for having abandoned him to the Methodist Guardians, sorrier still for—

Mark heard himself laying the truth before Tad, but he cut himself off. Some things his son didn't need to know.

Rita Crowe had killed herself. On that gray, drizzling morning in January 1954, when Mark was but six weeks old, she'd left him in the waiting room of the Methodist Guardians Foundation in southeast Portland, the old tote bag beside him, a cryptic suicide note pinned to his moth-eaten blanket. She then walked a few blocks to Tacoma Street and caught a bus to Sellwood Park on the east shore of the Willamette River, where she got off. No one knew how long she lingered among the picnic tables and trees, perhaps weeping softly in the hopeless rain, perhaps praying for forgiveness for what she was about to do. Police records didn't deal with such things, so the officers of the Methodist Guardians couldn't speculate. The records showed only that Rita Crowe eventually climbed to the grimy rail of the Sellwood Bridge and jumped before any of the passing motorists could stop and grab her. Her body washed ashore on Ross Island the next day, less than a mile downstream, swollen and mottled and entangled with flotsam. The County of Multnomah buried it with minimal ceremony.

Yes, this could wait until Tad was older, *much* older, thought Mark.

The next item to come out of the bag was a humble little trinket on a delicate gold chain, a tiny silver amulet caked with tarnish. It was, quite possibly, the same trinket that Rita Crowe wore in the photograph. Mark handed it to Tad, who examined it carefully, holding it close to his face. Barely discernible through the tarnish was the head of a lion with a snake draped around it—a strange and somber piece of art, Mark had often thought.

Tad handed it back abruptly. "It's warm," he said with puzzlement in his face.

"What do you mean?" Mark let the amulet lie in his palm a long moment. It was indeed warm, warmer than it should be—almost hot. "Maybe the trunk was sitting over a heating vent," he said, not believing this himself. No heating ducts led into the attic, and the weather wasn't cold enough to require turning on the furnace, anyway. Mark dropped the amulet into the tote bag and suppressed the tingle of horror that had taken root deep in his stomach. *Okay, it's warm. No big deal. Just let it lie.*

The final item was the book. It was flat and thin and bound between hard covers, a storybook for kids, full of ham-handed pictures painted by a watercolor artist who had long since died. Cranbrook & Sons of Seattle, Washington, said the imprint inside the front cover. *The Kitty-Tale Series, Suitable for Kids Ages 3–6.* The publication date was 1939.

Mark stared at the faded blue cover as he had so many times before, knowing that he could damn-near recite the text from memory. The main character stared back at him with piercing, oversized eyes, a grinning cat whose cartoonish head was far too large for his body, whose outlandish grin consumed most of his face. The artist had intended the expression to be both friendly and full of innocent mischief, but today it seemed anything but friendly. Or even innocent. It seemed different somehow.

The Tale of Snacky Cat.

Mark pressed his lips together hard and stared at the picture. Snacky Cat's grin *was* different, no question about it—wider than he remembered it, and toothier, less full of harmless mischief and more suggestive of—what? *Hunger?* The green eyes were sharp and glinty, despite the fading ink.

The story concerned a feline named Snacky Cat, who more than anything else in the world loved to eat. He'd tired of the bland kibbles dished out by his rosy-cheeked mistress, Prissy. He envied the plowhorse, who received juicy red apples from the farmer's wife; the dog, whom Farmer Pete favored with succulent ham bones; the squirrels for their tasty walnuts and acorns; the cows who got molasses with their silage; and most of all, the humans, who feasted on an endless variety of mouth-watering food. He'd tried to convince Prissy to give him some of the wonderful things others ate, but she'd always replied, "Oh, Snacky Cat, be happy with what you have. After all, you're just a cat, and if cats won't eat their kibbles, then they can always eat mice!" The thought of eating cute little mice revolted him, so he decided that if he was indeed a cat, and if cats couldn't have what others ate, then he would just have to become someone *else. . . .*

The narrative plodded on in mostly one- and two-syllable words, recounting the hero's ludicrous adventures in impersonation, how he tried to pass himself off as a horse, a dog, a cow, and even a human in order to score more interesting eats. Mark found himself wading through it with eyes wide and hungry, reading aloud to Tad, turning the brittle pages with trembling fingers, devouring the juvenile prose and wondering why this little story now seemed so full of hidden meaning. *To become someone else . . . !*

Then it was over, and Mark packed the tote bag and its contents into the trunk again. Tad stared at him with his huge, earnest eyes, silently asking, *What does all this mean, Dad Bear?*

Mark felt obliged to say something. He tried to remember what he'd rehearsed. He tried to remember exactly why he'd thought it so important to show his son this sorry parcel and its contents. For some reason he found it hard to think clearly.

"I wanted you to understand that it's not such a huge deal to be adopted, Tad," he said at last, his voice shaking. "I wanted to share what I know of my real mother, to let you see her picture and . . ." *And show you how little she left me.* "Do you see, Tad Bear, that this is all there is to it? Only that bag, a few odds and ends. That's all I have of her, and that's all I need. Ever since I was twelve, I've had Gram and Gramp, and they've been the best parents any kid could want. Actually, I think of *them* as my real parents, because they're the ones who loved me and gave me a home to grow up in."

The boy nodded as if he understood, but Mark saw nothing in his face to suggest relief or enlightenment, no sign that troublesome demons had been purged. Instead, he saw the same wonderment at the amulet's warmth that lay cold against his own heart, the same unspoken feeling that something strange had just happened, something tinged with evil.

"Come on, Tad Bear, let's get out of here."

iii

John Lansen called around eleven and asked Mark to join him at his law office. As he'd said yesterday after Kristen had left for the Nehalem Mountain Inn, he had something Mark should see.

Mark left Tad under Marta's able supervision and strolled down the hill on Tillamook Way to Clatsop Street, wearing the faded Dodgers cap he'd found in the attic. He bore right and walked past the Kalapuya County High School, which stood in the shade of towering noble firs and Garry oaks. He turned left on Chinook and continued past the county courthouse to the Lansen law office, which occupied the second floor of a converted Victorian house on the corner of Main and Chinook. A pair of elegant Pacific dogwoods stood in the front yard, attended by beds of blossoming devil's club.

"You look a little peaked," said John, ushering Mark into his personal office, which boasted an ancient Persian carpet over a squeaky hardwood floor. "Want some coffee or a Diet Pepsi? Maybe a leftover bear claw from Katie's?"

Mark declined the offers. He'd eaten a big breakfast, he said.

John seated him in the big chair behind the ponderous oak desk and went to a file cabinet. He returned with a brown file folder that he placed on the blotter before Mark. Inside were three sets of documents, each held together with a paperclip.

"By way of preamble," he said, slipping out of his camel-hair sport coat, "I'll point out that the Gestern family has been a strong economic force in this town since the very beginning, which I'm sure you know, since you're writing a history of Oldenburg. As a matter of fact, the original Clovis Gestern—"

"Is *that* what this is all about?" interrupted Mark. "You've got something on the Gesterns?"

"What else would it be about? I'm trying to show you why I don't want Kristen associating with that family." He placed his palms on the glossy surface of the desk and leaned forward slightly. "Take a look at what I've got, and hear me out, okay? Then if you think I'm ready for the drooling academy, you can say so. I may even go peaceably. Deal?"

"Deal."

The Gesterns were the first white family to settle on the land that eventually became Oldenburg, John continued. They had originally put down roots well to the south, in the region of

Tualatin, now engulfed by the Portland metro area. For some unknown reason they had left that settlement for the remoteness of Nehalem Mountain, where they had eventually rebuilt their ancestral house, Gestern Hall. To make a long story short, they had bankrolled many of the enterprises that fueled the development of Oldenburg.

The first salmon cannery, for example, founded by a German immigrant named Heinrich Olden in 1875, the man who gave the town its name. John Lansen had seen nineteenth-century bank records showing that a man named Clovis Gestern owned a large share of the original cannery. When Olden went bust after twenty years, thanks to river pollution, overfishing, and tough competition from Alaska, he sold out to a Norwegian named Haaken Hilde.

And where did Hilde get his money? Much of it from the Gesterns, said John. The Gestern family's share of the enterprise grew even larger.

Another example—the German Point Sawmill, built in 1915 by yet another German immigrant, Robert Kuchenbrod. Again, the Gesterns were in for a large percentage.

"All very interesting," said Mark, "but it's ancient history. What does any of this have to do with Kristen and Skip Gestern?"

"Bernie Pellagrini isn't ancient history," replied John, straightening up and pocketing his large red hands—hands that could easily have belonged to a logger. "He's dead, yes, but his estate is very much alive. And so are his heirs, some of whom I represent." He went on to reveal that Clovis Gestern, presumably the grandfather of the present-day Skip Gestern, had lent Bernie Pellagrini the money he needed to found the family appliance business. Moreover, the Gesterns and the Pellagrinis had entered into several real estate ventures together.

"Every single person I've mentioned—the people who went into partnership with the Gesterns—met with personal disaster. Heinrich Olden shot himself after selling his cannery to Haaken Hilde in 1895. Old man Kuchenbrod fell into a circular saw in 1935, presumably by accident, and ended up in two large pieces at the end of a conveyer belt in his own mill. Hilde was found dead in 1945, the day after the war ended, asphyxiated in his Packard. No one ever determined whether it was an accident or suicide, since he was a doddering old man by that time. You *know* what happened to Bernie and Fran Pellagrini."

Mark laced and unlaced his fingers nervously, wondering just what the hell his father was driving at. Did John actually believe that doing business with the Gesterns carried some kind of curse?

"You don't need to say it," said John. "I know what you're thinking. Do me the favor of looking at the documents in front of you before jumping to conclusions."

The first appeared to be a death certificate, printed in French.

"I know you're a competent linguist, so I won't bother to tell you what they say," John added, motioning his son to start reading. As a medievalist historian, Mark could read not only modern French, but also the ancient French of the Valois kings. And German and Latin, too, for that matter, as well as Old English, which he'd found as foreign as the others.

Mark scanned the document, struggling here and there with the elaborate ministerial script. The decedent was a man named Clovis Gestern, who had died of cardiac arrest on November 22, 1974, in the province of Burgundy.

Atop the next batch of papers was a similar document, this one printed in standard German, dated July 21, 1935, from a town in Bavaria called Rothenburg ob der Tauber. This particular Clovis Gestern died of *Schlaganfall*, or stroke.

The third was a death certificate in English, noting the passing of one Clovis Gestern, marked with the seal of a magistrate in York, England, dated March 1, 1888. Death befell as the consequence of maladies related to advanced age, it said.

Each of the three certificates bore the signatures of an attending physician and a municipal official who had accepted it for the public file. Attached to each were photocopies of official records from Kalapuya County—probate documents, John explained. These recorded the disposition of the departed Gesterns' property, both "personal" and "real." The estates were huge.

"Seems like the family has been partial to the name Clovis," Mark observed wryly while thumbing through the papers. "It was the name of the first Christian king of France. I wonder if they've ever named a kid anything else."

John merely grinned and said that all three death certificates were phonies. Mark glanced up and stared at his father, looking skeptical but waiting for more.

"It's true," said John. "I got a hunch when I perused the probate documents on file with the county clerk of court. It wasn't too hard to notice that every time a Clovis Gestern died, the whole estate went to just one heir—another Clovis Gestern. Sort of jumps right out at you, know what I mean? There weren't any other heirs, which is damn-near unheard of with estates this large."

"It's what I call taking primogeniture to the extreme," said Mark, chuckling.

"No kidding. But that in itself wasn't what set me to sleuthing. I noticed that in all three cases, the decedent Gestern left the country to die—went to Europe, as you can see from the death certificates. The fact that it happened three times to three consecutive Clovis Gesterns seemed a little too symmetrical to be coincidence, almost as if it was planned. . . ."

"Oh, come on, Dad! Are you suggesting that these guys *knew* they were going to die and that they wanted to do it in Europe? Doesn't that seem a little farfetched, even to you?"

"I'll let you draw your own conclusions. I wrote to each of the jurisdictions and requested copies of the death certificates. I didn't really need any, since our own courthouse already had these on file with the probate records. I merely wanted to confirm that the certificates were genuine. Imagine my surprise when letters came back telling me that none of these agencies had recorded the death of anyone named Clovis Gestern—not *ever!*"

John paused to take his pipe from the pocket of his sport coat, which he'd draped over a chair. He made a production of filling the pipe with tobacco and lighting it, forcing Mark to wait while the suspense built up.

"I then wrote to the national medical associations of each country," he went on, gesturing with the lit pipe, "France, Great Britain, and the Federal Republic of Germany. I asked for information on the attending physicians noted on the death certificates. And guess what? None of them had any record of these gentlemen practicing medicine in their countries, not in 1974, not in 1935, and not in 1888, not *ever.*

"Now, I wouldn't be suspicious if only one of the jurisdictions had lost the death records of someone named Clovis Gestern, especially if the death had happened over a hundred years ago. Agencies have been losing records since the very birth of bureaucracy. But I find it impossible to believe that all three agencies lost the records of three different Clovis Gesterns, all in different countries and each a generation apart. It just doesn't make sense.

"As for the doctors, the same reasoning applies."

And what did John do next? What any other lawyer would do—sent copies of the death certificates to each of the agencies in Europe, asking whether they could confirm authenticity.

"The British and Germans wrote back, saying they doubted these could be copies of genuine documents, but they wouldn't say for sure without comparing the originals with genuine samples. The folks in Burgundy were less circumspect: The French death certificate was definitely a skillfully executed forgery, and they said so flat out."

Mark leaned back in his chair, removed his baseball cap, and massaged his scalp through dark, bushy hair. With a weary voice he asked the obvious question: Why would someone go to all the trouble of dummying up death certificates?

John could think of only one reason—to convey an estate to an heir before death actually occurs.

And why would someone want to do *that?*

The possible reasons were multitudinous, and most involved money.

"Let me ask you something, Dad. What got you started? I mean, why did you start digging in the Gesterns' probate records in the first place?"

The probate proceedings on the Pellagrinis' estate had revealed that the Gestern family still owned a major share of their business, John explained, per the original agreement the Pellagrinis had signed with old Clovis Gestern. The two families also held joint interests in some local real estate. John needed to find out the names of the dead Gestern's heirs, because those heirs could be due a portion of the Pellagrinis' estate. Jointly held property interests needed liquidation and disbursement.

But there was more to John's story, something he'd just found out today. He pulled up an old oak chair, sat on it backwards, and loosened his tie, his face flushed with excitement. "Today I took on a criminal case, my first in years. I only did it as a favor to Judge Kelstad, in order to spare him the hassle of finding a public defender for the guy. It's an obvious plea bargain, anyway, hardly any work at all. But I need to swear you to secrecy, Mark, at least until the case is finished."

Mark swore, and John related the incident of two nights earlier at Poverty Ike's. Two guys had driven into town. They'd checked into the Hotel Luxor and gone to Poverty Ike's for dinner. Beer had flowed. A fight had broken out, involving the two guys and Gary Bayliss, of all people. Poverty Ike had called the sheriff's office, and Deputy Will Settergren had answered the call. John's client had a gun in his hand, and it went off in the melee. Will fired back, hitting John's client in the left shoulder. An ambulance rushed the man to the hospital in Astoria, where he'd undergone emergency surgery.

"Fortunately for him the round only nicked his clavicle and took a small notch out of his shoulder blade," said John. "It'll hurt like a son of a bitch for a week or two, but there won't be any permanent damage. Will and another deputy drove over to Astoria this morning and brought him back to the Kalapuya County lockup. I talked to him as soon as they booked him. His name is Robert Gammage, and he's a licensed private detective from New York. He's also a former New York City cop, and he owns a valid permit for the gun he was carrying. Swears up and down that somebody at Poverty Ike's slipped him a Mickey Finn, and that he was only trying to break up the fight between his buddy and Gary Bayliss. I believe him, but I don't see any way we could beat the D.A. on an assault charge. I told him he's better off with a plea bargain and thirty days in the county jug. Besides, he says he doesn't have time to hang around for a trial, which would take longer than the time he'd serve under the deal."

"Are you telling me there's some connection between him and Skip Gestern?"

"Gammage specializes in runaway kids, Mark. He's looking for a teenaged girl from New York, named Skye Padilla. The guy who was with Gammage, apparently the one who started the fight in Poverty Ike's, had gotten a tip on the street in Portland and had sought out Gammage. The girl was in Oldenburg, this tipster said, in a place called *Gestern Hall*." John leaned away from the chair, gripping its back with his ruddy hands, looking maddeningly pleased with himself. "Need I say more?"

Mark exhaled air through pursed lips. "So what are you suggesting—that we call out the National Guard to storm Skip Gestern's house? So *what* if there's a runaway teenager up there?

There could be dozens of innocent explanations, if it's even true."

"Oh, I intend to find out if it's true, never fear. I also intend to find out *why* that little girl is up there. And I intend to get Kristen away from that place. Don't you see, Mark—it's just one more drop in the bucket, just one more reason to be leery of that place and that family. Given what we already know about the Gesterns—"

"I hope you're not referring to all those old Halloween stories I used to hear when I was a kid."

"I'm referring to the family's record of committing fraud. Besides, this isn't the first time that house has been associated with runaway girls, kids off the street, kids no one can check up on. I could tell you stories, Mark. . . ."

"And that's just what they'd be—*stories.* I don't see any reason to go off half-cocked on the basis of old folktales, especially where Kristen's involved. I've heard about her recent bad dreams, Dad, and I think it's important that you and Mom reestablish a good relationship with her. I want to smooth things over with her, talk her into visiting you on a regular basis. But that won't happen if you barge into Gestern Hall with wild stories about missing girls."

John rose and paced to the other side of the room, looking antsy and impatient. He stood for a moment with his head thrown back and his eyes clenched tight, as if he had a headache. "None of this makes any sense to you, does it, Mark? None of what I've said causes you the least apprehension over your sister's welfare."

"Dad, I can understand your worry up to a point. Kristen's growing up, and she's taking her first steps toward making her own life. You feel as if you're losing your little girl—"

"That's *not* it, I can assure you."

"Okay, but don't you owe it to yourself and to your daughter to get a few more facts before you start a war with her? That's exactly what'll happen if you pursue this thing, you know—a war. And Kristen will win it."

"Where do you suggest I look for these *facts?*"

"For starters, how about Gammage's buddy, the one who started the fight in Poverty Ike's. Shouldn't you at least talk to him?"

"Not possible," answered John. The guy managed to escape

through the back door of the bar while Will Settergren was busy giving first aid to Gammage. The sheriff's office was still looking for him. "Gammage told me not to expect too much from this guy, even if the cops manage to find him," John added. "He's been living under a freeway in Portland, and apparently he's paranoid as hell. Thinks the FBI is after him. Whatever he has to say is probably—"

"The *FBI?*" Mark's eyes became wide and round. He felt a cold breath on the nape of his neck. "Living under a freeway, you say?" He endured a quick flashback to the meal room of Baloney Joe's in Portland, to the bizarre conversation he'd had with a man who believed that the FBI was after him.

"A homeless fella," said John, eyeing his son quizzically. "Gammage hadn't known him until a couple of days ago." He walked to his desk and picked up a legal pad on which he'd jotted notes during his interview with Bob Gammage. "Name's right here somewhere, kind of an unusual one. Here it is— Darkenwald. Sam Darkenwald."

Mark put his hand on the wall to steady himself. A horrible moment ensued, during which he doubted his own sanity. Suddenly he knew fear as he'd never known it in the broad light of day.

PART II

There is something at work in my soul
which I do not understand.

—Mary Shelley,
Frankenstein

17

In the Bowel of the Beast

i

Kristen Lansen sat up in the canopied bed and rubbed her eyes. A glance at her watch actually frightened her. It was nearly two o'clock in the afternoon. She couldn't believe she'd slept this long—almost fourteen hours!

For a moment her surroundings seemed alien, and she felt as if she'd awakened in the middle of a Gothic novel. From the peak of the vaulted ceiling hung a crude chandelier made of hammered iron bands. Electric bulbs occupied the holders, which in the days of yore probably held candles. Heavy brocaded curtains denied the daylight, and an ornately patterned carpet covered the floor. The abundance of tapestry gave the chamber a smothering atmosphere that made her want to cough.

The far wall was full of books on sagging shelves—thick old books with frayed leather covers. Kristen could almost smell the dust. Near the bed stood a small antique desk, flanked by iron-frame chairs with backs bent into Gothic arches. On the desk were a pitcher of orange juice, a bottle of Excedrin, and a box of Kleenex.

Am I sick? she wondered, *or just hung over?*

Her head ached, so she availed herself of the Excedrin, washing the tablets down with the orange juice, which had warmed to room temperature. She'd drunk only one glass of red wine with last night's dinner, so this couldn't be a hangover, she told herself. She'd eaten very little, so food poisoning was equally unlikely. Mrs. Drumgule had concocted something called country beef pie, a round mess that was awash with fatty gravy and peppered with bits of gristle. Just looking at it had made Kristen nauseous. She'd managed a bite or two for the sake of politeness, and had made a sparing meal of an unbuttered muffin.

And then—what?

Her recollection shimmered and grew fuzzy, like badly shot videotape. Skip had toasted her—she remembered that. He'd called her the "hope of the Nehalem Mountain Inn," the one who would notify the world of the earthly delights available here, the bed-and-breakfast with a difference. The four of them had raised their glasses, and—

The *four* of them?

Skip Gestern, Mrs. Drumgule, Kristen herself, and—who else? *Oh yes, the young girl. What was her name?*

Skye. That was it. Kristen couldn't remember the girl's last name, but she recalled that it sounded Hispanic, that it seemed appropriate to the child's dark, handsome features. She had a small white scar near the corner of her mouth, a flaw that actually accentuated the melancholy perfection of her face.

Panic gripped Kristen when she found a bandage on the inside of her own left forearm, a wide adhesive strip over a Tefla pad. She jumped from the bed, darted to the window and threw back the heavy curtain. Sunshine flooded the room, and a harsh reflection jerked her attention away from the bandage. She stared uncomprehendingly at the chrome gurney that stood in the opposite corner, at the canvas straps that hung from its thin mattress and the tall vertical assembly attached to its frame.

The straps, she knew, were meant to restrain whoever lay on the gurney. And the vertical shaft of chrome was an intravenous delivery rack.

ii

She showered in the bathroom adjacent to her room and dressed in an olive drab poplin romper with knee-length cuffs and button-flap pockets, a comfortable outfit, almost business-like. She stood a moment at the tall, arched window, which had diamond-shaped panes and thick, imperfect glass that distorted the outward view.

The second-story window faced north, toward the valley and the town below. An arching tangle of blackberries bordered the lawn, giving way to a forest of red alder, noble fir, and cedar. Here and there stalks of bear grass poked through a thicket of holly and leathery licorice fern. For a mad moment Kristen thought she saw movement in that wilderness of afternoon shadow, then doubted it. A trick of the eyes and nerves, she told herself, or a crazy refraction of the ancient glass.

She rubbed her arm where the bandage had been. Beneath it she'd found a small puncture in the center of a blue bruise, the kind of hole an IV needle would make. She stared at the wound again, as she'd stared at it in the shower, wondering, worrying, pushing down outrageous suspicions.

Yesterday seemed a lifetime gone. A mere twenty-four hours ago she'd felt feisty and confident as she stood up to her parents on whether to take the job offered by Skip Gestern. She'd showed them she couldn't be bullied, that she was her own person. She'd stomped out of their house, leaving them with their mouths hanging open and the stinging knowledge that they'd underestimated her.

At this moment, though, studying the small hole on the inside of her left forearm, she regretted the way she'd treated them. She didn't feel feisty now, or confident. She didn't feel like her twenty-year-old self, but more like a little girl.

iii

Skip Gestern welcomed her into his study with the offer of a glass of freshly squeezed lemonade, which Kristen gladly accepted. Dressed in a bright blue polo shirt and neatly pressed khakis, his hazel eyes reassuring and kind, he looked like a young pediatrician on vacation.

"I'll bet you're ready for some breakfast," he said, grinning perfectly. "Or maybe I should call it a late lunch."

"I'm really not very hungry," Kristen said, letting him lead her to a brocaded settee. "The lemonade sure tastes good, though."

From behind her came a voice that gave her a start. "And how are you feeling today, my dear?" Mrs. Drumgule emerged from a shadowy corner of the walnut-paneled study, wearing the same long drab dress she'd worn yesterday, or one exactly like it. In the light of the stained-glass windowpanes, her face seemed sallow and sickly. "I'm sorry if I startled you," she whistled through her bad teeth. "I was doing some dusting when you came in."

"I-I think I'm okay. It's not like me to sleep so long." Kristen turned to Skip. "I really am sorry. I'd planned to start work bright and early today. I can just imagine what you must think. . . ."

"Hey, there's nothing to be sorry for," he said, lighting a cigarette. "Everyone has bad dreams now and then. And you're certainly not the first to go sleepwalking, believe me."

"Dreams? Sleepwalking?"

"Surely you remember, dear," said Mrs. Drumgule, smiling crookedly. "You got out of your bed around two in the morning and walked the length of the second-floor corridor. You ended up on the rear staircase, where we still have restoration work under way. Apparently you tripped over some loose flooring and tumbled down the steps to the first landing."

"Which isn't very far, fortunately," said Skip. "But you did cut your arm on a carpet nail. I see you've taken the bandage off." He gently raised her left arm and examined the tiny wound. "There doesn't seem to be any sign of infection. Lucky that Mrs. Drumgule heard the thump when you fell."

"My room is just down the hall from yours," put in the older woman. "I found you on the rear stairs, and I called Clovis— uh—Mr. Gestern."

"And we cleaned up the cut. Gave it a good dose of antiseptic spray and slapped a bandage on it. We weren't sure how badly you'd hurt yourself at first, so we used our trusty first-aid gurney to take you back to your room. You seemed as if you were awake, so I'm surprised you don't remember. At any rate, I'm glad to see that you're apparently no worse for wear."

Kristen tried hard to recall some small fragment of the incident on the rear staircase, but could not. She explained that she had a history of bad dreams, that she'd been known to get out of bed occasionally and do weird things. She could rarely remember such an episode the next morning. Fortunately they didn't happen very often.

"Well, enough of this!" exclaimed Skip, tapping his cigarette ash into an ashtray. "The day is still young, the sun is bright, and there's work to be done!"

"I really do appreciate your putting up with me," said Kristen.

"I deem myself fortunate to have you aboard," said Skip reassuringly.

Mrs. Drumgule excused herself, apparently sensing that public relations talk was about to begin. After she'd closed the door behind her, Skip leaned close to Kristen and whispered, "I noticed that you hardly touched your country beef pie last night. Don't feel like the Lone Ranger. I can't stand it, either. That's why I had a pizza earlier—so I'd have an excuse not to eat!"

They shared a quiet chuckle.

"I don't let her serve that particular dish when we have paying guests," Skip added, "and as you know, we're empty right now."

Kristen asked whether Mrs. Drumgule handled all the cooking, even when paying guests were in residence. Yes indeed, answered Skip. Actually the woman was skilled in several Continental cuisines. Her country beef pie was her only real failing, a throwback to her working-class roots. He added that Skye Padilla, their newly hired maid, helped in the kitchen when needed.

"If I can help with the work around here, be sure to let me know," said Kristen. "I can drive a riding mower, and I've had lots of practice doing housework."

"I appreciate your willingness to help, but I didn't hire you to do manual labor, Kristen. Your first job is to soak up the ambience of this house, just as we talked about yesterday. You'll want to learn its history thoroughly. We have literally hundreds of books on the subject, most of which I've put on the shelves in your room, just so you'll have them at your fingertips."

"*Hundreds* of them?" Kristen was aghast, and her face showed it. "God, this place is more famous than I thought!"

"Well, not *all* the books deal directly with Gestern Hall. Most of them are old, limited editions that relate the exploits of Gestern ancestors. The story of this house is woven into the history of the family, of course. And therein lies the appeal, I think. I'd like every guest to feel as though he's living a little piece of the romantic past the very moment he steps in from the porte cochere. I want every guest to feel like a member of the Gestern family."

He rose from the settee and moved toward a wall, where hung a framed diptych. He pointed to the left panel, which showed Christ in the Garden of Gethsemane. A tall male figure in black was whispering something to the Son of Man.

"Take this painting, for example. It depicts an ancient legend concerning our family—one which I'm sure must be apocryphal—about the founding of a religious order that our ancestors led for many generations. Have you ever heard of the Gethsemanites?"

Kristen shook her head.

"You'll learn all about them in your reading. Their history is very colorful, believe me." He pointed out other features in the medieval paintings that hung on the walls of the study, all showing versions of the man in black, always in the company of divine figures. "The story of the Gethsemanites has captured the imagination of many an artist through the centuries, Kristen. I'm sure you can adapt it to a modern audience. It has all the ingredients of a first-rate epic drama."

"Sounds like a real challenge," said Kristen weakly. The unease she'd felt earlier surged again.

"It's a challenge, yes. But I'm confident that you're up to it. The books will tell you everything you need to know." For the briefest moment a shadow of sadness passed over Skip Gestern's eyes, but he banished it with a dazzling smile.

iv

Kristen retired to her "office," which was actually an anteroom off the cavernous kitchen in the rear of the mansion. It seemed less medieval than the rest of the house, thanks to airy beige paint on the plastered walls and contemporary berry-colored carpet. No ancient paintings or suits of armor here. No arched-back chairs or battle-axes. A computer, a flat-bed scanner, and a laser printer occupied most of the room, along with modern office chairs on rollers.

She snapped on the computer and booted a graphics program, needing something to do. She suppressed her doubts over whether a carpet nail could produce a puncture as small and neat as the one on her arm, not to mention the fact that she'd found no other bruises on her body, bruises that a reasonable person might expect if she'd fallen down a flight of stairs.

The door opened, and Skye Padilla appeared, wearing the same sort of vaguely medieval dress that Mrs. Drumgule favored. She hesitated at the threshold, smiling warily.

"Oh, hi," said Kristen, glad for the interruption. "Come in and take a load off."

The girl pulled the door closed behind her. "Sorry to bother you, Ms. Lansen, but I—" She stammered and cleared her throat.

"You can chill that 'Ms. Lansen' shit. As long as you don't

make me call you Ms. Padilla, you can call me Kristen. Just don't call me Kristy or Kris, okay? I hate those nicknames even more than my real one."

Skye settled on the edge of a chair, her limbs gathered close. She reminded Kristen of a kitten whom someone has mistreated—a kitten with a beautiful, distrusting face. A knowing glint in her eyes suggested that her girlhood had ended long before it should have, as did the ragged needle tracks on her wrists.

"I just wanted—y'know—to talk to you a minute," said Skye, with an accent that sounded like Brooklyn. "If you have stuff to do, I can—y'know—come back some other time."

No problem, Kristen assured her. This was as good a time as any.

"I don't quite know how to say this," Skye began, "but I think you ought to get out of here. You ought to get out of here as soon as you can. It would be best if you could do it before dark."

"Why in the world is that?"

"This place isn't good. I'd get out myself, if I could. I've seen things around here that would make—" From somewhere came a soft bump, which sounded like Mrs. Drumgule cleaning upstairs, and Skye flinched.

"It's okay," assured Kristen. "We're alone. So, what exactly have you seen?"

Skye's facial muscles twitched, wiggling the milky scar near the corner of her mouth. "You don't want to know," she breathed. "Just get the hell out before something else happens to you."

Something *else*? Kristen could see that the girl was thoroughly terrified, and suddenly she felt fear worming in her own gut. She took a deep breath and chose her words carefully. "If I left, would you come with me?"

"I can't. Mrs. Drumgule and Skip would never let me leave. But *you*—you can come and go whenever you want, right?"

"Of course I can, Skye." She studied the girl's pretty face a moment. "How long have you been here?"

"About three weeks. I ran away from home four months ago. I was living on the street in Portland, and this old dude comes up to me and asks me if I want a job, y'know? I thought for sure he wanted a date, because I was doing dates then, y'know, just to buy burgers and stuff. So I went with him, and he brought me here. It was night, and I don't even know for sure where this place is. I've been here ever since, working with that awful old woman, doing everything she says."

Kristen suggested that Skye call home, that she ask her parents to come for her. But Skye couldn't do this, even if she wanted to. The house had only one telephone, and that was in Skip's study. When Skip wasn't around, the study was always locked.

Then why not wait until Mrs. Drumgule and Skip were asleep? She could slip out of the house and walk down the mountain to Oldenburg in less than two hours, even in the dark.

Skye's answer turned Kristen's flesh to icy pinpricks. "There's people around the house at night—*weird* people, a man and a woman, y'know? Once I saw them watching me through the window, like they wanted to get in here and come after me. Sometimes I hear them poking around in the bushes near the back door. They look *bad*, Kristen—I mean they look like they've been in some kind of humungous accident or something, y'know, all bloody and mangled. No way you're gonna get me outside this house after dark."

Kristen wanted to tell this confused kid not to listen to the wild tales the locals told about Gestern Hall and Nehalem Mountain. She wanted to assure her that she had nothing to fear from Skip Gestern, a man who bought uniforms for the high school band, who gave money to restore the old courthouse. She wanted to hear these words from her own mouth, but they wouldn't come, as if blocked by her own worming misgivings.

"I've got to get back to work," said Skye, standing. "Do like I say, okay? Get the hell out of here, and never come back, man. I don't want them to—" Another soft thud came from somewhere, and Skye bolted out the door before Kristen could reach out to stop her.

18

The Nehalem Mountain Raiders

i

From early morning until high afternoon Mark Lansen struggled with the final outline of his history of Oldenburg, even skipping lunch (which Marta didn't approve of at all). For all his struggling, he made precious little progress. He sat at his computer in the curtained twilight of his boyhood room and pecked halfheartedly at the keyboard, or stared at the screen or rummaged through notes. Time and again the terrors of the past week reared up and made him squirm.

Shortly before three o'clock his stomach growled, so he snapped off the computer and went downstairs. He found Tad in his grandfather's favorite wicker swing, a book about the planets open in his lap. He wore a loose basketball shirt, baggy orange shorts, and his Walkman headphones.

"How about you and I get off our dead butts and go somewhere fun, Tad Bear? Things can get a little quiet around here—maybe a little too quiet. A change of scenery might do us both good. Up for it?"

Tad removed the headphones and smiled faintly. "I guess so. Where is this place, anyway?"

"That's a surprise. We'll go on our bikes. All you have to do is follow me, assuming you can keep up. You ready?"

"Let's do it."

ii

They coasted down Tillamook Way to Clatsop Street, where they bore left, skirting the eastern edge of Kalapuya County Park and crossing Floral Avenue, where the First United Methodist Church and the old Hilde mansion faced each other on opposing corners. Birds sang in the trees overhead, and the sun shone in yellow bars between the leafy branches. The summer air felt friendly on Mark's face. When they reached Main Street in the heart of Oldenburg's business district, they turned left toward the river. They cruised by the Burger King, Baldridge's Family Eatery and McCullen's Texaco. Main Street dipped beneath U.S. 30 and emerged into a quarter that was weedy and old and tumbledown.

Mark pointed out the deserted machine shops on the left—long, leaning buildings with high windows that had no panes and with yards overrun by blackberries. Hundreds of men had once worked here, he said, making parts for the machinery at the old Hilde cannery, which stood on the river shore straight ahead.

Beyond the B & R Railroad tracks lay the Chinese section, which dated back to 1875, when Heinrich Olden founded his fish cannery and his town. The low clapboard houses were mostly in ruin now, mere sticks piled atop crumbling foundations.

"We're going to a place full of history," he said to Tad. "It also serves the best burgers in town."

The place was Poverty Ike's, cool and cavernous beneath its high, smoke-darkened ceilings. Tad took it in with wide eyes: the intricately carved back-bar with its umpteen rows of glistening bottles, the caryatids at either end of it, the painting of a nude fat woman in its center. On high stools half a dozen old men sat with their paws around long-necked beer bottles, their elbows resting lazily on the marble-topped bar.

Mark saw that the mirror had been repaired, after a bullet had destroyed it on Monday night. Nowhere did he see any evidence of the fight that had erupted between a local brute named Gary Bayliss and a psychotic street-dweller named Sam Darkenwald. Country-western music thumped from an ancient jukebox behind the pool tables.

"Wow, this place is awesome, just like an old movie or something," breathed Tad. "What's that smell, Dad Bear?"

Stale beer and tobacco smoke, Mark replied. And *history*, too. In fact, Poverty Ike's saloon fairly reeked of bygone days.

Only one table was occupied, since the lunch hour was long gone. Five men, all from the James River sawmill, Mark figured from the look of their hard hats, leaned back on the rear legs of their chairs, drinking red beers and smoking cigarettes. They chuckled loudly now and again over some off-color remark.

Mark and Tad took a table near the bar.

"Well, if it isn't John Lansen's boy, Mark," said the old man who came to take their orders. He was tall and angular, and he wore thick, rimless bifocals. He offered a bony hand, which Mark found capable of a young man's grip. "Haven't seen you in a month of Sundays, or maybe a lot longer. This must be your pup—Thaddeus, I hear his name is. Fine-looking lad, if you don't mind my saying so."

Mark did the introductions, and Tad grinned with his perfect white teeth. "Only my mom calls me Thaddeus. Everyone else calls me Tad."

This was the famous Poverty Ike himself, Mark said of the old man, someone who remembered as much of Oldenburg's history as anyone. If any man personified the town of Oldenburg, Ike was he.

"How he keeps from aging no one can figure out," added Mark, awed by the fact that Ike seemed no more wrinkled or rickety than he'd seemed fifteen years ago. If anything, his muddy eyes were even sharper, more alert.

"Your old man here was one of my favorite customers, back when he was a young buck," said Ike, winking at Tad. "He used to bring his girlfriend in for hamburgers and malts, and they'd sit over there next to the jukebox and talk about history."

"Did you really have a girlfriend, Dad Bear?" asked Tad, as if the idea sounded preposterous.

"You bet he did," said Ike before Mark could answer. "Pretty one, too—prettiest in town, maybe. I always liked having you kids in here—nice change from the usual run of doddering old beer hounds and loud-talking millmen. You kids always behaved yourselves, which is a credit to you and your families."

Mark said that Ike had always been willing to sit down and talk about the old days, about frontier families and the river trade, maritime adventures and gamblers and medicine shows. "He knew so much about the old days that if you didn't know better, you'd almost think he'd lived through them himself."

Poverty Ike merely smiled. "Decided what you're hungry for?" He pulled a pad from a pocket in his grease-spattered apron.

Mark ordered a chicken-in-a-basket, and Tad ordered a cheeseburger with lettuce and tomato but no onions. Poverty Ike shouted the orders in his own personal code to the cook, who shouted them back through a small window in the wall between the kitchen and the bar.

"Squawk box on one, stretch one through the garden, hold the Oh!" Ike grinned at Mark and Tad, then headed back to the bar to draw their Cokes. Mark whispered a confession to Tad: One reason he'd come to Poverty Ike's over the years was to hear the old man shout those crazy orders. Among the menu offerings were brains and eggs *("He needs 'em!")* and Mulligan stew *("Under the bridge on one!")*. A glass of milk was *moo juice.* Tad laughed, even though the one about Mulligan stew made no sense to him.

When Ike returned with their food, he asked after John, Marta, and the rest of the Lansen family.

"Everybody's just fine," answered Mark around a mouthful of coleslaw. "Mom and Dad miss Father Briggs and the Pellagrinis, of course, but they're surviving, getting on with their lives." Then, to change the subject, he mentioned the first time he'd come to Poverty Ike's—this for Tad's benefit. "It was on Halloween of 'sixty-six, and I hadn't lived here in Oldenburg very long. In fact, my parents had only adopted me a little more than a month before. In those days, Tad, just about everyone in town brought their kids to hear Ike tell a scary story on Halloween. The place was all decorated with witches and goblins and pumpkins, and there was a big water barrel right in the middle of the floor there, with apples floating in it. . . ."

He saw Tad's face grow very sober at the mention of adoption. The boy even stopped chewing to listen.

"I can even recall the story you told, Ike," Mark went on. "It was about an Englishwoman whose husband worked for the Hudson's Bay Company—a witch, actually. She and an old Indian woman, Queen Molly—"

"She's the one in the park!" exclaimed Tad. "I've seen her statue! There's a metal plate on it that tells all about her."

"The very same one," confirmed Mark, pleased that Tad was showing an interest in something historical.

"So you remember that story, do you?" asked Poverty Ike, drawing up a chair and sitting. "Funny that you should remember it, after all this time. I called it 'The Witch of Mesatchie Illihee.' "

"It was the last Halloween story you ever told, wasn't it?"

"Yup. Haven't told one since, and I don't aim to, at least not in public."

"Why?" asked Mark. "The whole town loved your stories."

"Not *that* particular one," said Poverty Ike, studying the scarred wooden tabletop. It had disturbed some people, offended others. It had lacked a happy ending. "Anyway, things change. Towns change, too. People aren't satisfied with the simple things anymore. Nowadays, a story needs to be *video*, or kids won't sit still for it. *Most* kids, anyway—present company excluded." He lightly touched Tad's hair with an osteal hand.

"I wish I'd come to Oldenburg earlier," said Mark. "I would've liked to hear your other stories. I've always been a sucker for a good Halloween yarn."

Poverty Ike gazed at him steadily with his magnified eyes. "You heard the one you needed to hear. I'll tell you a little secret, though. I didn't really finish telling it, back on Halloween of nineteen sixty-six."

What a weird thing to say, thought Mark: *the one I needed to hear?* "Are you saying there's more to it?"

"Oh, there's more, all right. I didn't finish it because there were people here in nineteen sixty-six who'd been involved in it, and others with relatives who were involved. I was respecting the privacy of everyone concerned."

Mark couldn't keep from smiling. "So, you're telling us that it was all true—the bit about the witch, that business about burying the new baby alive in the ground?"

"Wow, this sounds like a really cool story!" interrupted Tad. "I wish I could've heard you tell it, Mr. Ike."

The old man's muddy eyes twinkled behind his thick glasses. "You can leave off the 'mister,' son. But to answer your dad, yes—it was all true. I don't say everybody should believe it merely because I told it, but I know what I know. Living as long as I have, you learn about certain things, and sometimes you feel as if you should pass them along. Some folks don't want to know about them, and that's their business. Other folks *need* to know about them. . . ."

There it was again, thought Mark: *a reference to something I need to know. Why is he looking at me that way?*

"What would it take to make you tell the rest of the story?" asked Mark on impulse, not dreaming for a moment that Ike would actually do it.

"Not much, if I thought you were ready."

"We're ready for it, aren't we, Tad?"

"Right!" Tad squealed eagerly. "We're ready for it! Please tell the story, Ike. *Please!*"

Poverty Ike stared fondly at the boy, his face crinkling with glee. "All right, if that's what you both want. . . ." His next words went to Mark specifically, though something beneath the surface of his grin wasn't even remotely gleeful. "If that's what you really *need*."

iii

From the death of Queen Molly the story about the Witch of Mesatchie Illihee leapt forward seventy-nine years to the day after New Year's Day, 1942, with the arrival in Oldenburg of a young man from the War Department. He got off the train and went straight to Mayor Phil Laughlin's office. He asked the mayor to call a meeting of all the men in town who were eighteen or older, and it took place that very night in the gymnasium of Kalapuya County High. Poverty Ike attended, of course.

"It was for civil defense," Ike explained to Mark and Tad. "The Japanese had bombed Pearl Harbor less than a month before, and the War Department thought that the Imperial navy might send a submarine or gunboat up the Columbia to reconnoiter or land saboteurs. Naturally, every fighting-age man in the county had either joined the service or was about to, so the gentleman from the War Department directed his remarks mainly to us oldsters. He said we could do a great service to our country if we were to set up a guard post and keep an eye on the river. The government would train us and furnish any equipment we needed—binoculars and compasses and telephones and so forth. All they required from us was the manpower.

"Naturally we were eager to do anything we could to protect our country from those dastardly Japs, so we did as he asked. We formed a group, elected leaders, and found ourselves a guard post to man. The War Department sent in some fellas to tell us how to spot enemy activity, both in the air and in the water. Same thing happened in nearly every other town up and down the Columbia and along the coast. Old men who couldn't do any real fighting got together to become America's eyes in the night."

The Oldenburg group called itself the Nehalem Mountain Raiders, Ike said. They set up their guard post on the highest available spot with a good view of the river: the northwest face of Nehalem Mountain.

Though it was a logical choice, several of the men grumbled about it and suggested setting up the guard post somewhere else. Nehalem Mountain seemed an unfriendly place, and rumors abounded about Gestern Hall, which stood less than half a mile from the guard post. Too, there was the legend of Mesatchie Illihee, an enchanted piece of ground that supposedly lay somewhere near the summit on a forested plateau. Back in 1942, Oldenburg boasted more than a handful of living citizens who remembered the tale of the young English witch who had buried her living child in the ground of Mesatchie Illihee. A few of these had actually claimed to hear the scream of the Catamount, the demon-cat who still served the witch, supposedly.

"But in the end, logic and tactical considerations prevailed," chuckled Ike. "The Nehalem Mountain Raiders set up their guard post in a clear-cut on the side of the mountain, almost within spitting distance of Gestern Hall. It wasn't much of a guard post, really—just a glassed-in shack with one of those army-issue kerosene stoves, a couple of folding cots, and a telephone connected to an army unit over in Astoria. Didn't even have an indoor privy."

They lacked uniforms, but they had army helmets of World War I vintage (issued by the War Department), which they painted white. They designed their own shoulder patch to wear on their jackets, which the city council paid a tailor in Portland to make. They carried their own weapons, hunting rifles and shotguns, mostly, though several had pistols that they wore in holsters on their hips. If the Japanese had made the mistake of landing saboteurs anywhere near Oldenburg, the Nehalem Mountain Raiders were ready. They took their duty seriously, even though a few of them were uneasy about going up on Nehalem Mountain or venturing close to Gestern Hall.

"One man was more scared than the rest," said Poverty Ike. "His name was Alois Conrad, and he worked in the machine shops up the street. Everybody called him 'Skutch,' and he had a whole tribe of kids. One of them, his youngest boy, Lawrence, grew up to become the sheriff of Kalapuya County, a job he holds to this very day. Skutch's shiftmate was Vernon Yngstad, who owned the local nursery and left it to his son when he died back in 'fifty-eight. They had the six-to-midnight shift, every fourth day.

"On the night of January 30, 1942, something strange happened to them. . . ."

iv

Skutch Conrad's 1935 Plymouth jounces over the muddy washboard of Queen Molly Road and nearly lurches into the ditch as it rounds the curve below Gestern Hall. Vern Yngstad barks at Skutch to slow down, saying that he would appreciate living to see the rest of his grandchildren born.

"We don't want to be late for the start of our shift, do we?" asks Skutch. "Wouldn't be fair to the other boys."

"Don't give me that bunkum," retorts Vern. "You always speed up when we come within sight of the Gestern place. It's downright strange, seems to me, that an old codger like you shivers in his socks over a lot of whispered claptrap. Why don't you admit it—you're *scared* of Gestern Hall!"

"You wouldn't be so all-fired cocky if you'd've heard the Catamount scream," mutters Skutch.

"And I suppose *you've* heard it, is that so?"

Skutch says nothing more for now and halts the Plymouth behind Norm Satterlee's pickup, where a logging trail meets Queen Molly Road. The two men pile out of the car, bearing dinner pails, guns, and flashlights. They trudge a hundred muddy yards up the trail to the guard post, which stands amid a host of mossy tree stumps on the mountainside. Below them the lights of Oldenburg twinkle in the gathering night, and behind them looms Gestern Hall.

Upon arriving at the shack they trade small talk with Norm Satterlee and his shift mate, Erwin Spurlock, who are glad their shift is ending. "She's going to storm tonight, sure as hell," says Satterlee, pulling on his overshoes. "I can feel it in the joints of my thumbs. Lucky you boys got here before she hits full-force."

"It's already raining pretty good," says Skutch, setting his ten-gauge Ithaca shotgun in the corner behind the kerosene stove.

"Drive careful on Queen Molly Road. It's slicker'n a gob of spit."

"I can't believe my ears!" laughs Vernon Yngstad. "Old Mr. Leadfoot, here, telling you to drive carefully. You should've seen him a few minutes ago. Damn-near ran us in the ditch!"

After Satterlee and Spurlock depart, Vern settles into a chair at the wide window in the north wall of the shack, binoculars hanging around his neck. His is the first watch, and he leans forward until his nose is only inches from the glass, staring into the night. Beyond the lights of Oldenburg lies the wide Columbia, a black expanse of emptiness.

Skutch switches on the table-model RCA Victor radio that one of the Raiders has contributed to the cause, and tunes in "The Musical Dinner Hour," a selection of orchestra music broadcast from Portland. The music almost covers the soft patter of rain on the shingles above.

"Sometimes I wonder why we bother with all this," grumbles Vern, squinting. "When the sun goes down, you can't see a blessed thing on the river from up here. The Japs could float their whole damn navy all the way to Portland, and we wouldn't see 'em if they just kept their lights off."

"I said as much at the start," says Skutch, biting into a ham sandwich.

"You said so simply because you were scared to come up here. My only worry is a practical one. Keeping men on this mountain at night is a waste of precious manpower, since nobody can see anything from up here anyway."

"Maybe so, but at least we'd still hear an airplane, if the Japs sent one."

"What the hell good would *that* do? If you can't see the plane to identify it, you can't report it as an enemy plane. Use your noggin, man!"

They spell each other every hour at the window. They eat their sandwiches and drink their coffee. A few minutes after ten o'clock, Vern calls Skutch to the window.

"Tell me this isn't the damnedest thing you ever saw," he says, pointing to the sky over the river. The storm clouds have parted briefly, letting a smattering of stars shine through. A bright red gem beams down on the valley, casting a rosy glow over the nightscape. "It doesn't even look natural, does it? Looks like a badly done painting. Must be Mars, but I can't say I've ever seen it that bright."

"It's the Blood Star," says Skutch under his breath. "A man doesn't want to be out on a night when the Blood Star shines like that."

"By Jesus, I wish you'd stop this kind of talk! It's Mars we're lookin' at, and that's all it is! *Blood Star*—I'll be goosed!"

"I've seen it like this once before, back when I was a kid. It was the same night I—"

"The same night you what?" Vern turns to look at Skutch and winces when he sees how white his face is. The old boy looks ready to faint. "Skutch, I'm losing my patience with you. I wish you'd tell me just why the hell you're behaving like a scared little schoolboy."

Skutch places a palm against the windowsill to steady himself. He swallows and licks his lips, which have gone dry. "When I was a kid, we lived in a cabin down on Benson Creek. My pa called me outside one night to look at the Blood Star, and it was like it is now, so red and so strong that the moon looked pink. Even the *trees* looked pink, I swear. Later that night, around midnight, I think it was, we heard the Catamount scream. It was something I'd never heard before, and something I hope never to hear again. . . ."

V

"A few minutes later the storm hit, and it hit with a vengeance," continued Poverty Ike. "The wind blew so hard that the shack started to creak and lean, and it took some shingles off, so the roof started to leak. The rain fell so thick that Vern and Skutch couldn't even see the lights of Oldenburg. As if all this wasn't enough, their power line blew down, and they had to use a kerosene lantern for light. Their radio went dead, of course, since they didn't have any battery-powered, transistorized radios in those days. All in all, things looked pretty bleak."

Skutch decided that it was time to go back to town, and made for the door, but Vern stopped him. It would be suicide to drive in that storm, Vern said. For all either of them knew, the road had washed out. The smart thing to do was to stay put and wait out the storm. The shack stood in a clear-cut, so they were safe from falling trunks and limbs, Vern pointed out.

"Skutch Conrad let himself be persuaded," Ike continued. "He sat near the stove with his Ithaca across his knees, his eyes as big as dollars, like he expected the Catamount to burst through the door any moment. But then the wind died suddenly, and the rain quit. It was as if the god of storms simply flipped a switch on his control board. In the space of a few dozen heartbeats the mountain became as quiet as a graveyard. . . ."

vi

"I heard something," says Vernon Yngstad, cocking his head.

"What was it? I didn't hear anything. I swear I didn't hear anything, Vern. Are you *sure* you really heard something? I tell you I didn't hear—"

"Stop your damn yammering and listen, will you?"

Now Skutch hears something, too, a cry in the blackness beyond the walls of the shack. The two old men stare at each other stupidly.

"There's a child out there," whispers Vern.

"A *child?* Out *there?* Up *here?* That doesn't make any sense."

It makes no sense, but they both hear the cry again, the unmistakable sob of a small child who sounds frightened and lost. The sound ignites an ache in their hearts.

Vern rises out of his chair and gathers up his coat, his helmet and his flashlight. He pulls on his rubber boots and buckles them up tight, knowing the storm has generated streams of mud down the mountainside.

"Where are you going?" asks Skutch, his voice shaking.

"Don't ask stupid questions. I'm going out to find that kid."

"V-Vern, I'm not so sure that's a good idea. You don't know what else might be out there."

"There's a little kid out there, probably lost and cold and soaked to the bone. I don't know about you, but I can't sit here and listen to her cry. I'm going to find her and bring her in."

Skutch tries feebly to talk his friend out of this and fails. Then he gathers his coat, helmet, flashlight, and boots, knowing that he can't stay behind. He brings along one thing more: his Ithaca.

Outside the shack they find that the sky has begun to clear as the final remnant of the storm passes through. Mars now hangs near the western horizon, tinting the night eerily. The sound of the child's crying draws them generally toward Gestern Hall.

Between the clear-cut and the old stone mansion lies a band of red alder and noble fir that marks the Gestern property line, and the men plunge into it, beating aside rain-heavy ferns and tall stalks of bear grass. They head uphill, their boots squelching through a litter of fallen branches and cones, but they stop frequently to listen for the sobbing.

A spotted owl hoots from its roost in a cedar snag. "Damn," says Vern, "I thought we would've found her by now. I wonder if she's on the move."

"I don't see how a little kid could move around in this stuff. It's denser than a hawk's nest in here. I don't mind sayin' my pants are soaked right through to my skin."

The sobs seem louder now, and the men fight their way through a clump of skunk cabbage to the base of a hemlock that towers high into the night. Next to it, weathered and rotting and mossed over, stands a totem pole. At its top is a winged image carved by men when the hemlock was not yet a cone.

Skutch draws a breath and holds it, not daring to speak.

"I'll be damned," whispers Vern, staring up into the red night. "I've heard stories about this place all my life, but I never thought I would live to see it with my own eyes."

"You're thinkin' what I'm thinkin', aren't you?"

"This is a place that the old Cathlamet Indians thought was sacred. They put this pole here to warn people away, to keep mere mortals from defiling it." Vern moves toward a ravel of fallen trees, beyond which lies a clearing.

"You're not going any farther, are you?"

"I'm going to find that child. You coming?"

"This ain't a place where white men are supposed to be, Vern. Don't you think we better—?"

"For the love of God, man, there's a child nearby who needs help! If we don't help her, she'll probably die! Now you can stand there and shake in your boots like a yellow-livered coward, or you can act like a man and come along."

They slowly work their way over the fallen trees, pushing back the leathery licorice ferns that grow in riotous colonies out of the bark, stepping carefully over and around branches and snags. Finally, they emerge into the clearing, where a mist stings their faces and the pungent smell of buckthorn invades their noses.

They see her—a stripling of a girl standing in the ground fog on the low knoll in the center of the clearing, naked as she was on the day of her birth, bathed in the ruddy glow of the Blood Star, her face turned skyward. "Jesus, Mary, and Joseph," whispers Vern Yngstad.

She appears no older than seven or eight. Her dark hair cascades down her slender back, almost covering her bare bottom. In her arms she clutches a bundle of something that the men can't really see from their vantage. Her sobs touch both old men to the quick.

Vern ventures forward gingerly, fearful of frightening the child. "Little girl, are you all right? Th-there's no reason to cry—"

A scream erupts from the throat of a creature that should exist only in nightmares—a scream that could damn-near sear the lichens from a stone, Vern would later say. It stirs a mob of woodland creatures to flight, and when it dies, it leaves a silence as dense as lead.

vii

"Vern and Skutch stood there like their feet were frozen to the ground," Poverty Ike continued. "I suspect their legs felt like rubber, and that their hearts were trying to climb up into their throats. But they didn't cut and run. Maybe they figured that a creature who could scream like that would have no trouble running a pair of rickety old men to earth. Somehow Vern Yngstad made himself take a step toward the little girl, and then another and then another. . . ."

Ike paused to sip from Tad's Coke. Mark glanced at his son, whose mouth hung open in wonderment. No doubt about it: Old Ike could tell a story like few others could. Tad hadn't even heard the full tale of Queen Molly and Elspeth Carey, and yet he sat as if mesmerized, his arms folded on the table. Mark hadn't seen the boy so absorbed since the first issue of Super Mario Brothers hit the Nintendo market.

Mark himself had a case of the chills.

"And finally he reached her. He went down on one knee, feel-

ing his old joints creak and pop as he did so. He felt sweat running down his back. Truth is, old Vern Yngstad was shaking like
a newborn lamb on a frosty night. When she turned to look at
him with her tearful eyes, he saw that she was wearing a silver
pendant on a golden chain. His spectacles were spattered with
water, but he was just able to make out the head of a lion with
a snake draped around it."

viii

Vern gathers the girl in his arms and struggles to his feet
again, wincing with arthritic pain. His hand moves over the bundle that she clutches to her chest, and he shivers from the sensation that the bundle is alive, as if it's made of living human skin.
He turns and starts down the knoll, looking toward Skutch
Conrad who stands waist-deep in ground fog, his doughboy helmet gleaming pink in the glare of the Blood Star. Skutch's face
hangs in terror.

"Take it easy, little one," Vern whispers to the child. "Your old
Uncle Vern is going to get you inside where it's nice and warm.
He's g-going to g-give you a hot bowl of soup and a—"

A hand fastens onto his shoulder, and he knows that this is
why his friend is screaming like a mindless animal, that Skutch
has seen the owner of the hand, a creature that must be the ugliest in God's creation. Vern struggles not to swallow his tongue,
fights to hold on to his reason. His heart hammers in his chest
like a steam piston, and he forces another step forward. The fingers tighten on his shoulder, digging into his spare flesh and
causing pain.

"Give her to me," whispers a voice like a winter wind. "She
doesn't belong to you."

Vern spins around to confront the speaker of these words and
sees a face that's uglier, more damnably ancient than any human
face has a right to be. Somehow he keeps his feet and holds onto
the whimpering child. The owner of the voice glares at him and
her hand crawls toward his throat, leaving knots of pain in the
muscles of his shoulder.

ix

Mark felt a spasm take root in his gut as he listened to Ike's description of the creature.

She was old, ninety at least, maybe older. She wore a toilworn overcoat of tattered wool. Her hair was wild and hoary where it poked out from a furry winter hat. . . .

Mark saw her face in his mind. *Did she have a spinning wheel?*

If she'd had a spinning wheel, it would've been the last straw, because the hag he'd seen outside Cramer Hall also had a spinning wheel, and the presence of a hag with a spinning wheel in Poverty Ike's story couldn't possibly be a coincidence. If *this* hag had a spinning wheel, then Mark couldn't deny that she was the same hag he'd seen outside Cramer Hall, which was pure lunacy, yes.

"That twisted old woman," Poverty Ike went on, "held onto Vern with just one hand, but in that one hand she seemed to have the strength of ten healthy men. As if this wasn't enough, she held a *spinning wheel* in the other—held it high over her head, actually, as if it weighed no more than a little sack of hazelnuts. . . ."

There it was. The spinning wheel. Right alongside the little silver pendant that he knew so well.

Mark felt faint.

x

The great wheel rotates on its axle as if moved by the hand of a ghost, and the drive band rotates the spindle. As it spins ever faster, its spokes begin to whir, shooing away the fog in fingerlike wisps. The aged wood of the spindle sings a squeaky song.

Vern feels a change in the air, a tingle that suggests the venting of some incredible power. The hairs on his neck stand on end, and his skin prickles. From somewhere far away Skutch screams again.

A tall figure stands in the clearing a few paces from Skutch, a man whom Vern recognizes. Clovis Gestern wears a dark robe with a cowl that lies in a bundle around his shoulders. From his eyes issues a light that reminds Vern of golden lightning. To confront the legendary Clovis Gestern in the black of night is bad enough, but to confront those *eyes* ...

"Give the child to me," commands the hag again, and Vern feels her grip tighten. *"She doesn't belong to you!"*

"I-I can't. I can't give her to you." Vern fears that his cervical vertebrae are about to snap, but he cannot hand over the child to someone as loathsome as this. He would choose to die first, which doesn't seem altogether unlikely now, inasmuch as his body has begun to jitter and crumple. A boulder of pain forms in the center of his chest. His pulse crackles in his ears.

The Catamount screams again, and something huge rustles the thicket on the far side of the clearing. Through the veil of pain Vern senses a struggle taking place in the air, a clash of unseen forces loosed by the hag and the man he's always known as Clovis Gestern. They're tilting over possession of this little child, this naked innocent whose skin is caked with mud, as if she's been buried in the ground and only recently freed.

"You can't have her!" he tries to roar, but his voice falters before the words leave his lips. He twists around to face Skutch, gropes toward his friend. "Help me! D-don't just *stand* there, man! Help me!"

He sees something in Skutch Conrad's face that he knows isn't Skutch Conrad. Something has crawled into Skutch's simple mind and taken it over, something owned by Clovis Gestern.

Skutch moves smartly through the swirling ground fog toward Vern, the child, and the hag. He chambers a shell, then brings the Ithaca to his shoulder. He advances to within a few paces and levels the muzzle at the hag, who is shrieking now in a language that sounds like gibberish, calling on powers that swirl and roil in the air like noxious clouds, exciting the demon-cat in the thicket. But Clovis Gestern's voice booms even louder, invoking yet other powers to hold the hag's at bay.

Vernon Yngstad twists away from the hag and plunges to the ground, mere fractions of a second before Skutch's ten-gauge shotgun belches flame and thunders. The hag's head rips away from her shoulders and tumbles into the weeds on the knoll. Her body staggers backward, spouting gore. The spinning wheel falls to earth and dies.

Vern lies in the weeds with the child across his chest and feels his consciousness slipping away. He glances again at Skutch, who stands rigid with his Ithaca at the ready, inanimate and soul-

less as a mannequin. More terrible is the spectacle of the headless hag, groping through the fog until finding her pulpy head,
then staggering away toward the wood line, clutching it by the
hair. In his final seconds of consciousness, Vernon Yngstad as-
certains that the naked child is still breathing, and for this he
thanks his God. But a cold horror settles over him as Clovis
Gestern lifts her from his helpless arms.

xi

"Vern Yngstad and Skutch Conrad stumbled out of the forest
the next morning," said Poverty Ike. "The search party found
them at the side of Queen Molly Road, barely able to move, but
alive. Nobody believed Vern's wild story, of course—or at least
nobody *admitted* to believing it. Two old men had gotten confused in the storm, most folks figured, and had gotten lost looking for their car.

"As for Skutch, he never uttered a single word for the rest of
his life. Whatever had gotten into his skull the night before had
eaten his mind. His family committed him to a mental home
down in Eugene, and he died there in 'fifty-two.

"Some people did find it strange, though, that Clovis Gestern
turned up with a young foster-child, a little girl sent by distant
relatives to be raised by him and Mrs. Drumgule, supposedly. No
one saw much of her in town, except at school, and it seemed as
if Clovis raised her well enough. From outward appearances, she
never lacked for food or clothes. Besides, nobody was willing to
poke his nose into Clovis Gestern's affairs. And if anyone sus-
pected that the girl came from a hole in the ground in a place
called Mesatchie Illihee, he kept those suspicions to himself."

Thus ended Poverty Ike's story. Mark Lansen thanked him,
paid him for the food, and made ready to leave, feeling as if he'd
just awakened from a nightmare. Before he could rise from the
table, Poverty Ike caught him by the elbow.

"Think about the story I've just told you. Make of it what you
can."

"I will."

"And be *careful*," charged Poverty Ike, glancing toward Tad,
who waited out of earshot near the swinging bat-wing doors. "Be
careful of people who would hurt you, and be careful of *your-*

self." Then he grinned amicably, almost lovingly, showing teeth that Mark figured were dentures, so white were they.

"I will," Mark answered. "I'll be careful."

Outside again, astride his mountain bike, Mark found that he was too weak to pedal. He and Tad walked their bikes home.

19

A Disciple of St. Joan

i

Tressa had just tidied her desk in preparation for leaving the office for the day when she noticed a small envelope in her inbasket. Enclosed was a sympathy card from the county commissioners' receptionist, Ginger Truax, embossed with pretty floral patterns and religious iconography.

My prayers are with you in this sad time, the young woman had written in the space below the flowery poem. Tressa appreciated the thought and stopped at the reception desk on her way out to tell Ginger so.

"We all know how much you loved Father Briggs," said Ginger sweetly, "and I just wanted to say how sorry I am—" She coughed into her fist.

Lately Ginger's normally rosy cheeks had looked pale and slightly sunken. Today the edges of her eyes were inflamed, crusty. She looked wrung out, as if she should be home in bed, drinking juice and getting lots of rest. Tressa asked whether she was well.

"Summer cold or maybe the flu. I should probably megadose some vitamin C, don't you think?"

Tressa told her to take care of herself and meant it. "If you need to take a few days off, do it. No sense in letting a little cold turn into something big and ugly."

ii

Tressa walked briskly from the courthouse down Chinook Avenue, relishing the late afternoon sunshine and the squeal of robins in the trees. Instead of turning right and walking a block south to Clatskanie, which was the route home, she crossed Main and continued up Chinook, climbing the short hill to First Street.

She stopped at a tattered-looking, two-story house that needed a new roof and paint. The yard had gone to seed, and blackberries had taken over the hedges. A brooding old weeping birch dominated the front yard, casting a bleak shadow across the sagging porch.

This was the home of the Bayliss family, such as it was. The sight of it caused Tressa's cheery mood to evaporate.

The doorbell didn't work, so she knocked. Freddye Ann Bayliss answered, looking every bit as tattered and insubstantial as the house in which she lived. Forcing a smile, she invited Tressa inside. She offered coffee, which Tressa politely declined.

Freddye Ann was six years her senior. Tressa remembered her as a strikingly pretty high school girl with lustrous brown hair and a cheerleader's willowy body. She'd gone steady for more than a year with the leading heartthrob at Kalapuya County High, Gary Bayliss, who had also been the school's premier running back. Years later, after Gary had washed out of Oregon State and served a stint in the army, having accomplished none of the wonderful things the whole town had expected of him, she'd married him.

The decades had not been good to Freddye Ann. Bearing two daughters, Marnie and Gretchen, had left her shapeless and worn. Living with Gary had turned her into a cowering wraith who slunk around corners and seldom spoke loudly enough to be heard. Tressa thought she looked acutely anemic.

"Gretchen's sure not short of company today," said Freddye Ann, leading Tressa through a dingy hallway. "Brett's here, too, but he won't be staying long. He's due at the ThriftyKwik by six." Brett Omdahl was a sixteen-year-old skateboard fanatic who worked for Gary Bayliss at his convenience grocery store on Commerce Way. He and Gretchen Bayliss had been pals since grade school.

The bedroom door stood open. Freddye Ann motioned Tressa toward it and ambled back toward the kitchen, limping slightly. "Gretch'll be glad to see you," she said flatly. "Holler if you want anything."

Tressa knocked twice on the doorjamb and poked her head into the room. Gretchen sat in her motorized wheelchair next to the open window, wrapped in a white sheet. Even on the hottest days she needed a cover, since her thin blood never circulated well through her bony, misshapen body, and her stunted legs always seemed cool to the touch.

When Gretchen saw Tressa, her huge blue eyes brightened, and her delicate face broke into a smile. Tressa could see that she'd been crying.

Brett sat near her on the edge of the bed, a lanky boy with barley-colored hair and a deep sunburn, as tall as a grown man but as open-faced as a child. Across his lap lay his pride and joy, a Vision skateboard with a Thunderstruck "truck" and Slime Ball wheels. On its surface was a grimacing skull with a viper coiling out from between its sharpened teeth. At his feet lay Fudd, a seven-year-old cross between a collie and a rottweiler—blunt-nosed, long-haired, and powerfully built. Fudd whined a hello when he saw Tressa and thumped the floor with his tail.

"Wow, am I glad to see you, Tress," said Gretchen. "I've had all the tales of skateboard heroics I can take for one day." With great effort she managed to turn her head and throw a teasing look at Brett.

"Hang with me, you talk skateboards," retorted Brett with mock anger. "Besides, you should see some of the daredevil crap she pulls with this tricked-out wheelchair of hers. *She's* the one who should be telling stories."

The chair was a customized Rolls Arrow that Gretchen's father had given her last Christmas, after spending three years' worth of family savings. It had a joystick on the armrest and fat, high-traction tires. Brett had pronounced it gnarly.

Stacked in neat piles around the room were scores of books about St. Joan of Arc, many of which were scholarly pieces penned by noted historians. Having read them all, Gretchen had gained an encyclopedic knowledge of the martyr. Too, she'd collected more than a hundred likenesses of Joan, mainly prints of ancient paintings and photos of statues born entirely of the artists' imaginations, since no real portrait of the saint had survived the fifteenth century. The pictures covered nearly every square inch of the walls, leaving no space for the pop posters and airbrushed portraits of rock stars commonly found in the bedrooms of fifteen-year-old American girls. This room was a veritable shrine.

The books and pictures, Tressa knew, were Gretchen's vehicles to another world, a better world, one full of bright medieval flags, chivalry, and romance. Gretchen's deformity had denied her what others consider routine joys—a simple walk in the park, a bike ride on a sunny day, a game of Frisbee. In place of these and all the other simple joys that make life livable for most, she had Joan of Arc.

The Baylisses were long-standing parishioners at St. Pius X, and like Tressa, Gretchen had shared a special relationship with Father Charlie Briggs. When she'd first learned to read, Father Charlie had lent her a slim biography of Joan from the parish library, one written for children and full of fanciful illustrations. For months afterward all the child could talk about was Joan of Arc, and the fascination evolved into an avocation that showed no signs of weakening, even now.

"Hey, I gotta take off, man," said Brett, standing. "I need to go home and change before I go to work. Your dad won't let me wear stuff like this in the store." He wore ultra baggy shorts and an even baggier T-shirt with the rotting face of a ghoul stenciled on it. *Is it live, or is it dead?* read the caption. "See you later, Gretch," said Brett. "You too, Tress."

He and Fudd were nearly out the door when Gretchen said, "Remember what we talked about, Brett. No messing around after work, right? You promised you'll go straight home."

"Yeah, right. Be cool."

After he'd gone Tressa asked what *that* had been all about. Gretchen replied that she'd extracted Brett's promise not to go skateboarding after his shift ended, which was at midnight. She didn't like the thought of his traipsing around town after dark. This made good sense, agreed Tressa. If he were to hit a pothole or a parked car, he could end up in the hospital or worse.

"It's not potholes or parked cars that I'm worried about." Gretchen closed her eyes and said nothing for a moment. Then she opened them suddenly and asked, "Do you think Father Charlie would've been pleased with his funeral—the archbishop coming and everything?"

"I didn't see you there."

"I wanted to go, but Dad was working at the store, and Brett was in Portland with his folks, so I didn't have a way to get there. Mom, of course, was in no shape to take me."

Tressa sat down on the edge of the bed where Brett had been and spoke quietly. "Has your dad started hurting her again, Gretch? She looks—well—God, I guess I should just say it: She looks terrible, thinner and paler than ever. She appeared to be limping."

"It's beyond anything that has to do with Daddy," Gretchen whimpered, tears forming anew. "It's so bad I don't even know where to start."

iii

"This little girl needs a guiding hand," Father Briggs had told Tressa over bread pudding and tea in the parlor of his rectory, not long after she'd returned to Oldenburg. *"She needs someone who'll give her the kind of love and nurturing a child would ordinarily get from her parents. She won't get much of it at home, Tressa. Her father isn't equipped for it anymore. Gary's become a very bitter and self-centered man, I'm afraid. And her mother—well, let's just say Freddye Ann has changed. . . ."*

Father Briggs had known Gretchen from the day she was born.

"She's amazingly bright, a lot like you were at that age. Inside that wretched little body lives a mind with incredible potential. And she's such a good girl, Tressa. She needs an adult who'll take responsibility for her and help her realize that potential, someone who knows the ropes. . . ."

Someone like me, right Father?

"My point is simply this: It would be criminal to leave her fate entirely in the hands of Gary and Freddye Ann Bayliss. She'd only end up in some drab institution somewhere, with nothing but television, magazines, and canasta for stimulation. She needs someone to stoke her imagination and show her the possibilities that are waiting for her, someone who can point her in the right direction. . . ."

Someone like Tressa Downey, you mean. Why not come right out and say it, Father?

"It would be good for you, too, girl. I don't care what the shrinks say, the best therapy for the wounded soul is to do good for someone. It gets your mind off your own woes, makes you strong. . . ."

iv

". . . and like I've told you before, Gretchen, your mother doesn't have to stand for it. No woman does. We have strong laws now, and we can get court orders to keep men from hurting us."

Gretchen raised her face and stared straight through Tressa—this misshapen child who had such beautiful blue eyes that sometimes Tressa wanted to cry when she looked into them. They reminded her of another little girl's eyes.

"Would you mind closing the door?"

Tressa obliged and returned to her spot on the bed.

"It isn't Daddy anymore. Haven't you been listening to me? Daddy's never even home, except to sleep. He works late at the store every night, then goes to Poverty Ike's to drink beer. He gets up early the next morning to open the store, before anyone else is even awake. I hardly ever see him, and neither does Mom."

This took Tressa aback. If Gary wasn't responsible for Freddye Ann's sorry condition, then who or what was?

The sound of church bells danced in through the open window. Six o'clock, tolled the bells of St. Pius X Roman Catholic Church, only three blocks away. Gretchen counted each bong aloud, savoring the silver-tinged sound.

"Joan so loved the music of bells," she said dreamily. "It was when the church bells rang that she first saw the light of St. Michael and heard his voice. After she became a general, she ordered the bells to be rung continuously while she was praying, because their sound brought her closer to God. . . ."

"Gretchen, *please*. I'd like to hear more about Joan, but I want to help you, really I do. Now that Father Charlie's gone, you *need* someone like me. But you've got to level with me, okay? Tell me what's wrong in this house, and we'll face it, you and I. We'll do it together."

"You wouldn't want to face *this*," said Gretchen. "But I'll tell you. Yes, I'll tell you, if that's what you want. I don't expect you to believe me. Sometimes I'm not even sure I believe it myself."

V

For the past six months she'd heard strange noises in the night—scrapes and thumps on the wall outside her room, the sounds of a man climbing up to the spare room at the rear of the house, the one directly above her own. Gretchen's mother had taken to spending her nights there, rather than confront her husband when he finally stumbled in during the small hours.

The noises betrayed a man's progress up to the rickety dormer in which Freddye Ann Bayliss waited, a man's heels thumping against brittle old siding, his fingernails scraping for purchase at the eaves and gables. After these came the unmistakable sounds of a man and woman doing what men and women do in the night, mingled with the sounds of agony. Heaves and groans. Thrashing and flailing. The squeaking of overhead floorboards. Then, after several minutes of silence, came the noises of the man climbing down from the window.

"Last night I stayed awake and sat by the window in my chair," Gretchen went on. "I had a flashlight. I heard the guy go up the wall—"

"Gretchen, no human being could go up the side of this house the way you've described. You know that, don't you?"

"I didn't say he was a human being."

Tressa blinked stupidly, and Gretchen went on. She'd lacked the nerve to pull the curtains aside and stick her head out the window, and didn't muster it until the intruder was upstairs with Freddye Ann, making her shriek and scream as he'd done so often. This was what Gretchen had found scarier than the idea of the intruder himself—*Freddye Ann actually welcomed him into her bed, time and time again.*

The torture ended orgasmically, and the noises of climbing began again. Gretchen waited until the intruder seemed close to ground level, then threw the curtains aside and leaned out the window with her Everready flashlight in her fist. She snapped the light on as a man-shape dropped the final few feet to the grass below.

Now the girl's voice became a whisper as she described the creature. "He had incredible hands, with long, long fingers. I swear to God, Tressa, he had suction cups on the ends of his fingers, and he was all covered with mucus or something. He was naked, like he'd left his clothes on the ground, I guess. And his *face . . ."* She stopped to draw a fresh breath, to collect herself, to dredge up more gumption. The thing's face was covered with blood, Freddye Ann's blood, presumably. The eyes were bright and golden. The mouth was oversized and full of sharp teeth, the kind she'd always imagined a shark might have. A tongue dangled from the mouth—it might have been a foot long, and it was covered with round suckers like those on the underside of a leech.

Tressa felt ill, and she placed a finger over Gretchen's lips. "No more," was all she could say. She turned toward the window, praying for a breeze, but none came. "No more."

Gretchen managed to pull Tressa's hand away, the hard edge of anger in her eyes. "You made me tell you! You wanted me to level with you so we could face this thing together. That's what you said, Tress—*together*. You made me tell you even though—" She whimpered miserably.

"Even though what?"

Hissing around its incredible tongue, the golden-eyed monster had warned her never to tell anyone that she'd seen him—not if she cared about her mother, not if she cared about herself. "His voice made me cold," Gretchen added. "I felt like he could kill me with that voice, like he wouldn't even need to touch me. Something told me that killing wasn't the worst thing he could do to someone, if he wanted to."

Tressa wanted to wrap Gretchen in her arms and assure her that no golden-eyed monster would ever get her, but she felt weak, and she didn't trust her muscles to move her off the bed right now. She braced herself with an outstretched arm against Gretchen's heavy wheelchair and breathed in long, slow breaths.

"Gretchen, I need to tell you something," she said, having gotten control of herself. "I first wanted to be your friend because Father Charlie suggested it. As you know, I was going through a pretty bad time myself then, and he thought that a relationship with you could help me. I'm glad to say that it *has* helped me. Going places with you, talking with you—it's been good for me, and I'm grateful to have a friend like you." She fought down a wave of emotion that could easily have crested in tears. "Now it's time for me to give something back. This is a bad time for you, I know. You're having dreams, you're having . . ." She cast around for a term that wouldn't insult the girl.

"Hallucinations. You think I'm having hallucinations, don't you?"

"I didn't say that."

"But that's what you're thinking. Actually, I shouldn't be angry, because I can imagine what I'd think if someone told me the story I just told you."

"Gretch, I want to take you to a doctor. I'll make an appointment with Nat Schell, so you can tell him exactly what you've told me. He'll probably recommend that we see another doctor, someone who specializes in the kind of things you're feeling."

"I don't think Dad's insurance covers that stuff. I'm not even sure he's been paying the premiums."

"Don't worry. I'll cover the bills somehow. It's very important that we get help for you, and that we do it soon."

"I've told you, Tressa, this isn't something a doctor can cure. We'd only be wasting your money."

"Humor me, why don't you? I'll go home right now and call the Medical Center, then I'll call tomorrow and let you know when the appointment is."

"You don't believe a word of what I've said. You really think I've hallucinated all this!" Gretchen's mouth worked and yawned as she struggled not to start crying. "But if you really insist on taking me to a doctor, I'll go. I'll even go to a psychiatrist, if that's what you want. I'll prove to you somehow that I'm *not* sick!"

"You'll thank me someday," said Tressa, stroking Gretchen's hair. "You'll thank yourself, too."

20

Private Demons

i

On Friday morning John Lansen went to his law office as usual and Marta drove to Astoria to shop. Tad went out back to play on the two tire-swings that John had strung for him on the limbs of the tall oak. Mark found himself alone in the Lansen house and took advantage of the privacy to call his therapist in Portland.

He recounted to Dr. LeBreaux the slug dream he'd suffered four nights earlier, the worst ever. It had climaxed with the direful spectacle of a million slugs eating his sister alive. He'd awakened in Tad's room and had seen a smear of slime on the window, roughly the size and shape of a man's face—*after* dreaming that he'd pressed his own face against the outer surface of that very pane. Oh, and the room was on the second floor, by the way.

Was this good stuff, or what? he wanted to know. He visualized Kyleen LeBreaux twirling a strand of her long black hair between her fingers, looking intensely interested.

He told her about Wednesday's episode with Tad in the attic, when he'd dug out the few old odds and ends his birth mother had left him. He'd found the amulet unnaturally warm. In addition, the picture of Snacky Cat on the cover of the storybook had acquired demonic features. Mark had meant merely to help Tad work through his insecurity over the fact that Mark had been an adopted child, but he'd failed miserably, leaving the kid rattled and acting somewhat distant. Actually, Tad was probably no more rattled than Mark himself was, especially after hearing Poverty Ike's story about the Nehalem Mountain Raiders the following day.

On Wednesday he'd learned from his father that Sam Darkenwald, the bosom buddy of the dear departed Leo Fobbs, had come to Oldenburg with a private investigator who believed that a runaway girl was living in Gestern Hall, the bed-and-breakfast inn where his sister was now working, against the wishes of her parents.

After a long pause, Dr. LeBreaux said, "Tell me how you feel about all this, Mark."

"I can't believe you said that! Is that all they teach you people in shrink school? How the hell do you *think* I feel? I feel like I'm being sucked into a black hole, that's how."

"Mark, are you sitting?"

"I'm leaning against the counter in my mother's pantry, next to the wall phone. I'm wearing a rubber corset and black patterned nylons. Tell me what *you're* wearing."

"Get serious. I'm charging for this session, you know."

"Okay, I'm sitting. You may now spew your costly wisdom."

She wanted him to breathe slowly and deeply, to relax. She wanted him to say out loud what would make him feel better.

He told her that he wanted to find a rational, reasonable explanation for the string of synchronistic horrors he'd suffered since meeting the hag with the spinning wheel. He wanted some small assurance that he'd not lost control of his life, that some malevolent god wasn't maneuvering him into a giant meat grinder. He wanted to believe that he wasn't losing his mind.

"You're not losing your mind, Mark. You're simply suffering through the aftermath of a severe traumatic experience."

"Fobbs's suicide, you mean? That was only one thing among many. It wasn't even the first."

"But it was the thing that shook you. It would've shaken anyone. It left you vulnerable to the other emotional stresses you've been carrying around with you."

"*What* stresses?"

Like everyone else, Mark had tilted with his private demons, Dr. LeBreaux explained. The situation with Deidre and her lover was a prime example. He'd blamed himself for his inability to keep his wife's interest. He held himself responsible subconsciously for jeopardizing his marriage and subjecting Tad to the possibility of a broken home, the worst thing imaginable to a former orphan. This was the kind of stress that caused bad dreams, even delusions.

"I think you're full of shit, Kyleen."

"No you don't. I know you better than almost anyone, maybe even better than you yourself do."

Okay, fine. Dr. LeBreaux's explanation begged to be believed. But she hadn't explained why Leo Fobbs had stalked him, or what the hell Sam Darkenwald was doing in Oldenburg. The fact that Darkenwald was in *this* town, the town in which Mark had grown to manhood, could not possibly be a matter of pure chance.

"Why not?"

"Damn it, Kyleen, he's here because of *me!* Just like Leo Fobbs jumped off Ione Plaza because of *me!*" Mark exhaled explosively through pursed lips. "Something's going on, something dark and ugly. It's affecting my kid, my sister, and my parents. Hell, it might be affecting people I don't even know about yet. It may even have something to do with Father Briggs's suicide. I can't tell you how I know this, but I—"

"Mark, get a grip on yourself! I want you to listen very carefully to what I say. The mind is just a process, not a physical object. It's the *way* a hundred billion neurons operate. Things can affect that process—events, traumas, many other inputs. Certain parts of the process can get out of whack and change the way those neurons behave. In your case, a severe emotional trauma has distorted your perceptions. You're perceiving dark forces behind innocent coincidences. You're interpreting familiar old happenings differently than you did in the past."

"Will it go away?"

"Yes, Mark, it will go away. The mind can heal itself of these small glitches—not overnight, but in time. You can help the process along by consciously striving to normalize your life, by keeping yourself calm. Go on with your work. Write your book. Take care of your son. Just remember that you may experience some outlandish feelings from time to time. Don't let them get you down. Subject them to the test of logic, the same as you do with historical theories. Don't believe them if they fail to pass that test."

This could be more easily said than done, said Mark.

"True, but you have what it takes to do it. You're an educated man, a smart man. You're in control, Mark, as I've told you before. No one can steer your course but you." She paused a short moment, and Mark imagined her dressed in one of her snappy red outfits. Thinking about this made him feel a little better.

"One thing more," she said. "Don't hesitate to call me if you start to feel overwhelmed. I'll drive right out to Oldenburg, and we'll have a sit-down, face to face. We'll work things out, if need be." Underlying her optimistic tone was another, which Mark picked up—a tone of misgiving and concern. "You *will* call if things get bad, won't you, Mark?"

"Yes, Kyleen, I'll call if the world starts to cave in. Thanks for your advice. And send the bill to Deidre."

ii

Noon already. Mark wasn't hungry, but he figured that Tad was probably ravenous. He looked at his watch and wondered whether his father would come home for lunch. Marta had said she would return from shopping in Astoria around two or two-thirty, meaning that John, Mark, and Tad must shift for themselves at lunchtime. Fortunately the refrigerator was full of leftovers, and the microwave was idiot-proof.

He heated some canned soup and called Tad in from the back-yard. He gave the boy a chicken sandwich, a large bowl of soup, and a glass of apple cider. Mark ate half a sandwich himself and drank a can of orange Diet Slice.

While eating, Tad read the latest issue of *Star Knight*, an astronomy newsletter published for kids under thirteen. Deidre had forwarded it from Portland, as Tad had requested when she called on Wednesday evening. Mark had spoken with her only briefly, but long enough to learn that "business" would keep her away from Oldenburg next weekend. She hoped they hadn't planned anything around her. Maybe the following weekend, okay?

Whatever you say, Sweetstuff. Mark had held off saying something truly inelegant, like, *Say hi to Clay Burnham for me, if you can talk with his cock in your mouth.*

"Dad Bear, listen to this," said Tad excitedly. "Mars is coming closer to earth than it's been in seventeen years, and it won't be this close again until the year twenty-oh-three."

"That's great. When's it going to get here?" Mark tried not to think about Mars's role in the tale Poverty Ike told them.

"Not until September twenty-first—that's when it'll be closest. But we should have a great view of it all summer. It says here that the Pacific Northwest will have the best view of Mars in over a hundred years. Isn't that awesome?"

"Sure is. Good thing you brought your telescope, huh?"

"I hope the sky stays clear."

Seeing the grin on Tad's face and the sparkle in his eyes made Mark feel warm inside. For a moment he let himself believe all that Dr. LeBreaux had told him this morning on the phone, that his recent fears were merely the effects of the bruising his emotions had sustained a week ago.

Tad went out to play, and John arrived shortly before twelve-thirty, looking hot and sweaty. He announced that he planned to take the rest of the day off, and changed into plaid Bermuda shorts and a golf shirt. Over a sandwich and a beer he told Mark that the private detective from New York, Robert Gammage, had pleaded guilty as charged this morning in county court. In accordance with the plea bargain, Judge Kelstad had sentenced him to six months in the Kalapuya County Jail, with all but thirty days suspended.

"My guess is he'll be out in two weeks," said John. "On Monday I'll take a sentence-review petition over to the judge, citing extenuating circumstances, good behavior, and no criminal record. I'm pretty sure Kelstad will let him out."

"What about the derelict?" Mark asked, trying not to appear too interested. "Has anyone seen him?"

"Not to my knowledge. My guess is he's long gone—probably walked along the B & R Railroad tracks back to Portland." John took a swig of beer and stared at his son. "Mark, ever since I told you about this thing, I've had the definite feeling you know something you're not telling me, and that maybe it's something I *should* know."

Mark stared through the window at a pair of scrub jays on the bushy limb of an old hemlock and refused to look his father in the eye. "What could I possibly know?"

"That's what I keep asking myself. When I mentioned Sam Darkenwald's name the other day in my office, you turned four shades of gray and broke out in a sweat. I've also noticed that you haven't been your normal jovial self since then. Does this guy Darkenwald mean anything to you?"

Mark squirmed in his chair. "It's not something I feel comfortable talking about right now, Dad. Maybe later we can—"

At this moment Tad bounded into the breakfast nook and gave

his grandfather the high five. "Hurry up and finish eating, Gramp. I want to show you a trick I learned on the tire-swings. Then I'll challenge you to a game of badminton. I set up the net in the backyard."

John issued his trademark belly laugh. "I saw it when I came home. I don't think I've played badminton in twenty years. How about you, Mark? Care to join us in a game? Tad and I will stand you."

Mark accepted and thrilled to his son's joyful whoop. Tad bounded out of the breakfast nook and flew out the back door, letting it slam and causing John to wince. Mark laughed.

John reached into his back pocket and took out a folded sheet of paper, which he handed over. "Got this at the office yesterday, and I thought of you immediately." It was a printed invitation to an organizational meeting of the county Dukakis for President Committee—Velma Selvig, Chairperson, to be held at the Royal Kokanee Inn at six o'clock this evening.

"If I weren't a rock-ribbed Republican, I'd go," John added. "Velma Selvig is my nominee for the best cook in western Oregon, though I'll deny I said that if you tell your mother. The Royal Kokanee got three stars for the food from *Country Inns* last year. Trouble was, Velma used to eat most of it herself, until she started losing weight about a year ago. Now she's down to fighting weight and a fine specimen of womanhood, if I do say so. Don't tell your mother I said *that*, either."

Mark read the flier and wrinkled his nose. "I don't think I'm up for this, Dad."

"Well, go anyway. You need to get out and socialize a little, take your mind off that freak accident you almost had last week. Besides, a lot of your fellow bleeding hearts will be there, so you'll probably have a wonderful time trashing traditional American values."

"I'll go if you go. It doesn't say Democrats only. This is Oregon—you can't tell most Democrats from Republicans. You just might find yourself supporting Dukakis for president."

"Hope not for impossibilities," said John, quoting Thomas Fuller and winking, as he often did. "I have things to do tonight. You're a big boy now, so you go by yourself. Don't worry about me."

"Okay, I'll go by myself, if it'll make you happy."

Throughout the rest of the afternoon the three of them—John,

Mark, and Thaddeus, three generations of Lansens—played badminton. Occasionally they broke for cider. Tad swung on the
tires while hanging from his knees, and the men watched and
clapped. They laughed and talked and sweated and roughhoused.
They told bawdy jokes and cussed mildly, since no tender ears
were around. None knew that this was the last such time the
three of them would ever share together.

21

An Evening at the Royal Kokanee

i

"I think it's wrong of you to force that poor child into social occasions with normal people," said Cynthia Downey, frowning into the hall mirror outside the bathroom. She wore heavy cyan eye shadow and bright rouge that matched the flowers in her chiffon dress. "I for one can understand how going out could be a very hurtful experience to one who looks like she does, all twisted and deformed. That's why we have institutions, Tressa, so people like Gretchen Bayliss can live out their lives with their own kind." Cynthia scowled at the craggy image in the mirror.

Tressa stepped out of the bathroom, having put on a floral shirtwaist dress that she hoped was appropriate for a small-town political gathering. "I don't agree with you, Mother. I think it's unhealthy for her to sit in that dusky old room of hers for hours at a time, doing nothing but burying her nose in books about Joan of Arc."

"I wouldn't be so quick to ridicule someone's religious convictions, even if they are only a child's. Just because you've fallen away from the church doesn't mean—"

"I'm *not* ridiculing anyone's convictions, Mother. I want Gretchen to get out more, that's all. I want her to see more of the world. That's what Father Charlie wanted for her, too."

Early in the afternoon Tressa had called the Bayliss house to tell Gretchen that she had arranged an appointment for her with Dr. Schell on Monday. While making the call she happened to glance at her desk calendar, on which she'd noted Velma Selvig's organizational soirée for the county Dukakis campaign. She suddenly got the idea to invite Gretchen along.

Gretchen didn't want to go, of course, not at first. She detested social outings, because the same thing always happened: Everyone gawked at the pathetic little crippled girl, but quickly looked away to avoid eye contact. The silent storm of pity revolted her. But Tressa gently insisted, even employing the strength of the late Father Charlie's wishes to persuade her.

ii

The Royal Kokanee Inn stood downstream from Oldenburg, between the B & R Railroad tracks and the Columbia River. Kokanee Creek tumbled by its doorstep en route to the river, affording guests the undying music of splashing water and the sometimes distracting quacking of mallards. A dense stand of red alders and cottonwoods surrounded the inn, insulating it against the noise of passing trains and cars. Built by salmon-canner Heinrich Olden in 1881 to house unmarried Chinese cannery workers, the white clapboard building had a squarish, slightly institutional look that Velma Selvig had countered by painting the shutters and trim bright orange.

Tressa arrived with her mother and Gretchen a few minutes before six o'clock, driving Velma's Chevy van, which Tressa always borrowed whenever she took Gretchen on an outing. Using a plywood ramp that Brett Omdahl had fashioned for this purpose, Gretchen could simply drive her Rolls Arrow wheelchair right through the rear door of the van and park it behind the passenger's seat. The ramp folded up and fit nicely into the rear, so exiting was equally easy.

Velma led them into the main salon, where a long table offered a buffet worthy of royalty. Early comers had staked out positions around the table, from which they took turns swooping down on the array of smoked salmon, Dungeness crab, steamed Penn Cove mussels and all the other delicacies that Velma had expertly prepared. A small sideboard held the obligatory Brie and white wine, which immediately attracted Cynthia Downey. Tressa hoped her mother would behave herself.

Velma helped Gretchen to a plate of food and a glass of ginger ale, then pulled Tressa into a side room, where stood a magnificent old hutch full of delft earthenware. "Tell me if I'm overreacting," she whispered. "That goddamn Gary Bayliss is here. Can you believe it? I mean, is the guy brain-dead, or what? My skin is crawling so bad I'm afraid I'll slip right out of it."

Before Velma had lost weight, she'd "dated" Gary Bayliss, even though he was married. She'd been desperate, she confessed to Tressa later—a calamitously fat woman in her late thirties who had nothing resembling romance in her life and no prospects of ever having it. Gary's marriage was obviously in trouble, so Velma hadn't felt like a home-wrecker. After meeting Tressa, however, and after sweating off her excess poundage, Velma had gained a totally new image of herself. She'd acquired new expectations and standards. She'd seen that her relationship with Gary was nothing more than sweaty sex, and not even good sex at that. Moreover, the guy was a dirtball who beat his wife, drank too much cheap beer, and bragged incoherently about his heroics in Vietnam. With Tressa's enthusiastic blessing, Velma had rid herself of him, but not before telling him precisely what a lowlife he was.

"It was the flier you circulated," said Tressa. "He saw it and figured this was a good way to get a free meal. Look at him— he's so busy stuffing himself that he hasn't even noticed Gretchen's here."

"I guess ya takes yer chances when you send out invitations postal patron," said Velma, grimacing. "Everybody and his goddamn parrot gets one, and everybody and his parrot shows up! I still can't believe that he has the balls to show his face here, after what I said to him."

Tressa touched her friend's elbow. "Be thankful he doesn't have the face to show his balls," she giggled.

Velma asked how Tressa was. Had she gotten over the ugly episode at Gestern Hall, when someone or something had touched her intimately, uninvited and even unseen? Had she decided what to do about it?

"I have other things to worry about right now," replied Tressa. "I'm afraid that Gretchen is suffering some pretty severe emotional problems. I'm taking her to see Nat Schell on Monday. I brought her along because I wanted to get her out of that damn house, if only for an hour or two. I saw Freddye Ann yesterday, and she looked like death. Acted like something had eaten half her brain. I can't imagine how any kid could keep her sanity in a place like that."

iii

Mark Lansen refilled his glass from the keg. The ale was wonderful stuff, one of his favorites—Terminator Stout, brewed in a Portland microbrewery by the legendary McMenamin brothers. He wondered how Velma Selvig had managed to score a keg, since this stuff was normally available only to the McMenamins' brew pubs. Connections, probably.

He moved to the railing of the porch and leaned against it, hoping Gary Bayliss wouldn't follow. But Bayliss *did* follow, having drawn himself a fourth glass of ale. He sported a Band-Aid over the bridge of his nose and a shiny black eye that still looked swollen. For some reason he'd stuck to Mark like glue since the moment he came through the front door, behaving as if he'd found a long lost brother.

The two had never been real friends, partly because of the difference in their ages. Gary Bayliss was seven years older than Mark, and they had not actually become acquainted until Bayliss returned to Oldenburg after a stint in the army. Mark remembered him as a high school football hero, a guy who hadn't lived up to expectations. Now Mark thought him world-class vulgar.

"Velma knows how to throw a bash, doesn't she?" said Bayliss after taking a gulp of Terminator that left his Fu Manchu mustache white with foam. Shoving his sweating face closer to Mark's, he whispered confidentially: "You know, I used to fuck that bitch three, four times a week. She was a big woman then—I mean a *big* woman—weighed maybe two-oh-five. Then she goes on a fuckin' diet and gets skinny on me. Decides she's too good for me and drops me like a hot mortar round." He chuckled wheezingly, and Mark forced himself to smile through clenched teeth.

Just then a young girl in a powered wheelchair glided past the door toward the buffet table. She had an extraordinarily pretty face, Mark thought, with eyes big and blue enough to warm the stoniest heart. Mark saw Bayliss's own bleary eyes light up.

"Excuse me, will you, Mark? That's Top-Kick, my daughter. I wonder what the fuck she's doing here." Bayliss was off, apparently to chase down the girl, and Mark blew out a long sigh.

"Real prince, isn't he?" said someone behind him. He turned to face a rangy man in his early forties, whom he recognized immediately as Rick Omdahl, an old friend of the family. Rick's eyes twinkled with sarcasm. "Calls his daughter Top-Kick, like she's a first sergeant in the army. Isn't that cute?" He winked. "Gary gets even funnier as he gets drunker. We're in for a treat this evening."

"Hey, I'm in dire need of some sane conversation," laughed Mark, pumping Rick's outstretched hand. "For some reason Gary thinks we're old friends."

Rick Omdahl was a boiler shift supervisor at the nearby James River sawmill. He wore a freshly pressed work shirt and a yellow tie that he'd probably gotten for Christmas from one of his kids. "Was he telling war stories again? Did he tell you how he was captured by the North Vietnamese and how he escaped after killing six of them?"

"That and more. I've been here twenty minutes, and I've had enough blood and gore to last me into my next life. I also heard chapter and verse of the fight he got into at Poverty Ike's last Monday night. That's why his face looks like a Jimmy Dean sausage."

"Funny thing is, Gary didn't even go to Vietnam. He spent his whole enlistment in Fort Ord, California, working for a company clerk. He picked up the combat jargon from real vets who were back from the 'Nam. All those war stories are borrowed or made up."

"Are you kidding? None of that shit was true? How did you—?" Mark stared a moment at the older man's lean, rough face. "Wait a minute. *You're* a Vietnam vet, aren't you, Rick?"

"Twenty-fifth Division, Triple Deuce Mech." He glanced at his shoes, as if admitting this embarrassed him slightly. "Gary never learned that if you want to make out like a Vietnam hero, you shouldn't try it with someone who's been there. You mess up important little details that give you away quick. Besides, real Vietnam vets don't believe in heroes." He sipped his ale, as if to quell a troublesome memory. "Couple years back I ran into an old army buddy who knew Gary at Fort Ord, and he confirmed all my suspicions about his war record."

Mark couldn't hold back a lusty laugh. He asked how Rick's wife and boys were. Great, Rick said, and he thanked Mark for asking. Brett, his oldest, would turn seventeen, come August. Brett was a good kid, but his main interest in life was skateboarding, a fact that his father wasn't exactly thrilled about. Neither was he thrilled that Brett had taken a part-time job in Gary Bayliss's store, but a job was a job. The younger boy, Garth, had just turned fourteen, and Rick's wife, Nancy, was busy at the James River mill, where she worked as a safety engineer.

The two men took a slow walking tour of the inn's first floor, pausing here and there to admire antiques and old photographs. Historian that he was, Mark took pleasure in this. If he squinted and concentrated on shutting out the crowd noise, he could visualize the parlor thick with opium smoke from the pipes of the Chinese cannery workers who had once lived here. He could almost smell the oily aroma of Oriental cooking and hear the musical chatter of Mandarin tongues. This old building had seen much history, he knew—history that he yearned to soak up and take refuge in.

He stopped stone-still when he saw a woman standing against the far wall of the main salon. She was talking quietly with Dr. Nat Schell, who was obviously quite taken with her. She held a glass of ginger ale in one hand and a small plate of food in the other. Her eyes shone bold and her auburn hair hung in swirls around her cheeks and neck. She looked lithe and healthy in her flowered dress, and when she smiled, Mark felt a long-forgotten warmth somewhere in his chest.

iv

Tressa's knees went weak when her eyes met Mark Lansen's— those deep hazel eyes she'd seen so often in her girlhood dreams. She heard little of what Nat Schell was saying (something about wanting her to join him for a weekend on his sailboat). For the next thirty seconds a thousand sweet memories flitted through her head like a flock of startled sparrows, memories of a time so remote that it now seemed like fiction. Should she walk over and say hello? Should she wait for him to make the first move?

Jesus, what is this, anyway? she asked herself. *We're not high school kids anymore, and this isn't courtship!* Mark Lansen was a fully grown man, with a fully grown man's history and obligations. He was married, she'd heard. He had a son. He was teaching college somewhere—was it Portland? Besides, Tressa had her own history, and it was far from pretty. She wasn't in the market for romance, a point she'd tried time and again to impress upon Nat Schell.

Now Mark was moving toward her, striding through the crowd

in his long-legged way, smiling with his dazzling teeth. *He hasn't changed that much,* she whispered to herself. A little older around the eyes and mouth, more mature-looking. Brown hair fashionably short on top and full at the neck. He was slightly heavier, but still lean. He was still Mark Lansen, and Tressa's heart thundered like a kettledrum.

V

Ten minutes later, Nat Schell wandered off toward the buffet, leaving Mark and Tressa to talk about things he had no interest in, the kind of things people talk about when they go way back together.

"He appears to be sulking," said Mark. "I hope he didn't feel left out."

Tressa laughed. "Nat's my doctor now. Nice man, but he's decided he wants more from me than a doctor-patient relationship. I'm not ready for that yet. I'm not sure I ever will be."

The rumble of anger Mark felt in his heart surprised him. He shook it off and reminded himself that he had no right to feel angry or jealous or protective of Tressa. Their relationship was ancient history. But, oh, how Mark loved history.

They slipped out to lean against the porch railing and drink in the warm evening air. On the way Mark refilled his glass at the keg. "Want to know something?" he asked. "Seeing you is really good for me right now. I've had a week like you wouldn't believe, but you remind me of how good things used to be—back when we were innocent kids, I mean. It happens to be exactly what I need." He sipped his ale and looked apologetic. "Sorry to get schmaltzy on you."

Tressa said she knew how he felt, because she too had endured a hellish week, beginning with Father Charlie Briggs's suicide. They talked of the tragedy awhile and marveled that neither had noticed the other at the funeral. Then again, the crowd had been huge.

Mark asked her to bring him up to date on her life since their breakup fifteen years ago, so she did, albeit sketchily. She'd gotten her degree in fine arts and drama at Northwestern University near Chicago and had immediately entered the Landburne School of Acting in New York City. After graduating two years later, she'd played the Manhattan Theater Club and Trinity Theater, both in

New York. In 1980 she joined the Brattle Theater Company in Cambridge, Massachusetts, and later served stints with the Pittsburgh Playhouse and the Alliance Theater in Atlanta. Along the way she'd met and wed a playwright named R. J. Roscoe.

"Someday I'll tell you how I ended up as the assistant director of the New Community Theater in Pentington, Wisconsin," she said, smiling grimly and making it plain that she didn't want to give further details just now. "That's where the story becomes less upbeat, I'm afraid."

Mark nodded. He would be patient. "I admire you for doing what you always wanted to do," he said finally. "You always said you wanted to become an actress, that you wanted to play theaters in New York. You did it. You stuck to your guns, went out and got the training, and did it. You should be proud."

Tressa's laugh said that she was far from proud. And the term was *actor*, she said, correcting him gently—not *actress*. She disliked *actress*, because it was akin to *aviatrix* or *Jewess* or *Negress*. Who needed terms like those anymore?

"I stand corrected," said Mark with a little bow. "I hope you'll forgive this old lowbrow history prof." He offered to bring her a fresh drink or a new plate of food, since he was headed to the buffet. More ginger ale, she requested, and as much Dungeness crab as he could carry.

"It'll be your turn when you come back," she said, tossing her hair in a way that Mark had always liked. "I want to hear everything that's happened to you since the beginning of your sophomore year of college."

"Not while we're eating. It's pretty vile stuff."

"I'll just bet," she said, and he disappeared into the salon.

vi

From the porch of the inn Tressa gazed across the shady green yard to the driveway that led to a graveled parking lot. The surrounding glen had darkened with long, early-evening shadows. The cottonwoods and alders admitted only slim shafts of sunlight, and these tilted closer to horizontal with every passing minute. Night was not far off.

If Velma meant to make a speech, she'd better do it soon,

Tressa said to herself, because very shortly people would start to leave. Few braved the night in Oldenburg anymore.

She heard the sound of an approaching car, a latecomer to the soirée. She watched it turn into the drive, a monstrous old black sedan of a make she couldn't name. It rolled across the wooden bridge that spanned Kokanee Creek, frightening a pair of mallards into noisy flight from the water below. She caught sight of the driver, and her heart nearly stopped.

"Your Dungeness crab, mademoiselle—as much as I can carry, per your command," said Mark Lansen with a ridiculous French accent. "You okay?" he asked. "You look like you've just seen the ghost of Black Beard."

"Did you notice the car that just drove in?"

"Caught a glimpse of it. Nineteen sixty-three Imperial LeBaron, a real land yacht. Nicely preserved, from what I saw. Too bad my old man isn't here—he'd get a kick out of it."

Tressa took the plate and the glass he'd brought. "You're still a car buff, aren't you? Did you happen to see who was—?"

The ringing of someone tapping a glass with a spoon interrupted her, and the lowing crowd noise died. Velma's strong voice rang out, thanking everyone for coming (even the Republicans). She invited them to eat more, drink more, and—last but not least—to fill out the voter registration cards on the table near the front door. Tonight's event signaled the beginning of a spirited drive to carry Kalapuya County for Michael Dukakis next November, she said, and judging from the size of the turnout, that would be no problem. She then launched into the obligatory introduction of local luminaries, starting with Kalapuya County's state senator and representative, both of whom received hearty applause.

She'd just begun the introduction of a Dukakis campaign official from Portland when a scream ripped through the inn, a child's scream that sliced Tressa to the marrow. For a few seconds silence hung in the Royal Kokanee Inn like the stink of ozone after a lightning strike. Then the scream erupted again, more terror-filled now, a nightmare-sound that Tressa feared could jelly blood.

"Gretchen!" she hissed.

She tossed aside her plate and her glass, and charged from the porch into the salon. She elbowed her way through a mass of bodies to the buffet, spilling drinks and jarring plates from hands. She frantically scanned the room, but saw only startled faces with va-

cant eyes and mouths shocked dumb. The screams came from the
foyer, and she ran toward it, her heels pounding the carpet.

Gretchen's Rolls Arrow stood against an interior wall. Tressa
heard the whine of its motor, saw its wheels spinning uselessly in
reverse, leaving rubbery streaks on the hardwood floor. Gretchen
lay in the chair, her misshapen body coiled hideously against the
seat back, her face twisted in horror. Her right fist held the joystick
so tightly that her knuckles were white. Her left fist she pressed
against her yawning mouth, as if trying to swallow it. The joystick
was in the reverse position, meaning that she'd backed away from
something, that she was still trying to back away. She'd encountered the wall, but her terror wouldn't let her release the joystick.
Neither would it let her stop screaming.

Gary Bayliss lurched into the foyer from the opposite hallway,
his face red and his eyes stupidly wide, a half-full glass of ale in
his paw. He made for his daughter, but his feet became tangled and
he staggered crazily against Velma's prized grandfather clock, causing it to bong. While trying to right himself, he pressed his hand
through the glass front of the clock, shattering it. He bellowed like
an angry ox and pulled back his hand, which was gory with blood.

Tressa reached Gretchen and knelt beside the wheelchair,
grabbed her shoulders, and shook her. The girl's face was gray
with panic. Strings of spittle leapt from her lips as her head
jounced. Her left hand fought Tressa, tried to push her away,
tried to claw her face. This was fear like Tressa had never seen
it, an animal-fear that banished all reason.

"Gretchen, honey—it's me!" she shouted. "It's Tressa! I'm here,
Gretchen, and you're all right!" Still the screams came in searing,
rhythmic waves, cresting at the height of each breath, tearing the
girl's vocal cords, causing her to choke and sputter. "Gretchen,
please!" shouted Tressa. "What's wrong, honey? Tell me!"

The anguish in the girl's eyes touched a wound in Tressa's
heart, firing sorrows over another little girl, one much younger,
who had needed a mother's love and protection just as Gretchen
did. Tressa had failed that little girl. She would not fail *this* one.

She pried Gretchen's right hand away from the joystick, and
the wheelchair's motor immediately ceased its whine. Velma was
now at her side, trying to help, as was Mark. "Somebody get Nat
Schell!" Tressa commanded.

Suddenly Gary Bayliss bellowed again and clomped across the
foyer, flailing blood from his lacerated hand. "Top-Kick, baby,

I'm here! What're they doin' to you, Top-Kick? Your ol' daddy will take care of you!"

Nat Schell bounded in from the salon and caught Gary by the sleeve. "Sit down and be quiet, man! That's a serious laceration you have. If you don't let me take care of it, you'll go into shock."

"Forget him, Nat!" barked Tressa. "Help me with Gretchen!"

The doctor moved in the direction of the wheelchair, but Gary grabbed him and whirled him around like a limp rag. "What're you gonna do to my little girl?" He drove a hammy fist into Nat's midsection, producing a *whump!* that sounded like someone beating the dust out of an old armchair. Nat doubled up and went to the floor, gasping.

vii

Mark saw Nat Schell go down, and suddenly his anger rose like hot lava. He saw Gary Bayliss careen toward Tressa, bloody and bull-shouldered and drooling drunk, apparently meaning to yank her away from Gretchen. Didn't the son of a bitch know that these people were only trying to help his daughter?

Charged with adrenaline and anger, Mark bolted to his feet and moved between the advancing Bayliss and the wheelchair, fists at his side. For the first time in a decade he was mad enough to fight another man.

Bayliss charged into him, knocking him out of the way, outweighing Mark easily by forty pounds. Mark regained his balance by catching hold of Bayliss's shirt and just managed to duck under the haymaker the big man threw with his good hand. Mark came up with an uppercut into Bayliss's throat, which rocked him backwards, but Bayliss came back at him, blind with drunken fury. Mark hit him twice in the face, the second time with as much mustard as he could heap on it. Bayliss went down and stayed down, and Mark's knuckles hurt like hell.

viii

Gretchen finally stopped screaming. Nat Schell wrapped some ice cubes in a towel supplied by Velma and pressed them to Gretchen's forehead, then went to his car to fetch a sedative from the medical bag he always kept in the trunk.

Tressa held the girl's hands, stroked her cheeks, whispered reassurances. She was vaguely aware of the crowd, which had begun to disperse now. People talked in low tones, as if this were a hospital or a church. She was aware that Nat and Mark had helped Gary Bayliss into a chair, that they were bandaging his cut hand. She caught sight of her mother, who hovered in the doorway of the salon, wineglass in her hand, wearing an infuriating I-told-you-so face.

Finally she dared to turn toward the other end of the foyer, where she somehow knew the source of the trouble was. Clovis Gestern stood in the entrance, attired in immaculate casual clothing, his handsome face shaded with anguish. Tressa had known he would be there, for she'd seen him drive up in his old black Imperial. A cold thrill raced along her backbone.

She felt Gretchen tighten her grip on her hand. The girl's pretty blue eyes, now red and puffy, peered out from beneath the cold towel that Nat had placed on her forehead. She looked exhausted and pale. Her eyelids were heavy from the sedative. Her lips moved, but Tressa heard no sound, so she leaned closer.

"It's him, Tressa."

Knowing what she meant but unable to accept it, Tressa heard herself ask, "Who?"

"It's *him*. He's the one I saw outside my window, the one who hurts my mother."

"Honey, I think you should rest now. Mark and I are going to take you home soon."

"I can't go home, Tressa." Her voice was a labored, dreamy breath, hardly a voice at all. The sedative was working fast. "He'll come—for me."

Tressa started to say something comforting, but her own voice balked. She wished intensely for a glass of wine. "I won't let anything happen to you, Gretch." *Please God, don't let this be a lie. I didn't mean to lie to Desdi.*

"You don't . . . understand," said Gretchen, her head lolling to one side. She could no longer hold it up. "He's . . . the one. His . . . face . . . is normal . . . now. But I . . . know him. He's the . . . one, Tressa. He's . . . the *vampire*."

22

A Nocturnal Mission

i

On Friday evening, June 10, 1988, John Lansen did something he'd not done in almost four decades of marriage—he lied to his wife. He told her he had work to do at his law office, and asked her not to wait up for him.

Before leaving, he went into the rear parlor, where his grandson sprawled on a sofa, watching "Jeopardy!" on television. He ruffled the boy's hair and suggested an outing at the beach the next day. "What do you say we check out the wreck of the *Peter Iredale*? We could drive down to Seaside later and buy some kites. After lunch we'll fly 'em on the beach, just like real airheads. How's that sound?"

Excellent, Tad said. The *Peter Iredale* was a steel-hulled sailing ship that had run aground near Astoria around the turn of the century, and Tad was anxious to see it.

"Your dad should be home soon from that Dukakis party," added John. "Invite him along, why don't you?"

"Okay, Gramp. See you in the morning."

Marta gave John a little hug on his way out, and—with discernible worry on her face—told him to be careful (almost as if she sensed what he was up to). She reminded him that darkness would soon fall, not that he needed any reminder.

John wondered later whether Marta had believed the lie. Normally he brought work home with him, if he couldn't finish it during an eight-hour day. Years had gone by since he'd spent extra time in his office, a fact that could not have escaped his wife. Yet, she'd said nothing to indicate that she thought anything strange.

He left the lovely old Lansen house on foot and strolled down Tillamook Way to Kalapuya Avenue, passing between the high school and the county park. He crossed the old arched footbridge

that spanned Sunset Creek and continued east past the weathered
bronze statue of Queen Molly, which stood in a clearing on his
left. John tried not to look at the statue as he walked by, tried not
to visualize what had happened in the park just a week ago. A
shudder raced through him. He was glad that his route didn't
take him close enough to make out the irregular circle of black,
charred grass where his friend, Father Charlie Briggs, had
roasted himself to death.

He walked past City Hall, a white cement building with tall
pillars. He turned right at the corner of Kalapuya and Main,
where stood the post office and the venerable Hotel Cathlamet,
then continued up the steep hill to his law office. Once inside, he
opened his wall safe and took out a Smith & Wesson .38 revolver, a gift that a friend in the Oregon State Police had given
him years ago. He loaded it and stuffed it into his belt. Next he
opened a file cabinet and withdrew the folders and papers that
he'd shown Mark a few days earlier, the material relating to the
Gestern family, the phony death certificates and the correspon-
dence from civil jurisdictions in England, France, and Germany.
These he placed in his battered briefcase, which he put on his
desk.

Then he brewed himself a pot of coffee and fired up his pipe.
He switched on the radio and tuned it to an easy-listening station
in Longview, Washington. Smoking patiently, he listened to old
standards played by the Boston Pops and waited for the night.

ii

Darkness came with discomfiting suddenness when it finally
came. John Lansen picked up his briefcase and left the office,
locking the doors behind him. At the rear of the building stood
a metal shed in which he kept his 1981 GMC four-wheel-drive
Suburban, inasmuch as the garage at the family house wasn't
quite roomy enough for it. This was the vehicle in which he'd
taken his friends fishing, camping, and hunting—friends whose
ranks had begun to thin.

Charlie Briggs and he would never again hunt ducks down on
the river. Bernie Pellagrini would never again track elk with him
in the Cascade Mountains. The three of them would never again

play golf on sparkling Saturday mornings at the Astoria Country Club or cast for steelheads off Bernie's boat.

John had always thought of himself as a man with his feet planted firmly on the ground—hard-nosed and dispassionate. In matters involving his family and friends, however, he was neither. In matters involving Kristen particularly, he had trouble preventing his visceral, fatherly feelings from coloring his judgment. She was special to him. She was his little girl, the sole issue of his loins. More than once he'd admitted that in matters involving Kristen, he couldn't see straight.

Tonight John Lansen meant to go up the mountain to Gestern Hall—or the Nehalem Mountain Inn, as its owner now called it—and bring his daughter down. If she balked, he would show her the documents that attested to generations of Gestern probate fraud. He would tell her about Skye Padilla, the runaway girl sought by a private investigator from New York. With a little luck, he might even confirm that Skye really was at Gestern Hall, and maybe he would rescue her, too.

iii

He drove south past the intersection of Main and Yamhill Avenue, where the Benson Creek Baptist Church stood like an outpost on the fringe of town. Beyond this point Main Street became Benson Creek Road, potholed and twisty, hemmed in by forest and arching thickets of blackberries. The big Suburban rumbled over a bridge that spanned Benson Creek, and the forest broke into a clearing on his right, the municipal cemetery. The muddy picture of the Pellagrinis' violated graves took shape in his mind, and John felt the hairs stiffen on the back of his neck.

He turned left onto Queen Molly Road, which wound upward through a dense stand of Douglas fir interspersed with cedar. Occasional clear-cuts offered brief vistas of the town below, and John remarked to himself how dark and dead Oldenburg looked, even from up here.

He doused the headlights and parked two hundred yards short of the gate that led to Gestern Hall. After checking his bulky Coleman flashlight to ensure that it worked, he grabbed his briefcase and stepped out of the truck into an onslaught of cold moonlight. He trudged toward the gate, his Red Wing hunting boots crunching on the gravel, his briefcase brushing his leg. The moon was so strong that he didn't need to switch the flashlight on.

When he reached the gate, he laid eyes on Gestern Hall up close, the first time he'd done so in at least two decades. For a short, razor-bright moment he felt the sting of pure panic. The ancient Gothic house reared black against the night sky, its jagged angles violating the familiar sweep of stars. From within, its bulk seemed to radiate an insensate power that polluted all it touched, a power to distort the senses of living things, to deceive, to frighten. During this blind moment John Lansen could not doubt that whatever had gone wrong in Oldenburg in the past months, whatever had poisoned the night and driven the people to cower behind locked doors, lived *here*.

He remembered something his newest client, Bob Gammage, had told him several days earlier: Nobody Gammage had interviewed in Oldenburg had confessed any knowledge of Gestern Hall—not the fat woman who worked the registration desk at the Hotel Luxor, not the three old men whom Gammage had plied with drinks at Poverty Ike's. John Lansen had said this was absurd: Everyone in the town knew the mansion on Nehalem Mountain. It was a landmark that had presided over Oldenburg for a century and a half, for Christ's sake. How could anyone have missed it?

Cowering here in the shadow of its gatepost, John understood why those people had denied any knowledge of the place: Deep in their hearts they sensed that Gestern Hall was the home of something unmentionable. Gestern Hall was a tumor on the body of the town, the locus of the local disease. The people knew this in the instinctual way that a baby knows how to suck milk from a woman's breast, without being taught or told. This wasn't a matter to discuss with a stranger.

iv

A few interior lights glowed orange through the windows of the house, but the drive and the yard were unlit. Strange, thought John: This was supposed to be an operating business, the Nehalem Mountain Inn. Why hadn't Skip Gestern installed floodlights in the drive to help potential guests find the place, or

even a small illuminated sign to let them know they were welcome?

He walked briskly up the curving brick drive toward the porte
cochere and ducked into the shadow of the junipers that grew in
shapeless bunches along the west wall of the house. He could
just discern the outline of Kristen's Volkswagen Jetta, parked
close against the edge of the porte cochere. He'd given her that
car for her birthday last year, and her blue eyes had brightened
with joy. Seeing it now gave him a pang.

He turned from the main entrance and walked around to the
rear of the mansion, keeping close to the shrubbery. A covered
walkway led from the rear door to a pair of stone outbuildings,
the largest of which had undoubtedly been a carriage house, and
was now a garage. Both stood black and lifeless but for the lichens that grew on their walls. Beyond the outbuildings lay a
clear area that bordered the forest on its far edge—a parking lot,
judging from the gravel that covered it.

He heard a sound behind him, soft and breathy like a sigh. He
whirled on his heel, fully expecting to see someone standing
close at his back, but the moonlight revealed only the juniper
shrubs entangled with holly and Scotch broom. *The wind,* he
would have told himself, had the night not been so breathless, so
silent.

He gripped the flashlight hard enough to make his knuckles
ache, and contemplated beaming it into the shrubbery to search
out whoever was hiding there. But he didn't do it. Some deep instinct told him to get away from this spot, so he moved silently
through the weedy grass toward the rear door of the mansion. He
glimpsed a figure as it darted past a narrow window in the entryway, a young girl with raven-black hair, briefly silhouetted
against dim light. She wore a bulky dress and a light kerchief.
She disappeared within seconds, as if she'd come to the door
only long enough to check the lock.

A maid? A kitchen girl?

John felt that this girl was Skye Padilla, though he couldn't
say exactly why. He'd caught only a glimpse, but from what he
saw, she matched Bob Gammage's description of the young runaway from New York.

He mounted the low stone steps that led into the rear entryway. He was about to try the door handle when a sweet odor
came to his nose. Lavender, unmistakably. The smell conjured

the image of a woman he'd known not so long ago, a dark-complected and comely woman who loved to wear the scent of lavender, especially in warm weather. John couldn't remember noticing the scent on anyone else, but then he seldom noticed other women the way he noticed Fran Pellagrini, the wife of Bernie, his neighbor and best friend. In all the years he'd known the Pellagrinis, he'd never made a move toward Fran, or revealed to anyone how he'd felt about her. To do so would have risked hurting the woman he loved more than life itself, Marta. Still, Fran Pellagrini had often starred in John Lansen's fantasies, a safe and private realm where no one suffered dishonor or hurt.

Lavender. She'd worn lavender, both in the real world and in John's fantasy world.

He heard the sound again, the one he'd heard a few moments earlier, the sigh of someone very close. He turned slowly to his rear and saw a woman standing scarcely an arm's length away.

The smell was lavender, yes, tinged with sassafras, but laced with something else, too, something much stronger—wintergreen and cloves; and beneath all these, the acrid bite of formaldehyde. Embalmer's smells. Though the moonlight frosted her face and night dress, John recognized her. She was Fran Pellagrini.

He focused on her features, on her hellish grin, and felt a jarring revulsion. Bernie had beaten her to death with a golf club, and her misshapen skull bore the evidence. The nine-iron had crushed a cheekbone, had taken gouts out of her scalp and brow, which the mortician hadn't even tried to repair, since the funeral featured no open-casket viewing. She'd had a pretty aquiline nose: Now it lay grotesquely off-center and nearly flat against her face.

Every muscle in John's body went rigid as ice. His chest constricted, and his heart tried to climb into his throat. He strained to speak, but a mere grunt came out. The fright endured, like the moonlight.

"Hello, Johnny," whispered the woman hoarsely. "Nice to see you again. What brings you out on a night like this?"

With great effort John forced air through his vocal cords, forced his mouth to move. "Who are you?" he hissed, as if he didn't know. "Wha-what do you want with me?"

"Oh, come on, John—don't let on like you and I aren't acquainted." She moved a step closer, and her smell grew sharper in John's nostrils. Beneath the embalmer's stink was another that threatened to choke him, the gut-wrenching stench of putrefaction. No mistake now: This thing had come from the grave, and this was why the Pellagrinis' plots lay empty. "I have a confession, John," she went on. "I thought I would never see you again, at least not alive. And that pissed me off, it really did. You see, I've always felt the same things for you that you felt for me. And I've always regretted that you and I never got it together— know what I mean? My God, we lived next door to each other all those years. . . ."

John's body suddenly went weak and jittery. His head swam. He staggered backward against the heavy door. *Get control of yourself, man,* his brain shouted. *This isn't real. . . .*

But it *was* real. The reeking body of Fran Pellagrini moved closer.

"G-get away from me!" he gasped, fighting for breath. "J-just get away! Y-you're supposed to be *dead!*"

The thing that had been Fran Pellagrini laughed. "Johnny, Johnny—don't think about that." Her voice gurgled and bubbled. "It's not important. What's important is that we're here together, and we're *alone*. You don't have much time left to you, Johnny, so let's not waste it. Bernie will be here soon, and if he sees us doing *that*—"

John's stomach revolted. Vomit erupted from his mouth and splashed down the front of his light Vuarnet jacket. He dropped both the flashlight and the briefcase.

"That wasn't very nice of you, Johnny," the Fran-thing croaked. "Is *that* what you think of me? After all these years, after all the times you've watched me working in my garden— when I wore only shorts and a halter top, remember?—all the times you found excuses to go out to your garage, telling Marta you were looking for some old part for a car you were working on, when you really wanted to cop a peek at me over the hedge? *That's* how you react when I return your attention—you throw up all over yourself? Am I *that* repulsive, John?"

Emptying his stomach cleared John's head. His mind no longer fought the reality that Fran Pellagrini stood within touching distance. He could act now. He somehow knew that the moon-gleam in Fran's eyes wasn't really sex-hunger, that behind those eyes lay a craving to kill.

She reached for him suddenly with scabrous arms. Her hands closed around his Vuarnet jacket and tore it away. The force of the attack knocked the air from his lungs, and he heard the crackling of vertebrae in his neck as his head whiplashed.

"Come *on*, Johnny!" Fran Pellagrini wheezed desperately. "Let's *do* it, while we still have time! It's only fair after all those years of holding back—you with your pale, lumpy Marta and me with my scrawny Bernardo! I want your cock in me, Johnny! I want you to suck my beautiful tits! I want you to fuck me until I—"

John's rage exploded. The Fran Pellagrini he'd known could never have talked such filth. The Fran he'd mooned over from afar was the beautiful daughter of upstanding Italian immigrants, a woman who had reared two fine children. Hearing these outrages from the very mouth that Fran Pellagrini had owned was more than John could bear.

He shoved her away brutally, but she came back at him like a rabid cat, her face twisted with rage. He managed to sidestep her, but her hand caught him across the jaw, leaving hot nail tracks. He jerked the Smith & Wesson from his belt. She lunged at him again, and he fired—two shots, three shots, four. The surrounding forest crackled with echoes, and a night bird cried. The bullets tore gruesome chunks from her neck and chest, but still she came at him, fueled by the same force that had reanimated her and rousted her from the grave.

This isn't Fran! John's mind raged. *This isn't the woman I knew! This is something from hell!*

He fired again, hitting her square in the face this time and dislodging a gobbet of her skull with hair attached to it. She lurched backward crazily and crumpled to her knees.

"I can't take this, Johnny," she rasped, spewing globules of wet stuff through the hole in her face. "I can't take being murdered a second time, especially by you." She groped for him with clawlike hands. Something dripped like India ink from her wounds.

John twisted away from her. He ran toward the south corner of the house, huffing so hard that his sixty-two-year-old lungs burned. From somewhere behind him he heard a scream, a man's scream, a voice that sounded sick and angry and terrifyingly familiar. Bernie Pellagrini had found his wife.

V

John entered the porte cochere, escaping the moonlight. He plunged into a passage from which trickled feeble lamplight, and followed it to the main entrance of the house. A brass sign hung on the huge oaken door, welcoming visitors and bidding them to PLEASE COME IN. Pressing himself against the stone wall next to the door, he held his breath and listened.

Scraping sounds—irregular footsteps on cobblestone paving—echoed off the walls and arched ceiling above him. Someone had followed him from the rear of the mansion. *Bernie?* With his heartbeat pounding in his temples, John tried to remember how many shots he'd fired from his revolver. *Five,* he thought, which left him just one more round in the cylinder.

He tried the massive, curved handle on the door and found it locked. In desperation he threw his full weight against the door, rattling it loudly. The footsteps behind him grew louder, and he saw Bernie in his mind, lurching through the passage with his hands spread like predatory claws, the top of his head torn away by the rifle bullet he'd fired through his own palate. Bernie would be hunting the intruder who'd just shot Fran, yearning to tear that man limb from limb.

John forsook the locked door and headed for the short passage that led to the front of the porte cochere but stopped short. A figure stood stark-black against the moonlight that shone through the maw of the porte cochere. His head tilted oddly, and he had one arm splayed wide as if to block the way; a golf club lay on his shoulder—an iron, judging from the reflected moonlight. John backtracked toward the passage through which he'd just come, but this was the one from which footsteps issued. *Both* Bernie and Fran were coming for him. He was trapped.

He flung himself against the door again, knowing the hopelessness of doing so. The impact almost jarred him senseless and reverberated through the passages. He stood away from the door and gathered himself for battle. He had but one bullet left, but he was a big man, and powerful despite his age. At twenty-three he'd won the Oregon Law School arm-wrestling championship, and he'd kept himself in pretty good shape in the nearly four decades since then. Wasn't he known as the Big Square-Headed Norsky?

The echoes of footsteps came from both passages, louder now.

The Pellagrinis were closing in. He cocked the Smith & Wesson and balled his other hand into a fist. His cheek burned from the rips of Fran's fingernails, and abysmal thoughts lumbered through his head. The world outside Gestern Hall seemed a vague theory, a distant abstraction that lacked any relevance to the brutal Gothic power of this place. All that mattered to him was the here and now, the frantic need to survive. He meant to fight these monstrosities who wore the bodies of Bernie and Fran. He meant to beat them, and having done so, rescue Kristen from the clutches of Gestern Hall.

Fran Pellagrini emerged from the rear passage into the orange glare of the overhead lamp in the entryway. She halted a moment, and John quailed when he saw the nightmare sneer on her ruined face. Footfalls came from the passage on his right—the lurching and yet purposeful strides of the thing John had known and loved as Bernie Pellagrini. *The moment of truth,* John said to himself. *The jig is up. Time to show what you're made of, old man.*

A loud clank startled him—the throw of a dead bolt in the lock of the door. He heard the shriek of hinges as the door pulled inward. He spun around to see a face peek through the opening, a face timid and pale, a young girl whose dark eyes radiated pure panic. She had a small white scar near the corner of her mouth.

"Quick—inside!" she whispered. "They'll kill you! You can't fight them!"

John pushed through the door and slammed it behind him. He just managed to throw the dead bolt home before something thudded hugely against the outer surface. His nerves jangled as eager fingernails clawed the lock and handle, as lifeless fists boomed angrily against the wood.

vi

They sat at an ancient, carved-mahogany table in a dusky cubicle off the foyer, a suit of thirteenth-century armor guarding the door. Skye smoked a cigarette, and its ash brightened every time she took a drag.

"You can clean up, if you want," she said, eyeing John's vomit-stained golf shirt. "There's a bathroom on the other side of the registration desk." She indicated the way with a toss of her pretty head.

John leaned forward on his elbows and cradled his head in his hands. He tried to make himself stop shaking and almost succeeded. "You're Skye, aren't you?" he asked weakly. "Skye Padilla. From New York."

How did he know this? she asked, and he answered that it didn't matter how he knew. He promised to tell her the whole story later. He introduced himself, told her he was Kristen Lansen's father, that he'd come to take Kristen away from this place.

"That's good. I tried to talk her into splitting. I just hope it's not too late, y'know?"

John stared into Skye's face. What did she mean, *too late?*

She lowered her eyes, avoiding his, and sucked again from her cigarette. She obviously didn't intend to answer him.

"Why did you let me in?" John asked, wanting to start her talking again.

"When you came up the driveway, I was watching from the window in my room—upstairs." She pointed upward. "I saw you go around back, and I went downstairs to the kitchen to look out through the window by the door. Then I got scared when I saw—" Here she halted for a drag on the cigarette and blew out a cloud of smoke. She shook her head, as if clearing out an unwanted image. "Anyway, I heard some shots or something, and then I heard you trying to get in through the front door a minute later. I guess I knew you were okay, y'know? I knew you were on my side, because the hamburger people were after you."

"*Hamburger* people?"

That's what they looked like—hamburger, like they'd been in a plane crash, she said. They prowled around the windows and doors at night, peering in, watching her. She knew they were bad. They were the reason she hadn't tried to escape this place.

She told him how she'd come to be here, how a skinny old man had approached her on Portland's riverfront, offered her a job, and brought her here in his car. Since then her life had been hell—slaving for the ugly old woman, Bellona Drumgule, jumping every time the hag barked, eating the awful food she cooked. The work wasn't even real housework, but digging in the garden, mostly, uprooting strange herbs and gathering berries that Mrs. Drumgule needed for whatever strange purpose. Or lugging in foul-smelling chemicals and powders from vats and bins in the stone building out back.

"I think she's a witch or something," said Skye with unsettling matter-of-factness. "She has a room in the basement where she goes every night. I hear her down there, moaning and screaming—almost like chanting, y'know? And the smells that come out of there you wouldn't believe. It's like she's brewing up spells, y'know—potions or something."

"What about my daughter? What did you mean a minute ago when you said you hoped I wasn't too late?"

Skip and Mrs. Drumgule had *done* things to Kristen since she'd arrived here, Skye said, not looking at him—every night since the very first. Peeking through a crack in her door, Skye had seen the pair of them haul the unconscious Kristen from her room on a gurney, the kind hospitals use. They'd taken her downstairs, having drugged her, apparently, for Skye had heard Mrs. Drumgule whisper about the "dose." Skye couldn't force herself to follow them down those old stone stairs.

Each time they'd kept Kristen down there for an hour or more. They'd always brought her back to her room again, still unconscious. Later Kristen had seemed upset about a puncture wound on the underside of her arm, which she usually kept bandaged. Skye had seen the wound once, and it looked like the mark of a hypodermic needle, which was something she knew about. Her own arms bore the tracks of shooting crank and chiva into her veins. Skip and Mrs. Drumgule had lied to Kristen about the wound on her arm, telling her that she'd sleepwalked and fallen on a carpet nail.

John Lansen listened to this and paled. "Listen, Skye, I'm going to take you out of here," he said, catching her small hand in his huge one. "You don't belong here. You belong with your family or someone else who cares about you, and I'm going to see that you get there. But I want to get my daughter out, too. Do you know where she is? Do you know where Skip and Mrs. Drumgule are?"

"They took her downstairs about half an hour ago. I don't think they'll bring her up for a while yet."

"She's unconscious then?"

"She was the last time I saw her."

"Is there anyone else in the house—besides Gestern, Mrs. Drumgule, Kristen, and you?"

"I don't think so, man. I've never seen anyone."

"Okay, now listen to me, Skye. I want you to take me to the basement. I want you to show me where they took Kristen."

"Hey, I can't go down there. I don't know what's down there, but whatever it is, I don't want to see it."

"It's very important that we stay together, Skye. Right now, you and I have nothing but each other, but that's okay. If we stick together and do what we need to do, we can get out of here in one piece, and we can bring Kristen out, too. Now take me to—"

"Didn't you hear what I said? I can't go down there!"

"You *can*, Skye. You'll be with me. I won't let anything happen to you. Trust me."

"Hey, like I've heard that song before, man. Old people have been telling me to trust them all my life, and every time something goes down wrong, they come back at me, y'know? It's always *me* who fucks up, right? Well, not anymore, man. If you want to go down those stairs, you can do it with yourself, because *I'm* not going."

John sighed with exasperation. "Okay, okay. I don't have time to argue with you. Can you at least show me where the stairs are?"

vii

The stairwell curved downward to the right, walled with chiseled granite blocks that produced unnerving echoes with every scuff of boot. Every ten feet hung a naked light bulb, and some of these had burned out, leaving cold, shadowy stretches.

John descended the steps slowly, holding the pistol in front of him. En route to the door of the basement, Skye Padilla had led him through the kitchen, which was a tiled expanse with a massive island counter in the center. John had swiped a long Henckel butcher knife from a rack on the island counter. He gripped the knife now in his left hand, hoping he wouldn't need it. With a little luck, his one remaining bullet would see him through the rest of the night's work.

The stairway ended in a low, narrow passageway. He headed into it and then stopped after going a short way, but only long enough to let his eyes adjust to the gloom. The ambient glare from the stairwell helped a little. The passageway turned left at a ninety-degree angle. He saw a doorjamb on his right, festooned with cobwebs and barred with wrought-iron spikes. A tarnished brass sign identified it as CAVE À VIN, which he recalled was French for wine cellar. He went on, passing two more massive wooden doors, both unmarked and stoutly locked.

The passage took a right turn now and descended half a dozen steps. A weak glow filtered out of a passage to his left, and John paused to peek around the corner before plunging in. This passage, too, descended a flight of a dozen stairs, straight as an arrow. At the base gleamed a bare bulb from the ceiling.

John ventured downward, his flesh crawling. Sounds came from a door in the passage ahead—low, urgent whispers distorted with enough echo to be unintelligible. Shadows danced across the threshold of the door, cast by firelight. John thought he saw the image of a man's head cast briefly in shadow against the granite paving stones. The whispers became louder, more urgent. He heard a moan that sounded young and feminine, but heavy with sleep—or was it thick with passion? He knew that voice: It was Kristen's.

With his heart pounding, John descended the stairs deliberately, one foot in front of the other, taking pains to make no sound. He reached the door through which the shadows danced, then stopped and peered around it.

Kristen lay naked and unconscious on a gurney in the center of a long room, an ugly, doughy woman—Mrs. Drumgule, no doubt—stroking her brow. An IV tube curved upward from a needle in Kristen's arm to a holder atop a tall chrome rack. Silhouetted against a massive, crackling fireplace stood a man naked and deformed—so deformed, in fact, that John wondered if he was a man at all. As John watched, the man vomited into a heavy black kettle on a table next to the gurney, filling the room and the hallway with heaves and grunts. What came out of the man was red and thick and steamy, like the blood of a freshly butchered chicken. The man then ladled the liquid—John wasn't ready to let himself believe that it was blood—from the kettle into a glass jar until it was full. He stoppered the jar and inverted it atop the chrome rack next to the gurney. With his deformed hands he attached the IV tube to the jar and stood back to survey his work.

Realization burst in John's mind like a thunderclap. This man, this *thing*, had drunk blood from something or someone, had regurgitated it, and was now feeding it intravenously to his daughter. Why this was happening, John could not guess. What was important, what was *critical*, was to get Kristen out of here.

He lurched through the door and leveled his revolver at the monstrosity that hovered next to the gurney. "You—hold it right there!" he screamed, his voice cracking. "Make one goddamn move, and I swear by everything holy I'll blow your filthy head off!" He glared at the old woman, whose oily face twitched with shock. "That goes for you, too, you ugly old cow. I'd just as soon kill you as—"

His eyes now fully took in the face of the naked man, twisted with hatred. This wasn't the face of a man at all. Even as John stared open-mouthed at that lunatic face, it changed; became more heavily browed; became golden-eyed, like some living idol, and toothy with yellowed needles sprouting out of its gums.

John suddenly *knew* that face, recognized its owner, despite the transformation it had undergone. This man had never *seemed* like a monster, had never seemed anything more than an ordinary mortal. Before John could mouth the name, a scabrous arm slid around his neck from behind. Long-nailed fingers caught hold of his clothing, and dead weight forced him down.

He fought with the knife and gun, fought with his fists. He fought with all he had, but still he went down, coughing and gasping from the sickly sweet scent of lavender. He managed to raise his head and scream his daughter's name just before a golf club whipped the air. Its steel head connected with his skull, and John Lansen's world went black.

23

Necessary Evils

i

The sexton left the village of Liernais at half past five in the evening, having stopped at the *poste* as his master had instructed. Sure enough, a letter had arrived. He'd only glanced at the return address long enough to see that it came from America, from a priest in Oregon.

The sun hung low in the western sky as he drove the wheezing old Citroën up the road that led from Liernais into the mountains. The glare hurt his aging eyes, causing him to drive more slowly than he wanted, but he arrived at the abbey with minutes to spare. He parked in the muddy clearing that had once been a courtyard and quickly picked his way through the ruins toward the ancient church.

L'Abbaye du Sang Sacré, what was left of it, occupied a wooded plateau in the foothills of the Morvan Mountains in central France, less than thirty-five kilometers from the city of Autun. The ruins overlooked Lac du Brinon, a shimmering body of water fed by artesian springs and mountain streams, a year-round source of irrigation for the scores of farms that dotted the valley.

The sexton entered the shadow of the ruins and moved through the nave to the bell tower, dodging collapsed columns and piles of debris that had long ago fallen from the ceiling. Built in the mid-eleventh century when Capetian kings ruled France, the original church exemplified the simple cruciform plan favored by the Cistercian monks who had commissioned it, a design that typified their austere spirit. Little of those original Romanesque walls were still visible, however. Subsequent embellishing by Cluniacs and Augustinians had given the interior intricate Gothic tracery and sculpture. Centaurs, goblins, and apes lurked over doorways and capitals. Stone carvings of Old Testament prophets flanked the altar and the stairway to the choir. Here and there headless or armless statues of Christ's disciples clung to segments of vine-covered walls.

The sexton halted in the bell tower and squinted at his watch: exactly six o'clock. Time to ring the bell to announce compline, the last of the canonical hours. He tugged on the fraying rope, and the old bell gonged feebly, not nearly as boldly as it had when both he and the bell were young, but loudly enough to notify the master that compline was at hand.

The sexton labored with the bell a full five minutes, wondering as he often did why the master still observed the canonical hours after all these years. L'Abbaye du Sang Sacré was no longer home to any monks. The crumbling church no longer served a parish. For that matter, the Vatican had excommunicated the master himself long before anyone in the surrounding villages was even alive.

What was the point of it? the sexton wondered. Why should the master care about ringing the bell for matins at three o'clock in the morning, or for lauds at dawn, or for vespers in the afternoon? The sexton would have bet that observing the offices was the master's way of reminding himself that time does indeed march on, that minutes and hours eventually become centuries and millennia, that nothing in creation lasts forever.

ii

The sexton left the bell tower and moved toward the altar, rubbing his shoulder to work out the ache of pulling the rope. He came to a passageway behind the altar. A stone carving of the head of the prophet Jeremiah guarded a heavy wooden door, which had hinges of squeaky leather. Centuries ago some imbecile had taken a chisel to the marble facing above the carving and etched: *La Barrière d'enfer.*

The passage led beneath the cloister and ended in a chamber adjacent to the wine cellar of the priory. The sexton negotiated the route with no need of light, so many thousands of times had he done this. He climbed a curving stairway to the main level of the house, which lay mostly in ruin. He entered an inner suite that was still intact and made his way to the chamber that served as his master's study and music room. Before knocking, he leaned close to the massive door and listened for some clue as to whether it was appropriate to intrude. He heard a complex drum rhythm, the metallic strains of a tenor saxophone, and a husky voice singing in the impenetrable English of an American black man. The master's one passion of the outer world was American jazz.

The volume of the music suddenly lowered.

"Come in, Lucien," said a deep voice from within before the sexton could knock. "I've got a fire going. It may be warm out there, but in here it's cold, as always."

The sexton entered the windowless room, which smelled tartly of birch smoke and old books. Lining the walls were hundreds of volumes, some of them dusty and covered with webs, as if no one had touched them in centuries. Others looked clean and well used. Among them were the seminal works in astrology, alchemy, and magic, old knowledge from an age when science was an infant. The sexton himself had read some of them under the master's tutelage—Euclid's *Elements*, Ptolemy's *Optica*, and arcane Arabic works by Alkindi, Rhazes, and Alfarabi.

The master stood next to the blackened fireplace, holding a bulky, leather-bound volume in his hands, which the sexton recognized as the most notorious in the vast collection, *The Book of Rahab*, to which legend ascribed a formula for bringing back the dead, as well as other dreadful bits of knowledge.

Gautier Le Fanu was a sinewy man whose face appeared much older than his body, whose spare cheeks were pale from seclusion in the sunless priory. His dark eyes glittered wetly from deep sockets beneath silvered brows. Thick, white hair swept back from his patrician forehead to curl tightly at the edges of his stiff Roman collar. The wrinkles at the corner of his mouth and eyes suggested that he smiled often, maybe even laughed occasionally.

The sexton gasped upon seeing that Le Fanu was not wearing his customary black cassock, but rather a natty tweed sport coat and well-pressed tan trousers. All that remained of his usual garb were the Roman collar and his wire-framed spectacles.

"You may close your mouth, Lucien," said Le Fanu. "You don't want to catch any flies."

"Forgive me, *monsieur le curé*. It has been so long since I've seen you wear anything other than your—"

"Yes, yes. I understand. If you look more closely you'll see that I've shaved and bathed as well. I can't very well go into the world looking and smelling like a mendicant friar, now can I?"

The sexton glanced at the leather suitcase that lay open on the Persian carpet. Arrayed in and around it were neat piles of underwear, socks, toiletries, and, of course, the books that Gautier Le Fanu could not do without. Nearby lay a compact stereo tapeplayer, a "boom box," the Americans called it, and a short stack of cassettes labeled with names like B. B. King, Koko Taylor, and Albert Collins. The master obviously meant to make a journey, and he meant to take along suitable music.

iii

"The letter, if you please," said Le Fanu, holding out his hand. The sexton pulled it from his pocket and handed it over. Le Fanu placed the heavy book on a nearby cherrywood desk and opened the envelope. He wandered to the far wall, reading silently as he went. He absently switched off the expensive Japanese stereo that occupied a niche among a collection of vials, bottles, glass jars, and earthen jugs on the shelves.

"My worst fears are confirmed, Lucien," said Le Fanu, removing his spectacles and fixing the sexton with a hard gaze. "My servant in America has obviously failed to kill the heir of the Sire de l'Hier. Her magic isn't strong enough, apparently, which means that I must go to America and do the job myself."

"And this is why you've packed? You knew what the letter would contain before it arrived?"

Le Fanu smiled in his self-satisfied way. "You should know by now, my good Lucien, that I have many ways of knowing things." He moved to the cherry desk, which had clawed legs that rested atop waxen blocks. On its surface was a cloth of red satin, embroidered with a pentagram around a Star of David. In the center of the two stars, resting atop a smaller block of wax, lay a small wooden cabinet. Mounted in a ring of pewter on its surface was a disk of glossy obsidian.

"Ah, the scrying mirror told you this."

"Of course. Time and distance are no barriers to those who are adept with the mirror. I've never set foot in America, Lucien, but I know well the place I must go. I've seen the hills around the

village, the great wide river, the forest on the mountainside, even
the faces of the people. I won't be lost when I arrive there."

"Will you go alone?"

"Yes. You must stay here and care for things, keep our household running. Now if you'll assist me. . . ." Le Fanu gestured toward a tall steamer trunk that stood behind the door through
which the sexton had just entered. The sexton went to it, pulled
it open, and coughed after inhaling the musty air that came out
of it. Some craftsman from long ago—the sexton's own grandfather, perhaps—had fitted the trunk with scores of wooden parti-
tions and crannies, many of which now housed spiders, judging
from the gauzy webs that draped the handles on the drawers and
hinged panels. Each compartment bore its number on a band of
tarnished copper.

"Surely you don't plan to take along this relic, *monsieur le
curé.*"

"Oh, but I do. I'll have need of magic, where I'm going. To
use magic properly, one needs the right ingredients. One cannot
carry one's ingredients in just any old suitcase."

"I suppose not. What do you want me to do?"

Le Fanu slipped his spectacles on again and hoisted the heavy
book from the table where he'd placed it. "I'll read to you those
items I must take with me, and you will fetch them and place
them into the compartment I specify. Also, you will record on
paper the number of the compartment into which you place each.
Shall we begin?"

"Very well, *monsieur le curé,*" said the sexton without enthusiasm. He'd witnessed many horrors while serving Le Fanu, but
handling the substances of the old priest's arcane craft still made
him nervous. He went to an antique secretary that stood along
the wall behind Le Fanu's desk and rummaged through the top
drawer for a pen and a pad. "I am ready," he said, squaring his
shoulders.

"Come now, Lucien," said Le Fanu, his eyes twinkling. "Such
a face."

"I won't pretend that I enjoy touching these things."

"Don't be a child. They are only spices, most of them—
innocent powders and oils, things one can buy in any *marché.*"

"But some of them are not so innocent." The sexton pointed
to a jar on the shelf behind Le Fanu, one that contained a shapeless mass floating in a cloudy yellow liquid.

Le Fanu chuckled indulgently. "Not to fret. I'll have no need of the brain of a hanged man, or even"—he reached up and pulled an earthen jar from the top shelf; he held it out toward the sexton, who shrank back—"the liver of an unbaptized child. Aside from a small vial containing the semen of an old wizard I once knew, I'll take nothing that will even raise the eyebrows of an American customs officer."

"I don't know how you tolerate keeping such things close to you," breathed the sexton. "As if life in this place is not bad enough, doing the things you must do."

"Really, my dear Lucien, your squeamishness over such trivia as a few pickled body parts amazes me, in view of the other horrors to which you've been a party all these years."

"I understand the horrors, as did my father before me and his father before him. It's the magic and its accursed accoutrements that make me uneasy, the very things for which the Holy Father excommunicated you. My soul is perhaps salvageable, if I keep from staining it with the abominations found in your books." He nodded toward *The Book of Rahab* that Le Fanu cradled in his arms.

"If one chooses to do battle with the Sire de l'Hier, one must use the weapons he does," replied Le Fanu gently. "And the chief weapon in his arsenal is the Old Truth—that is to say, *magic*. The church excommunicated me, Lucien, because it's blind to any truth but its own. The practice of magic is no mortal sin, as the church would have us believe. It's merely a necessary evil. Surely you can see that."

"You have never told me why it is so important to find and destroy this Sire de l'Hier."

The old priest stared at the sexton a long moment, his jaw unhinged, as though he could not believe this was true. He turned toward the desk and lowered the heavy book to its surface once again, then leaned against the edge and crossed his arms.

"All this time you've served me, Lucien, and you've never known? I have a faint memory of telling the story to *someone*—I thought it was you, but it must have been your father. When you've lived as long as I, your memory becomes a clutter."

"Tell me, *monsieur le curé*, who is this Sire de l'Hier, and why do you hate him so?"

The priest touched his fingertips to his cheek. The twinkle disappeared from his eyes. "You may think of him as the most vile heretic of all time, Lucien," he said finally, his voice low and full. "You may think of him as a wizard, a necromancer, a beast who reads the future in the entrails of young women. You may think of him as a poet and storyteller, a teacher, a man who seeks truth. But most importantly, Lucien"—Le Fanu's voice became even lower, and the sound of it produced a chill that the sexton felt between his shoulder blades—"you must think of him as a vampire."

24

Dust to Dust

i

News of John's accident had traveled quickly. By Sunday afternoon the Lansen house teemed with well-wishers and grievers, most of whom had brought casseroles, cakes, and pies that occupied every available square inch of the dining room table and the kitchen countertops. Mark recognized family friends and acquaintances who'd come from as far away as Coos Bay on Oregon's southern coast, from Portland, Salem, and Seattle—John's legion of friends, colleagues, clients, and admirers.

Mark tried to smile as he met each guest, but couldn't. He hadn't slept for two days; he felt empty and sick and anxious. Smiling was out of the question. He could feel the tremors of volcanic grief building inside himself, growing hotter, stronger, approaching the point of eruption. He wondered how much longer he could resist collapsing into a bawling, blubbering mess.

He'd recounted the details of the tragic story so many times in answer to sympathetic questions that by now he felt like a tape recorder: *Dad was working late at the office. He went out for some reason, maybe just for a drive in order to clear his head. The Suburban went off the Benson Creek bridge, and—* here he always breathed deeply to clear an ache in his throat. *—he went through the windshield. Will Settergren found him around two on Saturday morning.*

He went to check on Marta, who had retired to her bedroom. A family friend sat with her, holding her hand, as she lay on the bed. She looked depleted, exhausted.

"I've just heard there's to be an autopsy," she said with anguish in her eyes. "Do you know anything about this? The very thought of it makes me want to—" She coughed, took a deep breath. "Why do we need an autopsy if John was killed in a wreck? Isn't the cause of death perfectly obvious?"

Mark explained that Sheriff Conrad, one of John's oldest and dearest friends, had spoken with Nat Schell, the doctor who had examined John's body at the mortuary. Nat had seen something he thought strange, if not faintly suspicious—head wounds that seemed inconsistent with injuries someone would ordinarily sustain in a smashup. Nat was no pathologist, said Sheriff Conrad, and he didn't pretend to be, but the wounds reminded him of those he'd seen just three months ago on a murder victim. So the sheriff had officially opened an investigation and had ordered the body shipped to Portland for a medicolegal postmortem.

"A *murder* victim? He thinks John was—was *done in* by someone?"

"He didn't say that, Mom. He just wants the opinion of a forensic pathologist on the cause of death."

"Did he say what was so suspicious about these—these head wounds?"

"Do you really want to hear about it?"

"Mark, I wouldn't've asked if I didn't."

"You might recall that Bernie Pellagrini beat Fran to death with a nine iron. According to Nat Schell, the marks on Dad's head looked similar to the ones on Fran."

Marta looked dazed and sat up slowly on the bed. After taking a sip of water from a glass on the bedtable, she asked about Kristen. Had she surfaced yet?

Mark felt the ache in his throat again. He'd called the Nehalem Mountain Inn half a dozen times on Saturday morning to tell Kristen the horrible news about John, but he hadn't gotten past an answering machine. In exasperation he'd driven up to Gestern Hall that afternoon, only to hear from old Mrs. Drumgule that Kristen had packed her things and left the previous day. Where she'd gone Mrs. Drumgule professed not to know.

"No word from her yet," he answered miserably.

"Something must've happened to her," said Marta, pressing a handkerchief to her mouth. "She wouldn't run off without telling the family, no matter how angry she was with us." Fresh tears flooded her eyes. "It almost seems beyond coincidence that John should die and Kristen should disappear on the same day."

That same thought had crossed Mark's mind a thousand times since yesterday. He sat next to his mother on the bed, put his arm around her, and kissed her cheek. "Please don't worry, Mom. I talked to Sheriff Conrad about this, and he said there's no reason to consider her a missing person. If we don't hear from her by tomorrow, he promised to go up to Gestern Hall and ask some questions."

ii

"Blessed be the God and Father of our Lord Jesus Christ, the source of all mercy and the God of all consolation. . . ." Pastor Hjortlin's melodious voice echoed through the sanctuary of St. John's Luthern Church, where the friends and loved ones of John Lansen had thronged to hear words spoken of him, prayers prayed for him, and hymns sung to celebrate his life.

Mark sat next to Marta in the front pew, holding her hand tightly in his. To his left sat Deidre and Tad. The absence of Kristen, John Lansen's only child by blood, was conspicuous and painful. Arrayed behind them was a third of the population of Oldenburg, crammed into pews or standing shoulder to shoulder in the aisles, jammed into the narthex and streaming out into the churchyard.

"He comforts us in all our sorrows so that we can comfort others in their sorrows . . . ," intoned Pastor Hjortlin, a fleshy man who stood like a snowy mountain in his vestments. He moved to the bier and supervised a pair of red-robed acolytes in placing a pall over the coffin. John Lansen's body had arrived from the forensic pathology lab in Portland only minutes before the start of the service, but hardly any of the mourners in the church knew this.

"Thanks be to God," said the congregation.

No, thought Mark. No thanks for *this*.

His eyes found the red oil lamp on the altar, and he imagined that it was glaring at him, just as the Blood Star had glared at him in a dream only seven days earlier. Bloody ether swirled in his head like a potent perfume, making him dizzy and weak, but at the same time angry. He became nauseous and wished fervently that the service would end.

Pastor Hjortlin said something that Mark didn't hear, and the congregation got to its feet.

"O God of grace and glory," the pastor continued, *"we re-*

member before you today our brother, John. We thank you for giving him to us to know and love as a companion in our pilgrimage on earth. In your boundless compassion, console us who mourn."

"Alleluia," responded the congregation, reading from the Lutheran Book of Worship. *"Jesus Christ is the firstborn of the dead; to him be the glory and power forever."*

After the celebration of the Eucharist, the service adjourned to the Benson Creek Cemetery. Mark, Deidre, Tad, and Marta rode in the limousine behind the hearse through the hilly heart of town, past the Hotel Cathlamet and the Chamber of Commerce; past the Sons of Norway lodge, of which John Lansen had been a proud member; past the Lansen law office, the Kalapuya County School Board Association, and the Stadtler Funeral Home, whose owner and president was staging this funeral.

Rain beat down on the motorcade as it mounted the hills and rounded the curves through the business district. Mark listened to the dolorous pounding of raindrops and watched the sights of Oldenburg flow by his window. He was intensely conscious now that his father was gone forever, that the streets where John had walked, the café where he'd taken his daily coffee break, the building where he'd worked, would continue to exist, but John would not. This seemed both inappropriate and unthinkable.

"In sure and certain hope of the resurrection to eternal life through our Lord Jesus Christ, we commend to almighty God our brother John," said Pastor Hjortlin over the muddy hole in the ground, *"and we commit his body to the elements; earth to earth, ashes to ashes, dust to dust. . . ."*

Mark gazed at the expensive mahogany casket, which was beaded with raindrops, and said his final good-bye. John would have liked this, he knew, the pious ceremony and liturgy, the gathering of friends on his behalf, the mournful prayers. John was a man who believed in institutions. Though he harbored no illusions about their divine origin, he believed institutions represented the goodness to which mankind aspired. The church was one of these, the law another. Institutions gave men a formula for goodness, he had often said, a method for living peacefully together, a blueprint for pursuing justice.

Something made Mark raise his eyes to Nehalem Mountain. Gauzy clouds shrouded its summit, hiding from view the old stone mansion that stood there. Mark felt the stab of irrational

fear. This was part of it, he was certain—Nehalem Mountain,
Gestern Hall, the death of his father, and all the other insanity
he'd suffered in the past ten days. Some dreadful culmination
was at hand.

"Lord Jesus," prayed the pastor, *"by your death you took
away the sting of death. . . ."*

Mark scarcely heard the prayer. His gaze wandered to the edge
of the cemetery, where a bushy colony of elderberry held forth
its clusters of budding fruit, where massive black cottonwoods
towered over crumbling gravestones. His mouth dropped open
when he saw the figure that stood in the shadow of a tall tree—a
hoary old woman dressed in a sopping overcoat, bags slung over
her back, her white hair matted to her cheeks. Her hands were
blurs as they urged the spinning wheel in its rotation, creating a
windy whir that invaded Mark's mind and drowned the pastor's
voice. The hag's stare bored into his. Her ragged lips formed
words that he could hear as surely as if she were standing next
to him and not a hundred feet away: *"Root it out, Mark!"*

His knees buckled, and he almost swooned. With the help of
strong hands at his elbows, he regained control and backed away
from the grave, avoiding toppling into it under John Lansen's
casket. The mist in his head parted, and he looked back toward
the elderberries and cottonwoods, but saw only a smear of movement as something disappeared into the foliage. He swallowed,
straightened—

*"God of Peace—who brought again from the dead our Lord
Jesus Christ, the great shepherd of sheep, through the blood of
the everlasting covenant. . . ."*

—and turned to thank the owner of the hands that had shored
him up. The face he saw was ivory-skinned, with lustrous black
hair that hung straight to the shoulders. It had huge dark eyes
that looked suitable for hypnosis. It wore a faint smile that
seemed both wise and kind.

Mark felt raindrops hitting his tongue.

*". . . make you perfect in every good work to do his will, work-
ing in you that which is well-pleasing in his sight; through Jesus
Christ, to whom be glory forever and ever."*

"Amen."

And Kyleen LeBreaux, Mark's therapist, whispered hello.

iii

He held up well through the afternoon, considering what had happened at the cemetery. Acting on Kyleen's advice, he threw himself into providing hospitality to the throngs at the Lansen house. Velma Selvig, bless her heart, had taken command on the food front, having rustled up refreshments from the kitchen of the Royal Kokanee Inn. Tressa Downey was her vice commander, and between the two of them they catered the affair on short notice. No one among the horde went away hungry or thirsty.

Late in the afternoon Mark spotted his wife coming down the stairs with Tad in tow, her arms laden with Tad's luggage. He intercepted them before they reached the landing, and asked Deidre what was going on. She was loading Thaddeus's things into her car, she replied—to take him home, of course.

"Upstairs!" Mark seethed, poking the air with his thumb. To Tad he said, "You're not going anywhere, so take your stuff back to your room." Tad obeyed instantly, his eyes huge with concern. Mark herded his wife into his own room and closed the door heavily behind him.

"Care to explain this little drama?" asked Deidre, folding her arms across her chest.

"No problem: Tad's staying here with me—bottom line, end of discussion. You're free to go, of course. You probably have dinner lined up with your boss—old what's his name?—so you'd better get cracking."

Deidre rolled her eyes and went to the window to gaze into the gray afternoon sky. "We're not mincing words today, are we?"

"No, we're not."

She turned to face him again. "I just assumed it would be better for Thaddeus to spend the summer in Portland, under the circumstances. After what's happened, and everything you've been going through—"

"You assumed wrong."

"Oh, really? Do you think it's healthy for him to stay here, after losing his grandfather—*here*, where everything he sees and touches and smells reminds him of . . ."

"Yes. It's healthy for him. And healthy for me, too."

"You're not serious."

"I *am* serious. We promised him a summer in Oldenburg, and that's what he's going to get."

Deidre balled her fists and planted them on her slim hips. She wore a navy blue suit with a beige shirt of costly silk, topped off with a flouncy scarf of bright paisley—an outfit barely funereal enough to wear to a funeral, and then only technically. She looked wonderful, and Mark detested himself for thinking so.

"Mark, do me a favor and look at yourself," she demanded. "Have you done that lately?"

"I do it every time I shave."

"Don't try to be funny. If you look at yourself, you'll see that you're not well. You're run-down, distraught. You're in no shape to handle a nine-year-old. I'm taking Thaddeus home, Mark, where I can take care of him properly. He'll have his own room, his own things, his friends—he'll have everything he needs to put all this sadness behind him."

"Deidre, I don't *want* him to put his grandfather's death behind him. I want him to remember it all his life. I want him to remember how much John Lansen meant to him, how much John Lansen loved him. More than that I want to be here for him, to go through the grieving with him and help him sort it out."

From beyond the window came a fulmination of thunder, deep and rumbling, though the rain had stopped. "My God," moaned Deidre, "I think you've totally flipped out. Don't you see what you're doing, Mark? You're using Thaddeus to hurt me. You're so damned angry over the sorry state of our marriage that you're willing to use any weapon to cause me pain, or to cause yourself pain, for that matter. You're doing this because you think we both deserve it, because it satisfies some perverted notion you have about justice."

"Gosh, I've underestimated you all these years, lamb chop. You're not only an architect, you're a fucking psychologist to boot. You're a regular Renaissance woman. You're so smart you could probably sit on an ice cream cone and tell me what flavor it is. Too bad you don't understand plain fucking English—Tad's staying with *me!* Unless you think you're capable of putting me on the floor two falls out of three I suggest you strap yourself into your Caddy and take yourself down the road, while you're still able."

Deidre shrank in the face of Mark's vehemence. Seldom had he ever stood his ground against her so squarely, so immovably.

Never had he implied that he might get physically ugly. Her face paled. She yanked a pack of Marlboros from the pocket of her suit and lit one with trembling fingers.

"Okay, as long as we're getting down to the bone," she said, "you may as well know the latest. Clay and I have decided we want to live together, maybe get married. I've talked to a lawyer, and he's drawing up some papers to lay on you. I'll probably file for divorce within the next few weeks. If I were you, I'd get a lawyer, since custody of Thaddeus will no doubt be an issue. We'll need to reach some kind of understanding, don't you think? I'm willing to give you a bunch of money, enough to set you up for a long time, but I'm not willing to give up Thaddeus. In fact, I'm going to fight for exclusive custody."

Something must have happened to Mark's face when he heard this, some contortion that transmitted his rage in a way Deidre had never seen it. He felt the fury spew silently out of him. He saw Deidre's own face go ghastly white as she stared at him, her eyes wide and unblinking, her mouth hanging open.

"You must be dreaming, you miserable bitch," he heard himself say in a voice he didn't quite recognize—deep, sonorous, raspy. "*You're* the one who's been doing the extramarital porking, not me. *You're* the one who's filing for divorce and breaking up our home. *You're* the one who's an unfit parent, and I'll make that point abundantly clear to the court."

"Yes, but you're the one who's crazy! I'll show that you—" Fright choked off her words at the sight of Mark's face, and she slapped a hand over her mouth. "My *God!*" she exclaimed under her breath. Suddenly she made for the door, and Mark made no move to stop her.

25

Children of Clay

i

Kristen Lansen closed the heavy book and leaned back from the small reading table in her room. Her eyes were bleary and her head ached. She couldn't read another word, so she snapped off the reading light and dressed to go downstairs.

In the six days she'd been at Gestern Hall, she'd managed to plow through only this and one other old book among the hundreds that Skip Gestern had made available to her. The latest was *Ecclesiastical Writings Pursuant to the Cult of the Gethsemanites*, a huge volume compiled by someone named Horace Fleischmann in 1820, translated by none other than Clovis Gestern in 1935. The translator must have been Skip Gestern's grandfather, Kristen supposed.

It was challenging reading—flowery language, archaic syntax, and subject matter that seemed woefully irrelevant to the late twentieth century. Most of it was morbid stuff about a religious cult that Skip had said figured in the history of the Gestern family, the Gethsemanites. Thus far, Kristen had found no mention in either book of anyone named Gestern, however, except for the translator of the second volume. Both works concerned the Roman Catholic Church's attempts during the Middle Ages and the Renaissance to annihilate a movement called the Gethsemanite Heresy. An early leader of the cult was a mysterious, almost mythical figure named Lord Yesterday, to whom legend attributed the most vile, gut-turning atrocities Kristen had ever heard of. Many churchmen had actually thought the man a vampire and a sorcerer.

To her surprise, Kristen had found all this arcane folderol mildly interesting, even at the outset. The more she read, the more fascinated she'd become. Now she was downright enthralled, and couldn't wait to begin the next book on her list, an ancient tome with a frayed cover and tarnished brass corner guards: *Commentaries on the Old Truth and Gethsemanism* by—who else?—Clovis Gestern.

She could read no more for now, however. Her eyes couldn't take it, and she felt hungry. Besides, she had errands to run, the most important of which was popping in at home to show her mom and dad that she was alive and in one piece. She felt a little guilty for not getting in touch with them since leaving so abruptly. Maybe she would even stay for dinner.

Wearing white linen walking shorts and a Hard Rock Café T-shirt, she left her room with her car keys dangling from her fingertips. She was about to turn onto the staircase when she saw movement at the far end of the corridor. Skye Padilla stood there and stared at her condolingly, as if Kristen had some terrible disease. When she made a move toward her, Skye bolted and ran down the rear corridor.

Strange girl, thought Kristen.

Kristen descended the stairs, and Mrs. Drumgule met her at the lower landing. "I was just about to fetch you," she said, her S's whistling. "Mr. Gestern wishes to see you in his office before dinner." She smiled in that god-awful, snaggletoothed way of hers, and Kristen even managed to smile back.

ii

Skip Gestern listened to her progress report with a faint smile on his face, his elbows resting on his knees and his fingers tented under his chin. When she finished, he leaned back in the settee and lit a cigarette.

"I see that you're finding this work every bit as fascinating as I knew you would," he said. "But you've only just scratched the surface, you know. The story of the Gestern family gets even better." He winked faintly. "And *juicier.*"

"I'm frankly surprised that I could ever get into this kind of stuff," said Kristen. "I've never been much of a history fanatic. That's my brother's department—"

"Your brother Mark."

"Yeah. How did you know that?"

"I get around a little," chuckled Skip. "I'd like very much to meet him sometime. Sorry to interrupt—go on."

"I was just saying that I never thought I'd get into stuff like ecclesiastical letters about some old cult. I really don't know why I find it so fascinating. It's almost like—" She wasn't sure what she wanted to say. Her head swam a little, as if some drug had fouled her synapses. Was it the red wine that Skip had poured for her? She felt as if a warm film had dropped over her eyes, making everything slightly fuzzy.

Kristen shook her head and blinked the feeling away. "Tell me something," she said, setting aside her glass. "Do you believe all that stuff about Lord Yesterday? Do you think he really read the future in the entrails of women—what's the word?"

"Antinopomancy."

"Right. Or that he was a vampire or a werewolf?"

"*Was?*" he asked.

"Okay, okay. I know that 'Lord Yesterday' was a title taken by every leader of the Gethsemanites—it couldn't've been the same guy from the time of Christ all through the nineteenth century! I'll rephrase the question: *Were* these guys really vampires and werewolves?"

Skip drew a lungful of smoke from his cigarette and blew it out. Shafts of light flowed from the stained-glass window through the smoke cloud—amber, green, and blue. The sun was sinking low. Once again, Kristen had slept well past noon, which had become her routine since moving into Gestern Hall.

"I find it hard to believe in vampires and werewolves, at least as they're portrayed in literature," Skip said, gazing at her through the smoke. "I suspect that the legends surrounding Lord Yesterday had more to do with his heretical religious beliefs than any factual occurrences. The church hated him so vehemently, considered him so foul, that any outrage seemed possible if it concerned him, even vampirism and lycanthropy."

From her reading, Kristen knew this: Lord Yesterday and his followers believed that Christ, on the eve of his arrest by Pilate, retired to the Garden of Gethsemane to seek help from the ancient powers of darkness, not to commune with his Father in heaven, as the Gospels held. The basis for this heretical notion was an ancient scroll written by an unnamed "necromancer" whom Christ had secretly asked to accompany him to the garden, according to the cult's teachings. Employing the powers of the old "Dark Deities," claimed the cult, Christ rose from the dead after his crucifixion, not by any power given him by the God of the Jews. The Gethsemanites thus advocated a mixture of Judeo-Christianity with the "Old Truth," through which its followers could work miracles, using magic and folk spells. Orthodoxy found such an idea abhorrent, predictably.

"What about antinopomancy, then?" Kristen wanted to know. "Did they really practice a ritual so—so—" Words failed her.

"So bloody, so murderous? I think so, Kristen. As you keep on reading, you'll discover other features of the Old Truth that seem easily as disgusting, all of them necessary to achieve true power. The Gethsemanites believed in these things and practiced them."

Kristen made a face. She suggested that this was a subject best left out of the public relations campaign for the Nehalem Mountain Inn. Skip chuckled and agreed with her.

They stood, and she felt a bit tipsy. Skip guided her to the door of the study and said he hoped to see her at dinner. She replied that she planned to have dinner at her parents' house this evening. Maybe she would see him later that night—she hoped so. Skip's face suddenly went blank, and he closed the door without saying another word.

iii

Kristen felt better when she pushed through the massive front doors into the passage that led to the porte cochere. The air was piney and rich with summer. She regretted that she'd not gotten out of the house earlier. Normally she was an avid outdoor person, not prone to staying cooped up inside.

She stopped cold when she passed through to the porte cochere. Her car was gone. She walked a few steps toward the front yard and saw nothing but an empty drive leading to the gateposts at Queen Molly Road. Skip must have moved her car into the garage, she figured, to make room for guests' cars.

Someone grabbed her by the shoulder as she stepped back into the foyer, and she gasped. Skye Padilla pulled her toward a small, dark anteroom, where stood a heavy carved writing table and padded chairs with pointed backs. They sat under the gaze of a suit of armor.

"What's this about?" demanded Kristen. "I'm kind of in a hurry, so make it quick, okay?"

"I need to tell you something," said the girl in a voice that was close to breaking. "I should've told you before now, y'know, but I didn't have the stones, man. I can't put it off any longer."

"I've wanted to talk with you, too, Skye. But when I saw you earlier, you acted like I had bubonic plague." She squeezed the girl's arm. "I've missed you at dinner, by the way. I hope that eating alone isn't a permanent arrangement for you."

"Look, I'm not s'posed to be talking to you, y'know, so I better get on with it. Three nights ago your old man was here—John Lansen, he said his name was. I let him in so the hamburger people wouldn't get him. I think he shot one of 'em, and I figured he was an okay guy, if *they* were after him. He was looking for *you*, man—"

"The *hamburger* people? He *shot* one of them?"

"They're the ones I told you are always spying on me through the windows. They've got faces like hamburger, I swear to God."

"You're sure it was my father?"

She described John Lansen with enough detail to convince Kristen.

"Skye, why didn't you bring him up to my room? I would've wanted to see him—you must've known that."

The girl explained why this hadn't been possible, that Skip Gestern and Bellona Drumgule had taken Kristen down into the basement of the house, where they'd done things to her while she was unconscious or drugged—things that Skye didn't dare guess about. John Lansen had gone down there to rescue her, armed with a gun and a butcher knife. Skye couldn't say exactly what had happened then. The hamburger people obviously had gotten down there somehow, maybe through a hidden entrance. She'd heard their horrible, gurgling voices.

At this point Skye's strength failed, and she could no longer hold back the tears. They spilled from the corners of her dark eyes and flowed down her cheeks, over the little scar at the corner of her mouth, and down her chin. They dripped onto her fisted hands, onto Kristen's hand.

She'd heard noises as she listened from the doorway to the basement stairs, she said, the gruesome noises of fighting and anger and pain. Hiding in the pantry and peering out through a crack in the door, she'd seen Skip Gestern and Bellona Drumgule bring the body of John Lansen up through the kitchen. They'd wrapped it in black plastic garbage bags and taken it out, presumably into the forest to bury it.

Skye had mustered the courage to dart outside to the spot where she'd earlier seen John Lansen shoot the woman with the badly bashed head. She was certain that he had carried something, a bag or a briefcase, but he'd been empty-handed when she let him in through the front door, except for his gun. Sure enough, near the rear entryway she'd found a flashlight and a briefcase, which she'd stashed behind the tapestry next to this very table. She wanted Kristen to take them, since they might be evidence, if anyone ever investigated John Lansen's death.

"Let me see them," Kristen said, her voice trembling.

Skye pulled the tapestry aside and brought out the battered old briefcase, the one Kristen knew her father had owned since passing the Oregon bar exam long before she was even a twinkle in his eye, a gift from his own proud father. Next came the flashlight, the old Coleman that had hung on a hook in the mudroom of the Lansen house.

Grief welled up inside Kristen, flooding her eyes and burning her cheeks. She would have jumped up and fled the house if Mrs. Drumgule hadn't appeared suddenly next to the suit of armor, doughy and urgent-eyed as always. A mean smile stretched her lips.

"Ah, my children of clay, I've found you. Dinner will be served soon, and I know you'll want to wash up." She walked a few paces away, but stopped and turned toward them again. "Skye, it's no longer necessary for you to eat your dinner alone. Since you've told Miss Lansen everything you've seen, or *thought* you've seen, there's no longer any point in isolating you." She giggled abominably. "We have no secrets anymore, do we? As for you, my dear Kristen Lansen, please don't plan to have your dinner anywhere but here." She spun on her heels and disappeared down the corridor.

Kristen shuddered and blinked away tears.

26

A Moonlit Hunt

i

When the janitorial crew at the Safeway store finished some-time around eleven, Bayliss's ThriftyKwik became the sole out-post of life and light on Commerce Way. The Drug Fair next door to the Safeway had gone dark at nine.

Sixteen-year-old Brett Omdahl had busied himself all evening with restocking the shelves and buffing the floor. Not one cus-tomer had dropped into the ThriftyKwik for a tank of gas, a six-pack of beer, or even a lousy pack of butts.

"You might as well hang it up, trooper," Gary Bayliss called to him over the howl of the buffer. "It's not quite eleven yet, but I'll pay you for a whole shift. A kid your age needs his sleep."

Brett shrugged out of his apron and went to the back room. He slung his knapsack over his shoulder and hoisted his skateboard from its place in a corner. "See you tomorrow, Gary," he called over his shoulder. "Tell Gretchen hi for me, okay?"

The air outside was thick and warm, and Mars glared bril-liantly overhead. Fudd, his "bodyguard," leapt up from his spot near the garbage Dumpster to meet him, to lick his hand, to dance around the hard asphalt.

"Ready to go, boy? Ready to hit the street?" The big dog whined and bowed low with his front paws far out in front of him, as collies do, baring his teeth in a rottweiler's "smile." Fudd was ready and had been for the past six hours.

Brett stepped onto his board and pushed off, filling the night with the clack and grind of his wheels. He rounded the corner of the ThriftyKwik to head for the front lot and Commerce Way, and Fudd loped after him, toenails ticking on the asphalt.

ii

As the crow flies, the distance between the ThriftyKwik and
the Omdahl home was about six blocks, but a skateboard is not
a crow. Brett customarily made the trip much longer than necessary, because nighttime was his one chance to really rip. At night
he had little or no automobile traffic to worry about, no pedestrians to get in his way, no cops to chase him down and hassle him
about the illegality of skating on the public roadways of Oldenburg. He'd skated these hilly, twisty streets for nearly ten years
and knew every curve, every chuckhole and rut, every crack in
the sidewalks.

His parents had begged him not to skate at night. They'd
begged him to walk directly home after work and spare them
hideous visions of their oldest boy splattered all over the grille of
someone's car, or imbedded in the trunk of a tree, or lying in a
gutter with a broken head. Even Gretchen had gotten into the act,
extracting his promise to go straight home after work.

He powered slowly up Church Avenue, past the International
Order of Odd Fellows lodge with its dirty yellow windows. An
old Willie and Waylon song rolled through the front door into the
street—something about someone running from the *Federales*.
He and Fudd made their way uphill toward the intersection of
Main and Church, where stood Baldridge's Family Eatery, and
across the street from it, the Lower Columbia Savings and Loan,
both dark. As he cruised into the center of the silent intersection
he glanced to his left, up the steep hill that carried Main Street
past Spurlock's Realty, Oldenburg Optical, and half a dozen
other small businesses that operated out of humble storefronts.
He saw not a soul, not a moving car, not even a wandering cat.

For some reason Fudd forsook his patrolling to trot at Brett's
side, which wasn't like him. "What's wrong, boy?" Brett cuffed
the big dog's ear. "You feeling spooky, too?" Fudd licked his
master's fingers and stayed close.

Spooky—was that what he'd said? Brett scolded himself, ac-
cused himself of getting as bad as Gretchen, who these days
talked about the Bad Thing that crept around town after the sun
had fallen. She didn't claim to know what it was, but declared
only that she could feel it in the river breezes. Or hear it in the
chatter of crickets and night birds. Or some such shit.

Everyone in town was conscious of it in his or her own way,

Gretchen insisted, which was why hardly anyone went out after dark anymore. The Bad Thing was responsible for the death of her beloved Father Briggs. She couldn't say how she knew this, only that she knew it. If she'd not seemed so deadly serious, or if her delicate face hadn't been so pale with grief, Brett would have scoffed and reminded her that Father Briggs had taken his own life. The man had obviously been sicker than hell, because only a certifiable sicko would subject himself to such an excruciating death, when a gun to the head would have done the same job with little if any pain and a much smaller mess.

iii

West of the intersection with Main, huge evergreens and weeping birches lined both walks. Respectable bungalows crouched behind clumps of azalea, rhododendron, and Indian plum. Within sight of one another stood the trio of churches for which the old avenue had been named.

St. Pius X Roman Catholic Church was a dinosaurian shadow against the night sky, a hulking dead space that blotted out the stars. Next to it was the rectory, dark and lifeless now that Father Briggs had launched himself toward his final reward. Farther west loomed St. John's Lutheran, an ornate monstrosity of locally quarried stone, the church in which Brett had been baptized and confirmed. A dull glow filtered out through its peaked windows, a weak mixture of color through stained glass—the light of an oil lamp on the altar, kept perpetually aflame to signify the presence of the Holy Spirit, the Comforter.

In confirmation class Brett had listened to Pastor Hjortlin explain the significance of the lamp, and had thought it crazy. Why have a lamp to signify the Holy Spirit's presence *here*, when the church taught that the Holy Spirit was everywhere? And where the hell was this Comforter when Gretchen Bayliss's body was forming in her mother's womb, taking on freakish bends and crooks that doomed her to a painful life in a wheelchair? Wasn't Gretchen entitled to a little comfort, even though she was a Catholic?

Farther west yet stood the First United Methodist Church, which was bigger and newer than either of the others, but not quite as grand. Kitty-corner from it was the town's pride and joy, the old Hilde mansion, built in 1895 by Haaken Hilde, the Norwegian immigrant who'd bought the failing Olden cannery from the founder of the town and turned both cannery and town into going concerns.

As he rounded the corner onto Clatsop, Brett felt a ripple of cold against his spine. *Movement* ahead. He thought he saw something float from the deep shadow of the shrubbery near the Hilde mansion toward the intersection of Clatsop and Floral. He continued across Floral Avenue, where Clatsop Street dipped slightly and rose toward its summit at the intersection with Kalapuya. The city of Oldenburg could no longer afford to maintain streetlights in the residential neighborhoods, and this was the darkest quarter of town. To his left loomed a wall of darkness that seemed even blacker—Kalapuya Park, which stretched another block south and several more east, toward the center of town.

An uneasy growl rumbled from Fudd's throat, pulsing in time to the rhythm of his trot, as if he sensed a threat, his hey-I'm-serious growl. Something rushed past Brett's shoulder and veered toward the park, passing close enough to leave its breath on his cheek and fan his hair. Whatever it was, it had size and bulk. It had moved soundlessly, leaving no footfalls.

Brett lost his balance, and the skateboard shot out from under his feet. Fudd snarled and launched himself in pursuit of the thing. Brett met the pavement with a knee and an elbow, felt eruptions of bright pain, heard his trusty Vision board clatter as it tumbled end over end. He lay still a moment, making sure that nothing was broken, and silence settled over him like a dream.

He got to his feet stiffly, rubbing an abrasion on his knee. Fudd's voice came from far away, from deep within the black void of Kalapuya Park—a long and pained yowl that ended with a sharp yelp. Brett's heart chilled as he visualized the dog caught in the grip of viselike claws, suffering and dying, spraying the night with his blood as something powerful shook him like a rag doll.

"Fudd!"

He bolted in the direction of the dog's cry, but stopped abruptly. The darkness of the park reared before him like a black hole in space, a maw into which a living thing might plunge and disappear forever.

"Fudd!" he screamed again, nearly crying now. "Fudd, come back, boy!"

The maw answered with silence. Brett wondered whether the

attacker watched him this very moment from behind a tree in the park, still licking its lips of Fudd's blood, giggling to itself and taking delight in Brett's terror. Was it sizing him up for another pass, meaning to do to him what it had done to Fudd? The thought sparked anger, and he bolted into the darkness of the park, his knapsack bouncing against him.

Before he'd gone twenty strides he collided with the boughs of a pine tree and sprawled onto the grass. He scrambled to his feet, panting, his face and arms stinging from the bite of needles. Dark though the night was, the red light of Mars seemed to brighten, and he could make out the black shapes of trees and bushes.

Another fifty strides brought him within earshot of Sunset Creek, and he pressed toward its splashing. His sneakers found the hard asphalt of a path that wound through the trees to a footbridge that spanned the creek, and he followed it, calling out for Fudd. Beyond the bridge the path ended in a clearing where Oldenburgers played Frisbee and badminton and croquet during the safe daylight hours. A band shell stood a hundred yards north.

He moved toward the center of the clearing, his sneakers whooshing softly through the grass, his neck prickling. Before him loomed a vertical pillar of dark metal set on a stone pedestal, the familiar landmark he'd known all his life, the bronze statue of the old Indian medicine woman, Queen Molly. She stood like a sentry, robed in ceremonial beaver skin and resplendent in beads, her right arm folded across her stomach. As a young boy, Brett had often climbed up to sit in the crook of Queen Molly's arm, where he'd felt a warm sense of belonging. *You're safe with me,* the kind old face seemed to say to him. *I'll always be here for you.*

He might have sought refuge in that silent promise even now, had he not suddenly remembered that on this very spot Father Briggs had soaked himself with gasoline and burned himself to death. Brett backed away from the statue, his leg muscles tightening.

Something moved from behind the statue and showed itself in the starlight, causing his heart nearly to stop. He forced his eyes to focus on it, forced himself to keep breathing.

A young woman. Barely more than a girl. Dressed in what appeared to be a Hard Rock Café T-shirt and white walking shorts.

She was tall and willowy, almost Brett's height. She had short blond hair that lay on her head like a cap. The light of Mars gave her hair and skin an unnatural rosy color, and her eyes—shit, oh dear, her *eyes*—were a cobalt blue that reminded him of atomic radiation. She stepped away from the statue and crossed her arms, tilted her head to one side.

"Hi, Brett. I see you've come out for a little fun tonight."

Brett swallowed wrong and choked, staggered backward a step.

"What's the matter?" she asked. "Forgotten how to talk?"

Brett wanted to run. He wanted to get as far from those blazing blue eyes as humanly possible. He tried to make his legs move, but they refused to cooperate. He felt sluggish, drugged, weighted with chunks of cement. He sucked breath to scream, but his throat produced only a strangling hiss.

"You don't really want to run away, do you?" She lifted her T-shirt over her head and tossed it aside, allowing her perfect breasts to bounce free. For a moment she stood marble-still, giving him time to savor the sight. Then she ran her palms over her breasts and kneaded them slowly. "God, you should feel how hard my nipples are."

Brett felt a surge of delicious panic, the kind he sometimes felt when hurtling down a steep hill on his skateboard, knowing that he could not stop, that he'd tossed his fate to gravity and sheer luck, and the best he could do was to avoid falling. The girl's hands went to the zipper of her shorts and inched it open. She pushed the shorts down over her lean hips, leaving white bikini panties that glowed pink in the weird starlight. After stepping free of the shorts, she began to rotate her hips and undulate her shoulders, dancing to some heathen song in her head.

Brett stood frozen, a tickling hunger in his groin. Something was taking hold of his will. Part of him struggled to get free of the grip, a part that sensed the danger, but another part wanted only to pull this girl to him and feel her bare belly on his.

She riveted him with that potent blue stare, chilling his bones and making him yearn for her warmth. The red haze in the sky grew stronger, colder, and Brett shivered. The girl grinned, showing perfect teeth that gleamed like ivory. She slid her hands under the band of her panties, slowly pushed them down. Brett's eyes went to the vee between her legs.

"I'm ready for you, Brett," she whispered huskily. "You should feel how hot I am. Wouldn't you like to *do* me, Brett? Wouldn't you like to push your cock into me?"

Brett probably would have fainted if the girl hadn't suddenly reached out to him. Though they stood at least twelve feet from each other, her warm hand found his cheek, his neck, his chest. Her arm simply grew enough to cover the distance between them, moving like a pink eel, taking no longer than the ordinary movement of a hand to a cheek.

Suddenly she was next to him, having glided to him like a leaf on the wind. Her hands caressed him, reached into the waistband of his pants. His pants were now open, and those amazing hands found his cock and pulled it out of his Jockey shorts. It stood like a steel shaft in the red night. She squeezed his balls gently and pushed her hard nipples against his bare chest.

Brett stared into those eldritch eyes, helpless. The hormones of a teenaged boy, overpowering as they can be, could not explain the strength of the spell. He was *wholly* hers now. He wanted only to fuck her. Nothing else in the world mattered—not Fudd, not his family, not—

Fudd! He remembered why he was here, and he realized that something else *did* matter. He might have shouted Fudd's name as the girl lowered herself down to where his cock begged for her mouth—*might* have shouted Fudd's name, but he couldn't know for sure. His head was so full of this girl that it had room for nothing else, not even—

Fudd!

Had he screamed the dog's name again?

The girl's tongue flicked maddeningly over the head of his penis and continued down the shaft. His hips rocked uncontrollably. Heat built up in his guts.

Fudd! Not again, for Christ's sake. Not *now*. She looked up at him, startled by the urgent cry that came from his mouth.

Fudd!

Brett's orgasm erupted, spattering her face and bare shoulders, the most delicious orgasm of his young life. At that moment he saw what her face had become. Her mouth was easily twice normal size, with teeth like ivory harpoons, viciously pointed and wicked. A sluglike tongue lolled between her lips, equipped with suction cups. Her hands had curving, eight-inch nails, and muscles writhed like snakes in her forearms.

Brett screamed as he came. The she-thing's hands slipped around his buttocks and gripped him hard, her sharp nails digging into his skin. Her face contorted into a gargoyle grin. Her yawning mouth hovered over his groin, poised as if to bite his genitals off.

Brett screamed again. The sound of his own voice shattered the spell that had held him rigid, and set free his hands. He beat at the face with his fists, tore at it and pushed hard against it, but God-almighty, she was strong. He felt the nip of her needle-teeth as she pressed her face into his groin.

Fudd's snarl reached his ears. Brett raised his eyes to see the big dog fly toward him in a high arc, like a living javelin hurled out of nowhere. The animal must have lain in the shadows of the bushes on the edge of the clearing, wounded and hurting, waiting to die, until hearing his master's cries. Fudd had mustered the strength to answer those cries.

Fudd hit the she-thing's shoulders like a cannonball and clamped his jaws into the back of her neck. She released her hold on Brett and whirled to fend off the attack, her claws whistling. Brett flung himself backward and rolled away from the fray. He scrambled crablike toward the street, struggling with his open clothing and knapsack.

The night came alive with snarls and growls and hisses. Claws and teeth slashed fur and hide. Brett glanced over his shoulder to see Fudd pressing the attack, covered with greasy blood, throwing himself repeatedly at the creature. She swiped at him with her outrageous claws, opening more wounds, but still Fudd attacked.

Brett screamed Fudd's name and screamed it again. The she-thing swiped at her tormentor to keep him at bay, then stared straight at Brett for a heartbeat or two, bathing him again with her blue glare, and in those few seconds Brett's brain labored like a dynamo. He *recognized* the woman. He knew now why she'd called him by name. She must have sensed this recognition, must have suffered for it in some unimaginable way, because she suddenly took flight toward the black clump of trees near the band shell, skimming the ground like a shadow-bird, scarcely needing feet or legs.

A heartbeat, a breath. She was gone. The night fell silent again.

Brett ran to his dog, who lay in a heap near the base of the statue. Though slick with blood and wheezing badly, Fudd was alive. He snuffled his master's hand. Brett pressed his face into the sticky fur and wept, then gathered Fudd in his arms for the long walk home.

27

Fungus

i

Tressa Downey couldn't sleep. Whenever she closed her eyes, her brain clicked into high gear and raced through the days' events like a VCR on fast-forward. She relived every moment of John Lansen's funeral and the reception afterwards. Having taken a day of sick leave from the county commissioners' office, she'd helped Velma Selvig with the food—no small chore, since hundreds had showed up at the Lansen home. Tressa and Velma had run themselves ragged between the Royal Kokanee and Fish Hawk Ridge, transporting pots and pans and trays.

Tressa had left the Lansens in midafternoon to walk Gretchen Bayliss to her appointment at the Oldenburg Medical Center. After Nat Schell's preliminary examination, the three of them had talked for nearly an hour, but had reached no real conclusions about Gretchen's recent emotional problems. The examination had revealed no evidence of physical sickness, aside from Gretchen's congenital malformations.

Around midnight Tressa got out of bed and went to the kitchen, where she rustled up a cup of hot chocolate. She sat at the dining room table and sipped, trying hard to relax. Her mind wandered to Father Charlie's journal, which still lay locked in a corner of her room. She'd carried the key with her since receiving it in the mail a few days after his death, along with a short letter from Father Charlie, his last words to her, a charge to read the journal and act on its message. Countless times since then she'd taken the brass key out of her pocket and simply held it tight in her fist, as if she could absorb from it the courage to unlock the book and lay her eyes on its pages. But the courage hadn't come.

"*I thought* I heard you get up."

Tressa started at the sound of her mother's voice. Cynthia

Downey padded to the table and took a chair opposite, having poured a cup of instant hot chocolate and laced it with Southern Comfort. Her hair was in curlers, encased in a pink rayon night-cap that matched her worn bathrobe. "I figured you'd be sleeping the sleep of the dead, considering the day you've put in—all that kitchen work at the Lansens, not to mention the hubbub of the funeral and all."

Tressa apologized for waking her.

"You sleep lightly when you get old," Cynthia said, lighting a menthol Virginia Slim. "If you ask me, you ought to send Marta Lansen a bill for all that work you did. God knows the Lansens could afford to pay you a little something."

"Mother, we've known the Lansens since I was a baby. They're good people. Velma and I only did what friends would do. Neither of us expects to get paid."

Cynthia opined that Velma Selvig would never get rich at this rate, donating hundreds of dollars' worth of food and service to funeral receptions. Tressa retorted that this was Velma's business, not Cynthia's.

"To heck with Velma Selvig," spat Cynthia. "I'm concerned about *you*. You're all wrought up about that little Bayliss girl, aren't you? Isn't that why you took her to Nat Schell's clinic today? You're all in a lather about that episode last week at the Royal Kokanee. Unless I miss my guess, and I seldom do, you feel as if you're responsible for her."

"Maybe I *am* responsible for her."

"I wish the Lord would tell me why you think so. Gretchen Bayliss has two parents of her own, a natural man and a natural woman. She's got a roof over her head, and she eats three squares a day, the way I hear it. A lot of children have less."

Tressa muttered something about love and charity, about helping those who need help, whether they belong to you or not. Besides, she'd come to love Gretchen as if the girl belonged to the Downey family. Gretchen was a good kid, sensitive and bright. She deserved more than what Gary and Freddye Ann Bayliss could give her.

"And you're the one who's going to see that she gets it, is this what you're saying?" Cynthia drank deeply of the boozy hot chocolate. "Seems to me you could've given the same consideration to your own little girl."

Tressa grimaced with the pain of an old wound ripping open,

one she'd carried for the past year and a half. It burned like a hot iron in her chest as she went back to a hellish winter night in Wisconsin.

ii

"... and so it looks like 1986 is going out like a lion, folks," warns the television weather guy. *"Moderate to high winds, lake-effect snow, and a wind chill of minus five."*

Tressa shudders. Oregon girl that she is, she has never toughened to the bone-slicing cold of the Wisconsin winter.

R. J. Roscoe, her husband and professor of drama at Pentington University, talks on the telephone in the kitchen. Desdi, a heart-faced pixie in her pajamas with sewn-in feet and a trapdoor in back, plays happily in the corner of the living room, where a Christmas tree should be. Her fourth birthday is a mere month away.

Tressa and R.J. have found neither the time nor the resources to shop this season, to send cards, or even buy a tree. Their sixth-floor condominium stands out like a missing tooth in the face of the building, having no strings of colored lights on its deck, no wreaths in its windows, not even a damned Christmas tree in the living room. Desdi has streaks of dried egg yolk around her mouth, and her tattered PJs are dingy. *I must've given her an egg for breakfast,* Tressa tells herself. *Or was it for lunch?* Tressa stares at her watch with disbelief: almost 6:30 P.M.

Desdi is totally absorbed with the box that her expensive Cabbage Patch doll came in—not the doll itself, which lies face down near an armchair on the other side of the room. She pretends that the box is the house of her imaginary friends, Elmer and George, who sometimes are elves, sometimes dogs, at other times sea monsters. Where she got those names, Tressa hasn't the foggiest. *No more expensive Christmas presents for that kid,* Tressa declares to herself. *All she needs is a damn old cardboard box to make her happy.*

She and R.J. should've been able to do much better this year. They're both decently paid. Desdi should have gotten new clothes and a tricycle, maybe, or a doll house with all the accessories. Tressa and R.J. should've been able to effect a real Christmas with a tree and a good dinner and a cheery get-together with friends, not only for Desdi, but for each other. But Tressa and R.J. are beyond Christmas, it seems. In place of Christmas, Tressa and R.J. have cocaine.

Tressa overhears her husband's telephone conversation with a dealer who lives near the Pentington campus. R.J. explains that yesterday he sold his and Tressa's whole stash at a handsome profit to a guy who was leaving town for the rest of the holiday break, which means that he and Tressa are fresh out. Can the dealer put something together for them?

He listens a long while, nodding and grunting occasionally, constantly tucking his shirt into his pants or pushing his hands deep into his pockets. R.J. hasn't shaved. He looks peaked. He has dark bags under his eyes.

The conversation ends, and he hangs up the phone, goes to the closet and pulls out his fur-trimmed air force parka. "Richie can't help us himself," he announces, poking his long limbs into the parka. "All sold out. That big bust in Milwaukee two weeks ago shut off his regular supply."

"So where does that put us?"

"He's found a new guy in Milwaukee, but he needs someone to pick up a quarter-pounder from him. He gave me the guy's name, told me where to meet him. Richie'll sell us an eight-ball from the shipment and give us an extra one for our trouble. That should hold us awhile, even give us some to deal. God knows we could use the money."

"Cripes, R.J., Milwaukee's a hundred miles from here. It's dark, and it's snowing, and it's supposed to get worse. You can't be serious about carrying almost ten thousand dollars of Richie's cash on a night like this."

"I *know* where fuckin' Milwaukee is! Cut me a break, Tress! Look, I'll be back before midnight, okay? Do you think you can hold out that long, for Christ's sake?" R.J. has been drinking beer most of the day, since finishing up the last of his blow around 10 A.M. He's tried a dozen times since early morning to reach Richie, his regular dealer, and has only just now succeeded. His mood is foul, like his breath.

Tressa's nerves are like loaded mousetraps, ready to spring with the tiniest jarring. At this moment she hates R.J. more than she has ever hated anyone or anything in her life. How could he have been so stupid as to peddle their whole stash? She watches him stride toward the door and slam it behind him, listens to him pound down the corridor to the elevators. Little Desdi whimpers, frightened by the storm of hostility, but Tressa hardly hears.

Midnight comes and goes, and by now Tressa can't think straight. The hours since R.J. left for Milwaukee have melted together into a meaningless puddle of non-time, hours that don't count because they lack the requisite cocaine-induced glow. Without cocaine Tressa can feel nothing but the need.

At one in the morning she steadies herself and takes stock of her situation: Desdi's asleep in bed, having eaten half a bowl of chili that Tressa warmed in the microwave (That was at—when? Three hours ago?); R.J. has undoubtedly run into trouble, which means that he won't be back for some time yet, or worse, he won't be back at all; the cupboard is bare of food and everything else worth having at a time like this, no whiskey or gin, which she and R.J. customarily keep in ample supply for the week or two after payday. No wine, no pot, not even so much as a lousy can of beer. The fact is, she and R.J. have "partied hearty" since the beginning of Christmas break, and all that's left is a giant Glad Bag full of reeking empties.

The need itself seems alive now, like a fungus growing under her skin. It neither burns nor itches, but she knows it will eat her alive unless she feeds it, satisfies it, puts it to sleep. The more it grows, the more dead she feels. Without cocaine, life is a walking coma.

She never dreamed it would come to this, especially not on that sunny summer afternoon five years ago when R.J. persuaded her to suck up her first hit of blow. It had felt good, yes, but not great—not great enough to convince her that the birds in the park were singing more sweetly or that the sun was shining more brightly. She doubted at the time that she could ever become an actual coke enthusiast, but the second hit was better, and the third better still. Within months she was willing to concede that the stuff did indeed make her feel good about herself, that it gave her energy and drive, enlivened her performances and her directing. Unlike marijuana or booze, both of which she'd used only lightly while in school, coke energized her and sharpened the sensations of day-to-day life.

Within a year she was spending several hundred dollars a week on her new "hobby." Within two years she was sucking up a good hard hit before every rehearsal, before every theater staff meeting, before every social gathering. Life was going swimmingly.

The first problem she noticed, other than the expense of the drug, is a rather nasty side effect: It makes her an Olympic-class procrastinator. It gives her the illusion of doubling or even tripling her output of work, which means that she puts off projects until deadlines loom dangerously close. Her work suffers. Actors complain about her crazy comments, her muddled directions. She makes commitments and promises she can't keep. She seems always to have the flu or the sniffles, or to be dog-tired, which causes her to exceed her allotted sick days at the theater. Her professional life is miring, and only lately has Tressa herself come to see this.

The couple's finances have crumbled under the weight of their drug life, which lately can cost a thousand dollars a week or more. American Express has canceled their cards, promising "aggressive legal action" unless they pay their delinquent balance immediately. Banks hound them relentlessly about long-past-due payments on their cars, condo, and tide-me-over loans. The gas company, the electric company, the water bureau, and the day care center are all threatening "interruptions." Thus has R.J. begun to deal coke himself, purely as a means to keep the wolf away from the door.

The fungus wriggles and writhes under Tressa's skin, letting her know it will devour her unless she feeds it soon. She feels herself moving toward the telephone in the kitchen, watches her hand as it punches out a number, hears the electronic buzz of a phone ringing on the other end. A familiar voice answers, and she answers back, trying not to sound desperate.

"Richie, it's Tress. Sorry to call so late."

No problem, the dealer assures her. He and his girlfriend are watching a late movie on the tube, William Holden in *The Bridges at Toko-Ri.*

"You haven't heard from R.J., have you?"

Negatron, but not to worry. The people R.J. is meeting in Milwaukee are mellow types. Besides, R.J.'s a big dude who can look out for himself—all growed up and haired over.

"You're right, I shouldn't be getting hot and bothered. He'll be here when he gets here. Richie, you don't suppose you could—well, you know—put something together for me until R.J. gets back?"

No can do, sweet stuff. All tapped, thanks to the Milwaukee drug squad that busted his main supplier a couple weeks back. Which is why he sent R.J. to Milwaukee in the first place, remember?

"Yeah, but I can't wait for him, Rich. I—I'm—well, you know—"

Oh, Richie knows, but when you're tapped, you're tapped.

"I'm not looking to score big. I'll take anything you can get. I'll take just one hit of blow, for Christ's sake. I'll even take a hit of crack! I'll go downtown, if I have to!"

Richie coughs, mumbles something about the difficulty of getting a deal together at one-thirty in the morning. But he doesn't want Tressa dealing with the scumbags on the street. How much money does she have?

"Almost seventy dollars," she answers, pawing through the handbag on the kitchen counter, finding a wad of bills, counting.

Not much to work with, but maybe this once Richie could make a call. He wouldn't go to such trouble for many people. Can Tressa find someone to look after her kid for half an hour?

"Let me worry about that, okay?"

Okay, but Richie can't imagine leaving a small child in a car in the parking lot of the Runway Lounge at two in the morning. No telling what might happen to a kid there, given the vermin the place attracts.

"Is that where I'm going—the Runway?" Tressa has never actually visited the place, but she knows its vile reputation: a strip joint on the edge of town that caters to Pentington males, as well as truck drivers, bikers, hard hats. Notorious for fights, knifings, drug deals, even gang rapes.

Go to the club, Ritchie tells her, knock on the office door near the stage, and ask for someone named Wicks, who'll hand her a package and take her money. Do a one-eighty and leave, talking to no one else. Don't stay for a beer, don't even visit the ladies' room. And above all, don't sit in the car and do a hit, because the parking lot is full of undercover cops and desperate crackheads.

The conversation ends, and she goes to the bedroom, sits on the bed and pulls on her Nikes. She moves into the bathroom to install her contacts. She catches sight of her image in the mirror, and it nearly stops her heart: A harridan stares back at her, wearing ratty brown hair and pale lips. An unhealthy haze dilutes the eyes—her father's blue Irish eyes, relatives have always told her—and the whites are dirty and slightly yellowed.

Into Desdi's bedroom now, where the little girl sleeps in a crib she has nearly outgrown. Butterflies and bumblebees adorn one wall, and posters of Disney characters hang on the other. Stuffed toys litter the carpet, worn and frayed, most of them. Among them is the brand-new Cabbage Patch doll, which Tressa trips over. Desdi stirs at the bump and comes awake, and Tressa damns herself for being so clumsy: She'd wanted only to check on her daughter before leaving.

"Hi Momma is Daddy back you going someplace can I come?"

Tressa bends over the crib, tucks the blanket around both edges of the mattress, and plants a cold kiss on her daughter's forehead. "Nothing to worry about, Wee Desdi. Daddy'll be back soon."

"Are you going somewhere?"

"Just going for a little walk. Need some fresh air, that's all."

"Are you gonna leave me?"

Tressa sucks in a breath and tries not to let her daughter's tiny voice wound her. She tells herself that what she's about to do does not make her a rotten mother. On the contrary, to remain in this state of deadness, infested with the fungus, would be truly rotten. In this state she can be no kind of mother at all.

Live again! she tells herself. *Just one more hit, and you can put an end to it!*

"Honey, I'll be right back, I promise. You'll be fine for a few minutes. Be a good sport and go back to sleep, okay? You won't even know I'm gone."

"Okay, Momma." Tressa pretends not to hear the quiver in the child's voice or see the gleam of tears in those blue eyes. "I'll be a good sport."

She touches her daughter's cheek. "Want me to bring the Cabbage Patch baby to keep you company? You might sleep better if you have a friend with you."

"I got Elmer an' George. They'll take care of me."

Tressa smiles: Elmer and George, the invisible duo. Her daughter's best friends. Better friends to her, certainly, than Tressa and R.J. "Are they dogs tonight, or sea monsters? Or maybe elves?"

Desdi holds on to her momma's hand as if she can keep her here if she squeezes hard enough. "Chiropractors. I think they're chiropractors tonight."

Tressa tries to laugh, but she can't. *Chiropractors.* Desdi must've heard the word in a television ad.

Tressa halts at the door before leaving the room and turns to look at her daughter, whose eyes are not closed, as she'd hoped they would be, but open wide and brimming. Desdi gives out not a whimper. She's being a good sport.

Outside, the night is alive with swirling, stinging snow. The wind moans and bites. The Wisconsin winter invades her body through her nostrils and eyes, but Tressa scarcely feels the invasion. She has only one need, and it's not warmth.

Driving is tough. The streets are rutted and slick, the traffic lights mere gauzy bubbles in the blizzard. Somehow she finds her way to the edge of town, where a tower of garish neon reddens the night and announces the Runway Lounge. She parks, trudges through snow to the front door, and pushes it open. Her mind recoils against a flood of foul sights and sounds and smells—the stench of beer, sweat, and cigarette smoke; the screech and thump of heavy metal rock over worn-out speakers; a buck-naked woman convulsing gracelessly on a lighted runway, wagging her ample breasts from side to side in time to the cannonading bass; a mob of scruffy-faced males hooting and whistling.

Tressa finds the door where Richie said it would be. She knocks, and worries whether anyone inside can hear her through the din. But someone does, a remarkably plain-looking guy with graying, blow-dried hair. The name's Wicks, he tells her, and, yes, he's been waiting for her, having gotten a call from his old pal, Richie. He hands over a packet wrapped with Handi-Wrap, but doesn't pull his palm back. Tressa digs into the pocket of her coat for the roll of bills and thrusts it to him, thinking vaguely that he looks like Jack Kemp.

The music ceases abruptly, and the bare-ass stripper wiggles off the runway. Tressa pushes through the all-male crowd, feeling the troglodytic stares cast at her, now that the runway is empty. Someone nearby whistles at her; someone else shouts, "Hey, baby, where you goin' in such a hurry?" Her stomach lurches, and she belches up bile that burns her throat. Fighting the dry heaves, she elbows her way to the entrance and throws herself against the door, which swings open too easily, and she tumbles forward onto the concrete threshold, which is icy and dusted with snow. She scrambles to her feet, having skinned a knee and a palm.

She now becomes acutely conscious of who and what she is. She doesn't *need* this, she screams silently. What she needs is Desdi. What she needs is to press her daughter against her chest and weep the night away, to await the dawn while the fungus burns itself out.

She staggers to her car, fumbles maddeningly with the keys, gets in. She guns the engine, snaps on the headlights. Her eyes fall on the dashboard clock, which tells her that she's been gone more than an hour. *Desdi, my God—!* Icy streets and blinding snow have made the going slow. *Desdi's been alone for more than an hour!*

The fungus magically dissolves, leaving behind uninsulated emotions. Tressa's shame becomes a proud sore. Going back to Wee Desdi—the good sport, the munchkin who plays with empty doll boxes and invisible chiropractors named Elmer and George—is all she can think about. She hungers for nothing but wrapping her arms around Desdi, and she knows that if she can do this, she will never again do cocaine.

She slams on the brakes. The car skids sideways on the snow-packed street, almost hitting a parked pickup. She rolls down the window and digs the Handi-Wrapped bundle out of her coat pocket, hurls it through the open window into the storm. With tears streaming down her numb cheeks, she swears out loud: *"God damn you! This is it! I'm gonna be free now!"*

She has left her child alone to score a hit of coke, a black truth that will always lurk in the cellar of her soul, stirring now and again to burn her with shame. In a way, it might be a blessing, because it will never again let drugs tempt her.

Please, God, let her be all right! Just let me get back to her. Don't let anything happen to my little girl.

She drives nearly six blocks before she realizes that she's actually praying—Tressa Downey-Roscoe, the clear-eyed humanist, praying over her steering wheel. *Imagine!* She sees the crinkled face of old Father Briggs in her mind, and she smiles through her tears. *"Train up a child in the way he should go, and he will never depart from it,"* she hears him say.

Please God, take care of my Desdi! Bless her, and bless Elmer and George, too! Bless all chiropractors!

No such thing as an atheist in a foxhole, is there, Father?

Lights ahead, pulsing red and blue, sharp beacons against the blizzard. A utility crew, maybe, called out to fix a power line that the storm has brought down.

No, no. Utility crews use yellow lights.

What then—cops? Ambulance?

An ache forms in her stomach as she draws close to the source of the pulsing color, as she sees three police cars, a fire truck, and an ambulance clustered in the parking lot of the condominium complex. The beams sweep across parked cars layered with snow, turning them alternately red and blue. The emergency vehicles block the way to the parking slot, so she sets the brake, gets out, walks toward the knot of people gathered in the glare of headlights and spotlights.

Movement now: White-faced men dressed in the dark jackets of firemen and cops, carrying a stretcher toward the open doors of the ambulance, not hurrying.

Tressa *knows*. Even before she shoves through the crowd to the hideous red blot in the snow, to the place where a small child's body landed after falling from a sixth-floor deck, Tressa *knows*. Her eyes pick out unspeakable details on the ground—a tattered hank of blood-soaked hair, a gobbet of bone, a mangled cardboard box that once held a Cabbage Patch doll.

"Elmer and George will take care of me...."

She feels hands on her elbows and shoulders. Someone speaks to her, tries to be her friend. He identifies himself as a cop. *"*. . . you Mrs. Roscoe-Downey?*"

"I—it's Downey-Roscoe."

"Sorry, ma'am, but could you please come with me? I'm afraid there's been an accident. . . ." An accident, yes. A little girl has fallen from the deck, which the kind policeman doesn't need to say, because Tressa *knows*. The next-door neighbor heard her cry just before she fell, heard her scream for Momma, as though Momma was somewhere near. *Of course! She thought I'd gone for a little walk! I told her I'd be only a few minutes! She got scared and went looking for me!*

"Apparently she climbed up on the railing and slipped over it. I'm very sorry, Mrs. Roscoe-Down—I mean Downey-Roscoe. If you'll come with me, we'll make arrangements for . . ."

"Elmer and George will take care of . . ."

Tressa goes with him, because there is nothing else to do, nowhere else to go. Her world has ended. All she has left is the fungus.

28

Kindred Spirits

i

Breakfast at the Lansen household on Tuesday morning was an unpleasant affair. Marta bustled between the kitchen and the dining room like a waitress at a truck stop, chattering while she worked—about how suddenly yesterday's storm had come and gone, about how badly her roses needed the moisture, about how nice the funeral flowers looked in church yesterday. Mark knew that she couldn't sit down. She needed to keep moving in order to stave off an onslaught of tears.

Later she attacked the breakfast clutter, fending off any offer of help. She shooed Tad outside and ordered him to play on the tire swings that John had strung up last week. Then she herded Mark into the rear parlor.

"Has the sheriff told you the results of the autopsy?" she asked, pressing her hands together as if she expected the worst.

"He called early this morning," Mark answered, knowing that he could put this hideous moment off no longer. "The medical examiner said the wounds on Dad's head were inconsistent with his other injuries. He also said Dad had some strange marks on his jaw, like fingernail scratches. It looked as if they'd festered before the accident. The sheriff wanted to know if Dad had been in any kind of altercation before going to the office that night, but I couldn't tell him anything since I wasn't here when he left. I promised to check with you and get back to him."

Marta stared blankly through the glass of her solarium, her head nodding weakly as if she suffered from Parkinson's disease. For a terrible moment Mark feared that she'd suffered a stroke. "No," she said finally, and Mark let himself breathe again. "John had no altercation with anyone that evening. When he left here, he didn't have so much as a scratch."

ii

The telephone rang, and Mark hurried to pick up the extension in the study. He didn't want Marta taking any calls just now, especially from the sheriff's office. He hoped keenly to hear Kristen's voice on the other end, hoped to hear that she'd stolen a weekend in a beach cottage with a boyfriend from the U. of O.

But it wasn't Kristen's voice he heard. It was Kyleen Le-Breaux's. She announced that she'd rented a room at the Royal Kokanee Inn for a few weeks. She planned to drive back to Portland this afternoon in order to tie up some loose ends with her practice, then come back to Oldenburg early tomorrow. When could they get together?

Mark was dumbstruck. He hemmed and hawed. He tried to tell her that he really didn't think he needed help this badly, that he was in control of his life, but the words came out weak and stuttery, unconvincing even to his own ears.

"Don't say any more for now," said Kyleen. "I think I know how you're feeling. I just want to hang around here for a while, in case you need a shoulder to lean on or an ear to fill. Anyway, I haven't gotten away from the practice for a long time, and this place seems to be exactly what I need. It's right out of Currier and Ives—peaceful as hell."

"Am I that bad off?" Mark wanted to know.

She paused a long moment, and Mark heard her breathing deliberately, searching for just the right words. "Mark, you've suffered more in the past two weeks than most people suffer in five years. I saw the effects yesterday at the funeral, and I won't shit you—you need some help. I want you to stay inside for a while. Take things easy until we can get together, okay? I'll call you as soon as I'm back in town tomorrow morning. In the meantime, stay put. Promise me you'll do that."

Mark promised.

iii

He broke the promise an hour later. After talking with Kyleen, he sat alone in the parlor next to a window, brooding and watching Tad play alone on the tire swings. The boy's actions seemed listless and halfhearted, which Mark could understand: Tad felt the loss of his grandfather as acutely as anyone.

Mark became angry with himself. He sprang out of the chair and dashed upstairs to change into shorts and a T-shirt. He went down to the yard and called to his son, motioning him to the garage.

"Let's saddle up the mountain bikes, Tad Bear. I think it's time you gave me the bike tour of Fish Hawk Ridge, don't you?"

Tad's face broke into an eager grin.

iv

From the Lansen house they pedaled south on Salmon Way to a nameless cul-de-sac on the steep side of Fish Hawk Ridge. A decade ago an overly optimistic developer had subdivided the bordering property into residential lots, but nothing had come of the project. The lots lay empty but for a few lonely Douglas firs and an impenetrable thicket of blackberries.

Tad led the way. "I'll show you a shortcut to the top of the ridge!" he shouted, gearing down for a climb. "It's pretty bumpy, though. Think you can handle it?" He grinned teasingly at his father.

"I'm right behind you, Hot Shot!"

A narrow trail led upward from the cul-de-sac, twisting and turning around boulders the size of Toyotas. Tad plunged into it, and Mark followed. Near the top of Fish Hawk Ridge the trail emerged onto Summit Drive, which was paved with ancient, potholed blacktop. Hardly anyone used this road anymore, apparently.

Mark's legs ached and his lungs burned, but the heat of honest exertion felt good. Spending time alone with his son felt even better. *This was a brilliant idea,* he told himself. They halted at the crest of Fish Hawk Ridge, where a break in the timber offered a spectacular view of the Columbia River and the town of Oldenburg. A gentle morning breeze cooled their faces.

"I'd forgotten how great the view is from this spot," said Mark, watching a naval vessel crawl up the river toward Portland. "I used to ride my bike up here when I was a kid. Sometimes I'd bring a sack lunch and a book, and I'd sit on one of these rocks and stare out over the valley. If I squinted my eyes, I could almost make myself believe there wasn't a town down there, or any roads or railroad tracks or power lines, that I'd somehow gone back in time about two centuries, when the only people around here were Cathlamets and Chinooks." He looked down at Tad and smiled. "Know something, though? I'm glad I'm living in the here and now. I'm glad I grew up with Gramp as my father, and that I've got you for my kid. I wouldn't trade places with anyone."

At the mention of Gramp, the boy's eyes moistened and his lips pressed tightly together. Mark wanted to wrap his arms around him and hold him close, but he didn't, because he was afraid that if he did so, he too would start to cry. He wouldn't let himself cry in front of his son.

Mercifully, the heavy moment passed. Tad darted away toward the windward side of Fish Hawk Ridge, his brown legs pumping the bike like steam pistons. From here the road wound downhill to the north, until joining Tillamook Avenue on the north edge of Oldenburg several miles away.

"Race you to the bottom!" he hollered. Mark accepted the challenge, knowing his chances of catching the kid were nil. Within a minute Tad was out of sight.

Mark pedaled gamely on, glad for the cool air in his face, for the sun's warmth on his shoulders, for the playful cawing of far-away crows. At this moment he felt capable and strong and sane. He felt equal to whatever had caused the emotional debacle he'd endured in the past ten days. If pure chance wasn't the culprit, as Kyleen LeBreaux insisted it was, then Mark would seek out that culprit and face him down.

Him?

He realized he'd just given his problem a gender, the first rudiment of an actual identity.

V

Mark rounded a curve where the road leveled out and became a narrow corridor through the timber. He hit the brakes hard. The bike skidded and the tires shrieked against the grainy asphalt.

In the ditch to his left lay the remains of an ancient De Soto, so brown with dereliction that he could hardly discern its make. On the front fender sat his sister, her elbow resting on a propped-up knee, her chin on a fist. Her mixing-bowl hairdo was tangled and matted, her Hard Rock Café T-shirt ripped and stained with what looked like dried blood. Though dirty and disheveled, she appeared unhurt.

"Hi, big brother. It took you longer to get here than I thought it would."

Mark swung off the bike and let it drop to the pavement. His legs felt wobbly as he approached her. His mouth hung open.

"God, you should see yourself, Mark. I never knew you could open your mouth so wide." She giggled and motioned him to come closer. "Can't you at least say hello? Why don't you sit down and take a load off? We can have ourselves a little brother-sister chat."

Mark ran a hand through his hair and blinked stupidly. "Kristen, where in the hell have you been? We've got the sheriff out looking for you, for Christ's sake. I went up to Gestern Hall on Saturday, and Mrs. Drumgule said you'd gone without saying where you were going."

"I know. She told a little white lie. She really didn't have any choice."

Mark went to her and took her hands in both of his. "Kristen, I'm afraid I have something really bad to tell you. There's no easy way to do this, so I'll just say it. It's about—"

"It's about Dad, I know. I heard what happened." She studied the weeds growing around the De Soto's tireless wheels. "Don't worry, I'm not going to cry. I've done all the crying I can do, at least for now. A person can only shed so many tears, know what I mean?"

Mark cupped her cheek and turned her face toward his. "Kristen, are you okay? Maybe I should take you over to see Nat Schell."

"There's nothing wrong with me that a long, hot bath wouldn't cure. I'll take one the minute I get back to the mansion."

"The mansion? Is that where you've been all this time?"

"Like I said, Mrs. Drumgule told a little white lie."

Mark leaned weakly against the rusty fender of the derelict De Soto. *Is this real?* he asked himself. *Is Kristen actually sitting here, talking to me?*

His hand dropped to the warm, brown metal of the fender. Something slimy touched his fingers, and he jumped back, his face slack with revulsion. A huge, caramel-colored slug had crawled out of a mound of leaves that had drifted against the grille of the old car. A glistening trail of mucus stretched behind it.

"Hello, little sister," Kristen said with a frightening smile. "Nice of you to put in an appearance." She reached over and caught the slug between her fingers, and held it close to her face. The creature writhed furiously and tried to pull itself into a ball. "Oh, don't be that way. We're all family here. We're all kindred spirits, aren't we?"

"For Christ's sake, Kristen, throw that fucking thing away!" Mark clapped a palm over his mouth.

"I used to hate these things," said Kristen dreamily. "I've even had nightmares about them all my life. Remember when I was a little kid, how I used to go out to Mom's garden with a spray bottle full of ammonia? I used to squirt every slug I saw and have fun watching them squirm and die."

"*Please*, Kristen! I-I can't take this. I-I have a phobia—"

"I know. And that's something you need to get over. I've gotten over mine." To Mark's horror, she popped the slug into her mouth, chewed it, and gulped it down. Then she smiled sweetly.

Mark felt dizzy and cold. He heard the sound of an engine in the distance—a big V-8, he thought. He clenched shut his eyes and drew a deep breath, trying not to let himself swoon. The roar of the engine drew close, and he heard the whoosh of tires on hot blacktop. He opened his eyes and saw an old black Imperial LeBaron roll to a stop next to his fallen mountain bike. He looked back at Kristen, who smiled horribly at him. The body juices of the slug stained her perfect teeth. Mark's body shuddered like a dying thing, and he fainted dead away.

29

Visitation

i

Tressa Downey used her morning coffee break to call Velma Selvig at the Royal Kokanee Inn and asked whether she'd heard the latest—that Gary Bayliss lay near death in the hospital in Astoria. Velma hadn't heard the news, and sounded shocked. According to courthouse scuttlebutt, Gary had met some sort of major misfortune last night after closing the ThriftyKwik, while driving to Poverty Ike's for his regular bout of late-night beer-drinking. Deputy Ron Fanning had found him in his pickup just before sunup, parked between the ruins of the old Brownsmeade Hotel and the railroad station, sprawled across the seat with his pants down around his knees.

"It sounds like he was cut somehow," continued Tressa, whispering into the phone. "Ron said he'd almost bled to death—that he was white as a sheet and barely breathing. The cops rushed him over to the medical center, and Nat Schell got him stabilized, then sent him to Astoria by Life Flight helicopter. I hear they're giving him whole blood, and it's anybody's guess whether he'll pull through."

"Wow. Any word on who the culprit was?"

That was a question only Gary could answer, said Tressa. His pickup was undamaged, which ruled out a wreck. The cops had found no signs of violence in or around the vehicle.

Velma waited a moment and said, "It wouldn't surprise me if he tried to kill himself. He's a dirtball, but he's a *proud* dirtball, Tressa. If I know Gary, he was depressed as all get-out after the show he put on here at the Royal Kokanee last Friday. He's probably fallen into one hell of a funk, knowing that the whole town is chuckling about how he cold-cocked poor little Nat Schell, and then got himself beaten up by Mark Lansen. On top of that, his store is about to fold, I hear, like half the other businesses in Oldenburg."

"I don't think it was a suicide attempt," said Tressa. "I've never heard of a man trying to kill himself *that* way."

"What way?"

Tressa breathed deeply to control her rebelling stomach. "It sounds as if someone tried to slice his genitals off with something sharp and jagged. Trouble is, the cops couldn't find a knife or any other kind of weapon."

"God in heaven!" Velma made slurping sounds that suggested a swig of coffee. "What about Gretchen and Freddye Ann? Is someone taking care of them?"

They were at Gary's bedside in Astoria, answered Tressa. A neighbor woman was with them. Tressa herself planned to monitor the situation closely and to spend as much time with Gretchen as possible during the next few days.

Velma said something about the town of Oldenburg being under a state of siege: First came the tragedy with the Pellagrinis last March, followed by Father Briggs's suicide, then John Lansen's accidental death, and now Gary Bayliss's misfortune. "I don't know who's doing the besieging, but I wish they'd call a screeching halt to it. It's starting to affect business. Normally I'd have all ten rooms rented this time of year, but now I've got exactly two guests in the whole place—a pair of real winners, too."

Tressa gave a strained giggle, trying to break the gloom she'd generated with the news about Gary Bayliss. "Anyone I know?"

"As a matter of fact, you may have met one of them—the shrink from Portland. She was at John Lansen's funeral, remember? Classy-looking lady, long black hair, red earrings and necklace, long and tall and disgustingly slim—kind of like you. Her name's Kyleen LeBreaux, and she drives a cute red Mercedes convertible."

Tressa remembered her.

"I suppose I should be glad to have the business," said Velma, talking in a low voice now, "especially since she rented the room for a whole two weeks. Even paid in advance with cash on the barrel head. I had to drag out the innkeeper's manual to figure out how to handle a cash transaction." She snickered, then got serious. "Look—you're probably busier than hell, so I won't tie you up. Let's get together real soon, okay?"

"But you haven't told me about your other guest."

"I'll give you a thumbnail sketch. Old priest from France, talks like Maurice Chevalier, looks like he came from Central Casting. Has a beautiful antique steamer trunk that I'd give my eyeteeth to own. It took two guys to drag it off the truck and up the stairs, so I figure he's a smuggler, right?—and the trunk's full of priceless Egyptian artifacts that he's stolen from museums in Paris. I plan to seduce him, get him to quit the priesthood, and marry him. Then I'll go south with his money. That's it for now, more later."

ii

Tressa had barely hung up the telephone when Commissioner Ed Nyberg rapped twice on her door and stuck his round, red face into her office. Emergency meeting, he said, and motioned for her to follow.

Tressa's heart nearly stopped when she entered Nyberg's office and saw none other than Clovis Gestern, resplendent in a chalk-striped business suit, a white linen shirt, and a club-print tie of red silk. Also present were the other two county commissioners and the county attorney, Don Gravely, whose toupee looked especially oily today.

The men all stood when Tressa entered, and Skip Gestern gave her a bright grin. "Nice to see you again, Tressa," he said, extending his hand. She had no choice but to shake it.

Everyone took seats on the fake-leather furniture, and Ed Nyberg got right down to brass tacks. This was an "off-the-books" meeting, he said, to discuss Mr. Gestern's latest civic-minded proposal: to tear down the ruins of the old Hilde cannery and the German Point sawmill, and to replace them with municipal parks and recreational housing. The Gestern family owned options on both properties, said the commissioner, thanks to investments made decades ago. Mr. Gestern was willing to deed a major share of the riverfront to Kalapuya County, provided the county government granted zoning variances that allowed residential condominiums and commercial tourist facilities. Mr. Gestern would even foot the bill for landscaping the park and building an access road for public use.

Nyberg's eyes glittered as he reminded everyone that the county had struggled for years with the question of how to rid itself of the crumbling industrial blight along the riverbank. After repeated failures to pass the needed bond issues, or to attract outside investors, a solution seemed finally to be at hand. Before going public with the good news, however, Nyberg wanted to make certain no one had any objections, political or otherwise.

No one had. So Commissioner Nyberg slapped his chubby hands together and grinned a chubby grin. "It's settled, then. We'll take official action at tomorrow's commission meeting." As everyone else shook hands and clapped each other on the back, Nyberg whispered orders to Tressa to prepare the necessary documents.

iii

Tressa retreated immediately to her tiny office when the meeting ended, needing to be alone with her newly developing headache. She'd just gulped a pair of aspirin when a knock sounded on her door. Expecting one of the secretaries, she shouted, "Come!"

Skip Gestern came through the door and closed it behind him, looking tall and patrician and elegant. He placed his palms on her desk and smiled in his odd, sad way. "Thought I'd stop by on my way out and say hi. Hope you don't mind."

"I-I really am very busy today, Mr. Gestern. I hope you'll forgive me if I don't—"

"Hey, I thought we'd gotten beyond the 'Mister' and 'Mizz' stage. I'm Skip, remember?"

"I really am sorry, Skip, but I don't have time to talk right now. I'm afraid I have a very busy afternoon shaping up."

"No, *I'm* the one who should be sorry, after what happened at the mansion last week." He straightened to his full height and clasped his hands obeisantly in front of him. "I feel responsible somehow, even though I don't quite know for what. I was serious when I invited you back for dinner, Tressa. I hope you'll accept the invitation soon, and let me make up for whatever it is that happened. Can you think of any real reason why we can't be friends?"

Tressa stood up abruptly and folded her arms across her chest. "Someone or something attacked me while you and I were talking in your study last week," she said evenly. "I don't know how he did it, and I don't know who it was. I can't even swear that I was in full possession of my wits at the time. All I know is that it happened. If I had any way of taking legal action, that's exactly what I'd do."

"And you think I'm the guilty one, naturally."

"It happened in *your* house, in *your* study."

"And I suppose you blame me, too, for little Gretchen Bayliss's outburst at the Royal Kokanee last Friday evening."

Tressa's mouth fell open.

"I was standing close enough to hear what she said about me after you got her calmed down," Skip continued. "I hope you don't really think I'm a vampire." He smiled again, but this time Tressa saw no charm in that smile. She saw only dazzling white teeth.

Skip leaned against the door, his hands pocketed. Somber now, he said, "She's a very sick little girl, you know. It's good she has you to look out for her. That *father* of hers—well, I shouldn't say anything bad about him. Let's just say I'm glad for her sake that Gretchen has you, because with a father like that she needs someone."

"Gary Bayliss is in the hospital in Astoria. Someone attacked him last night, and he may not live."

"So I've heard. He has my best wishes for a speedy recovery."

"I don't suppose you know anything about what happened to him?"

Skip Gestern stared at her a long moment, his eyes round and steely, his nostrils flaring ever so slightly. "My God, I think you actually believe her. You actually think I'm some sort of monster who goes around attacking people. Tressa, listen to me— Gretchen's a wonderful kid, from what I hear, but she's not well. She's delusional and hysterical, which shouldn't surprise anyone, given her physical disabilities. Under the best circumstances kids imagine all kinds of weird things. They dream up imaginary playmates . . ."

Tressa thought of Elmer and George, the daydream pals of a little girl she once knew—dogs, or sea monsters, or chiropractors. She bit her lip.

". . . and they dream up monsters to offset their real-life fears. For some kids it's a booger man or a bugbear, for others it's a troll or a goblin. For Gretchen Bayliss, it's a vampire. Don't you see?"

But Gretchen wasn't a little child, Tressa protested. Gretchen was a fifteen-year-old girl with a bright and lively mind, someone who had long ago outgrown the lore of kindergarten kids and grade-schoolers.

Skip shook his head. "We're not living in the Dark Ages, Tressa. We've come a long way since we stopped burning witches and pounding stakes through the hearts of corpses. Today we have modern medicine and satellites and computers. We have ways to help kids like Gretchen Bayliss." He reached across the desk and patted her arm, startling her. "We can't help anyone if we start believing the old lies again. Remember that, Tressa—for your own sake, as well as Gretchen's." Then he slipped away.

iv

For the next two hours Tressa threw herself into her work, but time and again her mind wandered back to the questions she'd tried so hard to suppress, worrisome questions about Gretchen's mental state, about Father Charlie's suicide, about the fright she'd endured last week at Gestern Hall. Maybe the most vexing questions concerned Skip Gestern, and what she did or didn't believe about him. Despite the aspirin she had popped, her headache flared again, so she popped two more.

At one o'clock she realized she'd taken no lunch break. Too late now, she told herself. She walked down the corridor to the vending machines that stood near the entrances to the lavatories, fed them coins, and took out a Mars bar and a Diet Coke. On her way back to her office she passed the reception counter, and Ginger Truax flagged her down. "Can we talk for a minute—somewhere private?"

"Sure, Ginger. How about my office?"

They stepped into her office, and Tressa nudged the door closed. Suddenly Ginger lashed out at her, knocking the Coke and the candy to the floor.

"Jesus!" hissed Tressa. "Why in the hell—?"

"Shut the fuck up!" Ginger balled her hands into fists. "I'm going to do the talking, and you're going to do the listening. Hear me, you slimy bitch?"

Tressa drew back until she hit the wall, until she could retreat no farther. She saw that Ginger's normally radiant blond hair hung loose and dirty, that her usually sparkling eyes were yellowed around the irises. The girl smelled as if she hadn't bathed in a week, which was frighteningly out of character. Worst of all was her twisted scowl of hatred.

"Ginger, I—"

"Shut up!" She positioned a fist in front of Tressa's face. "I'm only going to say this once, so listen good: Stay away from Skip Gestern. He's the first good thing that's ever happened to me, and I'm not going to let you fuck it up."

"Ginger, I don't understand. Skip Gestern is nothing to me. I don't even—"

"Do you think I'm fucking *blind?* I saw him follow you into this very room this morning, and I saw him close the door behind him. I saw the look on his face when he went in, and I saw it when he came out. Then he walked right by my desk and didn't say boo to me, like he'd never seen me before. So don't tell me that he doesn't mean anything to you."

That this young woman could be standing here just an arm's length away, spitting this absurd accusation into Tressa's face, seemed too horrible to be real. She could smell Ginger's gamy breath, and she could almost *feel* the heat of anger radiating from the girl's skin.

"Tell me what I want to hear," demanded Ginger, pushing her fist closer to her cheek, "or I swear I'll fuck you up good. Skip is *mine*, and he's going to *stay* mine. Tell me you understand this, and we'll let it drop, okay? *Tell* me!"

"Ginger, you're sick. I should've made you take some time off last week, when you weren't feeling well. I want you to go home now. After you're feeling better, we can—"

Ginger Truax reared back and let a fist fly at Tressa's face. Thanks to years of stage training, Tressa nimbly dodged it, rolling to one side with what was almost a dance step. Ginger's fist slammed into the plastered wall, and the girl bellowed like a wounded animal. She rounded on Tressa again, her eyes brimming with enraged tears, but she found only air to grab. Then her hands seized a desk lamp, the jointed kind that plugs into a base on the surface of the desk. She tore the lamp out of the base and came at Tressa, swinging it like a mace. Tressa just managed to duck under the first blow, and steeled herself to absorb the next one, since she had nowhere to flee. Suddenly the door burst open.

Drawn by the commotion, Don Gravely stepped into the fray and grabbed the lamp away from Ginger. He caught her wrist, folded it against the small of her back, and pushed her face into a wall. He shouted at Tressa to call the sheriff's office.

By the time Deputy Ron Fanning arrived, the county attorney had completely subdued Ginger Truax, but not before she'd knocked his oily toupee askew. It hung low over his left ear, exposing a narrow patch of shiny baldness on the right side of his head. Gravely didn't realize this.

"Better take her downstairs to the lockup," he told Fanning, "and let her cool off. Must be on drugs or something."

Tressa protested that the girl was obviously ill, and insisted that Fanning take her to the Medical Center. Tressa herself promised to see that she got home okay.

"Thanks for helping, Don," she said, sidling by Gravely to follow Ginger and Fanning. "You may have saved my life."

Gravely thrust his chin out, still unaware of the state of his toupee. "Glad to do it, glad to do it. Maybe we should get together for a steak or something, and rehash . . ." His words trailed off, because Tressa was already too far away to hear, and she wasn't looking back.

30

The First Taste

i

Your consciousness slips and dips as you strain to open your eyes.

You sense hard, dank walls. You hear wet, slithery sounds under the stones of the floor—snakes or lizards, maybe worse. You smell the smoke of candles, the breath and sweat of human beings close by.

The sounds of a retching man jar you fully awake, and you open your eyes: The scene has the texture and tone of a slug-dream, but you know that this is waking reality. You can make out ranks of ancient books along the walls, their gold-embossed titles stuttering in the candlelight. The stone faces of centaurs, trolls, and other medieval monstrosities grin down at you from their perches atop the walls.

An old woman sits near you in a wooden chair, her bad teeth peeking through her smile. She holds a weighty old book on her lap, its pages splayed. She strokes your cheek with a coarse hand, and you recognize her as Mrs. Drumgule, whom you met last Saturday when you came to Gestern Hall in search of Kristen.

Is that where I am? Gestern Hall?

A chrome rack towers above you, holding a glass jar and an IV tube that runs down to a point where your left arm stings. An ornate chandelier of tarnished brass gleams solidly over your head—no figment of a dream, surely. The vaulted stone ceiling that arches above is so real you can see the grime of at least a century's worth of burned candle wax.

How in God's name did I get here?

More gagging and retching to your left. A man hunches over a heavy wooden table, upon which rests a brass bowl. A gown of black satin hides his body, and a cowl covers his head. His shoulders quake as he vomits a red stream into the bowl, and a cloud of steam rises from it. A coppery scent invades your nostrils, and the first tendrils of panic tickle your ribs. The scent fires a hunger in your gut, a hunger for—

No! You won't say it. You won't even *think* it.

You try to sit up, but you're strapped to a gurney. Metal clamps encircle your wrists and ankles, and you feel like Frankenstein's monster in that grainy old movie you loved as a kid. You also discover you're naked as a newborn. The tendrils of panic you felt mere seconds ago become the bone-crushing tentacles of a giant squid. A croak escapes your throat.

"Easy now, easy now," soothes Mrs. Drumgule. "Let your hunger take its course, my young friend. Lie back and let us feed it for you. . . ."

Something inside you screams a warning, some inner voice that speaks for every notion of goodness or decency that you've ever had. You writhe against the clamps, igniting pain where the metal scrubs skin off your wrists and ankles. Inside your brainpan a collision occurs as the hunger meets the *real* you, as they come together at full tilt like a pair of charging locomotives. The concussion numbs you.

The cowled figure takes the IV jar from the chrome rack and fills it from the bowl, then places the jar back on the rack. He attaches the tubing, which turns red as the liquid courses from the jar toward your arm. You feel it embark into your vein, and your anger erupts in a howl that bounces off the stone walls and echoes through unseen corridors, through unseen rooms.

ii

Your body greedily sucks the tingling red liquid from the IV tube like a piglet at a sow's tit, despite your tears of protest and your groans. Every heartbeat pumps warmth deeper into the network of your veins and arteries, dampening the ache in your muscles, healing the abrasions on your wrists and ankles, soothing the nasty bruise that you took on the head when you fainted dead away on Fish Hawk Ridge. Your fears dissipate like morning mist, leaving the rosy glow of sated hunger. Your mind is clear, your senses sharp. You feel strong.

iii

"That's better, isn't it?" asks Mrs. Drumgule, leaning close. Her breath smells as if she's eaten a can of bathroom cleanser. "This is what you were made for, my young friend. This is what's been ordained."

The heavy book is still splayed on her lap. She directs her attention to a block of glossy wood on the table to her right, which she opens on hinges. She closes her eyes and mumbles words that you don't recognize, some ancient language, maybe, one that long predates the medieval tongues you struggled to master as an undergraduate. Despite her whistling S's and muffled diction you discern patterns and rhymes. She's *chanting*, you understand finally. She's doing magic, working a spell of some kind.

"It's called a *scrying* mirror," whispers someone to your left, and your head snaps back. It's Kristen, standing where the robed man had stood, next to the IV rack. She too wears dark, flowing satin, but no cowl. Her short, golden hair looks freshly shampooed, and her skin radiates a healthy glow. "It's a way to see through time and distance. A little magic, a little sorcery, and a block of wood with a black stone in it becomes a window. If you look into it, you can see things that haven't happened yet, things far away. That's how Mrs. Drumgule knew you'd be riding your bike on Fish Hawk Ridge today—by scrying. She told me where to wait for you." Kristen bends low and kisses your lips. "And I must say, I'm glad she wasn't wrong."

You brace for an attack of righteous shame, because this is *not* how sisters are supposed to kiss their brothers. You shouldn't feel an electric tingle where her lips meet yours, and your loins should not be warming. *But she's not really my sister, is she?* you say to yourself, and the wave of shame never arrives. *We're not related by blood. I was an adopted kid. . . .*

She draws away and stands upright, lowers the satin robe slowly over her breasts, and lets it drop to the floor. The candlelight kisses her nipples, and her lithe body begs for the touch of your fingers and tongue. The rust-colored mound between her legs begs for your cock, which is as hard as tungsten by now. You're sure that you could, like Frankenstein's monster, break the clamps that hold you to this gurney, so strong have you become. The part of you that protested all this—the part that struggled so hard against the delicious red flow from the IV tube—lies quiet now.

She's not really my sister!

The new you yearns to be free to press your eager hands over her wonderful breasts, to lick her belly in slow circles until she screams with pleasure, free to sluice your hard cock into her pussy and fuck her until hell won't have it. Suddenly Mrs. Drumgule sobs and slaps both palms to the tabletop. "Clouds and smoke and steam!" she blubbers. "All I see is fog! It's showing me only miasma! Someone has worked a spell against me!" She puts a hand to her doughy cheek and groans. Tears stream from her eyes, and she rocks back and forth slowly in her chair, cradling the huge book like a child, weeping as if all creation were ending.

"It's *you* she's looking for, Mark," Kristen says in a hushed tone. "She's trying to find you in the future, but something or someone is clouding the window. Her scrying spell has failed."

You try to speak, but the muscles of your mouth and tongue go dead. The heightened awareness dissolves, and a narcotic leadenness sets in. You feel as if the blood you've received intravenously is a drug that produces acuteness, but later brings sleep. Your eyesight dims. Your breathing slows. You feel Kristen's hand on your cheek, hear her voice in your ear, but you can't make out what . . .

"Soon you will know, Mark."

. . . she's saying, can't quite understand. . . .

"Soon you will know everything."

31

Nehalem Mountain Breakdown

i

"You're *sure* you won't let us call a doctor?" asked Skip Gestern yet again. He stood at Mark Lansen's bedside in a chalk-striped business suit, his arms folded. Backlit by noon sunlight streaming through a leaded-glass window, he seemed to have a halo.

"I'm sure," Mark answered, sitting up slowly. Helped by Kristen, he swung his legs over the side of the bed. "I want to thank you for your kindness. I've only passed out once before in my entire life, and that was when my wife said yes, she would marry me. I can't imagine why it'd happen now...."

He caught sight of himself in a gilded mirror that hung on the far wall. He had on the shorts and T-shirt he'd worn while biking up Fish Hawk Ridge, a mild surprise. A padded bandage stood out starkly against his tanned forehead, and another covered a small injury on his left inner forearm. Still, he felt remarkably good. In fact, he felt stronger than he'd felt in a long time. "I guess I'm lucky I didn't do more damage to myself than I did."

"Everyone has a fainting spell now and then," Skip said in an accent that Mark thought sounded like George Plimpton's. "A little too much exertion, a little too much heat—the body stages a short, temporary work stoppage. It's probably nothing to worry about."

Kristen looked newly scrubbed, Mark saw. She smiled at him warmly, and Mark found himself wondering if this was more than a "Glad-you're-feeling-better" smile. The dream from which he'd just awakened was still fresh in his mind, and he wondered whether he could ever again look at his little sister without suffering a rush of obscene thoughts.

"We put your bike in the trunk of the car, in case you're wondering," said Kristen. "We were in a hurry to get you here after you passed out, naturally, but I couldn't see leaving an almost-new Rock Hopper up there on the road."

Mark nodded his thanks, then froze. He worried that Tad might still be riding up and down the dusty roads of Fish Hawk Ridge, looking for his old man and wondering if he'd vanished from the face of the earth.

Kristen then told him about calling home not more than fifteen minutes earlier, having talked to Marta, having told her that she hadn't run away, that she hadn't been abducted. She'd explained that Mark had suffered a case of heat stroke or something, that she and Skip Gestern had evacuated him temporarily to Gestern Hall. "I made her promise not to worry about either of us, and I told her that you were sleeping like a baby in my own room here at the mansion. While we were talking, Tad walked into the house, looking a skosh bewildered and sweaty, Mom said, but otherwise okay. She put him on the line."

"You talked to him?"

"Of course. He sounded fit as a fiddle. He's anxious to see you, though, and he seemed worried about whether you're really sick. I told him to chill out, that you were just tired and that you'd be home soon."

Mark sighed with relief. "You're coming home with me, aren't you?" he asked Kristen. "Now that you know about Dad, I'd think you would want to be around to help take care of Mom. For that matter, we *all* need you, and I'd like to think that you need us, too. What do you say?"

"Not just yet," she replied.

She's changed, Mark thought. She apparently felt no need to come home and comfort Marta, and this pained him. It also frightened him.

Kristen looped her arm through his and led him to the door of the room. "You go on home and take care of things, big brother, and don't worry about me. Trust me when I say that everything's really cool, okay?"

Mark wanted to trust her, wanted to believe her, but he wasn't quite able.

ii

He got into the passenger's side of the grand old Imperial, though not without griping that he was well enough to ride his bike home, especially since the trip into town was all downhill from here. Skip Gestern wouldn't hear of it, and neither would Kristen. Skip would drive Mark home, and that was that.

Kristen stuck her head through the open window to give him a good-bye peck on the cheek (which is all it was, a *peck*, thank God). She asked him to give her best to all the family. Then Mrs. Drumgule leaned close to the window, reeking of cleanser and astringent cleaners, and for a horrible moment Mark feared that she too wanted to give him a good-bye peck. Instead, she gripped his forearm and whispered, "Take care of yourself, young man. And be watchful. There are some who wish you harm."

As the Imperial rolled away from the cool shade of the porte cochere into the heat of early afternoon, Mark saw a teenaged girl standing in the mouth of the covered stone passageway that led from the main door of the mansion to the porte cochere, a girl lean and dark. She wore a shapeless gray dress with a white apron, and she looked Hispanic. The name *Skye Padilla* flashed through Mark's head, and his gut cramped. Last week's conversation with John Lansen replayed itself in his mind—the last long, serious talk he'd had with his father.

"That's our cleaning maid," said Skip Gestern, glancing at him. "Sorry I didn't introduce you, but she was busy with her chores. Even though she's just a kid, she's really quite competent. I don't know why she's satisfied with the little we're able to pay her, but she is, and for that I'm glad."

Gestern swung the Imperial smoothly between the gateposts and turned right onto Queen Molly Road. Mark stole a final glimpse at Gestern Hall, which stood bleak against the blue sky like a modern-day Castle of Otranto. The sight of it tweaked his historian's imagination, and he felt a stirring in his soul like the one he'd felt when he first laid eyes on Mont-Saint-Michel on the rowdy shore of Brittany. The latter was like a vision out of Arthurian myth, a gigantesque construction of stone walls, battlements, and cathedral spires that thrust upward from a misty sea.

A *stirring*, yes, but it wasn't the same, was it? The sight of Gestern Hall loosed a thrill of panic and a crawling suspicion that behind those walls, perhaps deep within the viscera of the house, lurked something hellish. The mansion disappeared in a cloud of dust churned up by the Imperial's tires, and Mark turned forward again.

"That cleaning maid of yours," he said. "Her name is Skye Padilla, right?"

"How did you know that?"

"How did Kristen know that I'd be riding a bike up on Fish Hawk Ridge this morning?"

"I doubt she had any idea you'd be up there. It was pure co-incidence that you and she ran into each other."

"Then what was she doing there? And why did she look like she'd just lost two falls out of three with Hulk Hogan? And how did you just happen to come motoring along in your thunder lizard here, the very second I blacked out?"

"God, you sound downright suspicious of something!" laughed Skip. He stuck a cigarette between his lips and punched the lighter in the dash. "The fact is, I drove up to Fish Hawk Ridge to fetch your sister and bring her home, as I've done nearly every day since she signed on at the Nehalem Mountain Inn. She goes hiking every morning, which I assume you know. She tells me where she's going and when she wants to be picked up. I accommodate her, because I respect her need for a daily constitutional. I'm relying on her, you understand, to design a first-rate public relations package for the Inn, and I'll do anything necessary to keep her creative juices flowing."

A damned lie, thought Mark, *but a smooth one.* The first words out of Kristen's mouth this morning had been, *"Hi, big brother. It took you longer to get here than I thought it would."* She clearly had *expected* him. Besides, she hadn't been dressed for hiking. Kristen was an avid outdoorswoman, and she was positively anal retentive about outfitting herself properly. For hiking she would've worn proper hiking boots, carried a light pack with a plastic bottle of water, a first-aid kit, extra socks, energy snacks, and God only knew what else. She would've had her binoculars and bird book. Today she'd worn only a blood-stained T-shirt, shorts, and sneakers.

The lighter popped out, and Skip Gestern lit his cigarette. "Kristen tells me you're a medievalist, a historian. I assume you teach."

"I teach. I write."

"What's your area of interest?"

"France, twelfth and thirteenth centuries."

"Great! You really should come back to the mansion and spend some time. We have a ton of artifacts that date to that period, many of them from France. A lot of old books, too, which I'm sure would fascinate anyone who reads medieval Latin. Do you?"

"Do I what?"

"Read medieval Latin."

"Yeah, I do, along with medieval French, German, and English. I'm still working on medieval Esperanto." Mark's annoyance ripened quickly into full-blown anger. "Look, Clovis—*Skip,* or whatever the hell I'm supposed to call you—let's stuff the happy horseshit, okay? I know something's wrong with my sister, and I'm pretty sure it's got something to do with you. Why don't you just tell me what's going on with her? I'll find out anyway, whether you tell me or not, so you might as well clear the air and save us all some heartache."

"Why do you think something's wrong with her? She seems perfectly fine to me."

"She's *not* perfectly fine! She's kept herself hidden from the family for the past week or so, so well hidden, in fact, that I couldn't even track her down to tell her that our father was killed. When I talked to her on the road this morning, she acted strange, as if she didn't really care that Dad's gone or that our mother's sick with grief. Then she looked at me with this ungodly expression on her face, and picked up a live slug with her bare fingers, and"—Mark gagged—"and *ate* the fucking thing." He took a slow breath. "She's hated slugs all her life, just like I have. It's an outright phobia with us. If she was in her right mind, she would never even *touch* a slug, much less *eat* one!"

"You're right, this doesn't sound good."

"And another thing: Mrs. Drumgule lied to me when I came up to your house looking for Kristen. She told me Kristen had packed up and left the day before, destination unknown. I want to know *why*, Skip. I want to know why Mrs. Drumgule lied, and I want to know why Kristen has changed."

They approached the junction of Benson Creek Road, where Skip steered off to the right and halted. He cut the engine and turned in his seat to face Mark. The windows of the car were open, and Mark could hear the splashing of Benson Creek. A pair of thrushes chattered in a nearby tree. At any other time Mark would have relished these golden summer sounds, but now he hardly heard them.

"We *all* change, Mark," said Skip Gestern softly. "We're all becoming what we're programmed to become. It's true for Kristen, for you, for me. It doesn't do any good to fight it. The best thing you can do is let the change happen with a minimum of fuss, don't you see?"

"You're quite the armchair philosopher, aren't you? Well, here's a late bulletin: I don't happen to believe in predestination. In fact, I don't have a deterministic bone in my body. What's more, we're not talking about *me*, Skip—we're talking about my sister. She's the one with the problem, not me."

"You're absolutely sure about that? You're sure it's only Kristen?"

Mark's cheeks reddened. A film of sweat formed on his forehead, and he felt an insane craving to break Skip Gestern's handsome jaw. No, he couldn't say that Kristen was the only one with a problem. His *own* problem loomed like Godzilla on the horizon of his life: He was going off his knob, losing touch with reality. Somewhere along the line he'd thrown a lug nut. *Whom the gods would destroy, they first make mad,* right?

He wondered how Skip Gestern knew. He realized that his eyes were blearing, and wondered whether he was actually furious enough or scared enough to cry. His anger evaporated when Skip's face drew into a kindly, knowing smile. Mark heard himself say, "She *made* me faint up there on Fish Hawk Ridge. I know it sounds world-class silly, but I swear to God, she *made* it happen somehow. I don't know how or why she did it, but she . . ."

Suddenly he broke down and wept like a little kid. He sobbed. He shed huge, stinging tears that crashed down his cheeks and left damp splotches on his T-shirt. He didn't shrink from Skip's comforting hand on his shoulder, averse to touchy-feely types though he normally was. All the terrors, misgivings, and grief he'd suffered during the past two weeks bubbled up and gushed out of him.

"It's all right," said Skip. "I know how you feel." That Skip Gestern could know how he felt didn't seem preposterous at all. "It'll pass, Mark. Soon you'll look back on these difficult days and laugh, believe me. Until then, I'll be here, if you need help. So will Kristen."

"But I don't know what to do. My life's falling apart. My wife's divorcing me, and she's trying to take my son away from me. She'll probably succeed, because I'm going bats, hallucinating things. . . ."

"You're not going bats. You're changing, that's all. It was *meant* to be this way, Mark."

"But nothing seems real anymore. It's like I'm trapped inside a runaway locomotive, and somewhere up ahead there's a bridge out. I have this feeling that something horrible is about to happen, and there's nothing I can do about it."

"I'll give you some advice. Let your feelings rule you, Mark. Do what *feels* best, because that will be the right thing. Forget about trying to find rational explanations, because they usually don't work anyway—people only *think* they do. Last but not least, don't fight the change, because you can't beat it. No one can. Just relax and let it take you."

The spell of weeping lifted abruptly, and Mark rubbed the moisture from his eyes. Strangely, he felt not the slightest bit embarrassed over having broken down and blubbered his private lunacies to someone he'd only met half an hour ago.

Skip crushed his cigarette in the ashtray and restarted the engine. The Imperial rolled north again toward Oldenburg, past the Benson Creek Cemetery.

iii

Skip drove directly to the Lansen house without directions from Mark, as if he'd visited many times. He halted next to Mark's old BMW, got out and opened the trunk. "This goes in the garage, I assume," he said, holding Mark's mountain bike aloft with one hand.

Mark opened the BMW in order to reach the remote door opener, and punched it. The garage door rose noisily, and Skip carried the bike into the garage. He placed it next to one that was identical, except smaller—Tad's. He remarked about the Alfa Romeo roadster that stood in the garage, and Mark explained that it had been his father's pride and joy. On the rear bumper was a sticker that said *Legalize Lutefisk*.

Skip walked back into the drive and extended his hand. "It has been a pleasure, Mark. I hope our next meeting will be under more pleasant circumstances."

Mark felt as if he was shaking hands with a Pepsodent commercial. Nowhere had he seen teeth *that* perfect, *that* white, except maybe on—oh, yes. On Kristen.

"Skip, I want to apologize for—uh—for getting out of control back there on the road. I guess I've had a lot of strain the last few weeks, and I—"

"I understand. You have nothing to apologize for."

"Thanks for taking care of me this morning."

"You would've done the same for me, I'm sure."

Indeed, he would have, thought Mark. If the shoe had been on the other foot, if he had come across Skip Gestern lying unconscious on Fish Hawk Ridge, he would have bundled the man into his car and rushed him home. He would have called a doctor right away. He would have found John Lansen's old first-aid kit, which the family kept in a cabinet in the bathroom off the study, and taken out the smelling salts. He would have—

"I'd best get going," said Skip, sliding behind the wheel of the Imperial. "Why don't you come to dinner at the mansion on Friday evening? I'll give you a tour of the place and show off some of the artifacts I talked about earlier. Besides, I'd like to pick your brain about life in the Middle Ages. It's a subject I've really gotten interested in, but I'm a rank amateur. Maybe you could steer me onto some good books."

Mark accepted the invitation, and thought, *No doubt about it.* Had the shoe been on the other foot, he would've helped Skip Gestern, like a regular good Samaritan. He would've brought him *here* to the Lansen home, which was much closer to Fish Hawk Ridge than Gestern Hall. In fact, the distance between Fish Hawk Ridge and Gestern Hall was probably twenty times as great.

Why hadn't Skip and Kristen brought him *here?*

32

Father Charlie Speaks

i

The Personal Journal of Father Charles Briggs

"January 17, 1988: Back to the matter of breaking the seal of the Sacrament, a dreadful little chore that I can't put off any longer. Here it goes.

"Freddye Ann Bayliss has been a longtime parishioner of mine and a devout Catholic, at least until last week. She's the mother of two fine girls: Marnie, who graduated last year from high school and ran off to Seattle with her boyfriend; and Gretchen, who's barely fifteen. Gretchen is my favorite, inasmuch as she's the brighter and the more spiritual of the two girls. She's also the victim of a severe birth defect that has confined her to a wheelchair with no hope of ever walking.

"For more than a year, Freddye Ann has been confessing adultery. Her lover visits her at night in the Bayliss home, she says, sometimes two or three times a week. She has become estranged from her dreadful husband, Gary, which wouldn't be all bad, if not for the sin of adultery. She's losing weight and growing more pale every time I see her.

"It pains me that a simple, small-town girl whose heart was as good as gold has become a walking scarecrow with no heart at all. She deserves much better than Gary Bayliss. She also deserves better than some skulking paramour who won't be seen with her in the daylight.

"Last week she informed me that she would no longer come to confession or Mass, that she's leaving the Roman Catholic Church. I fought back tears when I heard this. I stared at her poor, emaciated face and her sunken eyes, and I tried feebly to reason with her, to talk her out of turning her back on a lifetime of faith. But it was hopeless. A member of my flock is gone, and I'm at a loss on how to get her back. . . ."

ii

Tressa laid the journal aside and listened to the tick-tocking of the old mantle clock over the fireplace. The clock bonged once, causing her heart nearly to stop. Eleven-thirty. She sat still a moment, dreading the possibility that the clock had awakened her mother. But the house remained silent as a tomb, and Tressa sighed with relief.

She'd sat in this armchair for nearly three hours with the journal in her lap, her eyes glued to its neatly handwritten pages. Her back was weary, her butt sore, and her body yearned for sleep, but her mind was wide awake. Having come this far, having learned of Father Charlie's torments over the past two years, she certainly couldn't stop reading now.

This wasn't easy. The words sprang off the pages and became spoken syllables that she heard in Father Charlie's voice. Most painful was the knowledge that Father Charlie had hidden his torments from her, breathing not a hint of his suspicions and fears. He'd clearly not wanted to burden her in the wake of cocaine addiction and the loss of Desdi, or to distract her from the task of rebuilding her life.

He'd written of the *change* that had come over Oldenburg.

iii

That afternoon, she'd driven Ginger Truax home from the Oldenburg Medical Center. Dr. Nat Schell had injected Ginger with a strong sedative and had prescribed a less powerful sleeping aid. Then he'd quizzed Tressa about the possible causes of the girl's wild behavior. Had she and Ginger quarreled? Had Ginger experienced any difficulties with other workers in the county commissioners' office? Had she spoken of any family difficulties?

Tressa answered no to all these questions and explained that, for some absurd reason, Ginger thought that Tressa was making a play for Skip Gestern. Tressa had worried about the girl during the past week or so, fearing that she was coming down with the flu or a bad summer cold.

"I'm afraid it's more than the flu or a cold," Nat had said, kneading his brow, "but I won't know for sure until I've given her a full checkup. She's obviously very stressed and may even be suffering from pernicious anemia."

Tressa had noticed the worry and tension in Nat Schell's face. He'd lost weight he couldn't afford to lose. Bluish pouches under his eyes made him look older than he was.

"I wish somebody would explain to me what the fuck is happening here!" he exclaimed suddenly, pounding a fist on the countertop hard enough to rattle a little vase full of artificial daisies. "I thought the Pellagrini tragedy was an aberration, the kind of thing that simply doesn't happen in a nice little town like this one. Three quiet months went by after it happened, and I said to myself, terrific, things are getting back to normal. Then, *whammo!*—Father Briggs burns himself to death! A week later John Lansen is killed under very suspicious circumstances! Last night someone attacks the older Omdahl kid on his way home from work, and damn-near kills his dog. . . ."

Tressa's knees went weak as Nat recounted how Rick Omdahl had brought his son Brett to the Medical Center for a quick once-over late last night, just to confirm that nothing was wrong with him other than a few superficial bruises. The kid's story was that he'd narrowly missed being hit by a car late last night while skateboarding. Brett had merely fallen and bruised himself, but Fudd had tumbled beneath the wheels. The driver hadn't stopped, supposedly.

Nat had gone out to Rick's pickup with a flashlight and had examined the animal. The wounds were neat, parallel furrows that curved in the arcs of long, deadly swipes—*claw* marks made by a big cat or possibly even a bear. He'd urged Rick and Brett to go immediately to the emergency veterinary hospital in Astoria, because the wounds were deep and Fudd had lost much blood.

"Now, we all know that there aren't any big cats or bears around here, especially not in the middle of town," Nat railed. "And if that dog was hit by a car, I'm Pee-Wee Herman. The kid lied, damn it! *Someone* or *something* attacked him, and the pooch came to his rescue. You don't need a doctorate in logic to figure that much out!" He took a tired breath. "Then just a few hours later, Deputy Fanning brings in Gary Bayliss, dangerously exsanguinated, more dead than alive. It's a damn good thing that Life

Flight had a chopper free in Portland, because Gary didn't have two minutes to spare in getting to the emergency room in Astoria. Wheels just wouldn't've been fast enough."

Having heard this, Tressa had decided to read Father Charlie's journal.

iv

What's wrong with Oldenburg?

Earlier she'd hoped merely to learn more from the journal about Gretchen, to benefit from Father Charlie's years of observing the girl. Now she knew that it contained much more.

She stood and stretched, then tiptoed into her bedroom to exchange her contacts for her glasses. On the way back to the living room she poked her head into her mother's bedroom just long enough to hear Cynthia's rhythmic snore. *Good,* thought Tressa.

She returned to the armchair and sat, tucking her feet beneath her. She started reading again.

v

The Personal Journal of Father Charles Briggs

"February 27, 1988: Bernie Pellagrini has never been a steady parishioner, unlike Fran, who attends Mass regularly on Sundays and comes to confession every Wednesday morning. Bernie spends the lion's share of his time and energy running the family business, Pellagrini's Appliance Mart, but now that he's nearing retirement, he relies on an assistant manager, which frees him to play more golf with John Lansen and me. We usually field our threesome at the Astoria Country Club, after which we treat ourselves to steaks, beers, and a round of locker-room jokes.

"I dearly value Bernie Pellagrini's friendship, despite his lukewarm Christianity. When he came to confession last week, I almost dropped my teeth. The surprise wasn't exactly pleasant, however. I didn't like the scared quiver in the voice that came through the screen of the confessional. . . ."

vi

"Bless me, Father, for I have sinned." Bernie's voice trembles, and his breath stinks of cigarettes. Through the screen of the confessional Father Briggs can smell his sweat. "It's been—God, I think it's been twenty years since my last confession. Father, listen to me. I think I'm about to do something bad, something *really* bad. I don't know—I'm not sure I can fight it. You've got to help me."

"Every man is free to choose between good and evil, Bernie. Tell me what you're afraid you'll do."

The bench on the other side of the screen squeaks as Bernie Pellagrini squirms and leans closer. "It's about Fran," he whispers hoarsely. "She's been seeing another man. It's not like it hasn't happened before, or like I haven't known about it, Charlie. Hell, you've probably known about it yourself."

This is true. Francesca has confessed at least three times to committing adultery, but she's always seemed contrite in the aftermath, always willing to do penance to secure absolution. For the sake of her daughters she has stayed with her husband, playing the role of dutiful wife and mother.

"I know it's my fault in many ways," Bernie goes on. "I've always been so damned busy with the store or going out with my pals to play golf or hunt or fish. I've been an okay provider for her and the kids, but I haven't been much of a husband, Charlie. Fran's a good-looking woman, a passionate woman. She gets her kicks growing champion roses and taking them to shows in Portland. That's where she's met some of the guys she's—well, you know what I mean."

"I understand."

"Lately, things have changed—gone from bad to worse. Fran's been like a stranger to me. A few months back she started sleeping in one of the guest rooms . . ."

Father Briggs winces, for Freddye Ann Bayliss has revealed that she too has started sleeping outside the conjugal bedroom. Gary often comes home late with a bellyful of beer and an urge to slap her around, it seems. Father Briggs cannot believe that the same problem afflicts the Pellagrini household.

". . . and I'm just glad the girls are grown up and moved out, so they can't see what's going on."

"Have you talked to her about it?"

"I can't talk to her about *this*. There's no way I can talk to her about what's been happening, about what I've *seen*."

"I know this is painful, but you've got to tell me. You've got to tell me what you've seen and what you're afraid you'll do."

Bernie gulps audibly and draws a raspy breath. "I'm afraid I'm going to kill her—no! I *know* I'm going to kill her! I can't let her live after what I've seen, Charlie. No man could let someone live after—" He coughs, spits into a handkerchief.

"Why, in the name of everything holy," Father Briggs manages to ask, "would you even *think* such a thing?"

Bernie explains, choking now and then on his own words.

It started with noises at night—thumps and scrapes on the roof above his bedroom. Several times he has actually gotten out of bed to investigate, going down to the backyard in his pajamas. But he has seen nothing on the roof or anywhere else that could explain the noises. *Must've been a raccoon,* he's told himself, *or maybe birds.* Scrub jays are known to crack nuts on the shingles of roofs. But at *night?* What he really believes deep in his heart of hearts, far deeper than the light of rationality can reach, is that somebody has been walking around on the roof of his house in the dead of night.

Living in a house for thirty years, one gets to know the little noises it makes—the creaking of a certain door, the click of a certain latch, the whine of a certain faucet. Bernie has heard the opening of the window in the guest room where his wife sleeps. The window frame is warped, which makes it tough to open. It makes a peculiar squeak. And that's when the *other* sounds begin, the ones that cut Bernie to the quick, the breathy grunts and heaves of sexual passion, the little cries of delight, the moans of a woman in ecstasy.

Bernie, who has never had much use for religion, pauses and crosses himself. Father Briggs blinks a stinging drop of sweat out of his eye.

"It's been happening two, maybe three times a week, right in my own house, for the love of God. At first I couldn't believe that some son of a bitch would have the guts to come right into my house and do this with me at home, just down the hall. It ate at me, Charlie, like a bad rash. Sometimes I wondered if I was going crazy. A couple times I almost jumped out of bed and barged into her bedroom, but I couldn't do it. I was scared. It's like I was frozen to the sheets in my bed. Something about the whole thing, the noises on the roof, the window—it scared the shit out of me. It seemed"—he gulps again—*"unnatural."*

"You still haven't told me what you saw."

Last night, shortly after one in the morning, he heard the thumps and scrapes on the roof, then the faraway squeaking of the window in Fran's room. A few long minutes of silence ensued, and the moaning began as usual. Bernie swung out of bed, his heart beating madly in his ears, his face streaming sweat. As if they had brains of their own, his feet moved him through the door of his room to the hallway, headed for the source of the sounds. His hand gripped the doorknob to the room where his wife slept. He twisted it and pushed. The door swung open, and the sounds grew loud—Fran's whispers, husky with sweet agony, and a sickening, liquid sound that reminded Bernie of a man sucking an orange. His fingers found the light switch, snapped it upward.

"And I saw her, Charlie, kneeling on the bed, with her nightdress pulled up around her shoulders"—Bernie sobs now—"and that *man*, Charlie, that son of a bitch who lives up in the old Gestern place."

Father Briggs bites his lower lip so hard that blood leaks down his chin. He grips the crucifix that hangs around his neck and prays urgently that he will not hear the next words out of Bernie Pellagrini's mouth. Terror rumbles through him like an earthquake.

"He was down between her legs with his tongue, Charlie, and he was sucking her so hard I thought she was going to die. She was damn-near screaming when I turned the light on. . . ."

And when the lights came on, Fran Pellagrini stared at her husband with a doll's eyes. Instead of pushing her lover away and shrieking with the shame of having been found out, she *laughed*. She cackled like a fishwife, hurling her laughter into Bernie's face like a fistful of gravel. Clovis Gestern rose from his sexual labor and turned his face toward Bernie.

"His mouth was covered with blood. He was sucking blood out of my wife's . . ." Father Briggs wills his eardrums to cease their function, wills his brain to block out the words, the truth. He fails. *Is this the Devil visiting . . . ?* ". . . and that's when I got a good look at his face, Charlie. I knew it was Gestern's face, but I—I don't know how to say this. I don't know if I *can* say it. It wasn't *human*, Charlie. It was all distorted. And the mouth—I don't know if I'm ready to talk about the mouth—it was a monster's mouth. It was like something you'd see in a bad movie!"

33

An Embarkation

i

From the dormer window of his boyhood room Mark Lansen watched the sun climb over the V between Nebraska Hill and Nehalem Mountain. Morning rushed downward into the valley like water over a dam, banishing the night in a surge of golden light that flooded the dark warrens of Oldenburg and made the town habitable again. Or so it seemed.

He wasn't sleepy, which was miraculous, because he had not slept all night. Neither was he hungry. He'd spent the night sitting in this straight chair, wearing only a pair of boxer shorts and staring through the window at the starry sky. He'd watched Mars cross to the western horizon, sometimes not taking his eyes off it for whole minutes. Throughout the night his head had buzzed with questions that would probably have kept him awake even if he'd been tired enough to sleep, questions about Skip Gestern, Kristen, and himself, about the string of horrors that had befallen him since Friday, June 3, only twelve short days ago.

"Let your feelings rule you," Gestern had advised. *"Forget about trying to find rational explanations, because they usually don't work anyway—people only* think *they do."*

As a historian, Mark had developed his own professional credo: *All questions have answers.* Some questions are difficult, to be sure, and the answers may be next to impossible to find. But the answers *do* exist, and they *can* be found. One diligent scholar or another will find them, even if it takes a thousand years.

He now resolved to follow his own credo. He vowed to find the answers, to recapture control over his life. Having made this resolution, he saw the world in a better light. Clothed in the soft rays of dawn, it seemed a blessedly normal place in which men wore yellow power ties and women bought packets of potpourri.

Little kids played baseball, and big kids played house. Cops gave speeding tickets, and dogs chased cats and . . .

And the hag sat in the leafy branches of the magnificent old oak from which the late John Lansen had strung two tire-swings, her spinning wheel wedged in a woody crook. She stared mutely at him like an armed sentry.

"Root it out, Mark."

Mark's hair stiffened on his neck as he stared back at her from his spot at the second-floor window. He and she were eye-level with each other, not more than ten paces apart. He could plainly see the urgency in that wrinkled face, the unblinking determination in those flinty eyes. Her skin was a webwork of wrinkles, her hands a blur of brown bone as she worked the spinning wheel. The rays of morning glanced off the huge silver ring she wore, etching bright trails on his field of vision with every movement of her hand.

The wheel spun. In his mind Mark heard its windy whir, felt its breeze on his cheeks. *She's spinning my destiny,* he whispered to himself.

An ember of anger flared in Mark's chest, the anger of frustration and fear. *She's the one!* screamed a voice in his head. *This whole sad, fucking story started with her, didn't it?—the very moment you first laid eyes on her outside Cramer Hall. Ten minutes later a man jumped off a high-rise building and nearly killed you. Less than a minute after he landed, he was talking to you, calling you by name—talking, yes—with his brain splattered all over the sidewalk, with his spine broken in God knows how many places. And it's been downhill ever since, hasn't it, Buckaroo?*

"This is where it stops!" shouted Mark Lansen, whirling.

He bounded from the room and pounded down the curving staircase into the first-floor hallway. His bare feet scarcely hit the floor as he darted through the kitchen into the rear porch, and the screened door slammed loudly behind him. The cool morning stung his skin as he sprinted wildly toward the old oak, his feet thumping the damp grass, the air fanning his hair. His hands closed around the rope that secured a tire-swing to a branch high above in the oak, and without thinking he hauled himself aloft, hand over hand, climbing like a chimpanzee or a superbly trained athlete. When he gained the branch to which the rope was knotted, he saw that the hag was no longer in the tree. He frantically scanned the leafy riot above and around him, listened hard for an alien heartbeat and sniffed the air hungrily, but he found nothing of the hag except a lingering trace of her warm reek.

Mark lowered himself down the rope and gasped when he landed. Thaddeus stood barefoot at the base of the tree, wearing his Portland Trail Blazers pajama bottoms, looking sleepy and bewildered.

"Where did she go?" asked Tad, rubbing his crusty eyes.

"She—she—" Mark's breath caught. *God! I just climbed a thirty-foot rope without breaking a sweat!* Realizations exploded in his brain like a string of firecrackers.

"My door was open, and I heard you run out of your room," Tad said. "I was afraid something was wrong—"

"Wait a minute, Tad Bear," breathed Mark, going down on one knee and laying hold of the boy's shoulders. "Are you saying *you* saw her, too?"

"I got up and followed you out. I looked out the door and saw you climbing the rope. You're really a great rope-climber, Dad Bear. I never knew—"

"You're sure you actually *saw* her?"

"Yeah, I saw her. Who was she? Why was she up in the tree?"

Mark pulled the boy close and hugged him hard. "You saw her, too. Your old Dad Bear's not loony after all. Did you see where she went?"

Tad had not.

Then she must've jumped, Mark said to himself. *A woman in her nineties climbs at least thirty feet into an oak tree, lugging a spinning wheel and a heavy bag of belongings, then jumps down when accosted. You see this kind of shit all the time. And Nancy Reagan is really Ernest Borgnine in drag.*

Mark and Tad headed for the house, arm in arm.

ii

Mark helped his mother with the breakfast dishes. She voiced her worry over the fact that he'd drunk only a glass of orange juice and had eaten nothing. He wasn't sick, was he? He assured her that he wasn't.

When they'd finished in the kitchen, Marta drew him into the solarium and closed the door. Lowering herself into a sofa, she said how glad she was to have him home safe and sound after yesterday's "accident," how relieved she was that he'd found Kristen. Mark protested that he had not found Kristen at all: She'd found *him*.

Marta told him that she no longer considered Kristen's employment at Gestern Hall an issue. If working up there made the girl happy, then that was good enough. "But promise me something," she said, patting the sofa seat next to where she sat. He scooted over close. "Promise you'll stay away from that place. If Kristen wants to live up there, that's her business. She knows how her father and I felt about it, and she made her choice. But *you*, Mark—just promise you'll stay away from there."

"First tell me what you know about that place. I can't promise to stay away from Kristen without knowing why."

"The *place* isn't the important thing."

Mark frowned skeptically. "Does this have anything to do with those old Halloween stories that Poverty Ike told for so many years?"

"It has more to do with Kristen herself," Marta answered, looping a hand through her son's elbow and resting her head on his shoulder. "I've been fighting with myself over whether I should tell you this, Mark, and it's not easy for me. I'll do it because I love you, but I don't want anyone else to know." A tear tumbled from her cheek and landed on his hand, causing him a twinge of apprehension. "Kristen isn't John's daughter. She's mine, yes, but John Lansen wasn't her father. I never told him, and I never told Kristen. I never told *anyone*. I loved John, and I was faithful to him ever after. Over the years, though, I lived in mortal dread that he would find out somehow. Luckily he never did. He believed Kristen was his up until the day he—he—died."

She sobbed quietly for a long moment and dried her eyes with a handkerchief that she pulled from the pocket of her smock. Mark sat woodenly, his heart aching. He would have demanded to know why Marta had revealed this *now*, why it was important after nearly twenty-one years, but he didn't trust his voice. He endured a temblor of intense grief for his dead father, a cuckold, a man who had lived a lie without knowing it for more than two decades.

"Who, then?" he asked finally. "Who is Kristen's father?"

Marta stared at him with anguished eyes. "I can't tell you that."

"Why the hell not? What does it matter now?"

"It matters, believe me. Please try not to hate me. I felt that knowing about Kristen might be important to you someday— maybe someday *soon*. And I want you to know that I love you, Mark. . . ." She wept again, but only briefly.

Mark studied her face and saw lines that had shown up only within the five days since John Lansen's death. Her blond hair had lost its honey-tinge to advancing streaks of dull gray. The rose in her cheeks had come out of a jar. The burgeoning anger Mark had felt a moment earlier dissolved. He kissed her forehead and stroked her hair. "I could never hate you, Mom. You know that."

"Then you'll promise to stay away from Gestern Hall?"

Mark agonized. He so wanted to comfort Marta, and he wished for the strength to tell her a white lie, especially if doing so would help her. But he couldn't lie, not to his mother. He had no intention of staying away from Gestern Hall.

iii

He whistled as he left the house, a notebook in his hand and his Dodgers cap on his head. He'd barely set foot on the porch stairs when he heard the telephone ring inside. That would be Kyleen LeBreaux, he knew, calling to set up a session with him. She'd promised to get in touch after returning from Portland.

Mark kept on walking.

Tad had seen the hag. This meant that Mark hadn't imagined her, that he wasn't crazy. The hag was as real as the ground under his feet, which in turn meant that his other problems were real, too. *No loose lug nuts here, Kyleen. My deck has fifty-two cards. Hell, I even climbed a thirty-foot rope in record time this morning, something I haven't done since I was in college. You're looking at a fine specimen of manhood, both physically and mentally!*

Mark had no idea who the hag was, or what interest she had in him. He couldn't explain the weird cravings he'd experienced in his dreams. He didn't know why Kristen had started to behave so strangely (she'd eaten a slug, for the love of God!). *But all questions have answers, don't they?*

Mark meant to find those answers, and he meant to start with a New York private investigator who sat in the Kalapuya County Jail.

iv

Bob Gammage sprawled in the common area of the tiny cell block, smoking a cigarette and watching the television set that was bolted to the ceiling. A breakfast tray lay on the card table next to him, empty but for a ravaged grapefruit rind and an unopened carton of apple juice.

Gammage's ugly face brightened when he heard the clank of the lock on the outer steel door. He welcomed *any* interruption of the mind-numbing nothingness of life in this ungodly little vault. He even welcomed the old fart who came every day to clean the toilet and empty the ashtrays.

The first person through the door was Deputy Will Settergren. On his heels trooped a guy in his mid-thirties, long-limbed, brown-haired. He wore a battered Dodgers cap, a green Oregon Ducks sweatshirt, and faded Levi jeans. He carried a spiral notebook. Settergren introduced him as Mark Lansen, the son of Bob's late lawyer.

"Don't get up," said Mark, smiling whitely and eyeing the cast on Gammage's left arm. He sat in a folding chair on the opposite side of the card table from Kalapuya County's only prisoner. "You up for some friendly conversation?"

"Gosh, let me check my schedule," chuckled Gammage. "Hold my calls, Will. And bring us a bottle of your best cognac."

"This dude's a real cut-up," Settergren said to Mark. "He looks like he belongs with the Manson gang, but we're pretty sure he's harmless. Stay as long as you want, Mr. Lansen. I know the sheriff won't mind, since we don't have any other prisoners or detainees. You're John Lansen's son, and that packs weight around here." Settergren went out, locking the heavy door behind him.

"You don't look like your old man," said Gammage, exhaling a drag of cigarette smoke.

"And you don't really look like a member of the Manson

gang. As a matter of fact, you look like a wholesome, upstanding member of the Hell's Angels." Gammage laughed and offered his visitor a cigarette, which Mark waved away.

"Know what, Speed?" Gammage wheezed. "I liked your old man, even though I didn't know him very long. I'm sorry about what happened to him. He didn't seem like the sort who'd drive a truck off a bridge."

John Lansen *wasn't* that sort, Mark confirmed. A medicolegal autopsy had raised the possibility of murder. The sheriff's deputies hadn't shared this news with him, Bob replied, his face becoming grave. He asked who was doing the investigating. The county sheriff, Mark answered, with help from the Oregon State Police. If they'd uncovered any leads, they hadn't told him.

"Unless they've got some physical evidence to work with, they're probably doing nothing more than interviewing people," Bob said. "They'll talk to all his friends and acquaintances, his clients, his former clients, people he's sued—trying to sniff out a motive. And they'll probably canvass the area around the death scene, looking for somebody who might've seen something."

"Dad told me you used to be a cop in New York."

"That's right. In fact, I was a homicide detective before I got into undercover investigations, so I know something about these things. I gotta tell you, Speed, it may be a long time before the cops dig up a lead, and they might not ever dig one up at all. A scary percentage of murders in this country go unsolved. Are you ready to deal with that possibility?"

"I don't know. I wasn't prepared for losing Dad, that's for sure. If you want to know the truth, I haven't had the time or energy to think much about the investigation, much less worry about it."

"Why's that?"

"Swear you won't think I'm crazy? I'm pretty sure Dad's death figures into a whole shitload of other things that have been happening around here recently—primarily to me, but to others, too—my sister, an old Catholic priest who was a close friend of our family, my parents' next-door neighbors."

Bob had heard about the priest—what was his name? Father Briggs? Burned himself to death in the park a couple of weeks ago, one of the deputies had told him.

"My chief interest at the moment is someone you know, a man named Sam Darkenwald," Mark said.

Now *there* was a piece of work, said Bob Gammage, jabbing a stubby finger at Mark and winking. He gave the short history of his relationship with Darkenwald. "I hope Sam's okay. The deputies say no one has seen him since he bolted out the back door of Poverty Ike's on the night I got shot. He's not really a bad sort, know what I mean? He's just a little . . ." He whistled like a flying saucer and fluttered his good hand in the air.

"Did he ever say anything about the person who sent him to you, or about his friend, Leo Fobbs?"

"Now that you mention it, that name rings a bell, but I'm not sure why. I didn't hear it from Sam, I can tell you that for sure. Fobbs . . . Fobbs. . . ." He scratched his beard-shadowed chin. "Okay, I'm stumped. Who is he?"

"Only a guy who jumped off Ione Plaza and almost landed on yours truly about two weeks ago. He was a derelict, and he had a knife in his hand. He'd been keeping a file on me—newspaper clips, newsletter stories, faculty roster, stuff like that. He was also the bosom buddy of the talented and lovely Sam Darkenwald."

"Shit!" exclaimed Bob Gammage, pressing his palm against his forehead. "I heard about that on the tube in Portland—the loony who jumped off the apartment building on the college campus. And *you're* the poor son of a bitch he almost landed on!" He hadn't paid much attention to the local news back then, since he was spending his nights hanging out on the streets, looking for Skye Padilla. But *this* particular story had caught his attention. "That was back when I actually had a client."

"You don't have one now?"

"You kidding? You think my client didn't fire me when I called to say I'd just been sentenced to thirty days in the Kickapoo County slam on a gun charge? Think again, Speed."

"It's *Kalapuya* County."

"Whatever. A jail's a jail, and that's what this is, in case you haven't noticed. I've got a hole in my shoulder that hurts like a motherfucker. I've lost my client, which means I'm losing money I don't even have. To top it off, I've now got a criminal record for a beef I don't deserve, something I'll have all my life. Don't let my pretty smile fool you—I'm pissed off, and I'm so bored that I'm counting the rivets in the doors. Which reminds me: Your old man said he was about to file a motion to get me released early. Know anything about that?"

Mark recalled that his father had mentioned his intention to file the motion on Monday. That had been impossible, of course, since John had died the previous Friday night or early Saturday morning.

"Fuck. That means I need to go through the public defender's office, which could take as long as I'm supposed to serve."

"Wait a minute. Dad had probably finished drafting the motion on Friday. If I found it in his office, I could take it to Sheriff Conrad, and he could make sure it goes to the judge. Might not be according to Hoyle, but it might work."

"If you do that for me, Speed, I'll owe you a big one. I'll buy you the biggest steak in Oregon."

Mark rose from his chair. "One more thing. I saw Skye Padilla up at Gestern Hall yesterday. I didn't talk to her, but I could see she was in one piece. She didn't look too happy."

Gammage clenched his right hand into a fist, then relaxed it again. "So old Sam Darkenwald was right. Skye *is* at Gestern Hall, after all." He stared at Mark. "Tell me something, Speed. What's wrong with this town? Will Settergren told me about that old priest who burned himself to death, like I said. Yesterday he told me about that Gary Bayliss dude, the one who mixed it up with Sam the night I got shot—says that somebody or something attacked him and nearly bled him dry. It's all part of it, Will says, all part of whatever you can feel around here at night. Naturally, I suggested that he was a raving idiot. I urged him to lay off caffeine and get professional help. But I have this nasty feeling that maybe he *wasn't* raving. What the hell was he talking about?"

Mark gazed unblinkingly back at Gammage. "I don't know. Maybe this is something we need to find out, you and I."

"Forget it. Once I get out of here, I'm hauling my rosy ass back to New York. I'm taking Skye with me, by the way, which might be tricky, with my arm in this cast. Whatever's wrong in this town is your concern, not mine. I'm curious, yeah, but not *that* fucking curious."

"You said you'd owe me one if I got you out of here. Were you serious about that?"

"I was serious, yeah. If you can pull it off, I'll owe you. Tell me what you want."

Mark gripped the back of the folding chair so tightly that his fingers turned bone-white. He leaned forward. "I want you to help me find out who killed Dad and why."

"How am I supposed to do that if the sheriff and the state police can't do it?"

"You'll have information they don't have, stuff Dad told me. You'll have a better idea where to look. With a little luck, you might get Skye Padilla in the bargain, along with the answers to a lot of questions I have. What do you have to lose?"

Bob Gammage looked thoughtful as he studied the plaster cast on his arm, absently tracing the ballpoint signatures of the jail staff with a fingernail. Then he offered his right hand. "If you get me out of here, and if you'll put me up and feed me twice a day, we've got a deal. But no guarantees, okay? I'll spend a week following up on whatever you give me, and if it pans out, wonderful. If it doesn't pan out, then I'm on my way. Can you agree to that?"

Mark agreed, and he shook Bob Gammage's hand.

PART III

~

We seem to move on a thin crust which may
at any moment be rent by the subterranean forces below.

—Sir James G. Frazer,
The Golden Bough

PART-III

34

Midnight Canyon

i

Father Le Fanu stood in the shade of an old elm near the corner of First Street and Chinook Avenue, his boom box in his hand, his earphones on his head. He wore a tweed sport coat that was much too heavy for this hot summer day, and a Roman collar that made it even hotter. He lip-synched along with Koko Taylor's molten vocal, but his mind was not on the jazz.

An old station wagon halted in the driveway of the house across the street. Two women passengers helped a man out of the rear seat—a hulking, bull-shouldered man who walked unsteadily. The women led him into the house, each propping him at an elbow. They returned to fetch a young girl from the car, one grossly misshapen by some tragic disease. They wheeled her into the house in a collapsible wheelchair, then came back for luggage and overnight bags.

Father Le Fanu waited a while longer, watching with dark, glittering eyes.

ii

A moment later, the woman who had driven the station wagon emerged and drove away, a helpful friend of the family who had done her good deed for the day. Father Le Fanu switched off his boom box, crossed the street, and climbed the squeaky steps to the Baylisses' front entrance. He tried the doorbell and then, not hearing it ring, knocked on the splintery screened door.

Freddye Ann Bayliss answered. The obsidian lens of the scrying mirror had done no justice to the pallor of her cheeks, the emptiness of her eyes, the fleshlessness of her limbs. Le Fanu knew that her days on this earth were numbered.

"Forgive me," he said in accented English. "My name is Father Gautier Le Fanu. You are Madame Bayliss, are you not?"

Freddye Ann nodded.

"I've come from France in answer to a letter sent me by someone you know. He is Father Charles Francis Briggs, the pastor of your parish, I understand."

"Father Briggs is dead. I don't belong to the parish anymore."

Le Fanu had known of the priest's death, of course. He'd actually seen it happen in the scrying mirror, a "replay" of a reality that had occurred in a different place and time. Such was the utility of scrying mirrors. While watching him burn and twitch and writhe, Le Fanu had admired Father Briggs's courage.

"I wonder if I might come in for a brief visit, madame. I wish to speak with your husband and daughter, and with you, too, of course. I won't be long, I promise."

Freddye Ann looked wary. Her husband had returned home from the hospital in Astoria only minutes ago, she said, and was in no condition to talk with anyone.

"This visit concerns your Father Briggs," Le Fanu explained. "It concerns your family and the trouble you've had. Please don't think me presumptuous, but I feel as if I can be of help to you. Your Father Briggs spoke of you in his letters to me." Le Fanu wiped sweat from his forehead with an immaculate white handkerchief. "He worried so about you and your little girl, madame. He dearly loved you both, and begged me to come here, having heard that I have considerable knowledge of—" He broke off and rethought his words. "He felt certain that I could help you."

After pondering the matter and deciding it was the least she could do in memory of her once-beloved Father Charlie, Freddye Ann pulled the door open wide and motioned Le Fanu inside.

iii

Gary Bayliss lay on the living room sofa, looking even more pallid than his wife. Days' worth of stubble covered his bloodless cheeks, and his ratty Fu Manchu mustache drooped over his upper lip. He hardly glanced at the tall, silvered gentleman whom Freddye Ann admitted through the front door.

"This guy's a priest from France," said Freddye Ann. "His

name is Father La—La—" She stumbled over the French name, and Le Fanu supplied it. "He's here because Father Briggs asked him to come, or something like that. He wants to talk to us."

Gary Bayliss set aside the sports magazine he'd been browsing, and looked squarely at Le Fanu for the first time. "Well, go get the man some coffee, for Christ's sake. And bring some for me, too." His wife shambled off like an oft-whipped slave.

Father Le Fanu placed his boom box against a wall near the door and pocketed the headphones. He took a wooden rocking chair and pulled it close to the sofa where Gary lay. "I'm honored to meet you, monsieur. Again, I am sorry to disturb you so soon after your return from the hospital."

Gary apologized for the clutter of the house. His goddamn wife had decided she was too good to do housework anymore, he added with a weak chuckle.

"If you don't mind, monsieur, I want to know precisely what happened to you. I speak of that which led to your present physical state, of course."

"And why would you want to know *that?*"

"If my suspicions are correct, what happened to you has happened to many others, and will happen to yet more people, unless we take the proper action. This is why I've come. You, your family, this whole town, as a matter of fact, may be in great danger. Now, please tell me."

"I didn't tell the cops, even though they gave me the third fuckin' degree. I don't see why I should tell *you.*"

"You feared that they wouldn't believe you, isn't this so? You feared that you would look like a fool, telling them something so outlandish. This is understandable. I can assure you, monsieur, that I will not scoff."

Gary Bayliss looked thoughtful, and Le Fanu sensed the working of this crude man's intellect, such as it was. Freddye Ann delivered cups of coffee. Le Fanu sniffed his cup and knew immediately that it was insipid American instant, but he took a sip to be polite. Gary ordered Freddye Ann from the room, saying that he and their visitor had private business to conduct, then motioned the priest to lean close. "I'd been noticing this girl around town quite a bit," he began, smirking. "Nasty little fox, too—blond, nice tits, a tad skinny to be ideal, but *young.* College girl. I knew her by name, of course, but I never really talked to her, except when she came into my place to buy gas. Anyway, I never dreamed she was hot for me. I mean, she never gave me any reason to suspect. She comes from one of the town's hoity-toity families, and I'm just a regular old workin' grunt. I've never had a pot to piss in, and I s'pose I never will. Guys like me don't have a prayer with chicks like that, or so I thought."

"Are you saying that it was this young woman who attacked you?"

Gary explained that he visited Poverty Ike's saloon every evening right after closing, just to sip a few beers and to shake the dice cup with old Ike. On Monday night (Tuesday morning, actually, because it was after midnight) he headed over to Poverty Ike's as he normally did, and had just turned onto North Main when he saw something out of the corner of his eye, something that just dipped below the top edge of his windshield. A bare foot rested against the glass, a small one, a woman's or a kid's.

"Christ Almighty, I hit the brakes, because I'm thinking that somebody's sitting on the roof of my pickup! It blows me away, because I can't see how someone could've gotten up there without me knowin' it, right? There sure as hell wasn't anyone on the roof when I left the ThriftyKwik. But before I could get the truck stopped, she slithered in through the passenger window—" Gary saw Father Le Fanu's eyes widen. "You heard me, Father— *slithered*, like some kind of Chinese acrobat, you know? Suddenly she's sitting right in the cab with me, grinning to beat the band and burning me up with those eyes of hers."

Father Le Fanu asked him to describe the woman's eyes, which he did. "A doll's eyes, Father—a doll that has a bright light bulb inside her head. They were *blue* like . . . like . . ." Gary shook his head, unable to think of an adequate word. "Yeah, she *was* the girl I talked about a minute ago—naked as the day she was born, too, and looking at me like she'd never had a good lay in her life. Well, I damn-near wrecked the truck. I finally got it stopped right in the middle of North Main, just on the other side of the underpass. The street was deserted, like it always is after sundown, and that's why I'm pretty sure nobody saw us."

The girl had talked to him, called him by name, suggested that they go somewhere more private. She'd known that he'd been looking her over for some time. She'd known that on several occasions he'd gone into the men's room of his store to "stroke the cougar" after she'd come in for a fill-up. How in the hell she could've known these things without reading his mind, Gary couldn't fathom.

"About this time my head was in a tizzy, Father. I couldn't figure how this chick had gotten onto the roof of my pickup. I hadn't heard anything land on it, no thumps or bumps or anything like that. I was thinking, 'Fuck, did she *fly* up there, or what?' I actually wondered if she'd dropped down off the overpass, but that seemed about as likely as a monkey learning algebra. And the way she came in through the window, it was like all her bones had turned to rubber. I've never seen anything like it in my life."

Gary sank back into the pillows beneath his head, looking exhausted. His face had become the color of a flounder's belly. After taking several deep breaths, he said that he drove to the alley between the ruins of the old Brownsmeade Hotel and the railroad station. By the light of the moon and stars, the girl made love to him, straddling him right there on the seat of his Chevy pickup.

"I must've come three, four times, and I didn't think I'd ever be able to come again, know what I mean, Father? No, you probably don't know what I mean, you being a priest and everything. Take my word for it, though, this was sex like no man has ever had sex. And just when I think I'll never get it up again, she goes down on me, and next thing I know, she's licking the old cougar and sucking it like a fuckin' milking machine. I don't know how many more times I came. All I knew was that I was getting weak, like when you've been in a hot tub too long. I could feel sleep coming on, but still she just kept sucking and sucking, and I'll be damned if I didn't shoot off one more time. This time I felt like my heart was gonna explode right out through my chest.

"I could feel myself sinking, Father, like I was falling in slow motion down a well, but I managed to open my eyes and look at her one last time. I suppose I should've been scared shitless, but I wasn't—I guess I didn't have the energy to be scared. She'd *changed*. She'd become something I didn't think was real, something that belonged in a comic book about monsters and demons. She had *teeth*, Father. . . ."

Father Le Fanu patted Gary Bayliss on the shoulder. "You needn't say anymore, my son. I've heard quite enough."

Gary grabbed the priest's sleeve in his fist and held on. "But I need to tell you one more thing, Father." His glassy eyes bore into Le Fanu's. "She was the best woman I've ever had. She was the best woman a man could ever *hope* to have. I don't care what she is, and I don't care if having her kills me. If she ever comes back, I'll let her take me again. In fact, I hope she *does* come back, because I'll be waiting for her with open arms. She can have my cock, she can have my blood! She can have . . ." His breath failed him, and his fist relaxed, letting loose Father Le Fanu's sleeve. A faint, mad smile quivered at the corners of his mouth.

"It's time for you to rest, my son," said Le Fanu. "You've told me everything I need to know."

iv

The whine of a powerful electric motor made Father Le Fanu turn away from the sofa. Gretchen Bayliss rolled into the room, having exchanged the collapsible wheelchair for an impressive powered one.

"Top-Kick!" wheezed Gary Bayliss when he saw his daughter. His eyes actually sparkled. "Come here, baby, and give this old trooper a kiss. Then I want to introduce you to Father Le Fanu, who's come all the way from France to visit us."

The girl motored past Le Fanu to the sofa and with great effort leaned low enough to plant a kiss on her dad's cheek. Gary introduced her, using her real first name and touting her as the smartest kid in Kalapuya County. "I call her Top-Kick, because she's the real boss around here," he added, grinning. "That's what a grunt calls a first sergeant in the army. This little girl gets straight A's, by the way. There's not a kid in school who can touch her in the smarts department."

Le Fanu rose and offered his sinewy hand to Gretchen, and she shook it feebly. Gazing into her startlingly blue eyes, the old man sensed something extraordinary in her, a raw power born of conviction or faith, beaming forth like lantern light from a distant midnight canyon. He had sensed such power in others, but only rarely. He doubted that this girl even knew she had it. It made her a force to be reckoned with.

"Would you like to see my room, Father?" she asked in her small voice.

"I'd be delighted, my child, if your father gives his permission."

Gary Bayliss saw nothing wrong with this. As Le Fanu and Gretchen left the room, he bellowed to Freddye Ann for more coffee.

V

Gretchen ushered the old priest into her room and bade him sit on the bed. Le Fanu, of course, could not help gaping at the array of likenesses of St. Joan of Arc that covered the walls, at the statues and busts displayed on tables and desks, at the collection of biographies and commentaries that lined the shelves.

Gretchen closed the door of the room and maneuvered her chair to face her visitor. "You're here because of what's happened to Mom and Dad, aren't you?"

"I am."

"How did you know about us?"

"The pastor of your parish, your Father Briggs, wrote to me. He begged me to come. I only regret that I could not arrive before he—"

"But why did he write to *you?*"

"My name is whispered among a small circle of scholars and clergy as belonging to a man with expertise in certain matters. Your Father Briggs consulted an acquaintance in the Vatican, a historian he'd studied with in seminary, and this man gave him my name."

"These *certain matters*—we're talking about vampires, aren't we?"

Le Fanu folded his spectacles and put them into a pocket of his sport coat. "I'm afraid this is true, my child. Unless I am grossly mistaken, one vampire in particular is at the center of your trouble here in Oldenburg, a very old man who once lived in France. In fact, he once lived near Domrémy, where he terrorized the population for many generations. In those times he was known as the Sire de l'Hier, that is to say, Lord Yesterday. He was the leader of a cult of heretics who practiced witchcraft and all manner of abominations."

Why had such a man come to Oldenburg? Gretchen wanted to know. Lord Yesterday wasn't merely a vampire, he was also a wizard, a sorcerer, said Le Fanu. A vampire's long-term survival depends on the use of magic as much as on the sucking of blood. Through magic a vampire can learn the future and in many cases influence it. Without magic, a vampire would eventually succumb to the ravages of time.

Lord Yesterday, according to legend, had made a pact with an English witch named Amanda Crowe in the mid-eighteenth century. In return for certain secrets that would enable her to live the equivalent of twelve normal lifetimes, Amanda Crowe was to bear Lord Yesterday's child. This child, in turn, would beget children, a line that would carry the blood of Lord Yesterday.

The pact established the fate of a particular child—the first female to be born of Lord Yesterday's and Amanda Crowe's line during the next "high cycle" of the Blood Star, which was the sorcerer's name for Mars. This child, who was to be a girl, would become Lord Yesterday's wife. Separated by several generations from Amanda Crowe, she would become the mother of yet another offspring, a full-blown vampire, born with a vampire's longevity and powers. This young vampire would be Lord Yesterday's heir. He would be capable of siring a line of full vampires, an actual dynasty.

"You must understand that most of the popular myths about vampires, those you see in films or read in cheap novels, are just that—myth," said Le Fanu. "A vampire cannot create another vampire simply by sucking someone's blood. Vampires are *born*. A true *primo* vampire, however, can only be born of parents who each have the needed degree of vampire blood in their veins. At least one of the parents must be more than half-vampire, meaning that his or her father or mother must have been a primo vampire."

"Did Amanda Crowe keep her part of the bargain?"

"Yes, indeed. She even cast a spell that guaranteed the birth of a woman-child during the next cycle of the Blood Star, which was nearly a century off. She could not have known, however, that her own daughter would turn against her. Amanda's daughter, you see, was also a witch, and she was determined to prevent her child from falling under the influence of her father, Lord Yesterday. She adamantly opposed his evil scheme to found a dynasty of vampires. Shortly after the birth of her daughter, she killed her own mother. Then she cast a spell on a spinning wheel, which enabled her to spin yarn from her very own skin. Her magic kept her alive long enough to weave this yarn into cloth, and to sew the cloth into a sack. She placed the infant in the sack and buried her in the ground, singing the proper incantations. The tiny child lay there for nearly a generation. The mother, of course, died soon after, because not even a witch can live long without her skin. In the meantime, Lord Yesterday's enemies drove him from England back to France."

"Are you saying that the child was still alive, even after being buried?" asked Gretchen, captivated.

"Yes, this is true. Her name was Elspeth, and she survived. The spell, you see, had put her in a state of suspended animation, so she didn't need air or food or water. According to her mother's instructions, relatives dug her up many years later, when any threat from Lord Yesterday seemed remote. Elspeth grew into a normal girl and then into a beautiful young woman. She married an ambitious young gentleman from Liverpool."

"What was Lord Yesterday up to all this time?"

"He kept close track of his granddaughter from afar, using a tool called a scrying mirror. By outward appearances, this device is little more than a block of wood with an inlaid disk of obsidian. In skilled hands, it offers views of both the future and the past. Through that dark stone one can see events taking place on the surface of a Jovian moon, if one wishes, or detect spells and ligatures cast by other witches and wizards. Using his scrying mirror, Lord Yesterday observed the comings and goings of Elspeth."

"Did Elspeth become a witch like her mother?"

"Yes, Gretchen, she did. In fact, she became a good enough witch to discover that Lord Yesterday was watching her from the dark cellar of his mansion in faraway Burgundy. She too was adept in the use of a scrying mirror, you see. She learned that Lord Yesterday meant to claim the first child that she herself would bear, in order to renew the pursuit of his scheme to start a line of vampires."

"Wasn't there anything she could do to stop him?"

Elspeth feared that her own witchy powers weren't strong enough to hold Lord Yesterday at bay forever, Le Fanu answered. Elspeth knew that she needed something more to use against him. "In a mere handful of spots on the surface of the earth are the loci of the dark powers, that is to say, the intersections of cosmic streams, the points at which spiritual forces intertwine and flow together. No one knows why these spots exist, any more than one can say why the moon spins in such a way as to keep only one side toward the earth. We do know that wizards and necromancers are drawn to such places. They're able to tap the powers that flow through these locations, assuming they know how to do so without annihilating themselves. Such a locus lies near here on the side of a mountain, the one you know as Nehalem."

Gretchen told him that the local Indian tribes had woven their own legends about such a place. They called it Mesatchie Illihee.

Primitive cultures around the world have often thought such pieces of ground enchanted or holy, Le Fanu replied. Weird manifestations occur in and around these spots—frightening noises and atmospheric effects, even voices.

Through her powers of divination, Elspeth discovered the existence of the magical locus on Nehalem Mountain in faraway North America, even though she herself had never left the misty shores of England. She persuaded her husband to seek employment with the Hudson's Bay Company, to which the English crown had granted control of the vast Oregon Country, for here was where the magical Nehalem Mountain lay. When the company hired him, Jordan Carey requested posting to Fort Vancouver, the nearest English settlement to the mountain. He built a cabin near an Indian village, where his wife became friendly with the native witches and soothsayers.

"Beyond this point, our knowledge of Elspeth Carey dims," said Le Fanu. "Whether she succeeded in actually reaching the locus on Nehalem Mountain, I don't know. I do know, however, that the Sire de l'Hier—Lord Yesterday—followed her here. Accompanied by a band of his disciples, he journeyed to America and traveled by ox-drawn wagon across the frontier to Oregon. He first established himself somewhere to the south of the locus—I don't know where exactly. Sometime later, he relocated to a site on the side of Nehalem Mountain, hoping to snare Elspeth or her child, I assume. I'm told that he even arranged the dismantling of his old Gothic mansion in Burgundy, and had it transported by ship to his new home, where he reassembled it."

"And you think that Lord Yesterday is the one who's been hurting my Mom?" asked Gretchen, her voice shaking slightly.

"I think so, yes. God only knows how many others he has victimized over the generations. But we have an added problem, unfortunately: *another* vampire, a female. She may not be a primo vampire, but she is in all probability a child of the Sire de l'Hier. She is the one who nearly killed your father. There may be yet others."

"What do we do now, Father?"

"We must kill them. Unfortunately, it is far easier to say this, my child, than it is to do it."

35

Sharpening Stakes

A few minutes after 1:00 P.M., Tressa Downey walked into County Commissioner Nyberg's office and told him she needed to take the rest of the day as sick leave. Ed Nyberg readily gave his permission, then remarked with a suggestive grin that Tressa looked as if she hadn't gotten much sleep last night, apparently thinking this was why she needed the time off. Tressa thanked him without smiling back, spun on her heels, and left without another word.

In truth, she hadn't gotten *any* sleep last night, but not for the reason that Nyberg envisioned in his filthy little mind. She'd stayed up and read Father Briggs's journal through to the bitter end. Having done that, she wondered whether she would ever sleep again.

She walked to the Omdahl house on the corner of Clatskanie and First. Brett Omdahl answered the door, wearing a work shirt and old blue jeans covered with sawdust.

"Brett, are you okay?" Tressa asked through the screen door. "I've been worried sick about you."

"You heard about it, huh? I suppose everyone in town has."

"Dr. Schell told me yesterday—the official version, that is. I'd like to know more. Can I come in?"

The boy let her in and offered her a soda. He and Fudd were alone in the house, he said, since his parents were at work at the James River mill, and his little brother had gone to the beach with friends. Brett had been busy in his father's shop downstairs when Tressa came by, which explained the sawdust on his jeans.

Tressa accepted a can of Orange Crush and followed him to the rear porch, where Fudd lay on a huge canvas pillow full of soft cedar chips. A vet in Astoria had clipped much of the fur from the big dog's shoulders in order to suture his wounds and had dressed them with thick padded bandages. Fudd thumped his tail against the pillow and whimpered a hello, begging for a pat and a scratch, which Tressa willingly administered, taking care not to touch the bandages. She sat in a wicker chair near Fudd's pillow, and Brett sat cross-legged on the floor on the dog's other side.

"About what happened two nights ago," said Tressa, sipping her Crush, "what you told your parents and Dr. Schell and the cops—the bit about the hit-and-run driver—that was all bullshit, wasn't it?"

"What if it was?"

"I want to know what *really* happened, kiddo. I want you to tell me the whole thing."

"No, you don't."

"I'll get you started, okay? Fudd didn't get hurt by any car. Those wounds on his back came from claws. Somebody or something attacked him, or he attacked *it* because it was after you. Why don't you take it from there?"

Brett ran a hand through his barley-colored hair and stared beyond the screened-in porch toward Nehalem Mountain, which loomed darkly in the east against a hot summer sky. "You've been talking to Gretchen again, haven't you? You're starting to believe all her wild monster stories, I bet."

Tressa hadn't talked to Gretchen since last weekend, she replied, which was before Gary Bayliss ended up in the hospital in Astoria. The Baylisses were due home sometime today, she'd heard. "Maybe I *do* believe Gretchen's stories," she added, studying Brett's earnest, young face. "Maybe you can give me good reason *not* to believe them."

Brett fidgeted, laced and unlaced his fingers. He started, then stopped. Finally he told the story slowly, apologetically, as if he didn't expect to be believed. Tressa heard him out in numbed silence—a tale of a young woman who accosted him in the park, seduced him with her cobalt eyes, who maybe had meant to kill him with her wicked claws and teeth. Fudd's condition was proof of her capability. When the telling was done, Brett's cheeks burned red.

Tressa wanted to hug him and tell him that everything would be all right, but she herself didn't know whether this was so. The world was topsy-turvy, unreliable. Insanity was afoot.

"You don't think I'm making it all up?" asked Brett, not yet daring to look up. "Can you see why I told everybody it was a hit-and-run?"

"I *know* you're not making it up. I think you're scared, and I think you have every right to be."

"Wrong. I was scared before, but not anymore. I'm going to take care of things, Tress. I'm going to do what somebody should've done a long time ago."

"Meaning what?"

He explained that yesterday afternoon and again this morning Gretchen had called on the telephone from Columbia Hospital in Astoria, where she and her mother had kept a vigil at Gary Bayliss's bedside. Gretchen had heard about Brett's "accident" on Monday night, which was the same night someone or something had attacked her father. She and Brett had compared notes, had talked frankly about what each of them had seen in the night. They'd decided what must be done.

"There's no doubt about what we're up against," said Brett, getting to his feet. "Vampires. At least that's what Gretchen says they are, and from what I've seen, I can't say she's wrong. The one I met didn't look like what I've always thought a vampire should look like, but what else sucks a person's blood, huh? What else can do things to your mind with its eyes? I guess it doesn't matter what you call them."

Tressa's guts twisted as the brutal logic sunk in. *Vampires.* Not so hard to say, once you put your mind to it. *Vampires were loose in Oldenburg,* and they were sucking people's blood in the dark of night, making them sick and terrorizing them, driving others to acts of desperate evil. The memory of the Pellagrini tragedy loomed obscenely in her mind.

"Brett, tell me what you plan to do."

"Do I need to spell it out for you? I'm going to *kill* them, that's what. I'm going to kill them before they hurt anybody else. I don't know how many there are—I know there's at least two of them—but I've got almost a dozen two-by-two stakes sharpened. . . ." He slapped sawdust off his jeans, and Tressa knew now what he'd been doing in his father's shop. He'd been preparing his weapons, sharpening stakes to pound through the hearts of vampires. "And if there's more than a dozen, then I guess I'll need to sharpen some more stakes, that's all. I'll be wearing my confirmation medallion, because it has a cross on it, so I'll be okay. And I've nailed together a wooden cross to carry along, just in case I need a spare. Gretchen and I'll go over to Saint Pie's before we leave, and she'll show me where the holy water is. I figure we'll need a couple pints of it, at least."

"I can't believe you're involving Gretchen in this!"

"She's already involved, okay? It'll be a hassle taking her along, that's a fact, lugging her wheelchair in and out of the car, but I'll need her moral support. Besides, she knows more about these things than I do. She's got Joan of Arc on her side, y'know? I'll be her Jean d'Aulon."

"You'll be her *what?*"

"Her Jean d'Aulon. He was Joan of Arc's squire when she was fighting the English." Brett smiled sheepishly, and he looked so young that Tressa wanted to cry. "Gretch calls me that sometimes. She's looking at this thing like it's a holy quest or something."

"Brett, listen to me." Tressa jumped up and grabbed his arm. "You've got to drop this crazy idea right now. You can't possibly know how dangerous it could be."

"Oh, I *know*, believe me. I've seen one of them face to face, remember? I've seen what she did to Fudd. I've felt her teeth on my—on my—" He stammered as a memory flashed in his brain.

"Brett, you can't just go around killing people, not even if you're sure they're vampires. Do you have any idea what'll happen if you actually pound a stake into someone's chest? You'll be arrested and tried for murder, probably as an adult. If you involve Gretchen, her life will be ruined along with yours. You'll get sent to prison or a home for the criminally insane, and by the time you get out, if you get out at all, you'll be old and weak and wrinkled. Is that what you want?"

"So what am I supposed to do—forget about everything that's happened? Am I supposed to forget that Skip Gestern is killing Gretchen's mom? Or that Kristen Lansen is sneaking around town at night, attacking people like me and Gary Bayliss?"

"*Kristen Lansen?* Is that who attacked you?"

That's who it was, confirmed Brett—Kristen Lansen: a real babe when she's normal. The kind every teenaged boy dreams about.

Tressa's mouth hung open. She drew her arms across her chest and clutched herself, as if the air around her had become cold. She remembered Kristen as a toddler in the Lansen home. Mark had been so proud of his little sister. Countless times Tressa herself had bounced that delightful blond moppet on her knee, had played patty-cake with her, had cooed to her.

"I don't know this for sure," said Brett, "but I think she lives with Skip Gestern up on Nehalem Mountain—up in that old mansion. I s'pose it makes sense that vampires stick together, you know? I plan to find out."

"And do you expect them to let you walk right in with your stakes and crosses and your holy water? Are you going to ask them to lie down on the carpet and close their eyes, so you can hammer pieces of wood through their chests?"

Brett muttered something about vampires staying in their coffins during the daylight hours.

"That's bullshit!" shouted Tressa. "Vampires aren't afraid of sunlight. They're not afraid of crosses or holy water, either. Ask anyone around town—Skip Gestern goes out during the day, just like a normal person. He goes shopping. He goes to meetings. He plays tennis. You've seen him yourself, I'm sure."

Brett gaped at her stupidly, and now *his* mouth hung open.

"None of that old vampire-movie stuff is true," Tressa went on urgently. "In fact, it's downright dangerous to believe in things like holy water and garlic and—" Her voice halted, broke. She was about to say *the cross*. Yes, it was dangerous to believe in the cross, as Father Charlie had found out. Despite his faith in it, the cross had given no protection at all against the "gentleman on the hill." Father Charlie had *believed*, and that misplaced belief had killed him. "There might be ways to kill vampires," said Tressa slowly, her throat aching, "and there might be ways to protect yourself from them, but I don't know what they are. And neither do you."

Brett stared at her a long moment, his eyes round and wide. "I can't believe I'm hearing this from you," he whispered. "You believe in them, don't you? You really *believe* in them!" He let out a little giggle. Then he let out a big giggle. Then he laughed long and loud, and Fudd whined and thumped his tail on the pillow full of cedar chips, thinking that everyone was having great fun.

Tears welled in Tressa's eyes as she watched him laugh, this handsome teenager who should be planning a date with his girlfriend, or skateboarding under the innocent summer sky, or shooting baskets with his pals in the driveway. Instead, he was busy planning the murder of vampires. Sharpening stakes, for Christ's sake. And scheming the theft of holy water from St. Pius X Roman Catholic Church.

36

Golden Eyes

i

"Fancy running into *you*, of all people!" exclaimed Mark Lansen as he caught up to Tressa Downey. She was walking briskly up Kalapuya Avenue toward Fish Hawk Ridge. Except for her sensible athletic shoes, she was dressed for work in a conservative suit of gray cotton twill. *She's beautiful*, Mark thought—clean of cosmetics, uncluttered of jewelry except for a simple gold strand around her neck. Her face was honest and kind. "The courthouse is back that way," he said, jabbing a thumb over his shoulder. "You walked right past it."

"I wasn't headed to work. Actually I was on my way to see you. We need to talk, Mark. Is now a good time?"

It was. Mark explained that he'd just left the courthouse, where he'd delivered a petition his father had drafted the day before he died, seeking release of Robert Gammage from the county slam. Gammage was the man Will Settergren shot during the altercation in Poverty Ike's, he reminded her. Sheriff Conrad had promised to take the petition directly to the judge, which meant that things were looking up for Gammage.

"Let's go sit in the bleachers," he suggested, pointing toward the Kalapuya High School playing field. "You look like you could use some sun on your cheeks."

They slipped through a chain-link gate and crossed the yellowing gridiron, which was as lonely as the rest of the campus, since summer vacation was in full swing. They chose seats on the fifty-yard line, where they'd often sat hand in hand during Kalapuya High's home games. The afternoon sun beat warm on their shoulders.

"I need to talk to you about Kristen," said Tressa, looking grave. "I don't quite know how to put this, but—"

"Is *that* what's worrying you? My God, word gets around fast in this town! Tressa, I know all about Kristen."

"You do?"

"I saw her yesterday, in fact. We talked. I even visited her at Gestern Hall, although I didn't quite go voluntarily. I wasn't able to persuade her to come home with me, but I think she'll come around if we give her time." He realized that Tressa was staring at him strangely, no doubt because he had a huge grin on his face.

"Mark, are you okay?"

He was more than okay, he assured her. He was *wonderful*. Seeing the sun in Tressa's auburn hair made him feel better still. "Sitting here with you makes me feel like a kid again. I feel as if I've found a piece of myself that's been missing for longer than I can remember." He wanted her to smile and said so, watched her try. The corners of her mouth widened slightly, but the smile never really materialized.

"Listen," she said, her voice trembling slightly, "maybe it's not such a good idea for us to talk right now. You probably have other things to do."

She gathered herself to stand, but Mark caught her arm and gently held her. "Wrong. I can think of nothing better than sitting here and talking with you, Tressa. I don't know why, but at this moment it's the most important thing in the world to me. I haven't felt this good since . . . since . . ." Had he *ever* felt this good?

He hadn't slept for more than twenty-four hours, and yet he felt energetic and razor-sharp. Neither had he eaten during the same period, if you didn't count the glass of orange juice at breakfast this morning. He'd felt no need for food or sleep since his return from Gestern Hall yesterday, where he'd dreamed of—

No, we can't let that word leak into our conscious thoughts, can we, Buckaroo? It's not the sort of thing that normal people think about.

"You look distracted," said Tressa. "Are you sure you're okay?"

"Know what? I've missed you. I didn't realize exactly how much until about thirty seconds ago."

"That's—that's very flattering."

"Sounds maudlin as hell, doesn't it? If I've made you uncomfortable, I'm sorry."

"I'm not uncomfortable, Mark. It's just that—well, I'm surprised, I guess, after all this time."

He understood. Fifteen years ago they'd gone their separate ways. Each had married, embarked on a career, built a life. And yet Mark felt as if those fifteen years had simply melted away like ice cubes in the afternoon heat. He felt as if he had finally caught up with the past.

"Let me ask you something," he said. "What in the hell did you ever see in me?"

ii

Not a hard question, thought Tressa: Mark Lansen was funny. He'd always made her laugh. Making people laugh was important to him, and he worked at it. But he was also funny when he *didn't* work at it, which endeared him to Tressa even more. Plus he was thoughtful and honest. He was brighter than anyone she'd ever known, but he'd been delightfully naïve about some things, among them females. He loved history, and he *cared* about the world. "I liked you mainly because you weren't a jock."

"And that's *it?*"

"Well, you were mildly good-looking, even though you were a skosh skinny. I liked your hazel eyes and your brilliant white teeth."

"Didn't my mind have anything to do with it?"

"No," she lied. "For me the attraction was purely physical." The shock in Mark's face made her giggle, and she thought, *God, he's doing it even now—making me laugh! I've come to tell him his sister's a vampire, and he's making me laugh!*

"You were a beautiful girl, Tress, a real star of the student body. You could've had any guy in the county. I've never been able to understand why someone like you wanted to hang out with someone like me." He glanced wistfully at the blue sky, as if he yearned to see some piece of wisdom written in the clouds. "We've changed a lot in fifteen years, haven't we?"

"Yes, we have. Happens to everyone, I hear. We change, we learn."

"I'm much wiser about women since you and I split the sheets, Tressa. I've learned some important do's and don'ts."

"Such as?"

"Well, I've stopped asking for an enema on the first date. And I no longer lecture over dinner about medieval criminal justice. And I never, *never* French-kiss while chewing Skoal. These rules have really helped me, Tressa. I landed a trophy wife, you know—one who's gorgeous and smart. *And* ambitious. *And* rich."

"You must love her a great deal."

"I did at one time." He bent forward, his forearms on his knees, his chin on his fists. "I've tried to keep on loving her, but I can't anymore. She wants a divorce, and she wants to take my son away from me."

Tressa felt a burst of sympathy and laid her hand on his back. Without even thinking about it she rubbed the area between his shoulderblades, just as she'd always done when they were boyfriend and girlfriend long ago. "Mark, I'm sorry. Last week when we talked—at the Royal Kokanee, and later at the Baylisses' house—I sensed that things weren't exactly wonderful between you and your wife, but I never guessed . . ."

Remembering that horrible night made her mouth dry. She closed her eyes and saw Gretchen Bayliss's wan face twisted with terror at the sight of Skip Gestern in the foyer of the Royal Kokanee. She heard again the girl's mind-shredding screams. Tressa and Mark had taken Gretchen home and had sat for more than two hours at her bedside. While Gretchen desperately clutched Tressa's hand, Mark and Tressa talked quietly of old friends, old enemies, old times. They'd touched only superficially on their respective recent lives, each sensing that the other was wary of the subject.

Finally Gretchen stopped twitching and crying out in her sleep. They left her in the care of her drunken father, who had passed out on the living room sofa, and her poor unsteady mother, who looked as if she longed to curl up and die.

"Deidre's been having an affair with her senior partner. They're architects, you know," said Mark. "She thinks I'm crazy—not as in 'He's a wild and crazy guy,' but crazy like a raving lunatic, a monster. To be fair, I guess I've been acting a bit strange, especially since Dad got killed. Deidre and I had a real pisser of an argument on the day of his funeral, about Tad. She wanted to take him back to Portland, and I sort of blew up. I think I scared her a little. . . ." He paused and stared at Tressa. "I'll take that back. I think I scared her a *lot*."

His mood was changing, Tressa saw. Just moments ago he'd been ebullient, on top of the world. Now she read desperation on his face, and . . . what? A craving for something? The change was dramatic, and Tressa felt a tickle of panic. She fought it and forced herself to think about why she'd sought Mark out. "Mark, we've *got* to talk about Kristen. What I'm about to tell you will come as a shock, I know, but two nights ago she attacked a teenage boy in the park. You probably know him—Brett Omdahl, Rick Omdahl's oldest boy? It was just before midnight, and—"

"She *attacked* him, you say? You mean she tried to seduce him?"

"No, that's not what I mean. She *attacked* him. She almost killed his dog. She . . ." Tressa's mouth became even drier, and she wished intensely for a drink of water. She struggled on, forcing out the story as Brett had told it to her, complete with a description of the thing that Kristen Lansen became on that night.

When she finished, Mark sat as if stunned, staring blankly across the playing field toward the park.

iii

"We're all becoming what we're programmed to become," Skip Gestern had said yesterday while driving Mark home from Gestern Hall. *"It's true for Kristen, for you, for me. It doesn't do any good to fight it."*

Mark heard those words in his head and verged on believing them. Could it really be true, he agonized, that every human being's destiny is programmed in advance, that each phase of a man's life is a cell in some cosmic spreadsheet? The idea assaulted everything he had ever believed.

"The best thing you can do is let the change happen with a minimum of fuss, don't you see?"

Tressa talked about what she'd read in Father Briggs's journal, about things too outrageous to be real. Skip Gestern had victimized Fran Pellagrini, and when Bernie Pellagrini discovered it, he killed both his wife and himself. Somehow Skip had brought the Pellagrinis back to life, and they'd dug themselves out of their graves. They'd accosted Father Briggs and had tried to frighten him away from his chosen course, which was to seek outside help against the "gentleman on the hill." The gentleman himself had approached Father Charlie and had demonstrated his evil power, vowing not only to kill the priest, but also to resurrect his body and force him into a kind of slavery, just as he'd done to the Pellagrinis. Thus, Father Charlie had committed suicide by fire, taking great pains to ensure that virtually nothing remained of his body.

Mark didn't recoil from this insanity. Neither did he recoil from the suggestion that little Gretchen Bayliss's sick ravings were true. He didn't reject the story of Ginger Truax, a young woman who worked in the county commissioners' office.

"It follows," concluded Tressa, speaking slowly and choosing each syllable with care, "that Skip has been *visiting* Ginger, just as he's been *visiting* Freddye Ann Bayliss, just as he *visited* Fran Pellagrini. He's victimizing her just like he victimized them. The unavoidable fact is that he's a *vampire*, Mark, and somehow he has turned your sister into one, too."

Tressa closed her eyes and rubbed her temples, as if her head hurt. Mark reached out to touch her face. As his fingertips brushed her soft cheek, he felt a charge of energy shoot through his arm to his shoulder, to his chest, to his groin. The hunger welled inside him, and he knew instantly what he must do.

iv

Tressa opened her eyes at his touch and almost choked with fright. Something was happening to Mark's face. The harrowing grin he'd worn a moment ago had returned, and his mouth seemed actually to be widening. His eyes were turning to *gold*.

Staring into those eyes, she felt a milky warmth settle over her, and the fright evaporated. Mark's golden gaze conveyed not only the urgency of his yearning, but also the love he felt for her—the cherishing, the wonder, the deep respect. She felt his deprivation and knew the frustration he'd endured for so many years, the torment of trying to love a woman who loved someone else, while all the time he craved what he'd shared years ago with Tressa. She knew the agony of wishing that clocks would run backward, that the past could live again, if only for an hour.

Suddenly a wisp of cold alighted on the inner side of her right calf under her skirt, and she flinched violently. The coldness coiled around her knee and slithered upward over her thigh, like an icy snake. She recognized it as the same invisible tendril that had attacked her last week in Gestern Hall, while she stood in Skip Gestern's study, or at least it was one of the same species. She'd gotten the hellish impression that the coldness was a living thing, an appendage of some creature who possessed a will and unspeakable appetites. She felt that same suspicion now.

But this time she didn't swoon. Some deep-rooted instinct spurred her to stand fast against it, to summon every calorie of energy to use as ammunition in the fight. She couldn't beat it with physical force, she knew, because it was too strong. She'd seen the source of its power in the ancient paintings that hung on the walls of Skip Gestern's study, paintings that showed a dark man in the company of various holy figures. The dark man wore some hideous secret on his face. She knew now what that secret was, for she saw it in Mark's face, too, one that enabled its owner to twist physical reality, that let a man reach out with cold, invisible tentacles to touch a woman in her warmest places. It was a secret that demanded the drinking of human blood.

Tressa bit her tongue to keep from screaming and dug deep for morsels of positive power to fight this thing. She thought of Gretchen and tried to glean strength from the example of the child's piety. She remembered her own efforts to make Gretchen's life better, her own love and concern. Only *goodness*, she somehow knew, could stave off the attack of the golden eyes. *God grant that I have enough goodness left in me.*

She thought of her own departed child, Desdi, named for Shakespeare's Desdemona. She clenched her eyes and saw Desdi's sweet face, heard Desdi's laughter, saw her dazzling smile. Tressa felt an onslaught of grief that eclipsed the terror wreaked by the icy coil now nestling in her groin. Desdi's lips moved, and Tressa prayed to hear her say certain words (*"I forgive you, Momma"*), but the little girl uttered something else, something that suggested inanely that Desdi was *here*, that Desdi was *now*:

"Don't worry, Momma, Elmer and George will take care of you . . . !"

V

"Let your feelings rule you, Mark. Do what feels *best, because that will be the right thing."*

Good advice. Has Skip Gestern ever steered you wrong? Besides, you doubt that you could control these feelings anyway. They'll get their way, regardless of what you decide—*that's* how strong they are.

You need Tressa. You need her more than you've ever needed a woman in your life. You mean to have her in a way that you've never had a woman before. You're already glorying in her moist warmth, though you don't exactly understand how, since you've kept both your hands to yourself. You discover that you have the means to project yourself, or at least part of yourself, like an invisible finger that can probe what you can't appropriately explore with your flesh-and-bone hands. Tressa feels it, obviously—this invisible probe against her groin. Her twisted face suggests that she's not enjoying it much.

You grasp her by the arm and pull her to you. She comes pliantly, her eyes still tightly closed, as if she knows the futility of resisting. Before kissing her, you glance around to ensure that no other humans are near, and your eyes confirm what your ears and nose have already told you: The playing field is deserted.

You press your lips against hers, and she opens her eyes to stare into yours. She's terrified, and she breathes in to scream, but you reach out with yet another of your wonderful, invisible appendages, and enter her mouth with it. A simple flick of its tip constricts her vocal cords, and she gives out only a tiny squeak. "I'm sorry, Tressa," you whisper. "I'll make it up to you."

She's the most beautiful woman you've ever seen. You appreciate not only her outer beauty, which any man would—her slim body with its small, beautifully curved breasts; her long legs; her delicate, heart-shaped face surrounded by lustrous auburn hair—but also her inner beauty. Her tenderness. Her intelligence. Her *goodness*. Your hunger for her throbs in every fiber of muscle, resonates from every pore of your skin. "Tressa, open your eyes," you whisper into her ear as you press her backward onto the bleacher bench. "Open your eyes and look at me."

Which she does.

vi

Mark's eyes were golden fury. Despite the distortions of his face and head, and the mouth that seemed too full of teeth, Tressa saw something wonderful in those golden eyes. She saw the Mark Lansen she wished she'd married when she'd had the chance. She saw the joyful parade of days and months and years that *could* have been, if only she'd had her head on straight, years of being married to Mark Lansen instead of R. J. Roscoe. They would've been *wonderful* years. Mark surely wouldn't have introduced her to cocaine, and this in itself would've spared her incalculable suffering. Mark wouldn't have become a self-centered tyrant. Mark wouldn't have abandoned her in the wake of the tragedy with Desdi, when Tressa most needed—

Desdi!

Tressa remembered that if she'd married Mark Lansen, her beloved Desdi would never have existed. There might've been other daughters and sons, but there would've been no Desdi.

"That's okay, Momma, I forgive you. And I really love you for going out on Christmas Eve to buy me the Cabbage Patch doll. I know that you wouldn't trade me for a life with Mark, even if you got a chance to do it. That's why I'm sending George and Elmer to take care of you . . . !"

vii

You peel away Tressa's jacket, then open the buttons of her blouse. Her bra lifts easily off, and her firm breasts stand proud to the sunlight. She writhes and squirms as you kiss them, first one and then the other, as your tongue massages the nipples to make them hard as ball bearings. Your hands are busy with the buttons of the waistband of her skirt, and you push it down, along with her panty hose and panties. Now she lies naked beneath you, wearing only her simple necklace, which is as golden as your eyes. You rise upright for a moment on your knees, just to gaze at her.

She's magnificent, a masterpiece of flesh and blood and bone. You hear the hammering of her heart and smell the hot spiciness of her sex. You feel the cloud of emotion that rises from her like steam from a newborn lamb, the terror and longing, the love and bewilderment, the crushing regret for some sin you can't even imagine. Never before have you been able to penetrate a woman so wholly, and you marvel that you haven't even started to fuck her yet.

Quickly you shed your jeans and sweatshirt and underwear (your clothes don't seem to fit right anymore), and the summer air kisses your skin warmly, lovingly, just as you kiss Tressa—first her neck, where her racing pulse causes her veins to bulge, then her breasts again, then her tummy where your tongue traces hot, moist circles that make her moan. You move down to her abdomen, and she pushes her hips off the wooden bleacher bench to meet you. You move down to her inner thighs, which she opens to you. And finally onto the haired mound of her sex.

If you didn't care whether she lived or died, you could simply bite into the femoral artery in her groin and feast until her heart stopped. But you *do* care, at least for now, so you decide to follow Skip Gestern's advice and do what feels best, which is to bite only a small incision inside her and suck it until your hunger cools. With care and a little luck, Tressa will live for months, maybe even years, giving up only enough of her blood a few times a week to keep you strong.

Your tongue protrudes from your mouth far enough that you can actually *see* it, and it startles you at first, because it's monstrous and covered with suckers. The moment passes. You understand now what has been happening to you since that day on campus when you first saw the hag. It has been happening since the day you were born, in fact. The slug-dreams figure into it, certainly, a symptom of the conflict within you, a conflict that is about to resolve itself forever.

But a part of you doesn't want to do this thing or to *be* this thing. Something inside you, maybe that part you've always known and cultivated as the *real* Mark Lansen, has sided with the hag. A war rages.

"It doesn't do any good to fight it," Skip Gestern said, and he has never steered you wrong. *"The best thing you can do is let the change happen with a minimum of fuss, don't you see?"*

The whirring stops you. In your mind you see the hag, sitting in the crook of a tree trunk with her spinning wheel, her horrible eyes boring into yours. She urges the wheel faster and faster with a bony hand, and the whirring grows loud in your ears. You know she's nearby, because her stink has crawled into your nostrils. This is no hallucination.

"Root it out, Mark Lansen!" screams a voice inside your head, and you know whose voice it is. But you push on, determined to get what you need from Tressa, hag or no hag. You press your toothy mouth into the warmth of her sex. You open your jaws to bite when you feel a tiny tug on your bare toes, then another on your shoulder, then another on your ass. You burrow on with your delicious business, but the tugs become painful pinches that dart up and down your back and legs. You jerk your head up and howl, but you see only a pair of smears of movement in flight—too small to be people, too small even to be children. You hear muffled giggles under the bleachers.

"Who the hell are you?" you scream with a voice you don't recognize.

And now you see the hag, sitting with her spinning wheel in the top row of the bleachers, sunlight dancing harshly off her huge ring as she urges the spinning wheel faster.

viii

Tressa screamed, too, when she opened her eyes and saw how hideous Mark had become. He looked exactly like Gretchen Bayliss's description of the creature outside her bedroom window—all teeth and slime and suction cups on the tips of his fingers. As she screamed, the golden light in his eyes faded, and the gorgonizing grin fell away.

He became himself again. The mental stranglehold in which he'd gripped Tressa softened. She saw no more of the golden images that had flowed from the thing's eyes. Rather, she saw Mark for what he was—the *real* Mark Lansen winning a fight with the part of him that was a vampire.

ix

They sat in the cool shade of the school building, fully dressed now. They'd wanted to get away from the bleachers and had retreated to the grassy school yard, which was full of tiny white clover blossoms.

Mark felt the need to talk, to explain. He tried. Tressa listened, but he could see that she was still thoroughly terrified of him. Incredibly, she didn't run away. Neither did she look directly into his eyes.

"Before I start, I want you to tell me something," he said, not daring to look at her. "Do you know anyone named George and Elmer?"

37

An Exquisite Torment

i

At the dinner table that evening, Mark suddenly excused himself and went to his father's study. He locked the door behind him, picked up the telephone on John Lansen's prized mahogany desk, and pecked out his home phone number in Portland. Deidre answered after the third ring, which surprised him. It was only seven o'clock on a Wednesday evening, and he half expected her to be at the office.

"It's me," he said. "Just listen, okay? I'm bringing Tad home tonight. I'd appreciate it if you would be there when we arrive. We'll leave within the next hour, so we'll be there by ten at the latest."

"Mark, what's going on?"

"I told you—I'm bringing Tad home. I've thought about what you said after Dad's funeral, and I've decided you were right. He would be better off spending the summer at home with his friends. I'll drop him off with you tonight and drive back to Oldenburg."

"Mark, are you all right?"

"What do you mean, am I all right? Of *course*, I'm all right. I wish to hell everybody would stop asking me that. I'm all-fucking-right!"

"You sound . . . weird. Maybe I should come there and pick Tad up."

"Look, Deidre, I don't want to fight with you. Everything's fine, honest. You've won, okay? I'm going to let you have Tad for the rest of the summer. For that matter, you can have"—Mark tried to swallow the painful lump in his throat—"you can have custody of him, too. I'm not so sure I'm fit to—" He couldn't finish that thought. It was all he could do to keep from breaking down. "We'll be there by ten." He hung up the phone.

ii

His father's sudden decision to whisk him back to Portland devastated Tad. He sat silently in the passenger's seat of Mark's old BMW, his face obscured by the night except when the beams of passing headlights swept across it.

"Dad Bear, are you mad at me for something?"

"No, son. I'm not mad at you. I just want you to be—" Christ, he almost said it. *Safe.* How do you tell your boy that you've become a monster who tries to suck the blood from living humans?

"Be *what*, Dad Bear?"

"I want you to be happy this summer. I want you to have fun with your friends. It was selfish of me to bring you here when I knew that I'd be spending the whole summer in front of a computer. There's no one in Oldenburg for you to play with."

"Is it because Gramp got killed? Is that why you're taking me home?"

"Maybe. Yeah, I guess that's part of it."

"Or is it because of that old woman we saw this morning, the one who climbed the tree in the backyard?"

"I can't really—Christ, quit cross-examining me, okay? Trust me when I say that this is the best thing for you."

"But I want to be here with you, Dad Bear. I don't want to spend the whole summer alone with Wonder Woman. She'll only leave me with a sitter most of the time, anyway."

"Listen, young man, I don't want you to call your mother that."

"But that's what you call her around your friends, when you don't think I can hear."

"I don't give a rat's ass. She's your mother, and she deserves your respect. Hear me?"

"Yeah. I hear you."

They traveled the rest of the way in near silence.

iii

It was almost midnight when Mark arrived back in Oldenburg. During the long drive from Portland, he'd felt empty and profoundly weak. A dozen times he'd wanted to turn around to fetch Tad back with him, but each time he performed the mental equivalent of grabbing his own lapels and shaking hard.

You don't know what you're capable of! he screamed at himself. *You don't know whether you could actually hurt him when you're in that . . . condition. If you're not really a monster (a vampire, Tressa calls you), then you're terribly sick. A man who's that sick has no business trying to be a father.*

He stopped at the corner of Industrial Avenue and Main and signaled left as if to return to the Lansen house on Fish Hawk Ridge. A desperate idea flashed in his mind, and he turned right instead.

iv

Poverty Ike's was empty of customers except for two men at the bar, one of whom was a craggy old sot who was so drunk he could hardly stay atop his bar stool. The other, incredibly, was Gary Bayliss. Mark remembered the story Tressa had told this afternoon about Bayliss's recent "accident." Gary had only today returned home from the hospital in Astoria.

"Well, I'll be fucked, it's my old asshole buddy, Mark Lansen!" hollered Bayliss, seeing Mark's reflection in the mirror behind the bar. He spun on his stool to face the bat-wing doors and almost fell off. "About the other night at the R.K.—no hard feelings, right?" R.K. was local shorthand for the Royal Kokanee. "I mean, you caught me pretty good with that right jab of yours, but I guess I had it coming, huh? Let me buy you a drink just to prove I'm not such a bad dude after all." He spun crazily again on his stool to face the barkeep, who stood off to one side, silvered and somber. "Ike, this guy's money is no good."

Mark walked toward the bar, ignoring Bayliss and focusing on Poverty Ike. Bayliss got off his stool and wrapped a hammy arm around his shoulder.

"I bet you're surprised to see me up and around," wheezed the big man into Mark's face. "You probably heard what happened to me, huh? Just spent a couple days in the hospital, getting my blood supply topped off. I've been telling Ike and Varney, here, all about it. Trouble is, Varney's so fuckin' drunk I don't think he's heard a single word I've said!" At that moment, old Varney's forehead thudded onto the cigarette-scarred bar. He started to snore.

Mark told Bayliss to get the fuck out of his face. Bayliss

stared blankly at him, shocked speechless. Mark repeated the command, and Bayliss stepped away.

"You too good to drink with me—is that it, Lansen?"

"I'm not here to drink. I'm here to talk to Ike."

"Well, what the fuck kind of attitude is that? You come into a bar, but you don't want to drink! Know what I think? I think you don't want to drink with *me*, because you probably got somethin' against people like me. You probably don't like Vietnam vets. Is that it? You a fuckin' war protester or something?"

"Why don't you go home and get some rest, Gary?"

"Go home? Not fuckin' likely. I intend to stay out real late tonight, Lansen. Know why? Because I'm hopin' to run into your little sister again, that's why. Maybe *you're* too good to have a drink with me, but your little sister doesn't feel that way at all. She likes to wrap her long legs around me and slide up an' down on the old cougar like a piston. Then she likes to take the old cougar in her mouth and—"

Mark grabbed Bayliss by the front of his sweaty shirt. He lifted him off the floor and pressed him hard against the ceiling. The ceiling was a good fourteen feet overhead. Bayliss blubbered, yowled with terror, begged for his life. He was nothing but a poor working man with a deformed kid at home, he brayed, thanks to the Agent Orange that he'd absorbed in Vietnam. And he hadn't meant what he'd said about Kristen. He was sorry, honest to God, sorry as hell.

"No need to kill him," said Poverty Ike, leaning across the bar. "For his kind, life means little enough, and you can't justify taking it from him recklessly."

Mark's mind cleared quickly, and he realized that his right arm had grown absurdly, that it had burst out of the sleeve of his green Oregon Ducks sweatshirt. He possessed the strength of an elephant in that arm.

He gently brought Bayliss to the floor, after which Bayliss scrambled for the bat-wing doors, bawling like a panicky heifer. Within seconds the bar was quiet but for Varney's snoring.

Mark stared first at his right hand and then at Poverty Ike. His arm and hand had shrunk to normal size, but the shredded sleeve of his sweatshirt hung ragged. He touched his fingers to his cheek and stared into the mirror behind the bar, finding his face normal but slick with sweat.

"What was *that?*" he whispered, not really expecting an answer. "What just happened to me?"

"From where I stood, it looked like you lifted a two-hundred-and-thirty-pound drunk off the floor and pressed him against the ceiling with one hand. In my recollection, that's the first time it's ever happened in this place. Care for a beer or something? It'll be on the house."

Mark accepted a beer and lowered himself onto a bar stool. He studied Poverty Ike's long, angular face, and stared deep into the old man's knowing eyes, which the rimless glasses magnified. He detected no fear in that face and nothing but fascination in those eyes. "You're not scared of me, after what you just saw?"

"Nope. Should I be?"

"I-I don't think so." Mark took a slow sip of beer. "You know why I'm here, don't you?"

"I've got a pretty good idea."

"That story you told Tad and me last week—the one about the Witch of Mesatchie Illihee—it involves *me*, doesn't it? That's why you told it, isn't it? You wanted me to *know*."

Poverty Ike didn't answer, but only studied a gnarly thumbnail, smiling faintly.

"Please, Ike—I've got to know something else. The little girl who Vern Yngstad found in the clearing after the storm—she had something around her neck, a silver amulet—"

"Lion's head with a snake draped around it. Must've been pretty tarnished, seems to me, after all those years buried in the ground."

"Who was she? What was her name?"

"I think you know the answer to that question."

"I need to hear it from you. I need verification, Ike. I'm trying to get a handle on what's happening to my life, and I can't trust what I feel anymore. I need to hear you say her name."

"Oh, but you *can* trust what you feel, son. If you know who you are, and if you know what you are, you can always trust your feelings."

"Clovis Gestern raised her in the mansion, didn't he? She went to school here in town, like you said last week. But something happened to her when she was a young woman—"

"I can't speak to that. I suspect that whatever happened to her, she brought it on herself."

"She got pregnant, didn't she? She got pregnant, had the baby, and took it to Portland, where she gave it up for adoption. Then she killed herself, didn't she?" Mark's voice grew thin. "She jumped off the Sellwood Bridge, isn't that right?"

Poverty Ike wore a maddeningly self-satisfied expression. "That's all true from what I hear. Pretty girl, too, as I recall. She had big bright eyes and thick, dark hair. Any man would've been proud to have her for a wife, seems to me."

"Her *name*, Ike. What was her *name?*" Mark fought the urge to grab the old codger by the collar and shake the answer out of him.

"You know it as well as I do. Her mother named her, I suspect—gave the girl her own family name, instead of the father's surname. That was common among witches in those days. Anyway, she was known as Rita Crowe."

V

The Lansen house was dark when Mark wheeled into the drive. He let himself in and stole soundlessly to the attic, needing no light. Darkness was no longer an impediment, but he turned on the overhead bulb anyway. He rummaged through the trunk that lay in a corner under the slanting roof, and pulled from it the mildewed canvas bag that Rita Crowe had left him. He took out the photograph and studied it a long moment. Rita's face was as pretty as ever, as deep-eyed and lovingly sad. Next came the amulet, which was cool to the touch, not abnormally warm, as it had been when he'd shown it to Tad. The tarnish was gone, strangely, as though it had burned away.

And finally, the storybook. The picture of Snacky Cat on the cover had become a thing out of a Lovecraftian nightmare—all slavering teeth and claws, with a body that had grown to gigantic proportions. Snacky Cat was now bigger than the barn in which he supposedly lived.

The Catamount, breathed Mark. *Snacky Cat is the Catamount. This is all part of it.*

He probed his memory for the details of Poverty Ike's tale about the Witch of Mesatchie Illihee. Upon arriving at the sacred clearing on the mountainside, he recalled, Elspeth Carey had compelled Queen Molly to make a promise—to place the amulet around her baby's neck at the very moment she was born. This indicated that the amulet offered some sort of *protection*—against what, Mark didn't know. Maybe it would ward off the hunger that had gripped him as he sat in the bleachers with Tressa. Maybe it would cool the rage that had boiled up in him when Gary Bayliss accosted him in Poverty Ike's saloon.

He slipped the trinket around his neck and went to his room, carrying along the old canvas bag.

38

Mumbo Jumbo

i

Kristen Lansen greeted the dawn with a smile and went down to the kitchen to brew a pot of tea. She took her cup to an alcove off the main dining room, where sunlight streamed through a leaded-glass window, and sat in an overstuffed chair.

Skip Gestern glided noiselessly into the chair opposite, his face taut with dolor. Sweat stains darkened his tennis sweater, and his khaki slacks were caked with dried mud.

"Good morning," said Kristen, eyeing the sorry condition of his clothes. "What did you do last night—go out and wrestle some cows?"

Skip dug for his cigarettes and lit one. "Ginger Truax died early this morning. She must've been under some sort of sedation. I tasted something in her blood. The combination of the drug and blood loss was too much for her."

"What did you do?"

"Buried her in the woods on the western slope of Fish Hawk Ridge. No one will ever find her."

"Why are you taking it so hard? They all die eventually, don't they?"

"Ginger should've had more time left to her. I should've been more careful." He sucked a drag of smoke and kneaded the back of his neck. "She was a fine young woman, hard-working, caring. I'd grown to love her. I'm not enthusiastic over the prospect of breaking in someone new. How about you? Did you get it done last night?"

"I had none other than the good Dr. Nat Schell. He was working late at the Medical Center, and I waited in the backseat of his Saab. He never knew what hit him until it was too late. I left him a very happy man."

Skip stared at her through roiling strands of tobacco smoke. "I hope you didn't do to him what you did to Gary Bayliss."

"Gary's alive, isn't he? And he can't wait to see me again."

"You took too much blood, Kristen, and you almost killed him. Moreover, you used poor judgment in selecting someone like him, inasmuch as he's prone to bragging of his sexual adventures. He's already talked to at least one person."

"Oh, don't worry. No one will ever believe a word that jerk says."

"But you can't be sure, can you? I suggest you exercise more caution in the future."

"Consider me properly upbraided," she answered, imitating his adenoidal New England accent. Then she cocked her head, listening. "What's that?"

"Don't you recognize the sound of a young girl crying?"

"Is it Skye? Why is she crying? Where is she?"

"Somewhere beneath the subbasement, I should think— probably locked in one of those cells that Father always called the dungeon. She's terrified, and with good reason."

Kristen set aside her teacup and leaned forward, frowning urgently. "Mrs. Drumgule put her there, didn't she? *Why?*"

"If you'd been doing your assigned reading, you'd know."

"Skip, let's drop all this horseshit about doing research into the Gestern family, okay? I know everything I need to know."

"I doubt that."

"I know that I was born half-vampire and that when I got my first taste of blood, I started living the life of a vampire. I know that you used the ploy about doing research to keep me here long enough to get some human blood into my veins."

"Not just *any* blood, Kristen—blood taken from a host by a primo vampire, then regurgitated for you. And forcing you to read those books was not merely a ploy to keep you busy. Those books contain information you'll need to survive and prosper in a world that can be very hostile to vampires. You should be reading them still."

"Yeah, right." She jumped up and strode toward the kitchen, headed for the stairway that wound down into the dark regions below. "If you don't mind, I'll wait for the movie."

Skip followed at her heels. "I hope you're not thinking of interfering in Bellona's work."

"Oh, I wouldn't *dream* of it. But I'm not going to let her hurt Skye, either."

"And what makes you think you'll have any say in the matter?"

Kristen took the stairs four at a time.

ii

She came to a passage lit dimly by a single electric lightbulb overhead. Located in the lowermost of the levels beneath Gestern Hall, it dead-ended in a T. On the left stood a heavy wooden door with a small barred window and a heavy Yale padlock. To the right yawned a vaulted chamber lit by fluttering candles.

Skye Padilla had ceased to sob, but Kristen could hear her breathing and heartbeat through the bars. She could also smell the tart scent of the girl's terror. Bellona Drumgule sat at a massive wooden table in the vaulted chamber, hunched over the volume that Kristen knew was the notorious *Book of Rahab*. Arrayed around her were bottles, jars, bowls, and saucers, each containing some noxious powder or ointment or liquid, or dried pieces of some long-dead plant or animal—things Bellona needed to work her vile magic. Behind her lay a long marble slab atop squat pillars of stone. A knife lay on the polished surface, its blade wickedly curved.

As Kristen watched, Bellona reached into the bag on the floor beside her chair and brought up a handful of thumbtacks, which she put into her mouth and chewed, as if they were popcorn. She appeared to be in a trance—eyes clouded with a milky film, her breathing labored, her old heart squeaking greasily inside her chest. Now she swallowed a fistful of what looked and smelled like Vick's VapoRub. She opened a jar and took out a live toad, which she stuffed into her mouth and chewed.

"Good God!" breathed Kristen, choking.

Skip drew up behind her. "So this makes you sick, does it? You'll forgive me if I find that amusing, since you apparently felt no compunction about sucking nearly two pints of blood from a man by biting him at the base of his penis. Your brother even tells me you eat slugs. Come on. Let's go back upstairs."

Kristen pressed her face against the bars in the window of the heavy door. Huddled in the gloom of the tiny cell was Skye

Padilla, her knees drawn up to her chest. "Kristen, is that you?" Skye whispered.

"Yeah, it's me. Don't worry, I'm going to get you out of there. Just hang tough, okay?"

"I'll try."

Kristen fumbled with the padlock, tasting the cold metal with her fingers, measuring the hardness. She wondered whether she was strong enough to rip it off the staple.

"Don't even *think* it," Skip Gestern warned, as if he'd read her mind, which he probably had.

"She's just a kid," hissed Kristen angrily. "She doesn't deserve to be locked up in there. And she sure as hell doesn't deserve whatever that abominable old bitch is planning for her."

"Kristen, look at me." Skip grabbed her arm with no-nonsense force and pulled her around to face him. "What that girl deserves has nothing to do with anything. I feel as badly for her as you do, but there's nothing I can do for her. And there's nothing *you* can do, either. Her fate is sealed, just like yours and mine, sealed from the moment she was born. If you try to interfere, you'll only—" He broke off, apparently reluctant to face that particular truth.

"I'll only what?"

"You'll only get hurt. *Badly* hurt, I might add." He stared through the arching doorway at Bellona Drumgule, who had begun to mumble a chant:

> "Hear me, my Goddess, my Lover, my Slave.
> Rosemary balm and marigold I bring,
> A nightshade concoction mixed o'er a grave
> With brain of a snake to sharpen the sting."

Kristen twisted out of his grip. "I know what this is. It's *an-antip*—" She stumbled over the twenty-dollar word. "—*antinopomancy*. That old cow in there is planning to slice open Skye and read the future in her guts."

"Not just *read* it, Kristen. *Shape* it. *Change* it, if need be. And it won't be Bellona who actually celebrates the ritual."

"Who, then? You?" She launched a claw at Skip's handsome face, but he caught her wrist and held it in a viselike grip. His jaw hardened, and his eyes took on a mean glister. "It doesn't

matter who actually performs the act. What matters is that the act
takes place, that the future is laid bare to us."

"*Why?* Why do you need to butcher that girl? She hasn't done
anything to you! She's no threat to anyone!"

Bellona Drumgule's moaning chant rose in pitch and echoed
off the surrounding stone walls:

> *"Wind-flight and raptus, the power to kill,*
> *Vision to peer beyond the mortal's pale,*
> *Of ligature to bind Thy potent will,*
> *Of talons to rend the physical veil. . . ."*

"You're absolutely right," said Skip, "the girl is no threat. But
we have our enemies, Kristen. They're all around us like sharks,
circling and watching, waiting for the right moment to strike. If
you'd stayed current with your assigned reading, you would
know that the cult of the Gethsemanites has inspired much hatred
wherever it has gone."

"It was because they've protected vampires!" screamed
Kristen. "They've preyed on people, for the love of God! No
wonder they've been hated!" She struggled to break free of
Skip's iron grip, but failed. Strong though she had become, he
was far stronger.

"The hatred of the general populace has always been bad
enough," said Skip, his voice descending. "But we have enemies
who are extraordinarily powerful, enemies who are versed in the
Book of Rahab. They seek to destroy us at every opportunity.
The cycle of the Blood Star always brings an assault, because
this is when their powers are strongest. We entered such a cycle
a few weeks ago, Kristen. Fortunately, *our* powers also are at
their peak during such times."

"What does all this have to do with Skye?"

"It has nothing to do with her personally. All we need from
her is her body. She'll be the vessel of our deliverance. Our enemies are close, probably right here in Oldenburg. Their magic is
swirling all around us, *powerful* magic that interferes with Bellona's scrying. They're seeking to kill us, don't you see?" He
dragged Kristen back toward the stairwell, clearly meaning to
take her upstairs.

"Isn't there some other way? Isn't there some way to fight
them without killing an innocent kid?"

"Don't cry to me about innocence! There's no such thing anymore, not in *this* world! To answer your question—*no,* there's no other way. The Spell of the Entrails is the most powerful weapon we have. We'll use it, just as we've always used it. We'll use it because we have no choice, and we'll win, just as we've always won!"

Kristen broke down and sobbed, but if her tears moved Skip Gestern, he showed no sign of it.

39

Kyleen

i

A firm hand shook Mark awake, and he opened his eyes. He saw Marta, bending over the bed, wearing a Turkish bathrobe.

"Someone's here to see you," she said. "Her name is Dr. LeBreaux, a friend of yours, I take it."

Mark sat up abruptly, glanced at his watch, and saw that it was not yet seven—in the morning, presumably. That he'd actually slept amazed him. His fingers went to the silver amulet around his neck. He felt almost normal, but this wasn't a feeling to be trusted, he knew. Maybe now was a good time to confide fully in Kyleen, his long-standing stalwart ally.

ii

The breeze fanned Kyleen LeBreaux's straight black hair as they headed northwest on Railroad Avenue toward the river shore. Mark had always loved convertibles, especially little red Mercedes-Benz convertibles driven by beautiful brunettes.

"I hope you can understand why I wanted to get away from that house," said Kyleen, not taking her eyes from the road. "I have nothing against your mother, of course. It's just that a person's childhood home is not the ideal setting for a therapy session, particularly with family members around. It's very hard to be open under those conditions—too many old strictures lurking in the unconscious."

"I can appreciate that," lied Mark. Sometimes Kyleen's psycho-babble annoyed him. What did *not* annoy him, however, was the contrast between the tan of her long legs against the white shorts she wore. He tried not to stare.

Railroad Avenue became a rutty, graveled trail after crossing the marshland behind Bergen's Landing, lying roughly parallel to the B & R tracks. Blackberries grew in profusion along both shoulders. Farther back from the road reared thick stands of cottonwood and birch.

They came to a fork, and Kyleen chose the branch on the right, which led quickly to the water's edge. She stopped the car next to the crumbling ruin of a bridge abutment, switched off the engine, and turned in her seat to face Mark. "This should be private enough, wouldn't you say?"

"That used to be a bridge over to Pancake Point," Mark observed, nodding toward the abutment. Beyond it the river shimmered in the morning sun as it lazed westward. "No Name Bridge, they called it. And that's Puget Island over there—great place for raising dairy cows and just about everything else you can think of. The bridge collapsed in 'thirty-nine, and nobody bothered to rebuild it, you see, because Oldenburg's only creamery had gone belly-up when the stock market crashed. So, to answer your question, yes, this should be private enough, because nobody comes out here anymore except to pick blackberries. All the river traffic stays on the other side of Puget Island, and blackberry season hasn't started yet. To sum up, I'd say you've probably found the loneliest place in or around Oldenburg."

"Something tells me I've also found the loneliest man."

"Maybe you have."

"That's probably as good a place as any to start this session— the fact that you're feeling so alone. Care to talk about it?"

In truth, Mark didn't care to talk about it at this particular moment, but rather than argue with her, he told her about his decision to take Tad back to Portland, about Deidre's reaction to it, about his own misgivings over whether he was a fit father in his present state. Kyleen probed about how he'd reached his decision concerning Tad, but his responses sounded shallow and incomplete, even to himself.

"Mark, you're holding back. I can't help you if you don't give me the whole story—you know that." She took off her dark glasses. "Don't worry about how it'll sound to me. I'm a big girl now, and a shrink to boot. I can take it, believe me."

Sure you can, Mark thought. Suppose he told her about seeing the hag in the tree outside his window yesterday morning; about metamorphosing into a blood-hungry beast while in the bleachers with his old girlfriend yesterday afternoon; about lifting Gary Bayliss off the floor and holding him tight against the ceiling at

Poverty Ike's saloon last night. Kyleen would make a beeline for the nearest phone, surely, which was less than an arm's length away, actually, nestled in the console of her Mercedes. And she would summon some beefy guys with long-handled nets and a straitjacket. While waiting for them to arrive, Mark could explain how the Witch of Mesatchie Illihee had buried her infant daughter on a mountainside back in 1846, to protect her from some stalking evil; about how the little girl came out of the ground a century later, still alive, to grow up and bear a son—*a son who sits before you right now; who is himself a vampire.*

Mark chuckled to himself. *Talk about your fast track to the drooling academy!*

On the other hand, if he got himself hauled away to an asylum, he would at least end up safe under lock and key, where the hunger couldn't drive him to hurt someone. He would have the benefit of long-term observation by professionals who could tell him whether he was in fact a vampire, or whether he'd simply developed a horrendous case of the zoonies.

He was about to open his mouth—to say what, he didn't quite know—when Dr. LeBreaux started to unbutton the front of her bright red shirt. Mark clamped his tongue between his teeth and shut his eyes tight, but he couldn't help opening them again. While her fingers worked, Kyleen stared at him as if entranced. Mark worried that he'd accidentally hypnotized her, as he'd apparently done yesterday to Tressa.

"Something important is missing from your life," she whispered huskily. "We both know what it is. We've talked about it, haven't we? Estranged from your wife, as you are, having no woman to turn to . . ."

The red shirt slid down her shoulders to reveal heavy breasts encased in a translucent bra. She opened the bra in the front, letting them bounce free, and Mark felt stirrings of panic in the region of his solar plexus. In his jeans something else stirred.

". . . but what I haven't told you, Mark, is that it's missing from mine, too." She lifted her hips and slipped out of the white shorts, revealing skin the color of alabaster, a phantom bikini bottom above the tan of her legs. Mark bit his tongue hard enough to hurt. She reached over and unbuttoned his Hawaiian-print shirt, and having done that, insinuated her cool fingers into the waistband of his jeans. Mark moaned as she opened his pants and freed his cock.

"Kyleen, I-I don't think we should be doing this."

"Don't think about it, Mark. Just let it happen." She knelt on the bucket seat and swung a leg over the console, straddling him. Then she kissed him, ramming her tongue deep into his mouth. Involuntarily his hands went to her breasts.

"K-Kyleen, this isn't like you. I'm afraid—" She stifled his words by pressing her mouth over his, but he broke away again. "I'm afraid that I'm making you do this. I'm making you want me in a way that isn't—"

She reached down and maneuvered his penis into her, issuing a breathy hiss. Her warmth and wetness engulfed him, and he couldn't speak. Kyleen owned him now, and she pumped him. He pumped back. As he approached orgasm, he felt a burning pain against the skin of his chest, and he opened his eyes. The amulet that his mother had left him, the tiny trinket that depicted a lion with a snake draped about its head, glowed red-hot against the coarse hair on his chest. The orgasm withered before getting started.

This was insane, he knew, because silver would melt before getting red-hot. Yet the hair on his chest actually smoldered and smoked. More insane was the sight of Kyleen LeBreaux—her body arched above him, impaled on his penis, pumping furiously while pulling an ugly little pistol out of the console between the bucket seats. She placed the muzzle against his temple.

"Sangue et sangue!" she screamed, her own orgasm shaking her. The medieval French barely penetrated Mark's brain, for he was busy with his own thoughts, wondering why his arms felt like lead, as if Kyleen had weighted them to prevent his fighting her; thinking that death might indeed be the best thing that could happen to him now, better than institutionalization and better than living in an irrational netherworld.

Creation slowed, as it had slowed nearly two weeks ago on the campus of Portland State University, when Mark raised his eyes to behold Leo Fobbs hurtling down at him from the roof of Ione Plaza. Now he watched Kyleen's finger tighten on the trigger, knowing that every passing fraction of a second brought him closer to the finality of a small-caliber bullet ripping through his brain, putting an end to the madness.

But the end of the madness never came. It only got worse. Large, rough hands loomed up from Mark's right and closed over great handfuls of Kyleen's wonderful black hair. The twist came with matter-of-fact swiftness, generating loud bony pops in her neck. Suddenly she wore her head backwards. Her naked body slumped, and her hand relaxed, letting the small semiautomatic pistol thud heavily against Mark's blistered chest. Kyleen twitched and flailed and flopped. She died, and Mark Lansen threw up.

iii

"You ready to go now, Mr. Larsen?" asked Sam Darkenwald, touching Mark's shoulder. They sat on the abutment of No Name Bridge, their backs to the little red car that Sam called a Mercy-Bentley. Bugs chirped and buzzed in the surrounding thickets of blackberries, and gulls patrolled the riverbank for bits of God-knows-what. Mark tried not to think about Kyleen LeBreaux's body, which Sam had heaved unceremoniously into the thicket, its head hideously askew, its skin torn and punctured by nettles and thorns. He tried not to think about Kyleen's final words. He even tried to ignore the painful blister on his chest where the amulet had scorched him.

Sam looked better than Mark remembered him at Baloney Joe's in Portland, except for his expensive sunglasses, which were held together with dirty white tape, having gotten broken somehow. He seemed cleaner, leaner. He wore a neat work shirt and dungarees rather than layers of cast-off clothing.

Mark's own shirt and jeans were wet, inasmuch as Sam had insisted on taking them down to the water's edge to wash away the vomit. Sam had also used Kyleen's red shirt to clean up the interior of the car. Mark had bathed in the cold water of the river, and now sat on the abutment, drying himself in the sun and trying to cobble together his sanity.

"No, I'm not ready yet. And how many times do I have to tell you? It's *Lan*sen. *Lan*sen, as in Hansen except with an L. *Lan*sen, *Lan*sen, *Lan*sen." He was talking, he knew, to prove he could still do it. A few minutes earlier he'd congratulated himself for not collapsing into a pile of quivering mush, after having undergone that rare sensation of having one's sex partner die violently at the moment of climax. *Hell, I can handle this,* he'd told himself while washing his own vomit from his skin, shivering. *I'm just a little queasy, that's all.*

A little queasy. Right. He could barely walk without help.

"Sorry," said Sam. "Maybe I should just call you Marv, huh?"

"Fuck, I don't care what the hell you call me." Mark rubbed his inflamed eyes. "I guess I should be thanking you instead of giving you grief, huh? You saved my life, for whatever that's worth."

"It's worth a lot, I think. And I'm not the only one who thinks so."

Mark studied his blocky face, which seemed less lined than Mark remembered it. Sam's wispy gray hair looked freshly shampooed. "How did you know Kyleen and I would be here?"

"Old Ellie's scrying mirror—that's a device for looking into the future and the past. Come to think of it, you can use it for looking into the right-now, too."

"And this Ellie person sent you, is that it?"

"Yup. Told me to wait for you and the lady with the Mercy-Bentley, and not to let anything happen to you. Told me to kill the lady, if need be." Sam gazed for a quiet moment at the thickly forested shore of Puget Island. "I'm sorry it worked out the way it did, Mr. Hansen, but she was ready to blow your head off. I had to do something."

Sam Darkenwald's eyes suggested that he wasn't really all *that* sorry. He explained why: Old Ellie's scrying mirror had played reruns of the meetings between his late friend, Leo Fobbs, and the lady with the red Mercy-Bentley. Sam had heard the lady telling Leo what to do weeks ago, even months ago, as if someone had shot the scenes on a camcorder—to kill Dr. Mark Lansen (Sam actually got the name right this time). She'd chanted strange words that sounded like black magic, mesmerizing Leo, taking control of his mind. She'd given him pictures of Mark and pages torn out of directories that told where Mark's office was, where he parked his car, where he lived. She'd forced Leo to memorize Mark's teaching schedule, his comings and goings.

"I guess I don't feel as sorry for her as I should," Sam confessed. "She stole my friend from me, and then she took his mind from him. Made him into a stalker and a killer. My theory is that she picked Leo because he'd already burned his own brain away with booze, and he wasn't able to put up much of a fight."

Mark believed him. Kyleen LeBreaux had tried to kill him, no doubt about it. She'd commandeered the efforts of poor old Leo

Fobbs, and when Leo failed to accomplish his mission, Kyleen had come after Mark herself. She'd spirited him off to an out-of-the-way place, disarmed him with her gorgeous body, and put a gun to his head. The operative question was, *Why?*

"I guess you're wondering why Leo ran amuck a couple weeks back," Sam ventured, and Mark nodded. "I saw the replay of that, too. Old Ellie had been watching him and the lady all along in her scrying mirror, and when the time came for Leo to make his move against you, Ellie made *her* move. She went to work on him with her magic, got hold of a little corner of his mind, I think. At least that's how she explained it. She managed to push him off course. The lady with the Mercy-Bentley was pushing him to do one thing with her magic, but old Ellie was countering with her own spell. The result was some pretty heavy hallucinations for Leo."

"Why did he climb to the roof of the building?"

"He went up there without even realizing it, Mr. Larsen. He didn't even know where he was, really—only that he needed to get close to you. He wasn't himself at all when he took the dive. It was like there was a wrestling match going on in his head between Ellie and the lady you call Kyleen, and it was causing a full-blown psychomotor fit, which I know something about, having had a couple myself. If he hadn't've jumped, he might've walked in front of a bus or stuck his head into a trash masher or something. Poor old guy was nothing but a pawn, Mr. Larsen, and like most pawns, he was doomed from the start."

Sam then abruptly changed the subject. He said that he'd once been president of the Illinois Chess Association, that only two years ago he'd achieved his life's dream, a rating of Grand Master. He now planned to acquire a chess set and start practicing again, with an eye to taking on the local competition.

Mark interrupted: "This friend of yours—this Ellie—was protecting me from Kyleen, is that it?"

"That she was. And doing a good job of it, I'd say."

"She has a spinning wheel, doesn't she?"

"She surely does. And the damn thing runs by itself. I mean, the wheel turns without anybody doing anything to it."

Sam related how old Ellie had accosted him initially in an alley in Portland, how she'd instructed him to contact the investigator, Bob Gammage, with news of Skye Padilla's whereabouts. He told of his trip to Oldenburg with Gammage and the ugly scene that had erupted in Poverty Ike's saloon, where Sam had "discovered" that the FBI had trailed him from Portland. During his melee with "Agent" Gary Bayliss, a cop had shot Gammage.

"I mean to tell you, I thought Bob was deader than a doornail, so I lit out the back door of the place. Headed for those old ruins on the riverbank—old Hilde Cannery, I think the locals call it. Laid low there a day or two, because I knew the feds were combing the town for me. Just when I thought I couldn't stand being hungry any longer, old Ellie pops out of a shadow and takes me under her wing. Pulled a meal out of her bag that was fit for a king. It was even *hot!* That magic of hers is really something."

Under cover of night, old Ellie led him away, keeping to alleys and fields and hidden paths through thickets and glens. Up the mountain they'd gone, past an incredible hulking house of stone, to a place in the forest with a name he couldn't remember.

Mesatchie Illihee, Mark guessed aloud, and Sam beamed. "That's the place. We walked past this old Indian pole on the edge of the clearing and then went way back into the trees again. Ellie has a little shack in there, hardly big enough to turn around in, but it's comfortable. Warm and dry and stocked with food. It's no Ritz-Carlton, but it sure beats any place I've lived in for the past ten years. I think you're going to like it, Mr. Lansen."

"We're going there?"

"Those were Ellie's instructions: save you from the lady, and bring you back to her place."

"What if I don't want to go?"

"Well, I don't suppose I can force you. Ellie said to beware of you, if you started growing big teeth and bending all out of shape. She also said you're stronger than twenty men if you get mad enough."

"Will I meet her?"

"That'd be my guess."

Mark suffered a twist of panic over the prospect of coming face to face with the hag again, but he knew that he couldn't refuse to go along with Sam. Old Ellie might actually be the Witch of Mesatchie Illihee. "Let's get going," he said. "I'll drive."

Sam slid down off the abutment and went to a nearby bush to pick up his cowboy hat. "If you don't mind, *I'll* drive, Mr. Lansen. I used to race the Formula One circuit back in the sixties. Drove Ferraris and Porsches, came in second at the Belgian

Grand Prix in 'seventy-one." He nodded at Kyleen's costly little convertible. "I've been dying to get my hands on this thing ever since I saw it, even though it does have an automatic. I much prefer manual transmissions."

"Are you sure you can drive? You can't even say its name."

"It's an 'eighty-seven Mercedes-Benz 450-SL. The FBI will never recognize me behind the wheel, so don't trouble yourself over *that*. We have one short stop to make on the way, if you don't mind."

"Where's that?"

"The Kalapuya County Jail."

40

Shadows, Maybe Dreams

i

"No answer," whispered Tressa Downey, hanging up the phone on the wall of the kitchen. She tried not to look as worried as she felt. After all, Ginger Truax might still be asleep, since it was still only minutes before eight.

Cynthia Downey glanced up from the skillet of scrambled eggs on the range. "You talked to her yesterday, didn't you? Maybe she's feeling better and has already gone to work. That's probably what you should do, too. You'll be late in a few minutes."

"I *tried* to reach her yesterday—three times, as a matter of fact. She never picked up the phone. I just figured she was still on sedatives and dead to the world." Tressa snatched up her shoulder bag and headed for the door. "I'd better check on her."

"Shouldn't you at least call the commissioners' office and tell them you'll be late?"

"You call them for me, will you, Mother?"

"I swear, you're going to lose that job, girl—taking sick leave when you're not sick, like you did yesterday. Showing up late without calling in. Acting strange, like you are." She followed Tressa to the front door, talking. "I hate to bring this up, but somebody has to. You're not taking something you're not supposed to, are you, Tressa? You haven't backslid on me now, have you?"

The questions ignited old animosities. Who was Cynthia Downey to accuse anyone of backsliding? Her drawl was already as syrupy as three shots of Southern Comfort could make it, and the morning was still young. *Addicts beget addicts, right? The sins of the mothers are visited upon the daughters, isn't that so?*

But Tressa did not whirl on her mother. She got into her Honda and drove away.

ii

Twenty minutes later she parked in the lot of Oldenburg Medical Center. She strode through the front door and met the medical assistant, a pretty middle-aged woman named Jessica. Nat Schell wasn't in today, said Jessica. Not feeling well. Some kind of bug, probably. Even doctors get sick.

Tressa explained that she'd just come from Ginger's place at the Nebraska Hill Mobile Home Court, where she'd found the front door unlocked. She'd gone inside, but had found no trace of the girl. "I wouldn't be as concerned as I am if her car wasn't still parked in front of her place. Can you tell me whether Nat has been in touch with her, or whether she's called in?"

No, Jessica answered, Ginger hadn't called in. If the doctor had talked with her, he hadn't made a note of it. Sick as he was, though, he might have forgotten to log the call.

A hideous thought struck Tressa. "Nat's okay, isn't he?" she asked. "I mean, whatever he's got—it's nothing serious, is it?"

"In all honesty, Ms. Downey, he didn't sound too good on the phone. Sounded weak as a kitten, if you want to know the truth. I've worked here since he first came on board more than four years ago, and this is the first time he's ever been too sick to work."

iii

Tressa sat behind the wheel of her car, staring through the windshield at the intersection of Kalapuya and Main, her freight-train imagination running wild. Nat Schell was sick for the first time in four years (". . . Sounded weak as a kitten . . ."). Always in tip-top physical condition, Nat was a devout runner, a gobbler of vitamins and health food, a believer in preventatives. That he was sick enough to miss work seemed sinister.

Please, God, let it be the flu.

She started her car and headed for home. Father Charlie's journal, she remembered, had mentioned that he'd written to an "expert" in France, an excommunicated priest who professed knowledge of vampires. Whether Father Charlie had ever received an answer from the man, the journal didn't say, and Tressa didn't recall whether it contained a mailing address or a telephone number. If the journal itself gave no help, then she would go to the rectory, enlist Mrs. Lidderdale, the housekeeper, and together they would scour address books and records for some clue about how to reach the priest in France. This was a faint glimmer of hope, but it was a glimmer nonetheless.

Her mother appeared at the front door even before Tressa engaged the parking brake, having heard her drive up.

"You just missed a call from Velma Selvig," Cynthia said, wringing her lank hands. "She sounded positively desperate to talk to you. And if you want my opinion, she didn't sound herself."

iv

The splash of Kokanee Creek seemed rueful in the absence of the mallards' playful quacking. As she drove over the arching bridge, Tressa wondered where the birds had gone. Despite its bright orange shutters and fresh white paint, the Royal Kokanee Inn emitted a gray foreboding that assailed her the moment she set foot on the front porch. The surrounding red alders and cottonwoods hissed lightly as if stirred by wind, yet Tressa felt no hint of a breeze.

Velma hadn't answered the telephone when Tressa called from home only minutes ago. *"She sounded as if she was fading away,"* Cynthia had said, her thin face paling beneath a layer of rouge. *"She sounded sick and weak, I swear. . . ."*

Inside the inn reigned a shadowy, dreamlike silence: rooms filled with polished antiques, but empty of life; Velma's prized grandfather clock in a corner of the foyer, inert and ticktockless since Gary Bayliss had put his fist through its glass front; a ripe smell in the air that Tressa couldn't identify. If the Royal Kokanee boasted any guests, they were but shadows, or maybe dreams, or maybe both—as formless as the memory of the Chinese laborers who'd once lived here. *A dream itself is but a shadow,* she thought, recalling the line from *Hamlet.*

She found Velma in the rear parlor, her naked body sprawled across an antique divan, her legs open wide. Terror tightened around Tressa's chest like a tourniquet. Velma's face stared blankly into nothingness, the mouth slack and slick with drool, the eyes filmy. Blood seeped garishly from between her legs onto the carpet. Tressa saw a scrap of paper clutched in Velma's hand,

and she gently pried it away—a slip from a notepad, embossed with the logo of the Royal Kokanee Inn. Scribbled with ballpoint on it was: *Tressa—my office.*

She climbed the rear stairs and found her way to a room with a brass plate on the door, on which *PRIVATE* was elaborately engraved. Velma had furnished the office like a mid-nineteenth-century lawyer's study. Here she had administered the Royal Kokanee Inn, written her articles for the *Oldenburg Clarion*, and plotted a strategy to win Kalapuya County for Dukakis.

Atop an antique desk Tressa found a short stack of papers held together with a clamp—Xerox copies of newspaper articles from the previous century. Clipped to one corner of the top copy was another note from Velma, written on a slip from the same Royal Kokanee pad with the same ballpoint. Headlines jumped out at her from the topmost copy, a story from the *Tualatin Tribune*, dated November 10, 1856:

CLOVIS GESTERN AND HIS DISCIPLES ABANDON ENTERPRISE IN TUALATIN

LAWMEN SAY VIGILANTE MOVEMENT SUBSIDES

"The Anti-Christ Is Cast Out From Our Midst."
—The Reverend Stanley Ames

Before she could read further, she heard a noise in the corridor behind her, a creak in the flooring beneath an Oriental carpet. The noise had purpose, she sensed, as a footfall has purpose. Someone was standing outside the door of Velma's office, waiting, listening.

She folded the Xerox copies and tucked them into her shoulder bag. Then she squared her shoulders and resolved to face whoever it was with a modicum of bravery. It could be the cops, she thought. Or it could be the thing that had ravaged Velma Selvig, having come now to sample the blood of Tressa Downey.

V

A figure entered the door frame, and Tressa blinked away tears to see him clearly. He was a tall man with spare cheeks and stormy eyes behind wire-rimmed glasses. His argent mane, which matched his disheveled eyebrows, swept elegantly back from his high forehead. He was old—*how* old, she couldn't guess. He wore a winter tweed sport coat and the Roman collar of a priest. Despite the laugh lines at the corners of his eyes, a mask of sadness hung over his face, suggesting that he'd suffered more heartache than should be required of any human being in a lifetime.

Their eyes met. Tressa saw that he carried an expensive-looking portable stereo. A pair of headphones protruded from a pocket of his sport coat.

Don't faint, she told herself, gripping the edge of Velma's desk. *An old priest with a boom box can't be somebody to be scared of.* Then she remembered a telephone conversation she'd had with Velma several days earlier—about the only two guests at the Royal Kokanee. One of them was a psychologist from Portland, and the other was indeed an elderly priest from France. *Talks like Maurice Chevalier, looks like he came from Central Casting.*

"Are you all right, my child?"

"Yes. I think so."

"May I assume that you have been downstairs in the parlor, that you have seen what is there?"

Tressa swallowed and nodded.

"I am Father Gautier Le Fanu, mademoiselle. And you are . . . ?"

Tressa introduced herself, dredging up every speck of stage-craft to keep from going entirely to pieces. The reality hit her as she shook the old man's strong, lean hand: Gautier Le Fanu was the expert whom Father Charlie had mentioned in his journal, the French priest to whom he'd turned for help against the vampires.

"Why don't you sit down, my child? You look pale, as if you might faint. Here. . . ." He set aside his boom box and helped her to one of the beautiful brocaded chairs that flanked Velma's desk. He offered to fetch a glass of water.

"No, really, I'm fine. Sitting helps." She took a handkerchief from her bag and wiped her eyes, then blew her nose. "You're here because of Father Briggs, aren't you?"

"Yes, my child. Did you know him?"

"He was my closest friend."

"And the poor woman downstairs—were you a friend of hers as well?"

"Yes."

He pulled a matching chair close and lowered his tall frame into it. He leaned close to Tressa and took her hand in his. "I am so sorry for you, my child. Please accept my condolences. You must take heart in the knowledge that your two departed friends are beyond suffering now."

"Thank you, Father."

"Tell me, do you know how your friend died—the woman downstairs? *Velma*, I think her name was. Such a beautiful name."

"I know how she died," answered Tressa, lowering her face.

Le Fanu nodded minutely, his lips pursed, as if he'd heard such things many times. "Can you tell me?"

"You already know, don't you, Father?"

Le Fanu's kindly face hardened, and his rich voice became as stern as an inquisitor's. "I must hear you say it for yourself, my child. Long ago I vowed never to spread the knowledge of a thing so monstrous except when absolutely necessary, having seen what this knowledge can do to a person's life. Sometimes it is best not to know. Do you understand?"

"I understand. It was a vampire, Father, or something close to what we've always thought of as a vampire. I was nearly a victim of one myself." She told him about yesterday's horror in the bleachers with Mark Lansen, and Le Fanu listened without interrupting, nodding gravely now and then. She started to tell him about Gretchen Bayliss's ongoing ordeal, but Le Fanu lifted his hand and shushed her.

"I know of the Bayliss family's misfortunes. I have spoken with Gretchen and with her father. I also know what happened to the boy, Brett Omdahl, in the park last Monday night."

"Then you know about Skip—I mean *Clovis* Gestern?"

"Gretchen gave me her theories, and they were very astute, I must say. She is an extraordinary young girl, very intelligent and spiritually powerful. This young Clovis Gestern must surely be a vampire, as Gretchen says, but clearly there is at least one other vampire in the vicinity, in addition to your friend, Mark. This other one is quite possibly a primo vampire, one who can sire another of his kind."

"You mean vampires are *born?*"

"That is the only way a vampire can come into existence, my child."

Tressa put her hand to her cheek. "But that means—" Her words withered as the enormity sunk in. It meant that Mark and Kristen Lansen had been vampires as children, as babies.

"This Mark Lansen—you love him very much, don't you?"

"I-I—" She fought back a fresh onslaught of tears. "I love him more than I thought I could. We were—a long time ago, before we split up—we spent so much time together. . . ."

"I understand. Now you find it nearly impossible to believe that you've been in love with a vampire nearly all your adult life."

Tressa acknowledged this. She'd made love to Mark countless times before she and he went their separate ways. Never had he shown any of the monstrousness he'd shown yesterday. "Why *now?*" she asked. "After acting perfectly normal for so long, why is this happening to him *now?*"

"I can only speculate. If he is not a primo vampire, he could have lived a long life, perhaps, and never felt the craving for blood. Such people often do not behave like monsters until another vampire introduces them to the 'bloody feast,' as they call it—that is, a primo vampire vomits up blood that he has taken from a living human and forces the uninitiated vampire to drink it. In modern times, some vampires have even done this through intravenous means. Thus tainted with the disease of the primo vampire, the initiate begins to feel the unholy cravings and quickly develops the powers and abilities of a vampire."

Nausea swelled inside Tressa, and her head swam. If she'd married Mark, which yesterday she'd wished so fervently she'd done, they surely would've had children together. The seed of a vampire would have lived in each of those children, she knew now. The thought revolted her. Was there any way to save Mark? she asked.

Perhaps so, said Le Fanu. He had witnessed a few such miracles in the course of his long career. "This young man of yours may be our secret weapon, Tressa. You see, long ago the race of vampires acquired the skills of magic, a very old magic that is written in the ancient *Book of Rahab*. Consequently, they are terribly difficult to kill. In most cases, mere physical means—guns, knives, and the like—are not adequate. I myself have knowledge of the magic needed to kill vampires, but I am uncertain whether I can succeed in this case. The primo vampire who founded Gestern Hall is a very old sorcerer known as the Sire de l'Hier. He is powerful beyond belief. If we had another primo vampire on our side, however, one who would commit himself wholly to destroying the Sire de l'Hier, we could perhaps succeed. If your Mark were that man, I could arm him with the proper magic. He could perhaps destroy the evil that afflicts the people of this town. Do you think he would be willing to try?"

Tressa daubed at her eyes with one hand and gripped Le Fanu's hand with the other. "If he succeeded—that is, if he actually were to kill this Sire de l'Hier—is there anything you could do to help him? I mean, is there any way to cure someone from . . . from this *sickness?*"

Le Fanu's face became grim, and he didn't answer for a long moment. "Yes, my child, as I said, I have seen such miracles. But the way is very difficult and extremely painful. I can only hope that your Mark possesses the courage and strength to survive it."

"He's brave enough. If he isn't strong enough, he doesn't *want* to survive."

"You're certain of this?"

"I've never been so sure of anything in my life, Father."

"Then you must take me to him. We haven't much time, since the Cycle of the Blood Star is well upon us. I'll explain the Blood Star to you later."

"What about Velma? Shouldn't we call the police?"

"There will be time enough for that later, my child. For the moment, it is best that the police remain out of our way. We will place a sign in a window of the inn, yes?—one that says 'Closed,' and we will lock the doors."

"But there's another guest here, I think—a doctor from Portland."

"No need to worry about her. She has gone, and I doubt that she will be back. She was a witch, an agent of a vampire, you see. I felt her magic in the air."

Le Fanu helped Tressa to her feet and led her toward the door. "Father, there's one other thing that worries me," she said as they went into the corridor. "Brett Omdahl told me yesterday that he's planning to kill Skip Gestern and any other vampires he finds at Gestern Hall. He thinks he can do it with holy water and wooden stakes. I tried to tell him that Father Briggs discovered that things like crosses and holy water don't affect real vampires, but I'm not sure I got through to him. I'm terribly worried that he'll—"

"You were quite right, Tressa. Such holy props have no effect whatsoever. But you needn't worry about Brett. Gretchen introduced me to him, and I've spoken with him. He is a brave young man who yearns to fight vampires, and I intend to see that he gets his chance. Gretchen, too. You see, I need their strength of spirit, their pureness, to enhance my magic. I need yours, too, my child. If we all act together, and more important, if we act quickly and wisely, we can defeat the Sire de l'Hier. But we must not waste time. Come, you have a car, yes?"

"I do."

"Then we'll take it. But first we must collect some things from my room."

41

Devil's Club

i

Deputy Will Settergren shook Bob Gammage's hand and showed him the door, which opened onto the parking lot of the Kalapuya County Courthouse. "Fanning and I talked the sheriff into releasing your gun to you," whispered Settergren, "so we locked it in the trunk of your car, along with your other personal effects. The county could've kept it, you know, under the law and everything, but we figured you'd need it someday, on account of the business you're in." He eyed the heavy cast that covered Gammage's left shoulder and arm. On it was scrawled the signature of every employee in the County Sheriff's Office. "Sure you can drive with that thing?"

Gammage clapped him on the shoulder with his good hand. "If my whole body was encased in concrete, I'd find a way to drive away from this fuckin' hellhole, Speed. No reflection on the congenial staff, of course." Then he walked through the door and became a free man. He breathed deeply of the sunny morning and drank in the blue of sky. He listened to the cooing of pigeons in the dome of the courthouse and told himself that there was nothing like two weeks in the lockup to make a man appreciate the great out-of-doors.

His '73 Charger waited for him across the lot, parked among cars belonging to county workers. Before he'd ambled half the distance to his car, a red Mercedes-Benz convertible glided into the lot and halted in front of him. Gammage's eyes widened stupidly: The driver was none other than Sam Darkenwald, and the passenger was his Angel of Liberation, Mark Lansen.

"Looks like the last two weeks have agreed with you, Sam," said Gammage. "What are you two doing, cruisin' for babes?"

"Oh, this isn't my car, Mr. Gammage," replied Sam, grinning with his stained teeth. "It belongs to a lady I killed earlier this morning. She was trying to shoot my friend, here, Professor Marv Landon, so I had to break her neck a little."

"I see," answered Gammage, though he didn't see at all. He figured Sam was having one of his schizo fits. Waving the release form in the air, he said to Mark, "You came through for me, Speed. The judge approved that petition you delivered and signed me out, which is pretty obvious, I guess. I'm ready to keep my part of the bargain now."

Mark stared at him as if he had no idea what he was talking about.

"Your old man—remember? You wanted me to snoop around and dig up something that might tell us who killed him. I'm ready to start if you are."

"I remember now," said Mark. "Sorry if I seem a little disconnected. I appreciate your wanting to keep our bargain, but I think Sam has other plans for us."

"*Plans* for us? Are you kidding? This goofball couldn't plan his way out of a men's room. It was because of him that I ended up in the county stinker, for Christ's sake. If he hadn't gone berserk in that bar, I wouldn't have gotten shot, and I wouldn't have just spent two weeks living like a gerbil." He glared at Sam, who cowered behind the wheel like a contrite puppy.

"Aren't you mildly curious about what we're doing here?" asked Mark.

"I figure you're here to collect on the debt I owe you. The sheriff probably called you and told you I was getting out, right?"

"Nope. It was Sam's idea to meet you here. I'm along for the ride, that's all."

"Somehow I find that hard to believe, but okay, I'll bite. Just what the fuck do you want from me now, Sam?"

"Old Ellie sent me here to fetch you," answered Sam. "She wants to show you a way to rescue that little girl from Gestern Hall—Skye Padilla's her name. You remember Skye Padilla, don't you?"

."Yeah, I remember. But who the hell is old Ellie?"

"She's the lady who sent me to see you in Portland, the one who told me to tell you that Skye was at Gestern Hall. Remember when I came and knocked on your door at the motel, and you—?"

"I remember. I'm no dimwit, okay? So you're telling me that

this old Ellie is here in Oldenburg, and that she can get me inside Gestern Hall?"

"That's it, more or less."

"Why shouldn't I just walk up to the front door of the place and ring the bell?"

"That might be dangerous," Mark put in. "Some fairly strange things have been happening around here." He giggled inappropriately, betraying frayed nerves.

"Well, I can be pretty fucking dangerous myself," said Gammage, scowling his nastiest, "bad shoulder or no bad shoulder. The only reason I'm not pounding on the door of Gestern Hall at this very minute is because I owe you a favor, Mark. If you don't mind, I'd just as soon pay it and get on with my life. I'm not really in the mood to talk to old Ellie or whoever the fuck she is."

"You can pay me off by coming along quietly," said Mark, incurring a grateful glance from Sam Darkenwald. "You and I both need to hear what she has to say, I think."

Bob Gammage stared first at Mark, then at Sam, as if he was trying to decide who was crazier. "Very well, if that's what you want. I'll follow in my car, since you're driving a two-seater." He headed for his Charger and shouted over his shoulder: "Not too fast, though. I've only got one hand for driving."

ii

Sam parked on the shoulder of Queen Molly Road and set the brake. "We walk from here," he said, nodding toward the wall of forest on the mountainside. "The going's not too tough if you know your way."

Mark climbed out of the convertible and surveyed the territory ahead: dense growth of tall Douglas fir and hemlock, moss-covered stumps barely visible amid the heavy growth of licorice ferns, the barest hint of an old logging road overgrown with skunk cabbage. He was no forester, but he judged the stand to be well over forty years old, meaning that this could be the clear-cut in which the Nehalem Mountain Raiders set up their guard post. The view of the valley below would've been spectacular in those days.

Bob Gammage pulled up behind the Mercedes, cut his engine,

and climbed out. He plugged a cigarette into his lips and lit it. "That old mansion we passed back there—" He gestured with his good hand. "That was Gestern Hall, I take it. But the sign in front said it was the Something Mountain Inn."

"It's Gestern Hall," Mark confirmed, staring at the dark gables just visible over the tops of hemlocks and firs. "The owner laughingly calls it a bed-and-breakfast now. The Nehalem Mountain Inn."

"And that's where Skye Padilla is staying."

"That's where she was two days ago, working as a cleaning maid, supposedly." He then thought of Kristen, and felt a pang; she too was at Gestern Hall, as much a prisoner as Skye but in a different sort of way.

Gammage exhaled smoke, his fighter's face ugly with nicks and scars, his expression thoughtful. Mark knew what he was thinking. It would be easy to turn around and drive right up to the porte cochere of Gestern Hall, to walk through the front door and demand to see Skye. Mark wondered what Skip would do to him. Was there any chance that he would simply say, *Oh, you're here to take Skye home? Well, give me a minute to write a check for her severance pay, will you?* Or would Skip grow arms like elephant's legs (as Mark himself was capable of doing) and squash Gammage like a bug?

"No sense wasting time," announced Sam Darkenwald cheerily. He beckoned the others to follow. "Old Ellie doesn't like to be kept waiting." Mark fell in behind him, and Bob Gammage fell in behind Mark, grumbling under his breath.

The air tasted piquantly of living evergreens and moldering plant matter, the smells of a forest in the process of simultaneously birthing, growing, and dying. Spears of warm sunshine angled into the glade through the canopy above, spotlighting blossoming wildflowers here and there. A faint trail lay nearly hidden beneath the billowy fronds of sword fern and devil's club, twisting around fallen logs, lichen-covered boulders, and thick colonies of buckthorn, until bursting into a clearing where the noontide sun glared hotly. Mark gasped when he glanced to his left and saw the totem pole that Poverty Ike had described in his story, its intricacies rounded by rot and rain and moss. Nearly hidden in the boughs of a gigantic hemlock, it leaned against the trunk of the tree, having long ago lost the strength to stand on its own. At its top roosted the winged image of a Cathlamet god, carved by people who had walked this forest long before Christopher Columbus was born.

The clearing, of course, was Mesatchie Illihee. At its center was the low knoll upon which Elspeth Carey had birthed her daughter, Rita. Mark waded toward it through waist-high stalks of bear grass.

"Not that way, Mr. Henson," warned Sam. "The trail starts up again over here. We're almost there."

"Hey, listen to what the man says," grouched Gammage. "This place gives me the fuckin' creeps."

Mark went to the top of the knoll and looked for evidence of a grave, as though he needed any. He found only wildflowers and grasses, together with a few wayward stalks of flowering devil's club.

iii

Not fifty yards up the mountain from Mesatchie Illihee, the ground leveled out, and the trail ended at a structure that Mark couldn't call a house, for it appeared too cramped to be an actual house. But neither could he call it a hut or a shack. It was too permanent-looking, too substantial, too extraordinary.

"Now we meet Hansel and Gretel, right?" wisecracked Bob Gammage.

"I suspect we're about to meet Elspeth Carey," said Mark.

The structure appeared to be built partly of wood, though not of lumber. The walls and timbers looked *alive*, as if they were extrusions of the surrounding hemlocks. Its lines lacked the straight-edged artificiality of a man-made building, and the walls seemed to meld with surrounding stands of buckthorn and holly. Nowhere was a right angle visible. Ferns and grasses interthatched to form curved sides that looked as watertight and impervious to wind as any brick wall. A stone chimney rose above radically sloping gables, and from it issued a ribbon of spicy-smelling smoke.

"Elspeth Carey," repeated Gammage. "Is she the same person as old Ellie?"

"I think so," said Mark.

They didn't have to wait long. She appeared at the door of her house, looking as bent and witchlike as any creature from a children's storybook.

"I'll be dipped in shit and rolled in paprika," breathed Bob Gammage, his face ashen. The cigarette he'd planned to light dangled from his lower lip and fell to the ground.

The old woman wore the shapeless furry hat that had by now become familiar to Mark and a moth-eaten smock that gave no hint about the shape of the body inside it. Hoary fingers of hair poked out from her hatband, and her eyes gleamed like chunks of polished stone. Mark's scalp tingled when her gaze fell upon him, and he saw the same fury in her eyes that he'd seen yesterday morning when she'd sat with her spinning wheel in the oak tree outside his window. He felt an odd sense of having found something he'd long sought, a sense of having come home.

"I did like you wanted, Ellie," announced Sam Darkenwald, "but it took some doing, I'll admit. I brought them both along, just like you ordered. I have a confession to make, though—I *did* have to kill the lady with the red Mercy-Bentley. I'm sorry about it, but I—"

"You had no choice, lad," said the old woman in an accent that Mark thought sounded faintly British. "I saw it all. You did what you had to do, and I'm thankful to you." She stood aside from the door and grinned inscrutably. Looking straight at Mark, but apparently talking to Sam, she said, "You may as well bring our visitors inside and make them comfortable. We'll proceed with the introductions and have a bite to eat."

Mark followed Sam inside, ducking his head as he passed through the low door frame. Bob Gammage followed closely behind Mark, muttering profanities under his breath.

The place seemed much larger within than it appeared from without. It reminded Mark of a carnival fun house or one of those "gravity defying" buildings advertised on rural billboards throughout the American West, where the angles of walls and floors create illusions that warp the observer's sense of up and down. Cubicles lay around every turn in the tight corridor, and the corridor sloped gradually downward, giving Mark the feeling that they were descending to a place below ground level, though they never encountered any stairs. The atmosphere smelled of candle wax, burning spices, and flourishing roots.

They came to a room far larger than any they'd seen in the upper level, lit by a blazing stone fireplace with wrought-iron racks for cooking, the end of the line, apparently. Just inside the hearth hung several bubbling kettles, from which issued the spicy smell that permeated the structure. Curiously, the room seemed cool despite the fire. To the right of the hearth stood the ancient spinning wheel that Mark had seen more times than he cared to remember, and beside it lay a large wicker basket.

The three men sat in chairs built of forest softwood, and the hag stood before them, looking as if she was about to introduce herself formally. Instead, she looked straight at Mark again and gave a little gesture with her bony hand, a kind of casual wave. From the corners of his eyes Mark saw Bob Gammage and Sam Darkenwald slump in their chairs, their chins plopping against their chests, instantly asleep.

"Now we can have a confidential talk, can't we, lad?"

"My God," Mark whispered, screwing his own eyes shut. "Is this real? Did you actually do what I just saw you do?"

The hag drew close and leaned low until her outrageously wrinkled face was mere inches from Mark's. He could feel her heat on his cheeks and smell her hickory skin, but he didn't dare open his eyes. "How can you have any doubt that it's real," she asked, "after what you've seen, after what you've felt in the course of the past fortnight?"

She moved away from him, and Mark opened his eyes. She sat cross-legged before the fire on a thick mat, as if she needed the warmth, firelight glancing off her huge silver ring as she prodded the coals with a steel poker. As Mark gazed at her in stark profile, he remembered that he'd thought her familiar-looking when he first saw her on that sunny day outside Cramer Hall. Now, despite the distortion of decades and maybe even centuries, he saw traces of a beloved face in a black-and-white photo that he'd kept in a mildewed canvas bag.

"Do you know who I am, lad?" Her voice was as dry as fallen leaves.

"Elspeth Carey."

"Ah, yes—Elspeth Carey. I can't recall the last time I heard that name from mortal lips. I haven't been spending much time with ordinary people, you understand." She grinned again, and Mark felt his sphincter tighten. "Do you know who *you* are?"

"I-I'm your grandson, I think."

"You know I've been watching you, don't you?"

"Yes—for at least—" Mark's throat felt clogged with bark dust. He gulped. "—the last two weeks."

"Oh, much longer. I can watch you from afar, you know." She reached into a straw basket that lay near the hearth and took out a block of glossy, well-oiled wood. It consisted of two halves held together with brass hinges, and it looked as ancient as Elspeth herself. Mark knew what it held.

"That's a scrying mirror, isn't it?"

"A scrying mirror, yes. You've learned much in a very short time, lad. You're a smart one, no doubt of that—a scholar, a professor of history. Your mother would have been proud of you, just as I am."

"Are you also proud of the fact that I'm a vampire, that I almost sucked blood from someone I love very much?"

"No, I'm *not* proud of that," she answered slowly. "I know how it feels to have the blood of a vampire in one's veins, and I'm sorrier for you than I can say. Unlike you, though, I've never felt the *hunger*, because the lion's share of my blood is human. I've kept the beasts away with magic, you see, so they've never had a chance to give me the first taste. My daughter wasn't as fortunate, I regret to say."

"Your *daughter*. My mother, you mean?"

"Your mother, yes. I lost her during the last cycle of the Blood Star. You've heard the story, I think."

"Clovis Gestern took her away from you. And then he raised her as his own."

"His *own!* What an interesting way of putting it! He raised her until she was old enough to bear a child, and then he forced her into his bed. He made her pregnant, lad—pregnant with *you*."

Mark's eyes smarted. "Clovis Gestern was my father?"

"I thought you'd guessed as much by now."

"Was he Kristen's father, too?"

"Yes, as a matter of fact he was. He made advances upon Marta Lansen, having courted her years before she married John, your adoptive father. There are few women alive who can resist a conquest by Clovis Gestern, once he puts his mind to it, and Marta was not one of them, even after she'd been John Lansen's wife for nearly fifteen years. You see, Clovis manipulated her into seeking you out when you were an orphan. Marta had kept careful track of where you were from the time of your infancy. When the time seemed right, she prevailed upon John to adopt you, all at Clovis Gestern's secret insistence. And then, she indulged herself with an intimate encounter with Clovis, which made her pregnant with your sister, Kristen. She kept the truth from John, of course, making him think that she was pregnant by him."

"Then Kristen and I are related by blood, which explains why we look so much alike."

"And why you both have such perfect teeth—one of the few physical attributes that all vampires share. I'll wager that all your life, people have remarked about your beautiful teeth, haven't they?"

Mark cringed. *Perfect teeth—all the better to . . .* He beat down a revolting thought. "And her dreams, *my* dreams . . . ?"

"Ah, the vile dreams, yes. The offspring of vampires are often plagued with nightmares about creatures that live inside them."

"*Inside* them? Are you saying that Kristen and I have *slugs* inside us?"

"They aren't really slugs, my boy. On those rare occasions when they take fleshy form, they appear sluglike to the uninitiated, which is why the old Lord Yesterday, Clovis Gestern, was called the Prince of Slugs in medieval times. The essence of the vampire, the thing that craves the blood of living people, exists as a separate entity inside the body. Its mind and intellect have merged with those of the human host to whom it has been born, enabling it to take control of the human in order to satisfy its hungers."

Mark shivered. "What about the changes—the arm that stretches twelve feet, and the teeth, and the claws . . . ?"

"An ancient ability, lad, that isn't limited to vampires. It's a form of physioplasty, which isn't even reliant on magic, though magic certainly helps. Merely mind over matter, as they say, and vampires are very good at it. Some of them, old Clovis included, can move things with their minds—psychokinesis, I believe it's called. Others can actually read people's thoughts. A powerful vampire can contort his body into virtually any shape in order to get what he wants or needs. Such a creature will become what he must become in order to satisfy his craving for blood, even if it means growing limbs that enable him to climb walls, or teeth to bite with, or claws to fight with."

"Or invisible tentacles to *feel* with."

"Yes, of course. You've discovered such powers of your own, haven't you?"

Mark had. He slouched forward and braced his forehead against his palms. "Is it true what Sam said about Kyleen—that she tried to have me killed?"

"You yourself saw her point a pistol at your head. Is it so hard to believe that she conscripted that pitiable derelict, Mr. Leo Fobbs? She may have been a witch and a sorceress, yes, but she had no wish to be caught and charged with murder. Using a surrogate like Mr. Fobbs is a favorite tactic among her kind, because it allows them to accomplish their black work without incurring the wrath of society. A poor beggar or wino gets the blame for some seemingly random murder, and no one ever suspects the witch."

"But *why?* She's been my therapist for over five years, a trusted friend. Why would she suddenly want me dead?"

"Because you are what you are. She served a powerful creature who felt threatened by you, someone who wanted you dead and still does. She was *never* your friend, lad—only pretended to be. She wasn't even a real physician—"

"But I was her patient! I've been to her office at least fifty times!"

Elspeth Carey wagged her ragged head and chuckled, a perverse merriment gleaming in her eyes. "Can you say that you really knew her? Be honest now. Think back to when you met her. . . ."

Which Mark did. A stress-management seminar at the Northwest Community Center in Portland, 1983. Open to the public. He'd sat next to the pretty woman in the red sweater. They'd chatted, traded business cards. Kyleen LeBreaux was a clinical psychologist who specialized in family matters, particularly marital relations. Later she'd called to ask what he'd thought of the seminar, and they'd gotten together for coffee. Shortly thereafter he'd suggested to Deidre that they go to Dr. LeBreaux in an effort to save their foundering marriage.

Had she actually contrived to sit next to him at the seminar? Had Kyleen solicited Mark and Deidre as patients? He had to admit it was possible.

"It was a well-executed ploy on her part," said Elspeth. "She sought you out, got close to you, preyed on your vulnerabilities. Her office was merely a set, a stage. Her diplomas were props.

If you were to consult the state association of clinical psychologists, you would find that it has no record of her. You and your wife were her only patients, lad. You won't even find her name in the telephone directory."

"But why did she wait so long? Why didn't she just shoot me years ago and get it over with?"

"As I said, she had no wish to be caught and charged with murder. And it took time to find someone as malleable as Leo Fobbs, more time to cultivate him and work her spells on him. Her main purpose was to learn everything about you—your habits, your wants, your fears. She kept careful track of your mental state, looking for any sign that your final stage of development had begun. She knew that you wouldn't be likely to exhibit the proclivities of a full-fledged primo vampire until the next cycle of the Blood Star, which is now well under way, I might add."

"A *primo* vampire?"

She explained the term, and Mark paled. A primo vampire could sire other vampires, passing on the progeny of the slug inside him. This meant that Tad must be infected with the same curse.

"Is there any hope for me?" he asked, scarcely whispering. "Is there any hope for my boy?"

Elspeth Carey rose from her spot near the fire and approached him, holding her twiggy hands out to him. Taking both his hands in hers, she crouched to stare level into his miserable face.

"I've not told you everything I know, lad, because to do so would endanger you. You will soon discover that others have designs on you, that they mean to use you in pursuit of an unholy purpose. You must fight them. You must *destroy* them. You must find the strength within yourself to foil their scheme, or else you will surely become the abominable thing that they have ordained you to become."

Mark remembered what Poverty Ike had told him exactly a week earlier, after relating the rest of the tale of the Witch of Mesatchie Illihee: *"Be careful of people who would hurt you, and be careful of yourself."* "Then there *is* hope," he said eagerly. "There's a way to beat this thing, isn't there? You know how to do it, don't you?"

Old Elspeth squeezed his hands hard enough to bring new tears to his eyes. "Whether you can beat it is up to you, lad. Whether you beat it depends on whether you remember the message that I've sent to you time and again—a message you've heard in dreams, in your mind, even on the lips of a dead man. Remember it and act on it."

She released one of his hands and touched the silver amulet that hung around his neck on a gold strand. Mark saw a shadow of deep sadness pass over her filmy eyes, and he supposed that she was reliving the last time she'd seen it around the neck of her newborn daughter.

"Keep this with you always," she whispered huskily, fingering the charm. "It will help you keep the hunger at bay, and may even offer some protection against evil spells. As for the book— you still have it, don't you?"

Mark nodded, knowing she meant the tale of Snacky Cat.

"It too is a charm. It was activated by the onset of the cycle of the Blood Star, but you needn't have it near you to avail yourself of it. If you find yourself threatened, simply think of the scene on the cover, and will yourself into it. The Catamount will be there for you."

Mark's head spun now. He longed for a breath of fresh air and a cool drink of water. When he spoke, his speech was slurred. "What *message*, Elspeth? And how should I act on it?" The vision of her face grew wavy and rippled, and he felt exhaustion settle over him like a warm blanket. The crackling of the fire grew dim in his ears. "W-what message?" This was the effect of some spell, no doubt, and it angered him. He didn't want to fall asleep now. He had more questions to ask. "T-tell me, Elspeth. How should I . . . ?" Sleep smothered his words, and his chin plopped onto his chest.

42

Penetration

i

Sam Darkenwald and Bob Gammage followed Elspeth Carey along the forest trail, dodging low branches and occasionally tripping over roots or stones. That someone so old could maintain such a pace amazed Gammage. Their going slowed as dusk thickened, but suddenly they were at the forest's edge on a steep hillside.

The old woman halted. "From here, you must go alone," she whispered, pointing with a crooked finger to the open area ahead. "Fifty paces straight and thirty to your right, and you'll find the tunnel. Inside it you'll encounter the barred gate and the lock I spoke of earlier. Do you have your tools, Mr. Gammage?"

"Sam's got 'em," answered Gammage. Sam held up the compact leather satchel that Gammage had fetched from the trunk of his car at the outset of this trek.

"And your light?"

Gammage showed her the long-barreled, big-lens flashlight, which he'd also fetched. He then pulled up his jacket to reveal the butt of his heavy Sig Sauer nine-millimeter, which he'd jammed into his belt before locking the trunk. "A little something to make up for my bum arm, in case of trouble," he told her, winking.

The old woman hardly glanced at the pistol. "Once you've opened the gate, remember to lock it behind you, and follow the tunnel into the house itself. Bear always to the right, and when you come to the stairs, follow them down to the lowest level. Where the lowermost passage ends, you will find a cell, and inside you will find the child, Skye Padilla. You must open the lock, just as you will have opened the lock on the gate. When you have freed her, retrace your steps and withdraw from the house the way you entered it." She then moved close to Gammage, and fixed him with a hard, deadly serious stare. "You must keep your wits about you, Mr. Gammage, and you must take care not to be detected. Hide if you hear someone coming, and don't stir until you're certain that the danger has passed. Under no circumstances must you confront anyone in the house, other than Skye Padilla. To be found out is to risk death. Do you understand?"

Bob Gammage nodded, but really he understood very little. He didn't understand exactly what he was doing here, or why he was going along with this madness. He didn't understand this weird old woman, her weird little house in the forest, or the fact that he'd apparently fallen asleep in a straight-backed chair for something like eight hours. He didn't understand why Mark Lansen had disappeared. He felt as if he were living in some surreal fantasy, that at any moment it would turn into an out-and-out nightmare with gremlins and ghouls and man-eating freaks.

"Very well then," said Elspeth Carey. She turned to Sam Darkenwald, who stood grinning beneath his battered straw cowboy hat. "You've done me great service, lad, and I shall always be grateful. Take this small token of my gratitude." She pressed a small, sealed envelope into his hand, which he stashed inside his shirt. "Open it only when you return safely from Gestern Hall."

With that, she turned and slipped away into the glen, scarcely stirring a leaf or a twig.

ii

The tunnel entered the hill three hundred yards north of Gestern Hall, which loomed bleak and silent against the fading evening sky. They stepped into it and went twenty feet before encountering the barred gate, which was locked, as the old woman had said it would be.

Sam held the flashlight while Gammage first studied the lock, then rummaged through his little "doctor bag" for various hooks and probes. Within seconds Gammage was at work, cursing the cast on his arm with every breath. Awkward though the cast was, he still had limited use of his left hand, without which he could never have picked the lock.

"Nice going!" exclaimed Sam when, ten minutes later, the lock clanked and the heavy barred gate squeaked open.

"Keep your voice down. This was an old model, a fairly easy one to pick. No telling what the next one will be like." Gammage ducked through the gate and beckoned Sam to follow, upon which Sam reminded him that Ellie had instructed them to lock the gate behind them.

"To hell with that. I don't want to waste time picking it again. We might be in a hurry to leave, know what I mean?"

"Heck, Mr. Gammage, I think we should do exactly what old Ellie says. She probably had a good reason for telling us—"

Gammage whirled on Sam and grabbed the flashlight away from him. "Listen, you fuckin' loony tune, you can come with me or you can go back. Or you can stand there like a frozen jar of piss, for all I care. Just don't give me any more shit, okay?— because I promise you I'll deviate your septum if you say one more word. Do we understand each other?"

They understood each other.

43

A Council of War

i

The sun had sunk well below Fish Hawk Ridge by the time Mark found himself at the front door of Father Charlie Briggs's rectory, his finger on the doorbell button. A light burned in the parlor, casting yellow rectangles through the windowpanes onto the porch. He heard the chiming doorbell, heard footfalls coming to answer.

Tressa Downey appeared as he knew she would, wearing jeans and a white cotton turtleneck, her dark hair brushed and shiny. When she saw him, she put a palm to her cheek and breathed, *"Mark!"*

"You don't have anything to be afraid of, Tress, at least not from me." He held up the silver amulet that hung around his neck on its gold chain. "I can't explain how or why, but this thing helps. It keeps me—*myself*. I won't hurt you, I promise."

"How did you know where to find me?"

"I—" How *had* he known? Had Elspeth Carey put the knowledge into his head, having first put him to sleep? He could scarcely remember waking up. His first solid memory since losing consciousness in front of her hearth was driving down Queen Molly Road in Kyleen LeBreaux's Mercedes. Without even thinking, he'd driven straight to the rectory, somehow knowing that he would find Tressa here.

"My God, what happened to your chest?"

The top of Mark's Hawaiian shirt was open, showing the ugly blister raised by the amulet at the moment Kyleen LeBreaux had tried to blow his head off. Strangely, the pain was gone now. "Long story. Sad one, too. If you'll let me in, I'll tell it to you." He studied her face and listened to her thudding heart. Images flashed through his mind, accompanied by cold sensations of grief, confusion, misgiving. He realized with horrid fascination that he was catching snippets of her thoughts.

"Something else has happened, hasn't it?" he ventured. "It's something terrible. Someone is—" He shook his head in a vain attempt to clear it of the invading grief, *Tressa's* grief, which had become his own. "Someone's dead, someone you love."

Tressa whispered Velma Selvig's name, and Mark repeated it, not quite believing. Velma Selvig was dead, which seemed unthinkable. Her van stood in the driveway of the rectory, which had led him to assume she was here with Tressa.

Seconds dragged by as they searched each other's faces, each groping for something to say. Mark wanted to blurt how sorry he was, but his vocal cords went numb as the image of Velma's body assailed him, lolling spread-eagled in the rear parlor of the Royal Kokanee Inn, bleeding obscenely. The scene came to him through Tressa's brain.

"It wasn't you, was it, Mark?"

"No!" He reached toward her, but she shrank back. "*God*, no! Tressa, please believe that. It wasn't me." *Why should she believe me?* he wondered. *She's seen what I can become.* But she'd also seen that he could conquer that thing, that he could resist it and throw it off.

"I believe you," she said finally, and motioned him into the foyer. She put her hand on his arm, a small gesture that gave him a simple joy. "We've been looking for you all day, Mark. We went to your parents' house, and Marta told us you'd gone off with your therapist. I was worried. You'll probably think this sounds crazy, but—"

"Hey, nothing sounds crazy to me anymore."

"Mark, listen to me. I think you should stay away from Kyleen LeBreaux. I think she could be dangerous. I have reason to believe that she—she's a—"

"A witch? A sorceress?" He chuckled bitterly. "There's no need to worry about Kyleen anymore. She's gone riding on that big broomstick in the sky." He related what had happened that morning out by old No Name Bridge, without actually mentioning that Kyleen had seduced him. He said only that she'd tried to shoot him, that Sam Darkenwald had saved his bacon by killing her with his bare hands. The amulet, for some reason that only a witch could understand, had become hot enough to scorch his chest.

Why? Tressa asked. Why had Kyleen tried to kill him?

"I found out that she wasn't really a psychologist at all, and that she has apparently wanted me dead since day one. The psychologist bit was only a sham, a trick to get close to me. Remember the guy I told you about—Leo Fobbs, the one who jumped off a building and almost killed me? He was working for her, or more accurately, he was under her *control*. And the old woman I saw outside Cramer Hall—"

"The one you saw yesterday when you were—" She swallowed heavily, and Mark felt the image of Mark-the-Vampire flash in her head.

"Her name is Elspeth Carey, and she's a witch, too, which probably comes as no surprise. I've just come from her house."

"Her *house?*"

"Witches have to live somewhere, I guess. Hers is in the forest up on Nehalem Mountain. I'll tell you about it sometime. Anyway, she intervened with some kind of counter-spell to throw Fobbs off course. What it boils down to is that she saved my life, Tressa. And she was the one who sent Sam Darkenwald to keep Kyleen from shooting me."

Tressa leaned against the fading floral wallpaper of the foyer, looking as if she was about to swoon. "Then she's been protecting you, not only from Kyleen but—"

"From myself, yes. She refers to me as a primo vampire."

Tressa quickly collected herself. "Mark, there's someone I want you to meet. Believe it or not, he's had experience with these things, and he wants to help us. Father Charlie sent for him. I've told him all about you, me, everything else that's been happening in this town. He's in the study right now with the others, and he's anxious to talk with you."

"The others?"

Gretchen Bayliss and Brett Omdahl, the other half of a newly mustered band of vampire hunters. They'd convened here because they'd had nowhere else to go. Tressa could not abide the thought of returning to the Royal Kokanee, where Velma's naked body lay in the parlor, and they certainly couldn't meet at the Downeys' house, or at the Omdahls' or Baylisses'. So Tressa had talked the housekeeper at the rectory, Mrs. Lidderdale, into letting them stay here.

"I'm sure she thinks we're neck-deep in some sort of black conspiracy," Tressa added, trying to smile again, "and it's probably killing her not to be in on it. But never mind that. I want you to meet Father Le Fanu."

ii

Father Gautier Le Fanu stood and offered his lean, pale hand when Tressa introduced Mark. From his nearby boom box came lively brass strains backed up with double bass, piano, and drums. Brett Omdahl leaned against a corner of Father Charlie's old rolltop desk, looking bored as only sixteen-year-old boys can, while Gretchen Bayliss sat in her motorized wheelchair near the center of the room.

"Sounds like Dizzy Gillespie," said Mark, shaking Le Fanu's hand. "You a jazz fan?"

"I am an ardent jazz fan, monsieur. And it is indeed Dizzy Gillespie—'Salt Peanuts.' Are you also fond of jazz?"

"Some I like, some I don't. I've always liked Dizzy. You're obviously French."

"I am."

"Désirez-vous me parler en français?"

"No, monsieur," replied Le Fanu with a spare smile, "I think it best if we speak English, for the benefit of the others. Your French is excellent, however, no doubt because you are a scholar of French history."

"I do my best." Mark turned from the priest and went to Gretchen. He took one of her hands in his and found her skin cool to the touch, but her smile was sweet and warm. He detected pity in her eyes. "How's it going, kid? I suppose Tressa has filled you in on my—uh—*problem.*"

"I know what happened with you and Tressa yesterday, but I remember what you both did for me at the Royal Kokanee last week, and afterwards at home. You're one of the good guys, okay? You wouldn't hurt any of us, I'm sure of that."

He then shook hands with young Brett and tried to remember when last he'd seen the kid. Ten years ago, at least, when Brett was scarcely belt-buckle tall. The uncertain look on Brett's face showed that he did not fully share Gretchen's faith. Mark turned back to Tressa and asked, "So what's this, a council of war?"

"That's exactly what it is. Father Le Fanu and I rounded up Gretchen and Brett because they're probably the only other people in this town who know what we're up against. I doubt anyone else would believe us. Except for you, of course."

"Your perspective is unique," added Le Fanu with a touch of irony.

"Because I'm a vampire, you mean." The remark seemed to numb everyone in the room, and a long silence followed.

"Father Le Fanu says you can be cured," said Gretchen cautiously, "but not until some other things happen first."

"What things?"

"Why don't you make yourself comfortable, monsieur," suggested Le Fanu, snapping off the boom box. "You must learn the whole story, certainly, but telling it will take time. Also, you have things to share with us, I'm sure."

Mark glanced around and saw hope in their faces, hope that he embodied. He was about to sit when he spied a bottle in the glass cabinet in the entry of the study. He went to it, pulled it out—a fifth of Jameson's Irish whiskey, bottled in 1971, more than half full. Father Charlie had probably nipped from it on special occasions.

"Anyone care to join me?" Mark asked. None did, so he sat in an armchair across from Father Le Fanu and took an ambitious swig. "Okay, I'm ready as I'll ever be," he said, coughing from the sting of the liquor. "Let's talk, Father. You lay it on me, and I'll lay it on you. And no holding back, okay?"

iii

"So Clovis Gestern intends for me to mate with Kristen, my sister, is that it?" said Mark much later, having heard Le Fanu out. He spoke slowly to keep from slurring. The bottle of Jameson's had been more than half full when he'd taken it from the cabinet, but now it was less than a third full. "He wants us to have a baby during the Cycle of the Blood Star"—he pulled another swig from the bottle and rendered a sour grin—"just so he can experience the warm fuzzies of perpetuating his line."

"That baby would be a primo vampire, just as you are," answered Le Fanu. "The child's blood would be more than half-vampire, and he would be capable of siring more vampires."

Mark eyed Le Fanu for a long moment. Thus far he'd involuntarily caught bits and pieces of what three of the four others had been thinking—Tressa, Gretchen, and Brett. The ability had grown more acute with every nip of Irish whiskey, he realized. Le Fanu's mind, though, seemed hidden behind a lead curtain, impervious. The priest had apparently learned some trick during his long dealings with vampires that let him keep his thoughts to himself.

"So you're totally certain that I'm a primo? Is there any way you and Elspeth Carey could be wrong?"

"There can be no question now, monsieur. If you are the grandson of Elspeth, which you must certainly be, as you yourself have said, and if Clovis Gestern is your father, then you have more than fifty percent of a vampire's blood in your veins. You see, the Sire de l'Hier is also Elspeth Carey's grandfather, which means that your mother carried the blood, even though her father was an ordinary human mortal."

"The *Sire de l'Hier*," repeated Mark. "Lord Yesterday in English." He chuckled miserably. "And *gestern* means yesterday in German. That little tidbit just hit me!" He stared a long moment at Le Fanu, who gazed back at him through his wire-framed glasses. "Tell you what, Walt—you don't mind if I call you Walt, do you?"

"Not if it amuses you, monsieur."

"In case you're wondering," said Mark in an aside to the others, "*Gautier* is the French equivalent of *Walter*, but that sounds a little too formal, it seems to me. And since I'm not a Catholic vampire, it doesn't seem right to call him *Father*." Turning back to Le Fanu again, he said, "Tell you what, Walt. I'll do anything you want me to do, or at least I'll try, and that includes killing Clovis Gestern and any other primo vampires around, if you'll do one thing for me in return."

"And what is that?"

"Promise to cure both Kristen and me of this—this—" He coughed and took another long pull from the bottle. "Promise me you'll help us get rid of the fucking *slugs* inside us! I don't care what you have to do. I don't care if it hurts like hell, or even if it kills us. I'd rather be dead than live with this thing, and so would Kristen, I know."

Le Fanu rose from his chair and stood before Mark, as straight and solid as an oaken piling. "None of us should make promises that he may not be able to keep," he intoned. "Each of us can promise only to do his best." He laid a hand on Mark's shoulder.

"It is possible, monsieur, that you may not be able to kill the Sire de l'Hier, which would mean the most dire consequences for us all. It is also possible that my magic may not be sufficiently strong to save you, even if you *do* succeed in killing him. As for your sister . . ." He shook his head. "I will do everything that is within my power. Perhaps the magic of Elspeth Carey, combined with my own, will be equal to the task."

Mark rose from his chair and wandered to the window, beyond which lay the velvety night, an Oldenburg night that seemed alive with menace. "If that's the best deal I can cut, then I guess I'll just have to live with it. What's next?"

"We must make preparations," answered Le Fanu. "I will require the baggage that came from my room at Velma Selvig's inn."

"The stuff is outside in Velma's van," Tressa explained to Mark. "Father Le Fanu and Brett brought it over from the Royal Kokanee this afternoon."

"If you and Brett would be kind enough to bring the trunk in, we may begin," said Le Fanu.

Mark and Brett went out to the van and carted in the trunk, which contained various vials, jars, bags, baskets, and books. Per the priest's instructions, they placed it in the front parlor of the rectory. Le Fanu took from it the items he needed and arrayed them on a low table. Tressa drew the drapes and locked the doors.

"Everything appears to be in readiness," said Le Fanu as he placed his scrying mirror in the center of the embroidered pentagram on the red-satin tablecloth. At each point of the star stood a candle of unbleached wax. "You may put out the light."

"Wait a minute," said Mark. "I'm having second thoughts about involving these kids. If this business is as dangerous as you say it is, maybe we should leave Gretchen and Brett out of it."

"No way!" protested Brett, his cheeks coloring. "One of those things almost killed my dog! If you could've seen what she did to him—if you could've seen her *face*, you'd know why I need to be in on this!"

"I'm only thinking of your safety, big guy. And you don't have to tell *me* what a vampire's face looks like. Besides, your parents will be wondering where the hell you are."

"No way you're sending me home, man! You didn't see what

she almost did to me! Kristen either gets cured or she gets killed, and I'm going to make sure that one or the other happens!"

"The same goes for me," Gretchen piped up. Her bold blue eyes attested to her resolve, even though she couldn't hold her head up for more than thirty seconds at a time. "Skip Gestern has been sucking my mother's blood, Mark. And your sister nearly killed my dad." She groped for Brett's hand, caught it, held it. "We *both* have a stake in this thing! We're staying!"

Father Le Fanu approached Mark and stood close to him, face to face. "They are right, monsieur. These young ones have a right to be here."

"But what if something goes wrong? You said yourself the consequences could be dire. I'm not sure I could live with myself if one of these kids got hurt, or—" Mark stopped himself.

Le Fanu's oily eyes hardened behind his rimless glasses. "Don't you wonder whether either of these young ones will ever again have a moment of peace, having seen what they have seen, knowing what they know? Can you believe that either of their lives will ever again be sunny and bright, or that either will ever enjoy a restful night's sleep? If their future is to be more than a living hell, they must have a part in defeating this monstrous evil. For the sake of their sanity, you must not deny them this chance for resolution."

"Sorry, Walt, but I'm less concerned about how they'll sleep than about keeping them alive."

"Then consider this: I *need* them to help me fight the Sire de l'Hier. I need their goodness, their pureness of heart, especially Gretchen's. She possesses a potency of spirit, a vitality of faith, that will strengthen my magic. Believe me, monsieur, I need every ally I can find, and so do you."

"Can you guarantee their safety? Can you give me some assurance that they won't get hurt?"

"As I said before—no promises, no guarantees. It would be wrong of me to lie to you, monsieur."

With that, Mark knew that the matter was closed.

iv

Le Fanu went back to the low table, the legs of which rested on blocks of wax, and sat before it. "Before we begin," he said, addressing the group, "I want to make certain that each of you is aware of what you will face in the hours and days ahead. You will see things that you never dreamed possible. You will be witness to evil of a magnitude that defies human understanding. You will know fear as you have never known it. You must cling to your faith, and you must resist any temptation to forsake the goodness that lives in you. I will give you magic, yes, but magic is nothing without a strong heart, a *loving* heart."

He turned in his chair and looked first to Tressa, who stood near the lighted portrait of the Blessed Mother that had hung on this wall since her earliest recollection. She felt his eyes boring into her soul, reading her sins and tabulating her failings, taking stock of her. She felt like an open book.

"You must not dwell on the past, my child," said the priest, speaking directly to her, as if this was a confessional and no one else could hear. "What's done is done. You have found your absolution for old sins, and they no longer matter. What matters now is the love you still bear for the little one you lost, a love that is alive and strong and growing, a love that is good. Hold it close, and be ready to wield it like a sword when the time comes."

v

To Brett Omdahl, he said, "Your soul burns with hatred, my son, but it is a righteous hatred, unflawed by selfishness or wantonness. You have been a good citizen of God's earth. You have been a friend to one who deserves many friends, but has few, simply because her imperfect body has confined her to a wheelchair. For your courage, God will reward you. Cling to your righteous hatred, my son, and hurl it like a killing stone when the time is right."

vi

To Gretchen Bayliss, he said, "Come here, my child." The electric motor of her wheelchair hissed as it conveyed her to the center of the room, where Le Fanu sat at his table. He gazed at her a long moment, as if searching her soul, his face paling a shade. "I cannot say what gift you possess, but I see it shining through your eyes like . . ." Like lantern light from a distant midnight canyon, he thought once again, ". . . like nothing I have ever seen before."

"Saint Joan had a gift," said Gretchen, bowing her head. "I'm not Saint Joan."

"But yours is the faith of a saint. You must let it be the wings of my magic, the vehicle of my spell. Can you do that?"

Gretchen closed her blue eyes and leaned back against the padded headrest. "I'm worried about something, Father. I'm worried that—" A tear plummeted down her cheek. "What we're going to do—it won't be a sacrilege, will it? I mean, all the magic and spells . . . it seems so un-Christian."

The old priest touched her cheek. "Do you remember what happened on the rainy morning of the thirtieth of May, in the year 1431?"

"Yes, Father. That was the day Joan was burned in Rouen."

"And was not the Bishop Pierre Cauchon responsible for her death? Wasn't it the charge of witchcraft and heresy that sent her to the stake, brought by the church that you and I love?"

Gretchen bit her lower lip and nodded, still weeping.

"Listen to me, my child. It was because our beloved Joan heard voices that the learned men of the church thought her a witch, no matter that these were the voices of Saint Michael the Archangel, Saint Catherine, and Saint Margaret. They found her guilty and burned her, simply because Joan's truth seemed different from theirs. I too have felt the wrath of the church, because I have used magic from the *Book of Rahab* to fight vampires, notwithstanding that the church has been powerless against these beasts since the very beginning. The holy men of Rome defrocked me and excommunicated me for witchcraft because I dared to recognize truth that doesn't happen to appear in scripture or in the canons of the church." He cupped her cheek in his palm. "Just as Joan heeded her voices and took up the sword against an unjust English king, you must confront the evil that has raised its ugly head right here in Oldenburg. You too must become a soldier, Gretchen."

The girl raised her head off the headrest and blinked away tears. "I'll try, Father. I hope God will help me."

Le Fanu raised her tiny, twisted hand to his lips and kissed it. "*Aide-toi, le ciel t'aidera*, my child. God helps those who help themselves."

vii

Finally, he turned back to Mark Lansen, who had collapsed onto the sofa. Mark felt queasy, which he didn't attribute entirely to the whiskey he'd pounded down since arriving. Magic, spells, vampires—*Christ, when is this fucking nightmare going to end? This is the late twentieth century! I should be home watching "Cheers" with my son, sipping a beer. Please, God, take me back to the real world. . . .*

"You do understand, don't you, monsieur, that only another primo vampire has any real hope of killing the Sire de l'Hier? *You* must be that man."

So much for the real world. "What do I have to do?"

"You must get close to him. You must pretend that you are willing to follow him in his scheme to sire a line of vampires with his blood in their veins. You must even pretend enthusiasm. Can you do that?"

"It shouldn't be too hard to get close to him, if it's Skip Gestern we're talking about. He's invited me to dinner tomorrow night."

"Ah. Then he means to initiate the next phase of his plan to-morrow. He will probably try to drug you at dinner, and may even cause you to imbibe more human blood that he himself has vomited."

"Christ, why would he do *that?*"

"To make doubly certain that the slug within you has been fully awakened. The initiation of a primo vampire normally re-quires only one dose, whereas the initiation of lesser vampires often requires several. With *you*, however, the Sire de l'Hier will no doubt want to make doubly sure."

Mark's head ached, which Tressa saw in his face. She sat next to him and began to massage the back of his neck and his shoul-

ders. "I don't have to go along with it, do I?" he asked plead-
ingly. "I don't think I could stand another dose of blood."

"This is what I shall do, monsieur: I shall cast a spell and de-
rive a potion that you will drink before going to Gestern Hall. It
will render you temporarily immune to any narcotic that the Sire
de l'Hier may try to give you. It will also guard against any magical means that he employs to put you to sleep."

"I'll need it. A couple of days ago my sister knocked me out
by just *looking* at me funny."

"She was using forced hypnosis, a power that even lesser
vampires possess to some degree. It's especially effective against
victims who are distraught or emotionally fatigued."

"That's me, right down to my shoelaces."

"Which brings up another matter, monsieur: You must take
care to prevent the Sire de l'Hier from looking into your mind
and detecting your actual motives. As you have probably discovered by now, primo vampires have a limited ability to hear the
thoughts of others. By concentrating, you can hide your real
emotions and goals. Unfortunately, it won't be enough to simply
hide them. You must actually project false thoughts that lead the
monster to believe that you are with him, because he will suspect
the worst if his probe encounters only a blank wall."

"Do I know how to do this?"

"You must teach yourself before you go, and you must practice. I myself have learned to shield my mind from a vampire's
probe—"

"I've noticed that."

"—but not being a vampire myself, I can only teach you so
much. You must utilize your instincts, monsieur. You must exper-
iment. It is critically important that the Sire de l'Hier believes
you have become his ally. I will help you as much as I can."

viii

With the room dark but for the glow of candles, Le Fanu
placed a massive, old-looking book on the table next to the scrying mirror. He opened it and carefully turned its crinkly pages
until he found the passage he wanted. The silence of the room
thickened as he recited some arcane ritual in a language Tressa
didn't recognize, some unholy appeal to a force that she sup-

posed any self-respecting humanist would scoff at. The murky scene reminded her of something out of an Expressionist play, some fantasy or nightmare or hallucination intended to reveal the "dynamics of the inner man." That she should recall such trivia from her college days seemed incredible.

Suddenly Le Fanu's body convulsed and stiffened in his chair. From the obsidian surface of the scrying mirror rose a faint, green glow that hovered mere inches away from his open eyes. Gretchen gave a muffled cry and pulled Brett closer to her. Tressa heard Mark gulp.

Staring into that cloud of smoky green, Le Fanu spoke: "I see graves opening, and things coming out. The Sire de l'Hier has summoned them. He will send them into battle against us, these creatures blackened with mud, these beings that carry the stink of the grave. They will try to dissuade us. They will try to shake our resolve—"

A low light flickered in the corner of Tressa's eye, catching her attention. She looked to the portrait of the Blessed Mother that hung over the mantle, and bit her tongue to keep from screaming. The Virgin's eyes had brightened with a golden glow, and her lips had stretched into a lewd smile. The artist had depicted Mary's sacred heart as if it clung to the outside of her garment, right between her breasts. Now the saint touched it with the fingers of her left hand. Long black claws grew from the fingertips as Tressa watched. One of the claws punctured the heart, and thick green pus oozed out.

"—and his loathsome power surrounds us even now, at this very moment, a power to distort our senses and perceptions, a power to make us doubt ourselves. . . ."

The Blessed Mother's face broadened and became beetle-browed. Yellow fangs protruded beneath her upper lip. The once-Holy Virgin winked at Tressa and reached out from the gilded frame as if to snare her. Tressa leapt up from the sofa and fled the room, choking with horror. She heard a stir behind her— Mark following, alarmed, but a loud *No!* came from Father Le Fanu.

"Let her go, my son! Your place is here! If you ever hope to rid yourself of the evil inside you, you must stay . . . !"

44

Dungeon

i

"Who's there?" whispered someone inside the cell.

A girl's voice, thought Bob Gammage. A teenager's. Everything was turning out just as old Ellie said it would. So far.

"Skye? Skye Padilla?" He aimed the flashlight through the barred window in the wooden door. The beam sliced along a damp stone wall, where here and there protruded iron rings that some ancient mason had mortared into the stones, points at which to attach chains and shackles and wrist irons. The beam finally found the young girl, who huddled like a frightened kitten in one corner, shielding her eyes with a dirty, scabby hand.

"Skye, listen to me. My name is Gammage, and I'm here to take you back to New York. Your old man hired me, okay? I gotta know if you're all right. I gotta know if you can walk."

"I-I think so. I'm so cold and so tired. I-I haven't tried to walk since"—she coughed painfully, and Gammage winced—"since she put me in here."

How could someone do this to a kid? Gammage's heart screamed. *I wish to God I could get my hands on the son of a bitch who—*

Sam Darkenwald whispered, "Poor thing doesn't sound too good, does she, Mr. Gammage? I might have to carry her."

"Let's get her out first. Here, take the light." While Sam shone the light on the heavy padlock, Gammage held it in his good hand, measuring its weight and strength. He pulled it tight against the staple to determine whether there was any give. There wasn't.

"Skye, I need to ask a question," he whispered through the bars. "Do you know where the key to this lock might be? I don't really need it to get you out, don't worry about that, but I could do this a lot faster if I had it."

"Mrs. Drumgule keeps it with her all the time," answered the girl weakly.

"And where could I find this Mrs. Drum—what did you say her name was? Drumgoo?"

"Upstairs in the house somewhere. She'll be coming down here soon. She—" Another cough—raspy, croupy, like pneumonia at worst or acute bronchitis at best. Sounds like she should be in a hospital, thought Gammage, grinding his teeth.

"Try to help me out, sweetheart. Does Mrs. Drumgoo ever open this door? To give you food, maybe? To take you to the bathroom?"

"She never opens it. When she comes down here, she just sits in the room behind you, moaning and saying some kind of prayers. Sometimes she makes flashes of light and bad smells. I don't know how she does it, except it's awful, and it scares me. Pretty soon they're going to take me out of here and slice me open so they can—so they can—" Another fit of coughing racked her.

"Slice you open? Is that what you said?" Gammage wanted to gag.

"S-so they can read the future in my guts."

"Christ Almighty. Listen, Skye, we're not going to let anybody hurt you, understand? We're going to get you out of here and take you home, where you'll be safe from these maniacs. Be cool now, and don't worry about a thing." To Sam Darkenwald he said, "We better get busy, Speed. Give me the tools, and hold the light steady. This is an old lock, but it's a Yale, and it's gonna be tougher than a son of a bitch."

ii

Nearly an hour passed while Gammage poked and prodded the lock with various picks, tweezers, files, and pieces of wire. He developed a gnawing headache, and his left hand—the one hindered by the cast—sore. The flashlight batteries started to dim, and Sam began worrying aloud about discovery by the owners of the house. Worst of all, Skye Padilla's wheezing sounded louder, more painful.

"I always thought picking a lock was easy, if you knew how

to do it," groused Sam, shifting his weight against the heavy door.

"Only in the movies, Speed. Some locks take hours, and some can't be picked at all." Just then the lock succumbed and fell away from the staple with a clank. "God, this one was a mother," Gammage huffed, flexing his hands. "I think it made a cripple of me."

He pulled open the door and stepped into the cell, while Sam gathered up the tools and shoved them back into the satchel. Inside, the smell was bad. It was clear that the girl's captors hadn't shown the decency to let her out to go to the bathroom. "Time to go, sweetie," Gammage said, kneeling next to her in a corner of the cell. "Before you know it, you'll be sitting behind home plate in Yankee Stadium, screaming obscenities at the ump."

"I'm a Mets fan," wheezed Skye, holding her hands out to him. "I hate George Steinbrenner."

"Tell you what. When we get back there, I'll take you and your old man to a Mets game, maybe when the Dodgers or Braves are in town. We'll load up on hot dogs and peanuts, and make perfect asses of ourselves like New York fans are supposed to. What d'ya say?"

With his help, the girl got painfully to her feet and leaned against him. Gammage's heart ached for her: She was weak and wobbly, and the shapeless gray dress she wore wasn't nearly adequate against the chill of this place. Marveling that she was even alive, he steered her gently into the corridor. Suddenly the hair on his neck bristled.

"Someone's coming down the stairs," whispered Sam Darkenwald. "What do we do now?"

"I've got ears, for Christ's sake."

"What if it's Mrs. Drumgoo?"

"Shut up and let me think!"

On the landing immediately above this one, the stairwell opened into the system of corridors and passages that eventually led to the tunnel in the hillside. Sam Darkenwald and Bob Gammage had used this route into the dungeon, following the hag's instructions to bear ever to the right. On their way out, they meant to retrace their steps, this time bearing left. Gammage had no way of knowing whether the owners of the hurrying feet had descended past the next-to-lowest landing.

Voices, echoing against the backdrop of dripping water—

louder, nearer: ". . . and then I saw that somebody had picked the lock in the gate. I figured whoever did it must still be in the tunnel, but I thought I should talk to you first, Mrs. Drumgule." The man's voice had a gurgly, unhealthy quality.

"You did well, Bernardo. And you, too, Francesca."

"Thank you, Mrs. Drumgule, but it was Bernie who saw it, not me. Bernie's such an observant man, and smart, too. That's why I married him, you know."

Gammage remembered the last thing old Ellie had said to him: *"Hide if you hear someone coming. . . . Under no circumstances must you confront anyone in the house. . . . To be found out is to risk death."*

"Back in the cell!" he whispered urgently, wheeling Skye around. "Come on, Speed—you, too!"

"Hey, I don't want to be locked in there," protested Sam, his eyes huge and white in the glow of the flashlight. "It stinks like hell."

"I don't have time to argue with you. Remember what old Ellie said—if these people see you, you're gonna get killed."

"If you'd done what old Ellie said—if you'd put the lock back on the gate like I wanted to—we wouldn't be in this pickle."

"That's spilled milk, Speed. Now get in here before I get pissed off. Press your ass into that corner next to the door, and I'll do the same in this one. They won't see us when they look through the bars, and if we're lucky, they won't notice that the hasp isn't locked to the staple."

Reluctantly Sam entered the cell and did as Gammage ordered. Gammage positioned Skye in the far corner of the cell, where she'd been huddled when they first found her. He stuffed the Yale padlock into his pocket, carefully pushed the door shut and took up his position across from Sam. "Keep the light off," he hissed to Sam, "and don't even breathe!"

iii

The footfalls approached the door of the cell, and halted. A stench drifted through the bars, one even worse than the pissy, fecal smell that was already pervading the place. *Smells like something dead—death-rot mixed with stale lavender,* thought

Gammage. His fingers closed over the butt of the Sig Sauer in his belt.

Someone held a torch up to the tiny barred window in the heavy door, and vertical shadows danced around the tiny cell.

"Are you all right, my little child of clay?" asked Mrs. Drumgule. Skye Padilla answered with a vacant stare. "I would bring you some food and some warm blankets if I could, child, but the Spell of the Entrails won't permit it. You must suffer appropriately if the spell is to work, as I've already explained. You may take heart, though, in knowing that your misery will not last much longer."

Spell of the Entrails, thought Gammage. *What kind of sickos are these?* His fist tightened on the Sig Sauer, and he seriously contemplated bursting through the door with his gun blazing.

"Mrs. Drumgule, look at this," said the sick-sounding man, his voice gurgling with phlegm. "The padlock's gone. Someone's taken it off." Gammage's heart sank as someone fingered the hasp and the staple on the door.

"Skullduggery!" snarled Mrs. Drumgule. "Someone has been here! Perhaps he's here even now." Shoes scuffled across the stone floor, and Gammage imagined the trio searching the vaulted room opposite the cell. *"Under no circumstances must you confront anyone in the house. . . ."*

"We must've surprised him," said the female, moving closer to the door of the cell. "He must've sawed through the lock to get the girl out, but become frightened when he heard us coming."

"But where did he run to?" gurgled the man. "He couldn't've gotten by us. And if he didn't get by us—"

Long seconds of agonizing silence passed, in which Gammage heard only the far-off sound of dripping water and Skye's pathetic wheezing. *They're putting two and two together,* he told himself. *The jig is up. Time to go to Plan B. . . .*

Suddenly he heard the squeak of the hasp, followed by a metallic click, a sound he knew well. Someone had just hung a padlock on the door.

45

Father Confessor

i

Tressa found herself in the sanctuary of St. Pius X Catholic Church, kneeling at the rail of the tiny chapel off the nave, trembling like a fallen bird in the snow. She'd fled the rectory in a blind panic, having lost her final calorie of self-control when the vile caricature of the Blessed Mother grabbed at her from the picture frame in the parlor.

Why she'd come here, Tressa didn't know. Maybe because childhood impulses and beliefs die hard; maybe because she'd always associated this old church with peace and salvation. She'd been on autopilot when fleeing the rectory.

". . . and his loathsome power surrounds us even now, at this very moment," Father Le Fanu had intoned while staring into the pale green cloud that had risen from his scrying mirror, "a power to distort our senses and perceptions, a power to make us doubt ourselves. . . ."

Is *that* what had gotten to her? she wondered. Had she suffered a hallucination at the hand of Lord Yesterday? Hallucination or not, she'd felt the wind of the thing's claws as it swiped at her cheek.

ii

A candle burned inside a red lantern on the altar, the only source of light in the church. Shadows stuttered across the faces of the statuary—Christ on the cross above her, suffering in marbled silence; the Apostles clinging to pillars in the nave, pointing the way to heaven; and, yes, the Holy Virgin herself, smiling beatifically from her perch in a vaulted alcove to Tressa's left. Tressa didn't like the way the shadows flickered against the statue's face. She didn't like the way the Holy Virgin appeared to be breathing.

She rose from the railing, genuflected (an old, unconscious habit), and walked toward the nave. When she reached the narthex, she stared through the open door into the dark of the Oldenburg night, thinking that it seemed thick and smothering, almost toxic. Tressa couldn't go out there just yet.

She turned to her left and headed for the confessionals, which stood against an outer wall of the nave, two closets of dark oak, ornately carved with Gothic arches and trefoils. She pulled open the door of the one nearest the narthex, the one she'd always used when she was a youngster, and slipped inside.

The interior of the confessional was far darker than the nave, maybe even darker than the Oldenburg night outside the church. But this was a *different* kind of dark, less dense, less smothering. This was the clean darkness of the womb, where absolution restored the guilty sinner to the innocence of an unborn babe. The silence was so profound that Tressa thought she could hear the rustle of air molecules against her ear drums.

"Bless me, Father, for I have sinned," she'd said countless times as a young girl (Was she saying it now?). *It's been*—God, how long?—*almost seventeen years since my last confession.*

She'd confessed the sin of hating her mother, which Father Charlie had assured her that she was incapable of committing. She'd merely *resented* her mother, he'd insisted, or grown impatient with her, but she'd never actually hated her. Five Our Fathers and five Hail Marys, he'd prescribed.

She'd confessed envying Gina Pellagrini, her best friend, for her nice clothes and her ponies and her seemingly endless supply of spending money. She'd envied Gina most of all for her two honorable parents, neither of whom was a drunk. Five Our Fathers and five Hail Marys.

She'd confessed taking the name of the Lord in vain during gym class. Five and five.

She'd even confessed letting Mark Lansen feel her breasts at the drive-in theater over in Astoria, during a showing of *The Godfather*. This one had drawn three full rosaries.

What would she confess now? she wondered, assuming that she could ever bring herself to *believe* again. Having fallen away from the faith? Having rejected the authority of the church in favor of a truth less rigid, a truth that continually unfolds with the attainment of knowledge? In the eyes of the church, this was a mortal sin, she knew, the sin of consciously rejecting salvation.

"You have found your absolution for old sins, and they no longer matter. What matters now is the love you still bear for the little one you lost, a love that is alive and strong. . . ."

How many Our Fathers, Father? How many Hail Marys? How many rosaries?

The panel between the confessor's side and the penitent's suddenly slid to one side, revealing the small screened window through which the penitent whispered his transgressions. Tressa's heart began to thud crazily as she realized that someone or something sat in the confessor's chair. She heard breathing, wet and wheezing. She smelled something that made her want to vomit.

A phosphorescent glow filtered through the tiny screened window. A part of Tressa's mind screamed silently that she should burst out of the confessional and flee for her life, but another part—the part that had always yearned for knowledge, for truth, the part that had driven her onto the stage to learn things about herself that she couldn't learn any other way—whispered that she should stay. She leaned closer to the screen, her eyes yawning for every detail.

She saw Father Charlie sitting there, though nobody but Tressa Downey would have recognized that charred mess as Father Charlie. It wore the white surplice and black cassock of the priesthood.

"I see graves opening, and things coming out. . . . He will send them into battle against us, these creatures blackened with mud. . . ."

The green glow issued from deep sockets in the grinning, fire-scarred skull, where eyes should have been. The flames had taken most of the flesh, but enough remained to let Tressa know that this was indeed Father Charlie, summoned from the grave by Lord Yesterday. A sob welled out of her, less from terror than crushing grief: Father Charlie had chosen the unspeakable agony of burning himself to death in order to escape this very possibility. She wept again for him, harder than she'd wept since the horrible night he died.

"Mustn't cry, my child," it said, raising a skeletal finger in the way that Father Charlie always did. "Time heals all wounds. And your time is very short."

The skeletal fingers made wet, squeaky sounds as they

clenched into a fist. The fist flew against the small screened window and burst through it, spattering splinters and bits of metal against Tressa's face. The fingers closed around her throat, and she knew that she was about to die.

iii

Unable to endure any more of Father Le Fanu's arcane mumbo jumbo, Mark Lansen strode from the parlor over the priest's loud protestations and went out through the foyer. He stood on the front porch of the rectory and drank deeply of the cool night air.

He wondered where Tressa had run to, what had frightened her so. He worried about her having gone out alone, and he scolded himself for not having gone after her.

A mental nerve twitched somewhere in his head, and an image flashed through his mind. His scalp suddenly tingled.

Tressa. Trying to scream. Tears and ...

Bones.

Ashes.

The nerve twitched again, and Mark knew that Tressa was reaching out to him, calling to him for help—not with her voice, but with her mind. He collapsed to his knees and pressed his palms against his temples. He saw the interior of the church in the bloody glow of the lantern. He saw the confessional and heard the scraping sounds issuing from it, the noise of struggling, of choking. He smelled the stench of the grave, and his heart climbed into his throat.

He sprang to his feet and bolted down from the porch to the flagstone walk. He scarcely felt his own footfalls as he dashed toward the dark hulk of St. Pie's, dodging Kyleen LeBreaux's Mercedes and Velma Selvig's van in the drive of the rectory. He was only vaguely aware of the crystalline moon overhead, of the song of the insect choir in the rhododendrons, of the burning amulet against his chest.

By the time he burst into the narthex of the church, his shirt and jeans were in shreds, ripped from the inside by the sudden change of his body shape. His nose led him immediately toward the confessional, and he sprang for it, covering in one stride a distance that would have required six by a mortal man. The wall of the confessional disintegrated in a storm of splinters under his fists, and he saw the thing in the cassock and surplice, the thing that was strangling Tressa through the tiny window of the confessional. It shrieked at him with demonic hatred, with plutonian anger.

Mark's rage reached its climax. The priest-thing squealed as Mark's huge hand closed over its ash-blackened skull, as Mark hauled the creature out of the confessional and ripped it as a psychotic child might rip a rag doll. He tore it limb from limb and flung its charred pieces in all directions. He tore and ripped until nothing remained of the thing but flinching slivers of blackened bone and shreds of holy cloth.

The church was silent but for his own husky breathing and Tressa's muffled sobs. He hungered to take her in his arms, to comfort her and care for her bruises, but a glance at his own hands caused him to bolt away into the dark.

He couldn't let her see him like this.

In the dark cloakroom off the narthex he sank to his haunches and cried like a little child.

iv

Tressa climbed out of the ruined confessional and leaned against a pew, gasping. She called out to Mark, knowing that it was he who'd saved her, but her voice gave a mere croak. After massaging her bruised throat and taking a dozen deep breaths of sweet air, she tried again, only to hear his name echo thinly throughout the empty nave.

She no longer felt the crippling grief for Father Charlie she'd felt only moments ago. Somehow she knew that he was truly beyond harm now, mercifully dispatched by Mark Lansen. Her concern had become Mark himself.

She headed into the narthex, stepping gingerly around gobbets and bits of what had once been Father Charlie, calling Mark's name, pausing now and again to listen. Near the entrance of the cloakroom she heard the sounds of a man weeping, and she went toward them, not caring about the darkness. If she'd wanted to, she could have snapped on the lights, for she knew where the switch was, but she decided not to do this. Mark wouldn't want her to see him in the body of a monster.

She found him in a corner of the room, sitting under a coatrack, his back braced against a wall. She groped for his hand, touched it, and sighed with relief because it seemed normal. No suction cups, no claws.

"Mark, are you okay?"

"I think so. You?"

"Bruised but alive, thanks to you. How did you know I needed help? And how did you know where to find me?"

"Your mind called out to me. I answered. I guess I just let my feelings steer me."

"Mark, I have to ask you this, even though I wish I didn't. Did you feel—I mean, when you attacked that . . . *thing*—did you feel the same toward me as you felt yesterday in the bleachers?"

"The hunger, you mean? No, Tressa, I felt only rage. I knew I had to kill that thing because it was hurting you." He pulled her hand to his chest, where she touched the small silver amulet that hung around his neck. It was still warm. "It was much hotter a few minutes ago. I know now that Elspeth Carey was right—it keeps the hunger away. It lets me be my—" He stumbled on the final word.

"You were going to say that it lets you be yourself, but you're not sure that's true, are you?"

"God, I wish I could be sure. I can't say whether I was *myself* when I killed that thing. I don't want to believe that the real Mark Lansen can become a creature that walked out of a nightmare. Or that the real Mark Lansen can read people's minds and hear their hearts beat, even when he looks like himself."

Tressa found his cheek and caressed it. "Know what I think? The important thing is that the real Mark Lansen is in control, no matter what his body looks like."

"But *is* he really? Maybe somebody or something else is doing the steering without my knowing about it."

"I don't think that's true. There's a way to find out for sure, you know."

"Oh? What's that?"

She slipped her fingers beneath the tatters of his Hawaiian shirt and ran them through the hair on his chest. "I'm willing to try, if you are," she whispered.

"T-Tressa, no. You've seen what can happen to me. I don't want to put you in danger again."

"But you're wearing the amulet. It'll keep us safe. It's important that you believe that, and more important that you believe in yourself." Her hand found his belly and slipped under his belt. She felt his penis come instantly alive at her touch, and she kneaded it gently, bringing it to full hardness within seconds.

"My God, Tressa, how can you do this? You've seen me when I—"

She pushed his shredded underwear and jeans down below his hips and bent low to kiss him lovingly, to lick him.

"My God, Tressa . . ."

She felt his hands on her body now, tugging at her cotton turtleneck, and she helped him remove it. The coolness felt wonderful against her bare skin, even better against her breasts when she got her bra off. She'd read somewhere that sex is unbelievable immediately after a close brush with death, thanks to the flood of adrenaline and lingering endorphins. Mark's hands cupped her breasts, as his fingers tweaked her hard nipples.

He had her jeans open now and was rubbing her between her legs. She kicked off her jeans and panties and straddled him, frantically maneuvering his cock into her. She groaned as it slid in deep, and she began to ride him, thrilling to the hardness and the friction and the heat. She rode him like a horse, and he gobbled at her breasts. They pumped furiously until their pleasure exploded together. For him it was a peal of thunder, for her a long string of staccato detonations. She sank against his chest, and they lay silent a long while, exhausted.

"You were right," Mark whispered finally, stroking her hair. "I never stopped being me. You've shown me that, Tressa. I don't know how to thank you."

She put her fingers to his lips, telling him that no thanks were necessary. She'd needed this herself, maybe more than he had—to recapture something she'd long yearned for, something she'd lost. Having done this, Tressa believed that she could face anything.

46

Crossing Paths

i

Early on Friday morning, Thaddeus Lansen got a telephone call from his best friend, Josh, who had just acquired the latest version of Super Mario Brothers and a state-of-the-art Nintendo Zapper for his birthday. Could Tad come over and play?

His mother had already left for her office, so Tad sought permission from the Lansen-Garlands' housekeeper, Stephanie, and got it. The only condition was that he come home for lunch at 12:30 sharp.

Tad biked the two blocks to Josh's house, which stood slightly lower than the Lansen-Garlands' on the hill above Portland. The boys played Nintendo for several hours, then broke to watch selected scenes from *Alien* on the VCR. Tad dutifully boarded his mountain bike at 12:15 and headed home for lunch, his Walkman headphones clinging to his head.

Pedaling up the hill reminded him of outings with his father in Oldenburg during the past week, and he felt a little stab of sadness. This was only his second day back in Portland, and already he missed his dad intensely. Since Wednesday night, he'd spent a grand total of two waking hours with his mother, whose schedule was jammed with meetings, business lunches, business dinners, and workouts at the exclusive Multnomah Athletic Club. Not much time for a nine-year-old boy in the day of a top-drawer architect like Deidre Garland, not when housekeepers and babysitters were crying for work.

As he rounded a curve on the steep hill half a block from his house, he saw a tall figure leaning against the fender of a huge black car at the curb. The man was old and leathery, and his hair shone like snow in the hot noonday sun, almost as white as the starched shirt he wore. His face broke into a grin when he saw Tad.

"Good afternoon, Tad Bear," he called. "That's what your dad calls you, isn't it—Tad Bear?" This was Poverty Ike, Tad remembered, the saloon keeper and storyteller from Oldenburg. Stubble covered his jaw like iron filings on a magnet.

"Yeah, and he's the *only* one," said Tad, braking to a halt and taking off the Walkman headphones. "If you're looking for him, he's not here. He's in Oldenburg with Gram. He's busy writing his book."

"I know where your dad is, Tad Bear. It's *you* I've come to see."

A pit formed in Tad's stomach. "Me? Why?"

The old man removed his bifocals and polished them with a calico handkerchief that he pulled from the hip pocket of his jeans. When he put them on again, the sun glared so hotly off the lenses that Tad had trouble looking him in the eye. "Suppose I told you your dad's in trouble. Would you believe that?"

"What kind of trouble?"

"Trouble of a kind he's never had before. Trouble of a kind no man should have."

"I don't know what you mean."

"Son, I can't tell you the whole story standing here in the street. I will say this, though. Your old man didn't want to bring you back here. He loves you more than anything else in the world. If that's been worrying you, don't let it."

"Then why did he do it?"

"Because he was afraid for you. He wanted you to be safe. Trouble is, he was mistaken—you're *not* safe here, not safe at all."

Tad suddenly got a lump in his throat to go with the pit in his stomach. "Safe from what?"

"Someday I'll tell you all about it, but for now I'll just ask you to trust me. Your dad's going through a tough time, Tad Bear, and he needs help. I intend to give him that help, but I want to make certain that you're out of harm's way first. You see, you and your dad are special people, and there are some in this world who hate people like you. It's very important that we don't let them find you. I'm asking you to come back to Oldenburg with me, where I can make sure you're okay."

The sun no longer seemed warm on Tad's back. A chill sliced through him. "I'm not supposed to go anywhere without permis-

sion from my mom or Stephanie. I'm supposed to be home for
lunch in five minutes."

"I understand your reluctance," said Poverty Ike, laying his
hand on the boy's shoulder, "and I won't try to force you. If this
was any other time, I'd tell you never to go anywhere with
someone outside your family, or someone you don't know well.
I'll bet your dad has told you the same thing a hundred times."

This was true. If this was any other time, Tad would have already darted away on his mountain bike, screaming at the top of
his lungs, just as Dad Bear had instructed him to do if some per-
vert ever tried to lure him into a car. But this wasn't any other
time: Poverty Ike was right about the fact that Dad Bear had
some big trouble to deal with, that much was clear. Besides, Dad
Bear had known the old man for years, even if Tad himself had
met him only a week ago, so he wasn't exactly a stranger.

"This trouble my dad's in—is there any way I can help him?"

"I expect there is. I won't lie to you and tell you it'll be easy,
though. I'm not sure he can get out of it even with *my* help."

"Will you tell me about it if I come with you? Will you tell
me how I can help him?" Tad's eyes were filling with tears.

"Yes, son. I will. It's the least I can do."

"Then let's put my bike in your trunk and get going."

ii

Having showered and packed a bag, Mark went into the late
John Lansen's study, knowing that he would find Marta there. He
could hear her heartbeat through the oaken door. She sat behind
her dead husband's ponderous desk, her arms extended and her
hands folded on the blotter. Her skin looked pasty, and her once-
vibrant blue eyes were dull and vacant. She brightened slightly
when she saw Mark, but she didn't stand or go to him. She
looked depleted, used up.

"You're back, Mark. I'm so glad. Come in."

He went to her side, bent low, kissed her cheek. "I can't stay,
I'm afraid. I just wanted to let you know that everything will be
okay. I hope you'll believe that."

"You've found out the truth, haven't you? I see it in your face.
You know about Kristen's real father, and—and—"

"It's okay, Mom. I know everything."

She turned her head with what appeared to be great effort and gazed up at him. "It's started, hasn't it? All my life I prayed that we'd be spared this terrible thing. So many years have gone by that I'd almost come to believe that we'd beaten it, that we'd succeeded in waiting it out." She pulled his hand to her cheek. "I let myself believe that if I never spoke of it, or even thought about it, it would simply go away, and that life would go on as it always has—blissful and quiet. But I was wrong, Mark. It's started, and there's nothing we can do about it."

Mark gently pulled his hand away and strode slowly toward the door. Before leaving, he turned and said, "I'm sorry, Mom. I'm sorry that it had to be you. I want you to know that it hasn't made me stop loving you."

iii

Tressa stayed away from the parlor of the rectory through the entire day, not wanting to lay eyes on the portrait of the Blessed Mother that hung there. Several times she approached the door and listened as Father Le Fanu drilled Mark in the art of hiding his true thoughts and projecting false ones to a vampire. Other times she overheard him mumbling rituals while in the act of scrying or casting some other kind of spell. Gretchen and Brett stayed close, listening in rapt attention to everything the old man said, watching carefully everything he did. They fetched things from his massive old steamer trunk when he needed them, and came out now and then to give Tressa reports on how the various preparations were proceeding.

Tressa appointed herself cook, bottle washer, and sentry. She prepared lunch for the group and gave them an afternoon snack. In midafternoon she went home to bathe and change clothes, and was relieved to find that her mother wasn't there. According to a note left on the mantel, Cynthia had gone shopping in Astoria and would return before dark. At the bottom was a P.S.: *If I don't hear from you by evening, I'll call the sheriff to say you're missing.* Tressa scribbled a note in reply, telling her mother not to worry about her, that she'd run into an "old friend" with whom she planned to spend some time. She deliberately omitted any mention of the friend's gender.

Upon returning to the rectory, she went upstairs to the guest room where she and Mark had spent most of the night, and sat on the bed. She took from her shoulder bag the papers that Velma Selvig had left for her at the Royal Kokanee—Xeroxed newspaper articles from the distant past. Clipped to the first page was the handwritten note that Tressa had not yet had a chance to read. She read it now, hearing Velma's voice in her head as she did so.

According to the note, Velma had done some research into the Gestern family, after hearing what had happened to Tressa in Skip Gestern's study. She'd used the archives of the *Oldenburg Clarion* (for which she wrote a column) and had even driven to the state historical society in Portland to glean articles from the long-defunct *Tualatin Tribune*. In Velma's words, the articles would ". . . prove that only an idiot would have anything to do with that family." The note concluded with a cryptic reference to a "surprise player" and parenthetical instructions to look at the final story.

The first item was the one that Tressa had glanced at briefly in Velma's study at the Royal Kokanee before Father Le Fanu interrupted her, the article from the *Tualatin Tribune*, dated November 10, 1856:

CLOVIS GESTERN AND HIS DISCIPLES ABANDON ENTERPRISE IN TUALATIN

LAWMEN SAY VIGILANTE MOVEMENT SUBSIDES

"The Anti-Christ Is Cast Out From Our Midst."
—The Reverend Stanley Ames

The so-called Reverend Clovis Gestern has gathered about him his family and followers, and has quit the colony he founded eleven years ago on the hill outside Tualatin. With household goods and farm equipment loaded into wagons drawn by ox and horse, the band that calls themselves the Gethsemanites took to the North Road and headed for a new site near the Columbia River, according to several local men who profess knowledge of the Reverend's intent.

Our Town Sheriff, Jarvis MacDonald, who has struggled mightily to prevent the eruption of vigilante violence against the Reverend Gestern and the Gethsemanites, delivered a speech at noon the following day, Monday last, to the Committee of Public Safety which was formed upon the disappearance of Jesse Wyler's young daughter a month ago (the fifth in as many years).

"The men of Tualatin may rest easy now," Sheriff MacDonald declared. "I have heard from men I trust that no one cares to pursue the matter of bringing the Gethsemanites to justice for the crimes attributed to them, quite simply, gentlemen, because no one has offered any evidence that would stand under a judge's eye. . . ."

The piece then summarized the gut-turning rumors that raged locally, that the Gethsemanites practiced "vampirism" among the local population. The Reverend Gestern himself was rumored to be responsible for kidnapping young women and girls, whom he'd sacrificed in rituals to placate some hellish god.

"The Anti-Christ is cast out from our midst," declared the Reverend Mr. Stanley Ames from his pulpit in the First Calvinist Presbyterian Church, where he officiated at an extraordinary meeting of the congregation on the evening of Monday last, the faithful having gathered to give thanks for their deliverance from the Gethsemanites. . . .

Other articles came from the early *Oldenburg Independent Gazette*, which was the first real newspaper to set up shop in the town. The earliest of these bore the date April 2, 1890:

CHINAMEN DEMAND ACTION FROM SHERIFF AND DEPUTIES

CANNERY WORKERS SAY SIX CHINESE GIRLS HAVE DISAPPEARED IN PAST YEAR

"Oriental Claptrap and Primitive Superstition."
—Heinrich Olden, Cannery Owner

It told of the demands that a delegation of Chinese cannery

workers presented to the sheriff of Kalapuya County. They wanted the sheriff's office to investigate the disappearance of half a dozen young women and girls, but the sheriff wasn't anxious to tackle the matter.

"... I have heard a lot of superstitious talk in this community ever since I got here, and now it's spooked the Chinamen," said Sheriff Raleigh Brislin when asked by this observer to comment on the demands. "My sentiments go along with those expressed by Mr. Olden. It's mostly a bunch of heathen Oriental superstition."

Mr. Heinrich Olden has made his views on the matter well-known. "These Chinamen aren't well-settled men, as everyone knows," stated Mr. Olden. "Their women and girls run off, given the slightest provocation, often without telling their fathers. Claiming that their family troubles are caused by Mr. Clovis Gestern is pure Oriental claptrap, the product of primitive superstition. Mr. Gestern is a fine man whose family has been here for generations. He is an honest investor and businessman who shares my vision for this community, that Oldenburg will one day rival Portland both in size and wealth. Now let us leave these other foolish matters alone."

Half a dozen more articles from the *Gazette* and later the *Clarion* described mysterious disappearances of young women and girls in and around the region of the lower Columbia River, the latest in Portland in April of 1934. In the final case, the Oregon State Police interviewed Clovis Gestern in order to determine whether he could account for his whereabouts at the time a teenager named Miranda Hennessy disappeared from the area of the cargo docks in Portland, where she'd last been seen. Like several of the other missing persons, she was a runaway, a prostitute in all likelihood, not someone the police looked very hard for in those days. A short follow-up article revealed that the investigators had found "not a shred" of evidence to support the notion that Clovis Gestern had been involved in Miss Hennessy's disappearance.

That the Gesterns had long been the focus of local stories

about missing females wasn't news to Tressa. Having grown up in Oldenburg, she'd heard many black tales about the mysterious family who lived in the great stone house on Nehalem Mountain, things whispered by wide-eyed kids when "sleeping out" in pup tents in the backyard or told around campfires with an occasional pause to devour a toasted marshmallow. Until recently she'd never taken the tales seriously.

She could now imagine Velma's horror upon uncovering and reading these articles. Like everyone else in town, Velma knew that a private detective from New York had come to Oldenburg in search of a runaway girl named Skye Padilla and had gotten himself shot during a scuffle at Poverty Ike's. And Tressa herself had told Velma about seeing a dark young woman on the staircase at Gestern Hall, a girl who must certainly be Skye. The old newspaper articles had probably convinced Velma that all the whispered rumors about Gestern Hall were true, that whatever had happened to those other victims was about to happen to Skye. Apparently Velma had been about to share this information with Tressa, when she herself fell victim to the hunger of Clovis Gestern, or to someone else of his kind.

The final article in the bundle, the one that Velma had labeled "surprise player," was an obituary from the *Clarion*, dated July 31, 1935.

SCION OF LOCAL PIONEER FAMILY SUCCUMBS IN BAVARIA

Munich, Germany—Clovis Gestern, scion of Oldenburg's oldest family, died last week in a Bavarian hospital after falling ill the previous day. A family spokesman, Mrs. Bellona Drumgule, said that a stroke claimed the elderly Mr. Gestern during a tour of a medieval city, Rothenburg ob der Tauber.

Mr. Gestern and a small circle of friends had been vacationing in Europe for several months prior to his death, Mrs. Drumgule said. She also confirmed that the Gestern family has business holdings in several European countries, and that Mr. Gestern often visited them.

Facts concerning Mr. Gestern's life are hard to uncover, owing to the family's well-known obsession with privacy. Mrs. Drumgule, longtime overseer of the family

estate on Nehalem Mountain near Oldenburg, declined
to provide any more information about her employer, except to confirm that he had a wife overseas and a son,
Clovis Gestern, Jr., who will inherit the businesses and
estates. The young Mr. Gestern, himself in Europe, will
return to Oldenburg before the end of summer, Mrs.
Drumgule said. . . .

The story itself was not what shocked Tressa, not even the reference to Mrs. Drumgule. (It couldn't possibly be the woman
she'd met at Gestern Hall, she told herself—it had to be an
earlier relative.) What shocked her was the photograph of the departed Clovis Gestern, a man with a face that Tressa knew well.
This was *not* the man whom she knew by that name.

iv

Father Le Fanu presented the potion to Mark in a small
earthen bowl, with the command to drink it in one gulp. Properly
imbibed, the priest said, it would not only protect Mark against
any sedative that Clovis Gestern might give him, but also thwart
minor spells.

The smell was a repulsive mixture of rotten eggs and ammonia, and the consistency was that of pea soup. The color reminded Mark of something one might find in the diaper of a
newborn. He leaned back on the sofa and refused to take the
steaming bowl.

"Come on, Mark," said Gretchen Bayliss, maneuvering close
to him in her powered wheelchair. "This is no time to get squea-
mish. Drink it, for Pete's sake, and stop behaving like a little
kid."

"That's easy for you to say. You don't know what's in it."

"Simple herbs," Le Fanu assured him. "You yourself saw me
mix them, monsieur—yellow wolfsbane, aloe root, monkshood,
and a trace of nightshade, a few others. None of the ingredients
could possibly harm you in these quantities and proportions."

"But I heard you chant something about the dried brain of a
cat. And something else about the semen of a wizard. And most
of the time you were chanting in a language I didn't recognize."

"What's the alternative?" asked Gretchen derisively. "Do you really want to face Skip Gestern unprotected? If I were you, I'd be less worried about this potion than whatever *he's* got planned for you."

She was right, Mark knew. Brett offered to hold Mark's nose for him, and he accepted. With nostrils squeezed shut and eyes screwed tight, he tipped the foul-smelling bowl to his lips and poured the mixture down his throat.

V

The effect of the potion was dizzying. Whenever someone spoke to him, Mark heard all echoes and reverberations, as if he were living inside a steel drum. He nodded and pretended to understand and even made replies, but his brain was busy with other matters. The potion enabled him to peer beneath the various layers of his own consciousness, and what he saw both amazed and disturbed him.

While dressing for dinner, he heard Tressa talking urgently about old newspaper articles and ambiguities about someone's identity, but he didn't soak up any of it. As he knotted his red silk tie, he stared at his own image in the mirror in the guest room and reminded himself that he owned a unique identity, that the man in the mirror was someone who could define himself in any way he chose. That man possessed the power to shape his own future.

Kyleen LeBreaux had made the same point countless times, which now seemed ironic if not downright hilarious. She'd been an imposter who'd meant to kill him all along. The irony tickled him, and he giggled, then guffawed. He laughed so hard, he couldn't manage the four-in-hand knot that John Lansen had taught him when he was a teenager. Tressa intervened and tied his tie for him, then helped him into his seersucker sport coat.

"You haven't heard a word I've said, have you?" she asked, looking worried.

"My darling, I've heard *every* word. I just haven't digested them yet."

"It's the potion. It's made you drunk or something."

"No, it's your *beauty* that has made me drunk." He pulled her close and kissed her deeply, savoring the taste of her mouth, the feel of her breasts against his chest. Then he drew away, leaving

Tressa slightly out of breath. "Alas, I dare not tarry, my sweet. The eighth hour draws nigh, and I must sally forth to have dinner and kill vampires. Wish me luck, okay?"

Tressa forced a smile that contradicted the worry in her eyes, and went with him downstairs to the foyer.

vi

Father Le Fanu shook his hand warmly and, to Mark's surprise, hugged him. He remembered that French males routinely hug and kiss each other on both cheeks when meeting and parting.

"Keep in mind all I've taught you, my son," said the old priest, not looking as optimistic as Mark would have liked. "The potion has elevated your mood, which is to be expected, but it has in no way impeded your intellect. If you keep your wits and your resolve, you may well succeed in tonight's dark work."

How inspiring, thought Mark. The intoxicated feeling had passed mere seconds earlier, as if someone had simply lifted a veil from his head. In its wake was razor-sharp alertness.

He glanced through the tall window in the door and noticed that the sky was unusually dark for this early on a June evening. A storm was gathering. He stooped to hug Gretchen in her wheelchair and shook Brett Omdahl's hand. "See you later tonight," he told them, grinning. "Don't be late, okay?"

"We'll come the very moment Father Le Fanu gives the word," assured Gretchen. "He'll be following your progress in the scrying mirror."

Mark was about to give Tressa a parting kiss when a smear of movement caught his eye through the window in the front door. Red taillights, glaring headlights—the unmistakable profile of a low Italian sports car with its top up. The car cruised slowly by the rectory, headed east on Church Avenue. Mark dashed out the front door in time to see it turn right on Main.

"What's wrong?" asked Tressa, her face paling. "What did you see?"

"That was a black Alfa Romeo, a *new* one," he answered. "That car belonged to my dad, or at least to the man I claim as my dad."

The others joined him on the front porch. "But your dad's—"

Brett Omdahl stopped himself. "I mean, someone else is driving it, huh? Someone who shouldn't be?"

"It must be my mother," said Mark, looking perplexed.

The evening smelled of coming rain. Ashy-looking clouds had piled up over Fish Hawk Ridge, their lower edges tinged pink by the setting sun. Mark sniffed the unsettled air, tasted the stirring wind. "Well, it's getting late," he said. "I'd better roll." He walked down the steps to the front drive and put his hand on the handle of the garage door to lift it. He looked back toward the porch and gazed a moment at Tressa, who stood under the yellow electric light with her arms folded across her chest. Even from this distance he could see the fear in her face. He tried not to read her thoughts, but he couldn't stave off the intense wave of feeling that came from her, a feeling for *him*—total unflinching acceptance of him and everything he was. The feeling touched a tender place inside him, and he smiled at her. Then he lifted the garage door and got into Kyleen LeBreaux's Mercedes.

47

Dinner at Eight

i

Rain fell heavily by the time Mark turned onto Queen Molly Road. The thumping of droplets against the fabric top of the convertible reminded him of microwave popcorn, and he thought of better times, happier times. He thought of Tad, whose favorite food was Orville Redenbacher's.

Mom will be glad for this rain, he mused senselessly. *Her roses need it.* Then the black reality of the moment exploded in his mind, and he wondered whether Marta would ever be glad of anything again. Old sins she'd committed with Clovis Gestern had caught up with her, sins that had given her a beautiful daughter of her own blood and an adopted son of someone else's. She'd loved both as intensely and wholly as any mother could love her children. Tragically, both were vampires, which probably meant that Marta Lansen had smiled her last sweet smile.

Mark's anger flared white-hot, and he clenched the steering wheel so hard that his fists ached. If ever a man needed killing, Clovis Gestern was the one—a man who wormed his way into the lives of innocent people, polluted them with his evil, twisted their desires and urges, drove them to deeds of unspeakable depravity. For the first time in his life, Mark Lansen tasted a genuine hunger to kill, a "righteous hunger," Walt Le Fanu would've called it. Mark thrilled to the prospect of wrapping his hands around Gestern's throat and squeezing the life out of him, of thwarting the beast's unholy scheme to found a tribe of demons like himself.

But then his breath froze in his throat: A man can't change the color of his skin, can he? Or the color of his eyes? A black man is always black, and a white man is always white. A child born to have hazel eyes dies with hazel eyes. Did the same reasoning hold true for vampires? If you're born with the slug inside you, are you condemned to die with it inside you?

Mark prayed that it was not so. He clung to the hope that old Elspeth Carey had held out to him yesterday when he sat before her hearth, breathing the fumes of her magic. *"Whether you can beat it is up to you, lad. Whether you beat it depends on whether you remember the message that I've sent to you time and again—a message you've heard in dreams, in your mind, even on the lips of a dead man. . . ."*

ii

He swung the Mercedes between the gateposts and drove slowly toward the yawning porte cochere of Gestern Hall, which reared huge against a stormy sky. Rare though electrical storms are in western Oregon, a real beauty was in progress this night. A jagged bolt of lightning plunged into the forest somewhere behind the mountain, illuminating the mansion's tower, its steep gables, its Gothic quatrefoils against stained glass.

He eased the car into the porte cochere and halted behind Skip Gestern's old Imperial, which gleamed wickedly in the glare of the headlights. He noticed another car parked in front of it, a low-slung sports car with a fabric roof. A small *Italian* sports car, no doubt about it. An Alfa Romeo. He got out and walked over to it, touched its smooth, rain-beaded finish. He told himself that this wasn't necessarily his father's car, that there were other 1988 black Alfa Romeo roadsters in the world. But then he saw the bumper sticker on the rear deck, just readable in the harsh ambiance of the Mercedes' headlights: *Legalize Lutefisk.*

It had to be Marta, he told himself, unless someone had broken into the Lansen family garage and stolen the Alfa—someone like Kristen, maybe. He pushed the mystery aside for the moment, feeling certain he would know the solution before the night was out.

He went back to the Mercedes to douse its lights and shut off the engine. While reaching for the keys in the ignition lock, he spied the wooden grip of a small pistol beneath the right bucket seat, the same semiautomatic that Kyleen LeBreaux had meant to kill him with. He pulled it out and saw some engraving on the barrel that told him it was a Beretta .25 caliber. The hammer was still in the cocked position, meaning that the gun could easily have gone off when Kyleen dropped it at the moment Sam Darkenwald broke her neck. Mark eased the hammer forward and, without really knowing why, tucked the gun into a pocket of his sport coat.

A gust of wind blew rain into the dark, stony passage that led to the front door of Gestern Hall, rustling the Oregon grapes and junipers that bordered the outer walls. Mark listened to the storm as he walked to the door, felt the sting of stray droplets on his cheek, and wondered how in the hell things had come to this. He steeled himself to hide his true thoughts and emotions as Walt Le Fanu had coached him, to project a false face that would make Gestern think he'd accepted his fate, or better yet, that he actually welcomed it. For a terrifying moment he doubted he was up to a lie this large.

Obeying the PLEASE COME IN sign that hung on the door, he reached for the handle, only to see the door swing open before him. Mrs. Drumgule stood in the entry, grinning with her horrible teeth and staring through him with her dark, urgent eyes.

"Come in, young master, please come in," she said, her words whistling through her teeth. "Mr. Gestern has been expecting you, of course. I can promise you a very good dinner tonight, a better dinner than you've ever had, I'm sure!"

iii

Father Le Fanu gathered together Gretchen Bayliss, Tressa Downey, and Brett Omdahl in the study of the rectory, where he stood before a window battered by rain. Only a small desk lamp burned, and the room was dim except when lightning flashed.

"The time draws close," he told them over the rumble of thunder, his face as grim as an undertaker's. "I must ask you to allow me a short while alone, for I must prepare myself for the ordeal ahead. I shall be in the parlor with the scrying mirror, and you may hear strange sounds from time to time. But you must by no means come into the parlor, for you could face considerable danger. I require your promise that you won't leave this room until I've come for you. You will be safe here, but only if you do exactly as I say."

Tressa felt a cloak of icy needles settle over her shoulders, but she gave her promise, as did Gretchen and Brett. The priest collected his boom box and left the study, headed for the parlor. A moment later they heard the opening licks of Dizzy Gillespie's "A Night in Tunisia" played loudly in the parlor, followed by an almost inaudible crescendo of wind and rain that suggested the quick opening of a door or window. Tressa could not suppress the sick certainty that someone or something had either left the house or entered it.

iv

Deep in the forest near a place that the Cathlamet people had called Mesatchie Illihee, Elspeth Carey stuck her nose out the door of her house and sniffed the wind. She tasted the rain and listened to the rush of the storm in the trees. The time was right, she decided, to go to Gestern Hall. Though she couldn't see it, she knew that the Blood Star glowered above the storm clouds, having reached the zenith of its cycle. She would need the full brunt of its power tonight, if she was to defeat Lord Yesterday.

She assembled the things she would need and stuffed them into the bulky sack she carried wherever she traveled, whether into the town of Oldenburg in the valley below, or all the way to Portland, where she slept among the street people in alleys and under bridges. Chief among these tools was the spinning wheel, the very same one her mother had used to spin the skin from her body into a living yarn, which she then wove into a living sack. The infant Elspeth had slumbered for nearly a century in that sack, buried in sacred ground and safe from Lord Yesterday, just as her own daughter, Rita, had slumbered inside it, buried in the dirt of Mesatchie Illihee.

Elspeth planned to use the spinning wheel again tonight.

Burdened with the utensils of her craft, she left her house and set out for the entrance of the tunnel that led into the bowels of Gestern Hall. The builder had intended the tunnel as a secret passage of escape, should the mansion ever come under attack by citizens enraged by the loss of their kin to the monsters who lived there. Elspeth smiled at the irony: The tunnel would prove to be Lord Yesterday's undoing, rather than his salvation.

She hoped intensely that Bob Gammage and Sam Darkenwald

had succeeded in rescuing the young girl from Gestern's clutches, thus depriving the evil lord of a source of power. Elspeth knew that Gestern was a skilled practitioner of the beastly art of antinopomancy, which involved reading and manipulating the future in the entrails of butchered women and children. The rescue of Skye Padilla would prove a major loss to him.

Unfortunately Elspeth had been unable to use her scrying mirror to find out whether Gammage and Darkenwald had succeeded, because the atmosphere had become cloudy with competing spells and forces, with conflicting ligatures and summonses from the unseen world. The obsidian lens of the scrying mirror showed only a swirling miasma, not unlike a radar screen awash with blips from a thousand nearby radar transmitters. Bellona Drumgule was one culprit, Elspeth had surmised. And Clovis Gestern himself was another. But she'd also detected the magic of a newcomer from far away, a magic that bore the scent of an old and potent wizard.

Elspeth Carey knew who he was. The mere thought of him caused her old bones to ache, her old heart to skip a beat.

v

Mrs. Drumgule served a meal fit for a maggot—overly boiled meat, scorched vegetables that appeared unwashed, and some kind of grainy mush ladled into chipped bowls. Mark only picked at the food with a tarnished silver fork and took an occasional whiff of red wine.

He and Skip Gestern sat at opposite ends of a long table that had clawed feet and carved scrollwork, a beautiful piece that looked thirteenth-century French. With its sweeping tapestries and dim candlelight, the dining room had a shadowy, almost dreamy air. Rain thrummed against a tall window of leaded glass, through which lightning sometimes flashed red, purple, and deep blue, the dominant colors of the biblical scene depicted there. Mark heard the low fulmination of thunder, the whistle of wind through cracks in the stone walls.

Gestern wore a velvet smoking jacket, a crisp white shirt and a black cravat. His lean features gave no inkling of the evil that lived within him, and Mark gave no hint of the hatred boiling deep in his own gut. In accordance with Walt Le Fanu's coaching, Mark concentrated on keeping his mental shield firmly in place. He forced his mind to broadcast a willingness, an *eagerness* to discover whatever Gestern had in store for him.

Gestern had said earlier that Kristen could not join them for dinner, though she'd promised to have a drink with them later in the evening after tying up some "loose ends" with her public relations project. The talk was mostly chitchat, a mere preliminary to the real business of this night. Skip smoked cigarettes and discussed the family history, the building and restoration of the house, the origins of its many priceless furnishings. Mark listened politely, asked questions occasionally, and pretended to be entertained.

Mrs. Drumgule cleared away the untouched dessert course (a spongy-looking block of cake drenched in yellowish cream), and Skip excused her from further work tonight. "By the way," he added, as she backed through the door into the kitchen, her doughy arms laden with dishes, "that was an excellent meal, Mrs. Drumgule. Wouldn't you agree, Professor Lansen?"

"Yes, it was very good. I don't suppose you give out your recipes, do you?"

The old woman grinned abysmally and promised to write them down for him. Then she disappeared into the kitchen. After a moment Skip said, "When I invited you here, I promised you a look at some of our artifacts. We could start the tour in my study, if you'd like."

"Oh, I think there'll be plenty of time later to examine the artifacts. Why don't we just sit here and talk for a while. I'm having such a good time."

Gestern's hazel eyes narrowed. In the space of a heartbeat Mark caught a telepathic fragment of his feelings, the tiniest fraction of a second in which Gestern's guard slipped. *Regret. Sadness. Reluctance.*

"You've learned a lot since we last talked, haven't you, Mark?"

"Well, you know how it is. Nature takes its course, as they say, and certain things become clear." Mark fingered a tarnished silver spoon that Mrs. Drumgule had left behind on the white linen tablecloth. "You might be interested to know that I've decided to take your advice."

"Oh?"

"When you drove me home a couple days ago, after my—uh—*accident* on Fish Hawk Ridge, you told me to let my feelings rule me, to relax and let the *change* happen. That's what I've done, Skip. I've stopped fighting it."

Gestern smiled weakly, and Mark thought he suddenly looked much older. *Maybe his age is catching up with him,* Mark mused behind his mental shield. *How old must he really be? Five hundred years? A thousand?*

"There's no need to lie, Mark. I know what you have in mind."

"I don't understand."

"Look, Bellona Drumgule is as good with a scrying mirror as anyone around. She knows about the priest from France, and she knows about the old woman in the forest—your grandmother, as I understand it."

"I'm afraid I'm not following you."

"Oh, I think you are. None of your alliances will do you any good, Mark. The change is under way, because you've had your first taste, and there's nothing in this world you can do about that. You'll become what you must become, just as I did, and your machinations and intrigues will prove useless." Skip tipped his wineglass to his lips and drained it. Then he lit another cigarette and watched Mark squirm.

"I know what you have planned for me," Mark said finally, trying not to betray his growing panic. "I know that you want me to have a child with Kristen. I'm willing to do that, providing you do one thing for me in return." He gulped, knowing he was venturing onto terra incognita. "I want your promise that you'll leave my son alone. Promise me that you'll never let him have the first taste. I want him to live a normal life, a good life. I want him to have—"

Skip Gestern suddenly broke into loud, ringing laughter. He threw his handsome head back and laughed to the ceiling. He squinted through tearing eyes and poured himself another glass of wine from the decanter, still chuckling. At length he took a drag from his cigarette and got himself under control. "Let me get this straight, Mark. You think *I'm* the one who wants you to have a kid with your own sister, is that right? Just who the hell do you think I am, anyway?"

"I think you're Clovis Gestern, known to some as Lord Yesterday. You're the one they called the Prince of Slugs back in the Middle Ages. You're my father, and Kristen's father, too."

"*Damn!* This is rich! You think *I'm* Lord Yesterday!" More giggles, and another long, howling belly laugh. "I suppose I shouldn't be surprised, given the little that you really know and the unreliable sources of information around this town. But let me set you straight, Mark: My name is indeed Clovis Gestern, just as my father's name is Clovis Gestern. You and I are half-brothers, okay? I was born in 1915, which probably doesn't shock you, knowing what you know about vampires. I don't look thirty-five, and I probably won't start aging for another fifty or sixty years. That's one of the few perquisites of this job." He paused for a drag on his cigarette. "Bellona Drumgule is my mother. I'm the first and only child she's ever had. She became a mother at the age of a hundred and twenty-eight, which is probably a record. I'm sure you've gathered by now that she's a witch—and I mean that in the most positive sense of the word. She's much better at magic than she is at cooking, believe me."

Mark's panic blossomed, but he kept it in check and reached for his wineglass. He remember what John Lansen had told him of the Gestern family's long record of probate fraud. Phony death certificates. Dummied up inheritance documents. Pieces of the truth were falling into place.

"The family has always needed a living male to play the role of heir," Skip went on. "It should be obvious when you think about it. Old man Clovis just goes on living and living, while his contemporaries get old and die. He's a primo vampire, right? Primo vampires can live literally thousands of years. If he didn't die, people would get suspicious, to say the least, so at some point old Clovis needs to stage his own death. That's where the official heirs come in, guys like myself. Actually, I'm the only son that he's sired with a normal, mortal woman since he and the Gethsemanites came over from France, but he'd produced several before me back in the old country."

Old Clovis had staged his own death in 1888 and 1935, Skip explained. On both those occasions, he'd arranged to be out of the country, which facilitated the use of phony death certificates. Who in the Kalapuya County Courthouse would know a fake German death certificate from a real one? the old vampire had reasoned.

On the first occasion, he'd simply come back to Oldenburg ten

years after "dying" in England, passing himself off as his own
adult son and heir. After all, few Oldenburgers had really known
him, thanks to his notorious penchant for privacy. He'd con-
ducted most of his business by letters, and had avoided face-to-
face contact whenever possible. Suspicions about what had really
happened never went beyond the rumor stage.

By 1935, however, old Clovis Gestern had a legitimate son
who had just turned twenty, Bellona Drumgule's boy, later to be
known as Skip. With the "death" of the old man in Bavaria, Skip
had inherited everything—at least that was what the phony probate documents said. In reality, old Clovis was still very much in
control.

"We produced a bogus birth certificate for my own 'heir' back
in the fifties," Skip went on, "and staged my first death in 1974,
in France. I stayed away from Oldenburg until just over a year
ago, when I came back as my own kid and heir. So here I am at
the age of seventy-three—rich, immaculately educated, and well
traveled, a true bon vivant with nothing to worry about until it's
time to die again." He blew smoke across a candle on the table.
"Life is grand, Mark. You'll see."

"Then why aren't you happy? Why am I catching so much
misery coming out of your head?" Skip Gestern's shield had
fallen away entirely.

"Hmm." Skip studied his wineglass with empty hazel eyes.
"Maybe I'll tell you, since you asked," he said, speaking slowly.
"I've gone to all the finest schools, both on this continent and in
Europe. I've earned the equivalent of four doctorates, one each
in history, philosophy, biochemistry, and sociology. I've learned
more about the world than any ten normal mortals could ever
learn. But wherever I've gone, I've left a trail of bloody victims.
Sometimes they die, as one did two nights ago—a wonderful
young woman, whose name was Ginger. I needed her blood to
live, and I took it, and now she's dead. If one is careful, such
tragedies occur only rarely, but they do occur. And sometimes . . . sometimes the guilt . . ." His voice broke, and he took
a long drink of wine, as did Mark. "Everyone has something to
atone for," he went on, "and each of us atones in his own way.
Me—I give money to the high school band so they can buy nice
uniforms. Not a big thing, but a *good* thing. I give money to the
county so they can restore the old band shell in the park. I fi-
nance the restoration of the courthouse. I offer to tear down the

old Hilde cannery and put up recreational housing and a public park. I do what I can to make the community a better place to live."

"You're a prince," said Mark. "Every town should have its own vampire."

"I'm not bragging, damn it! I'm telling you how I deal with things. I suspect you'll find your own way, once you feel the need. The problem, my dear younger brother, is that there's nothing you can do to replace a human life. Nothing can make up for the sickness that a woman suffers because you've been taking her blood. There's no way on this earth you can pay for the misery you cause."

"If the guilt gets you down so badly," Mark spat back at him, standing, "why don't you end it all?" He pulled Kyleen LeBreaux's Beretta out of his pocket and tossed it to Skip. "I can guaran-fucking-tee that I won't let myself go on living, if I have to do it the way you do. I'll kill myself before I'll suck some poor woman's blood!"

Skip screwed his face into a contemptuous scowl. "You pathetic little slug! Do you think it's that easy? Do you think it's as simple as putting a fucking gun to your head? Well, I'll show you how easy it is, how simple it is." He pressed the muzzle against his own temple and squeezed the trigger. Nothing happened, for the safety switch was still engaged. Skip rectified the oversight, then pressed the muzzle to his temple once again while Mark watched open-mouthed.

The report was deafening. The small bullet tore into Skip Gestern's right temple and made a radical turn out his left eye, landing in a basket of Bellona Drumgule's hard dinner biscuits. Skip merely sat and stared at Mark with his remaining eye, bleeding ferociously from the empty socket. Then he grinned and stood up, geysering blood over the linen, the crockery, the silver. He put the gun down and leaned forward with his palms on the table.

"See what I mean?" he asked, his voice scratchy. "Death is no simple matter when you're a vampire, Mark. It's even less simple for you, because you're a *primo* vampire."

Mark felt the room spinning. He wanted to faint, to die. He wished he'd fired a round through his own brain, instead of tossing the gun to Skip.

Skip's body began to contort and bend. Mark heard the sound

of ripping cloth as Skip's legs lengthened, shredding his costly wool trousers. His arms acquired freakish crooks and angles as they thrust upward toward the ceiling. Suctions cups made of living flesh plopped against the vaulted ceiling stones, and Skip hoisted himself up, extruded and spiderlike. He sped along the ceiling on his crazily jointed limbs like some mutant simian, and was above Mark in the time it takes to draw a breath. His one good eye had become a glittering golden slit, his mouth a snout that held a riot of razored teeth. Slime glistened off his skin and dripped from the rags of his clothing onto Mark.

Skip lowered a long hand, and Mark watched a claw grow from its index finger, long and curved, deadly sharp. The claw touched the front of Mark's shirt and slit it easily, splitting his tie when it reached his throat. Mark wanted to resist, but something had wormed its way into his head, something cold and deadening. He'd felt it yesterday out by No Name Bridge when Kyleen had tried to kill him, an invasion of some force that turned muscles and nerves to lead. The claw severed the thin golden chain around his neck, and the horrible fingers closed around the silver amulet.

"A nice piece of work," growled the beast on the ceiling above Mark, examining the amulet with its good eye. "Pure silver, early eighteenth century, I'd say. You don't mind if I keep this, do you, Mark?" The Skip-thing popped the amulet into its mouth and swallowed it.

48

Convergence

i

Gary Bayliss lay on the scruffy living room sofa and listened to the storm. The old TV set was on, but the sound was turned off, so he had only ghostly, shifting images for company. The weather had made the reception so bad that it didn't matter whether he had sound or not.

Now that he'd closed the ThriftyKwik for good, he had nothing to occupy his evenings. Worse, he had no money to spend at Poverty Ike's. Early this evening, Freddye Ann had expressed concern over how the family would live, but Gary had shut her up with a good hard right to her solar plexus. She'd buckled to the floor and writhed for a good twenty minutes, which surprised him. Having just gotten out of the hospital, he hadn't thought he was strong enough to do that much damage.

His concern at the moment was Gretchen, who'd been missing since yesterday. Brett Omdahl had picked her up in the early afternoon, Freddye Ann had reported, and the two had gone off somewhere together. Rick Omdahl had called late last night to ask whether the Baylisses had seen their son, who hadn't come home for dinner.

Brett was a good kid, Gary knew, having been his boss at the ThriftyKwik. Dropping out of sight wasn't like the youngster at all. Gary had said as much to Deputy Will Settergren, who'd come around this morning after the sheriff's office received a worried call from the Omdahls.

No doubt about it, the kids were missing.

You don't suppose they've gone off somewhere to do the baloney dance? Gary asked himself. *Brett Omdahl and my Top-Kick. Wow.*

He wondered what a red-blooded American boy like Brett

would see in a horribly twisted little cripple like Gretchen. Most people hated even to look at her, much less—

He heard something upstairs. A thumping sound, scratches and scrapes. From Freddye Ann's room, it seemed. So what? *Maybe she's packing to leave,* he chuckled to himself—which would be an answer to prayer! If not for Gretchen, Gary himself would've pulled up his tent pegs long ago.

Now that he thought about it, he hoped the kids *had* gone off somewhere to fuck. He hoped Brett was reaming his daughter good, because she would probably never get it again, the way she looked. Everybody deserves to get laid at least once, Gary mused, even a heavy-duty fan of Joan of Arc.

Another sound. A crash, and now a curious throbbing that reminded Gary of the spasms of a dying thing. He listened hard through the rustling of rain against splintered old shingles, the groaning of wind around eaves. *What the hell is she doing up there?*

He pulled himself to a sitting position and contemplated going upstairs to find out exactly what was what. Maybe the scrawny cunt needed help packing. Whether she was packed or not, rainstorm or no rainstorm, Gary figured that now was as good a time as any to throw her out in the street—no argument, no ceremony. He and Gretchen would get along fine without her, thanks, assuming Gretchen ever came back. Gary couldn't let himself think that anything bad had really happened to the girl.

A floorboard squeaked at the top of the stairs. From where he sat, Gary couldn't quite see into the upstairs hallway. Too dark. Bad angles.

"What are you up to, you silly fucking slut? I hope you're packing your bags, because I've got half a mind to throw your ass out. You read me, cunt? I've got half a mind to toss your scrawny ass out in the rain, and be done with you for good. If you don't think I'm serious, just try me. You just—"

Something flew down the stairs on deathly wings, its taloned feet scarcely touching the ragged carpet. It was on Gary Bayliss within seconds—so fast that he never had time to focus on it. As its claws sliced through his throat, he saw that its vile mouth was already smeared with blood—Freddye Ann's blood, of course. It had taken *her* before coming to take him, and in the final fractions of a second left to him, Gary Bayliss was glad of that.

ii

Bob Gammage heard the scuff of footfalls in the stony corridor. He drew Skye Padilla close and whispered a low word of comfort in her ear.

"Nothin' to be scared of, squirt." He took out his Sig Sauer and cocked it. "As soon as they open that door, we're out of here. You ready to go back to the Big Apple?"

"I'm ready. Get me out of here, and I'll even go see the Yankees with you."

Gammage had given her his jacket and had sat with his good arm around her for most of the past twenty-four hours, trying to keep her warm. But the girl needed more than warmth, he knew. She needed food, medicine, a doctor's care. She needed her family.

Sam Darkenwald sat where he'd sat throughout this nightmarish imprisonment, in the opposite corner of the cell. To ease the passing of hours, he'd told dozens of stories about his past careers, segueing into each tale without the slightest worry over consistency. Gammage had marveled over the man's endurance and had wondered how Sam could continue to talk with no water to drink, no food to quell his knifing hunger. Gammage's own throat felt like ground glass, and in his stomach lurked an unrelenting pang. He dreaded to think of how Skye's throat and stomach felt, having been imprisoned in this place at least eight hours longer than he had.

"Want me to jump them when they open the door?" whispered Sam.

"Let me take care of this, Speed. Get ready to grab Skye and haul ass when I give the word, okay?"

Gammage got up and positioned himself alongside the door. He pressed his back against the sweating stone wall and felt moisture seep into his shirt. A shiver throbbed along his backbone.

"We're ready, Mr. Gammage," whispered Sam.

The footfalls in the corridor drew close, bringing with them the jittering yellow glow of a torch. "Stop!" someone commanded, and the scuffing ceased.

A young woman's voice, thought Gammage.

"Something isn't right," said the young woman. Bob

Gammage's knees started to go weak. The pistol was suddenly very heavy. He yearned to be free of this damnable cast.

"You sense something," said another voice, and Gammage recognized this one as Mrs. Drumgule's. "What is it, child?"

"I don't know. Give me a moment." Gammage detected a curious change in the young woman's tone, a roughening of her voice. "I smell metal."

"It's the bars in the door, Kristen," said Mrs. Drumgule. "And the shackle rings in the walls of the cell. They're made of cast iron."

"I've been here before, you old witch, and I know those smells. This is a different kind of metal, oily, brassy. I think it might be a gun."

Jesus, Mary, and Joseph, she smells my fucking gun! screamed Gammage in his mind. *What kind of people are these?*

A hand insinuated itself between the bars in the tiny window of the door, and Gammage briefly considered shooting at it as it groped into the half-light of the cell. But then the arm to which it was attached started to grow insanely. Within seconds it was no longer a human hand, but the wickedly clawed tool of some hellish hunter. As it whipped through the darkness, it flung strands of slime, some of which landed on Gammage's face.

Skye Padilla managed to scream. Sam Darkenwald swore. Bob Gammage stood transfixed, disbelieving his eyes. The claw found Gammage's Sig Sauer and wrenched it out of his hand, nearly breaking his fingers. Then it withdrew through the barred window, leaving Gammage to crumple to his knees with his ruined fingers tucked into an armpit, blind with pain.

Jingling keys now, the click of the padlock, the braying of old hinges as someone or something pushed the door open. Mrs. Drumgule entered the cell with a torch held high, looking exactly as Bob Gammage knew she would—dumpy and drab in her shapeless dress. Something stood behind her on the other side of the open door, something that threw a shadow that Gammage couldn't believe.

"The time has come, Skye," said Mrs. Drumgule, whistling. "Your torment will soon end. You were *made* for this moment, my sweet child of clay. . . ." She reached down to the girl, but Sam Darkenwald swatted her hand away. Mrs. Drumgule's face instantly contorted into a mask of hatred, and she pointed a doughy finger at Sam. She shrieked a guttural foreign phrase in a voice that Bob Gammage believed could have frozen battery acid, and Sam went limp as a wet chamois, his eyes staring and glazed, his jaw slack.

As the old woman gathered Skye Padilla into her arms, Gammage launched himself at her. He meant to break her fat-rounded jaw with a good old-fashioned right hook. He meant to do the same to her nose, maybe make it flatter than it already was. As long as he was alive and kicking, this old bitch wasn't taking Skye anywhere.

Gammage's right hook would have connected if someone hadn't reached out and grabbed his fist from behind. He whirled around and saw a mere slip of a twenty-year-old girl with short blond hair and bright blue eyes. She wore a loose pullover and shorts. She smiled like the sun, and Gammage's heart would have melted if he could have forgotten that moments earlier she'd owned a clawed arm with which she could have ripped his head off.

iii

Elspeth Carey defeated the padlock on the iron gate with magic, using low murmurs, a whisper, a wave of her hand. The aged lock glowed hot and parted, then fell to the ground in a spray of sparks. During those few dazzling seconds she was able to see into the passage ahead, and she shivered under her ragged shawl, frightened not by the festooning cobwebs nor the scutter of rats, but by the knowledge that she stood at long last on the threshold of Gestern Hall.

She shouldered her bag and spinning wheel, then pushed through the gate and moved warily forward, keeping her shoulder against the right-hand wall. Now and then she stepped in a chuckhole filled with water, since the paving stones had crumbled here and there under the weight of years, but she never faltered, never fell.

The passage finally ended in a narrow arch that opened into a stone stairwell. Light came from occasional bare bulbs dangling from frayed cords strung overhead.

Elspeth paused before starting to climb. She'd waited a century and a half for this night, had lain alone in her forest den with its walls of living wood, scheming and scrying, weaving her spells and cementing her ligatures. And she'd wept a river of tears, which left an emptiness inside her that now ached like a broken bone.

She'd buried her tiny daughter in the cold earth of Mesatchie Illihee, shrouded in a sack woven of human skin, the skin of Elspeth's own mother. Worse, she'd fully intended from the start to let the old vampire have little Rita when the time was right.

The time came in early 1942, nearly a century later, when the Blood Star soared high in its cycle. Elspeth had lifted the spell that had protected Rita, pretending to lack the power to hold Lord Yesterday off any longer. Two old men had unwittingly helped in the charade while trying to save the child: One of them had even blown Elspeth's head off with a shotgun. So grievous an injury would certainly have killed anyone who didn't have the blood of a vampire in her veins, and fortunately Elspeth had possessed magic to heal herself. The healing had required nearly seven years, a banishment she'd suffered alone in her forest den, unable to eat or drink or even move. She'd nearly rotted away, but gradually her head had regenerated and reattached itself to her torso, making her whole again. Learning to walk and eat like a normal mortal had required yet another year.

In the meantime Clovis Gestern had taken little Rita Crowe, Elspeth's only daughter, and had raised her behind the dismal walls of Gestern Hall. The townspeople had believed that old Clovis's son, young Clovis, was Rita's foster parent, but Elspeth knew better. Old Clovis hadn't confused *her* with his contrived deaths and phony obituaries and forged probate papers. Even after he'd taken a completely different role for himself in the community, and had assumed a new identity, he still spent his nights in Gestern Hall. Old Clovis had taken Rita into his bed as soon as she was old enough to be fertile, not because he felt any love for her, but because she had a trace of vampire blood in her veins. Inseminated by a primo vampire like old Clovis, Rita had given birth to a child who was more than half-vampire, a primo vampire cursed with a hungry slug inside him.

Over the years Elspeth had shed anguished tears for her Rita, the innocent child who had suffered so abysmally because of an old witch's obsession. Now, as Elspeth raised a foot to begin climbing the stairs, she knew that she was beyond crying—for her lost daughter, who'd ended her own life rather than live with the reality of it, and for her grandson, the man she'd manipulated

and maneuvered to serve as the killing weapon. The time for
weeping was gone. What remained now was to finish the task
she'd begun.

iv

Marta Lansen spent a harrowing evening.

Deidre Garland, her daughter-in-law, called from Portland
around dinnertime to say that Thaddeus was missing. The boy
hadn't come home for lunch, and no one had seen him since he
left his friend's house shortly after noon. Deidre was certain that
Mark had spirited him away, having changed his mind about letting Thaddeus spend the summer in Portland. She'd notified the
police, of course, and told Marta to expect a call from the Kalapuya County Sheriff's Office shortly.

Indeed, a few minutes after she hung up, a sheriff's deputy
called, wanting to know whether Mark was there, whether he'd
mentioned bringing his son back to Oldenburg. Marta answered
no to these questions, feeling terror close around her heart like
an icy tentacle.

Later she managed to get herself upstairs, to take one of the
tranquilizers that Dr. Schell had prescribed for her last week. She
dressed for bed and lay on a satin pillow, sobbing softly and staring out the window into the fury of a rare electrical storm.

Thunder boomed, rattling the house. The lights flickered and
died. Feeling a tingling urgency, she rose from the bed and made
her way downstairs, needing no light. She went out through the
kitchen, through the covered porch, and walked down the flagstone path to her garden, where lived her beloved roses, her
flowering wisteria and ornamental allium. There she stood rigid
as a statue as the rain drenched her to the skin, knowing that this
was what she *had* to do.

Lightning exploded overhead, and she imagined that she stood
outside herself, that she was able to see her own rigid body
clearly, a thing to be sacrificed. She saw her own wide, hopeless
eyes and strings of sopping hair, the torment in her face. She saw
herself thrust a finger toward the garage, apparently having made
some horrendous discovery.

"It's gone!" she screamed over cannonading thunder. "John's
car is *gone!* Don't you know what this means?"

Oh yes, she knew. Marta Lansen, of all people, *knew*.

"It has *started!*" she shouted against another fusillade of thunder. "The graves are opening! There's no hope for us! There's nothing we can do!" She tried to move back toward the house, but her feet had become dead weight. She heard a rustling in the colony of azaleas to her right. Something brushed against her in the darkness—it felt vaguely like a fire hose in thickness. She realized that it had coiled around her arm, that it was dragging her toward the azaleas.

Lightning flashed again, and she shrieked when she saw that it had *hands*, but not like any she'd ever seen before. Claws tore through the sopping cloth of her bathrobe, and dollops of inky blood oozed out. Now it had her by the neck, and its spiky nails sank into her throat and loosed dark spurts of gore. When she saw the thing's golden eyes, she knew that all was lost. It leered at her as it ripped her heart from her chest.

V

As Bellona Drumgule muscled Skye Padilla out of the cell, the young girl kicked and screamed with more fury than Gammage had thought her capable of. Her screams reverberated dreadfully throughout the dank passages and corridors beneath Gestern Hall, arousing scuffling and scratching behind the walls. Even the rats were terrified for her, Gammage thought.

Kristen Lansen didn't follow them out of the cell, but nudged the door closed and set a torch in a holder in the stone wall. She turned to Gammage, who backed away until the wall stopped him. She smiled, and he felt something twist in his bowels.

"So you're the infamous Mr. Robert Gammage we've all heard so much about. It's really great to meet you. Mind if I call you Bob?" Her voice was velvet, and in the stuttering torchlight her face was a vision out of Norse myth.

"Lady, you better let us go," he managed, his voice cracking. "And you better make sure nothing happens to that kid, or . . . or I'll . . . "

"Or you'll do what, Bob?" She glided closer to him, and he caught the sweet scent of her body. "Whatever goes on across the hall has nothing to do with you and me." She untied the strings at the neck of her pullover and slipped it off, revealing the most beautiful breasts Gammage had ever seen. Giggling, she clasped her hands behind her head and twisted a half-turn in each direction, modeling in the torch light. "Feel free to touch. This is a petting zoo."

Gammage fought panic. He made a fist of his aching right hand and dug the nails into his palm. He couldn't pull his gaze away from Kristen's cobalt eyes. Breathing became difficult, and he felt as if his whole body was encased in warm tar.

Kristen wriggled out of her tan shorts and stood before him with her legs spread wide. "All yours, Bob," she said gaily. She took three steps closer, and he could feel her breath on his cheek. Her hands worked at his belt buckle, his pants, his shorts. His cock stood free like a spike, and he felt nineteen again. She pushed him against the wooden door of the cell and went down on him. His cheekbones rested against the cold bars of the small square window, and for some reason he opened his eyes. . . .

vi

Mrs. Drumgule crouched to one side of the marble slab, upon which Skye Padilla lay naked and bound. A man in a cowled robe of black satin entered from the corridor, momentarily eclipsing Gammage's view from the barred window in the door of the cell, then moved to the center of the vaulted chamber and positioned himself on the far side of the slab.

Gammage couldn't see his face, not even when a hundred candles flared to life suddenly, because it lay hidden deep in the shadow of the cowl. The man's hands were visible, though—old, gnarled hands with long crooked fingers and curving nails.

Gammage wanted all this to matter. He wanted to feel rage over the atrocity about to take place before his eyes, but he could feel nothing beyond the glory of Kristen Lansen's mouth around his cock. She squatted before him with her back braced against the wooden door, and he leaned over her with his face against the bars. She ministered to him in a way that produced colors in his heart and music in his mind.

A massive old book with an ancient leather cover flipped open as if it was alive, and the pages fanned with a crinkling sound. The robed man leaned over to consult the text, then mumbled some words that caused the candles and torches to flutter. Skye

Padilla cried out again as Bellona Drumgule handed him a wickedly curved knife. He gripped it with both fists and raised it over his head. His voice poured from the void of the cowl, a growling basso profundo that roused visions of slithering snakes:

> *"Hear me, my Goddess, my Lover, my Slave.*
> *Rosemary balm and marigold I bring,*
> *A nightshade concoction mixed o'er a grave*
> *With brain of a snake to sharpen the sting."*

Bellona Drumgule mixed the specified substances in a shallow bowl that rested on the marble slab next to Skye. As the chant mentioned other ingredients, she fetched them from a surrounding array of vials, jars, bottles, baskets, and cages. Occasionally the chant broke into a language that sounded like none Gammage had ever heard, and the old woman voraciously gobbled stuff that could have come from someone's bathroom cabinet—handfuls of Comet cleanser, mouthfuls of Liquid Plummer (right from the bottle), huge bites of Irish Spring soap, and a long squirt of Lysol toilet bowl cleaner.

> *"Wind-flight and raptus, the power to kill,*
> *Vision to peer beyond the mortal's pale,*
> *Of ligature to bind Thy potent will,*
> *Of talons to rend the physical veil. . . ."*

The glare from the knife momentarily blinded Gammage, and he tried to push himself away from the barred window, but Kristen jerked him back with brute force, pulling him even tighter to her. He felt the electrical pricking of her nails against his buttocks and hips, the raw power in her hands. Somehow he managed to lower his head to glance downward, and what he saw caused his heart to thud against his ribcage like a wrecking ball. Kristen's head was mostly mouth, full of dagger-teeth and a tongue like an octopus's tentacle, covered with suction cups and slathered with Gammage's blood.

She'd razored into the flesh at the base of his cock, and he was bleeding like a butchered pig. Now the pain arrived with blaring horns and fireworks, and Gammage writhed helplessly. The Kristen-thing lapped his blood like nectar, and he knew that she wouldn't stop until he was as dry and white as a pile of bones in the desert.

He would have howled his own damnation, if he hadn't looked up and seen what was happening in the vaulted chamber across from the cell. Bellona Drumgule hovered in the air above the marble slab like a tattered gray blimp, twisting and convulsing. The cowled man chanted:

"For sweet flag and spice bush and dog dung and jet,
For sandalwood oil art Thou still in my debt.

"For cubeb and clove pink and jasper and ale—
A mixture that summons Thee, never to fail.

"Thou dost hunger for outrage, this I do know,
So shalt Thou have it, Lover below.

"A thousand sins, which is a hundred times ten—
With these have I bound Thee, time and again. . . ."

Fires flared atop candle wicks and torches. Runic inscriptions on vessels and bowls glowed green and yellow. The air crackled with magic, and Skye Padilla gave a final scream as she saw through her tears what was about to happen.

"Lay bare tomorrow in a vaporous cloud,
As my blade opens this child, young and fair.
I bring forth her innards upon this shroud
To read what's destined, if only I dare.

"Of curses to smite my enemy's brow,
To arouse the fury of seas and skies;
This pow'r and more must Thou grant to me now,
By this child's blood, as she suffers and dies."

The knife plummeted, a silvery missile. Skye didn't scream as the blade entered her chest precisely between her breasts, but only lay open-mouthed a long moment. Her poor punctured heart pumped bright blood in a stream that spread like a plague on the marble.

She turned her head to stare directly into Bob Gammage's eyes, her cheeks going white and her lips working silently, as if trying to say, *You promised me this wouldn't happen. You prom-*

ised to get me out of here and take me to a Mets game. What happened, Bob?

Skye didn't scream in her final seconds, but Bob Gammage did. Greenish gas ascended from the gore and hovered before the hidden face of the cowled man, roiling like the plasma of a newly forming star. Within the cloud flickered reflections and refractions of realities past, present, and future. Somehow Gammage knew that within it swirled truth that only a truly evil man could see.

He brought his cast down hard on the Kristen-thing's head. He heard the sickening crunch of cracking plaster, felt a laser-bright twinge that flashed from the wound in his shoulder down to the fingertips of his left hand. The Kristen-thing roared and reared to her full height, dumping Gammage to the stone floor like a rag doll. She towered above him and glowered at him with angry golden eyes, then bent toward him as if to slice him to pieces with her claws. But something outside the cell caught her attention, some smell or sound from the vaulted chamber across the passage. She turned away from Gammage and threw open the heavy door of the cell. Her mouth fell open as she took in the grisly tableau lighted by torches and candles. She staggered backward. Teetering on her clawed feet, she drew a huge breath, then roared her anguish to the stone walls as Bob Gammage himself had done a moment earlier.

Her body shifted abruptly back to its normal shape. She sank to her knees, covered her bloody face with her hands and sobbed.

A hand touched Gammage's shoulder. Sam Darkenwald had revived and had crawled to him from the far corner of the cell. Bellona Drumgule's spell hadn't been lethal, thank God, but Sam's movements were slow and painful, as if he'd been hit by a truck.

"Mr. Gammage, you're bleeding!"

Gammage cupped his hands over his wounded genitals and rolled slowly to a sitting position. He knew that he'd lost more blood than anyone should. "Sam, you've got to help me. . . ."

Sam tore off a large section of his blue work shirt, wadded it, and handed it to Gammage. "Press this tight against the wound to slow the bleeding, and we'll work on getting you out of here. I just need a minute to . . . a minute to . . ." Sam shook his head to clear out the cobwebs. "Don't you worry, Mr. Gammage. Old Sam will get you out in one piece, you'll see. Trust me."

Gammage pressed the wadded cloth into his punctured groin. He pulled his shorts and pants up, still keeping the pressure on the wound, but within seconds a huge dark stain spread across the front of his pants. He felt weaker with every passing second.

"Damn you, lady!" he spat at Kristen Lansen, who huddled naked and miserable only a few feet away. "Damn *all* of you! I hope there's a special place reserved in hell for you."

Kristen looked up and tried to speak, but couldn't at first. She gathered herself, tried again. "I'm sorry for what I did to you," she whispered hoarsely. "When the hunger comes over me, there's nothing I can do except . . ." She stammered, as if the truth was too wicked to utter, even now. "I-I'm so very sorry."

Gammage's head swam, and his heart lugged lazily in his chest. His blood was leaking away, he knew, taking with it his life. Incredibly, the anguish in Kristen Lansen's face moved him. In that face he saw only tragedy—no evil, no lies.

"I didn't want this to happen to Skye," Kristen went on, weeping, "but there was nothing I could do. I'd even planned to help her escape. But when the hunger comes over me, like it did a while ago, all I can think about is taking a man's blood. Nothing else matters."

Gammage grabbed Kristen's arm. "Can you help us now? Can you get us out of here?"

A dark shape moved into the doorway of the cell and cast a cold shadow over Kristen, Sam Darkenwald, and Bob Gammage. A man's deep voice said, "The night's work isn't finished yet, Kristen. You've had your nourishment, and now you need the love of your man. Come."

The man in the cowled robe extended his hand to her, and Kristen stared up at him, her face streaked with Gammage's blood. She glanced back briefly at Gammage and Darkenwald, then got to her feet. She couldn't resist this man, whoever he was—that much was clear.

"Don't worry about these poor souls, my child," whistled Bellona Drumgule, peeking around her master's satin robe. "We'll leave them for Bernardo and Francesca. They'll make short work of them, you can be sure of that." She laughed in a way that made Gammage want to vomit.

The man in the satin robe draped an arm around Kristen and pulled her quickly away, headed for the stairs. Old Bellona Drumgule followed, carrying a huge bowl of something steamy in her arms. As she turned for a final mocking glimpse at the men in the cell, the contents of the bowl sloshed over the rim, and a small amount splashed onto the cold stones of the corridor. It landed with a *plap!* that sent spears of bright red in all directions. It was, Gammage knew, the blood of Skye Padilla.

49

Truth and Injustice

i

Skip Gestern looked anything but elegant. He'd come down from the ceiling and had reverted to his normal human shape, but he'd bled copiously from his self-inflicted head wound. His mangled left eye hung awkwardly from its socket, and his shredded clothing was sticky with slime.

"Just what do you intend to do now, my dear younger brother?" he asked, settling into his chair. "Your little amulet can no longer protect you from the hunger, thanks to the fact that it's resting comfortably at the bottom of my stomach. Very soon you won't be able to think of anything but taking a woman's blood. In fact, you'll do absolutely anything to get it, just as a crack addict will do anything for his next hit. You'll surprise yourself at how far you'll go, I'm sure."

Mark Lansen clenched his fists under the table. "You're enjoying this, aren't you? You get some kind of unholy rush from seeing people suffer, don't you?"

"Not true. I find these things interesting, that's all."

"*Interesting?* Was it *interesting*, what you did to Fran Pellagrini? Or to Freddye Ann Bayliss? Do you think their families found it as *interesting* as you did?"

"I never touched Fran Pellagrini or Freddye Ann Bayliss. They were long-standing *friends* of old Dad's."

"You're lying. Gretchen Bayliss saw you outside her window one night after you'd attacked her mother. She spoke with you, and you threatened her. That's why she went into hysterics when you walked into the Dukakis party at the Royal Kokanee."

"For God's sake, why would I lie to you, Mark? Gretchen *thought* she saw me. Actually she saw my father—*our* father, yours and mine. She recognized some vague family trait that we Gesterns have in common, even when we're in—ah, *hunting* trim, let's say. Maybe it's in the eyes or the nose. More likely it's something spiritual that an average person would never notice. Gretchen is world-class perceptive, you know, and she's anything but average. But does it really matter? Old Dad and I are vampires, the same as you, and you'll probably acquire the *look* yourself someday."

At this moment Mark would have welcomed a nuclear strike on Nehalem Mountain or a collision with an asteroid. He wished he could will himself to burst into flame and burn to a lifeless cinder. The patter of rain against the stained-glass window became pounding bison hooves in his brain. The distant rumble of thunder sounded like a volcano. He heard the ticking of clocks throughout the mansion, the scrabbling of mice in the basement below, the whimper of a young boy somewhere above—

A young boy. He cocked his head and listened.

"Ah—the ears of a primo vampire have no equal," Skip Gestern said, lighting a cigarette. "You hear things I'll never hear, Mark. Actually, all your powers are stronger than mine, and for that I envy—"

"Shut up!" Mark jumped out of his chair and marched toward the staircase at the far end of the dining room. The whimper came again, and he was certain that he recognized it now: Tad was somewhere near. Mark couldn't imagine why his son would be at Gestern Hall or how he'd gotten here. Panic seized him.

Up the carpeted stairs he went, past suits of armor on the landings and medieval shields on the walls, past candles in their polished copper holders, the only sources of light here, since the storm had killed the power. The second-floor corridor was nearly dark, but Mark could see well with his vampire's eyes. Heavy wooden doors stood in straight flanks. Brocaded tapestries adorned alcoves at either end of the corridor, where tall pointed windows looked out upon the night.

In a distant alcove sat Elspeth Carey at her spinning wheel, naked and ungainly, an ancient bird who had lost her feathers, seemingly. An occasional flare of lightning cast her in silhouette against the glass. The wheel spun and whirred under its own power. She'd pierced the skin above her right breast and looped it around the spindle. The spindle rotated in a bloody blur, and skin rolled off the crone's rattle-boned body in a single reddish strand, winding around the spindle to collect in a frothy bunch.

She appeared to be in a trance. She registered no pain, though the process must have been excruciating. As lightning flashed again, Mark saw that her hands worked furiously with some kind of primitive darning needles, even as the wheel and spindle turned. A closer look showed him that the old woman was weaving some sort of cloth from her own skin. Already she'd laid bare her flesh over one old and withered breast, and the pattern was spreading to the other. Her lower torso was blood-slick.

Mark heard a little boy's whimper from somewhere near, and he turned away from the horridly fascinating spectacle of Elspeth Carey at her spinning wheel. He dashed to the nearest door in the corridor and listened, then went to the next and did the same. At the fourth door he heard the clear thumping of Tad's panicky heart, the rush of air through his lungs, and another soft whimper.

He opened the door.

The familiar aroma of pipe tobacco invaded his nostrils as he stepped into the dark room, which was a guest suite with a canopied bed, a fireplace, and a window with panes sectioned into medieval trefoils. His nose detected more than burning tobacco now. The stink of putrefactive organisms hit him full-force, bacteria and fungus, the slime of the grave.

John Lansen sat in a rocking chair near the window, smoking his pipe contentedly, holding Tad in his lap. In the week since his death, John's skin had blistered and had mottled brown and green. His hair had loosened and fallen away in places, showing conspicuously where Bernie Pellagrini's nine iron had taken divots out of his skull.

"Hi, Mark," rattled John, smiling. "Glad you could stop by. Say hi to your dad, Tad Bear."

Mark felt his knees buckling, felt the foundation of all his hopes dissolve. Only Tad's tiny, terrified hello kept him from fainting dead away. He took a step closer.

"My God," he croaked, "this isn't possible." Rain drummed against the window, and the rocking chair squeaked as John Lansen rocked. "It was *you* I saw in the Alfa Romeo. Gestern did this to you, didn't he? Father Le Fanu saw it in his scrying mirror—graves opening up, and things coming out to fight us. Gestern sent you here, didn't he?"

"To be frank with you, I'm not clear on the particulars, son. But I do know that I'm here, you're here, and Tad's here. Kind of sweet, isn't it—two vampires and a zombie! Three generations

of monsters in the same room! I wish to hell I'd brought a cam-
era!"

"How could you *do* it, Dad? How could you let him send you
to fight me, your own son? How could you let him do this to
you, to *us?*"

John Lansen chuckled, spitting little gobbets of something
down the front of his starched funeral shirt. "Let me set you
straight on a popular myth, Mark. Death changes a person. The
dead don't see the world as they saw it when they were alive.
They don't keep on loving the people they loved in life, their relatives and friends and such. It's just the opposite, actually. Nobody would hire a fucking medium to throw a seance if he knew
what the dead *really* think. And it would curl your toenails if you
knew what the dead really *want!*"

Mark moved nearer still, a chill taking root between his
shoulderblades. "Let me have him, Dad. Let me take him away
from here. Then you can go back to where you belong, wherever
the hell that is."

"Oh, I don't think so, Mark. Stop right where you are. You
see, I'm on a mission here. My will isn't my own. I suppose you
could say I have a client"—the dead lawyer laughed foully—
"and I need to do what my client wants."

"Do you mind telling me what that is?"

"He wants me to take care of Tad until you do what you're
supposed to do."

Tad started to cry softly. Mark saw the stains on his Portland
Trail Blazers T-shirt, and knew that the boy had recently vomited, which was understandable. Sitting in his dead grandfather's
lap had made him physically sick.

"What if I don't cooperate? What if I come over there and rip
your maggoty head off? I can do it, Dad. You have no idea how
strong I am."

"Before you took two steps closer, I'd have broken this kid's
neck. Maybe I'm not as strong as you, but I'm sure as hell strong
enough to make a corpse out of old Tad Bear here. Is that what
you want? You want to see your only son dead and twitching and
turning blue? I'll arrange it, if you push me, I swear."

Acid rose in Mark's throat and for an unholy moment he
feared that he would metamorphose into a bloodsucker before his
son's eyes. His anger bubbled just below the point of explosive
release, and only his fear for Tad held it in check. He couldn't

take a chance with his son's life. He could only do what old Clovis Gestern wanted.

He heard movement behind him and turned around to see torchlight fill the doorway. A tall man in a cowled robe of black satin entered the room, his face hidden in the shadow of the rich cloth. Behind him came Kristen with a torch, naked and blood-smeared, looking as if she'd just seen the gates of hell. And finally came ugly old Bellona Drumgule, carrying a huge bowl of blood.

"It's good to know that you've started to think rationally at long last," said the man in the robe, apparently a telepath who could hear thoughts. "You're absolutely right, Mark. You have no choice but to do exactly as old Clovis Gestern wants. John, would you care to make the introductions?"

A rattling chuckle came from John Lansen's throat. "Allow me to present my client," he said as the man in the robe pushed back his cowl. "Mark Lansen, say hi to the one and only Lord Yesterday."

Mark exhaled explosively when he laid eyes on the long, wrinkled face with its gun-metal stubble and thick bifocals. This was a man who had hazel eyes and perfect teeth exactly like his own. Never had he dreamed that this old man could be his biological father, much less the evil Lord Yesterday. Mark had always known him as a gentle old barkeep named Poverty Ike.

ii

Tressa Downey parked Velma Selvig's van in the porte cochere of Gestern Hall, halting just a few feet from the little red Mercedes that Mark had driven earlier in the evening. Brett Omdahl hopped out the back of the van and unfolded the jointed halves of plywood that served as a ramp. Gretchen Bayliss then drove her wheelchair smoothly down the ramp and wheeled around to face the front entrance of the mansion.

"It's certainly *dark*," said Gretchen with a shiver in her voice.

"The power's out here, too," said Brett. He snapped on his flashlight, as did Tressa. "It's a good thing we brought these."

Father Le Fanu got out of the passenger's seat and joined them, carrying his boom box in one hand, his headphones in the other. "The rain has stopped," he observed, glancing up at the dark sky, "and the Blood Star is shining."

Tressa looked up and saw the rusty light of Mars beating down through a rip in the dying storm. Suddenly the moon came out of hiding, and the night brightened as the remnants of the storm scudded rapidly eastward. Blackness lay in the valley below like a carpet of ruined hopes. Not a single light burned in Oldenburg.

"All is ready, my children," said the priest, taking a step toward the entrance of the house. "Each of you knows what is expected, yes? Let us proceed, and may God help us."

They found the door open and went into the foyer, where Tressa thought the air seemed thick and unnaturally black. Sweeping tapestries soaked up the beams from her and Brett's flashlights, and suits of armor threw disheartening shadows against the wood panels of the walls. Tressa saw that Brett held tightly to Gretchen's misshapen little hand as he walked alongside the motorized wheelchair. Both their faces shone pale, their eyes round and glistening.

The beam from Tressa's flashlight fell across the face of a sixtyish man who stood on the landing of the curved staircase ahead. Her stomach flopped when she saw that it was Bernie Pellagrini. Dressed for his own funeral, he wore a dark suit, a tie of indeterminate color, and a shirt stained purple and gray from putrefaction. His head appeared cobbled together, inasmuch as he'd wedged a deer rifle under his chin last March and blown much of his skull away.

Bugs and worms had gotten to Bernie. Fungus grew in mottles over much of his skin. He leaned against the banister with a golf club resting jauntily on his shoulder, with one foot crossed over the other, as if posing for a sports catalogue. But there was nothing sporting about the wicked gleam in his dead eyes or the tight, malevolent grin on his mouth.

"Good evening, ladies and gents," he rasped, "and welcome to the Nehalem Mountain Inn, the ultimate bed-and-breakfast experience. I'm your host, Bernie Pellagrini. Very shortly I'll beat all your heads in with this nine iron. I'll be ably assisted by my charming wife, Fran. . . ." He motioned toward the reception desk, and Fran Pellagrini popped up from behind it, scarcely an arm's length away from Tressa. She lunged at Tressa over the oaken counter with scabrous fingers hooked into claws.

Tressa jumped away and bit her fist to keep from screaming. Francesca looked even worse than her husband—her skull, too, was oddly asymmetrical, since Bernie had beaten her to death with the same nine iron that now lay on his shoulder. She sported a bullet hole just below her right eye and several more in her torso, from which oozed something black.

Bernie stepped down from the landing and raised the golf club above his head. "I'll do a good job on you folks, you can be sure of that. You can ask my wife, if you don't believe me. She knows my work firsthand, don't you, dear?" He laughed unbearably, spraying droplets of filth from his mouth.

"Stop!" commanded Gautier Le Fanu. "You'll do no killing tonight!" Bernie and Fran both froze, Bernie with his nine iron held high and Fran with one leg over the counter. Tressa heard Gretchen whispering a Hail Mary. "You have no idea with whom you are dealing, my poor dead friends," said Le Fanu, standing tall in the glare of Tressa's flashlight. "I have only to say the word, and a creature so foul I cannot utter its name will seize your souls and take them away forever. It will torture you endlessly for the sheer joy of it, because it thrives on human pain. It will give you fleshy bodies so that it may feast upon you when it's so moved. If you attempt to harm one hair on the head of these innocent people, I shall call this creature, I swear."

"You don't scare us, you wrinkled old shit," hissed Francesca Pellagrini. "You can't do anything worse than what's already been done to us."

"It would be a tragic mistake for you to believe that, madame," Le Fanu replied.

"Well, pardon me," said Bernie mockingly, "but I'm not convinced. I think I'll go ahead and split your fucking skull, and worry about that creature of yours later." He came at Le Fanu, swinging the nine iron. Le Fanu raised his boom box, which emitted a burst of static that caused the hair on Tressa's neck to bristle. The air crackled with ionic energy, and the boom box glowed with the green halo of Saint Elmo's fire. Le Fanu's mouth formed some unheard name, and hissing snakes of light whipped out of the boom box and encircled both Bernie and Fran, then squeezed around them until their wretched, rotting bodies were encased in dazzling cocoons. As suddenly as they came, the snakes of light departed, withdrawing into the boom box and leaving the room silent and dark once again.

In the glow of her flashlight, Tressa saw the bodies of Bernie and Fran Pellagrini tumble to the floor, having become pathetic sacks of rancid meat.

iii

Mark watched helplessly as the corpse of John Lansen carried Tad into the adjacent room of the suite and disappeared into the dark.

"I'm sure you'll agree," said Poverty Ike, moving close to him, "that it's best if your son doesn't see *everything*. Don't worry—the big square-headed Norsky will take fine care of him." He patted Mark on the arm, and Mark felt his limbs go leaden.

Something was seeping into Mark's brain, some living force that was usurping his nerves and synapses. He dared a glimpse into Poverty Ike's oily eyes and knew instantly that the force came from *him*. The old vampire was taking over Mark's head, controlling his arms and legs and hands. Mark tried to resist, but couldn't. Poverty Ike was simply too strong.

Bellona Drumgule led him to the bed, pushed him down on it, and started to remove his clothing. "There's going to be a conception tonight," she whistled cheerfully as she pulled down Mark's pants. "It won't be long before we hear the patter of little feet around here again!" He managed to push her away, but the force inside his brain asserted itself cruelly. His arms dropped to his sides and lay useless.

Poverty Ike stood beside the bed and told him what he already knew: Resistance was silly. His fate was sealed. Less than half an hour earlier, the old monster had performed a ceremony called the Spell of the Entrails, which had enabled him to manipulate the future, to foil his adversaries before they could even launch their offensives. Mark heard these words with his ears, but he saw their reality in his mind, images broadcast to him by the creature himself.

The images made him choke and heave. *Skye Padilla, flinching as the knife plunges into her heart, writhing deplorably as it splits her from sternum to pelvis. A green cloud rising from her entrails, with diamond-bright flashes of knowledge orbiting its core. . . .*

GOLDEN EYES 435

His eyes picked out the gestalt gems one by one, and they reminded him vaguely of some elaborate connect-the-dots puzzle. He had no choice but to complete the picture, to stare reality in the face.

Mark Lansen would call the Catamount. . . .

The Tale of Snacky Cat was a charm, wasn't it?

"It was activated by the onset of the cycle of the Blood Star," Elspeth Carey had said, *"but you needn't have it near you to avail yourself of it. If you find yourself threatened, simply think of the scene on the cover, and will yourself into it. The Catamount will be there for you."*

Mark did this, feeling as if his last few shreds of hope were burning away like cheap sparklers on the Fourth of July. He visualized the cover of the book and saw the demonically toothed face of Snacky Cat. He willed himself into the picture and found himself standing before the ungodliest creature he'd ever seen. Nominally a cat, it was three stories tall, possessed of the teeth of a dragon, the eyes of a viper. Its fur wasn't fur at all, but long, needly scales that were jointed to bend and twist like hair. The creature stooped low to sniff him, then threw back its head in feline fashion and yowled loud enough to rattle every china closet in the valley below. It was a roar of agony, of terror. . . .

Mark now realized that he was seeing this vision in the cloud that had risen from Skye Padilla's entrails, seeing it through Poverty Ike's eyes. As he watched, the sky above Snacky Cat filled with growling black clouds. A bloody rain fell, drenching the creature with gore, each droplet growing a brown, slimy bud; each bud then blossomed into a slug with horrible groping eyestalks. The slugs covered the Catamount by the tens of thousands, then by the millions and billions. They devoured the creature as Mark watched, reducing it to oily insignificance on the stony ground, to a few sorry fragments of bone and nail.

So much for Mark Lansen's last hope. Tears welled in his eyes, and he tasted hopelessness as he'd never known it.

"I'm afraid you're right," said Poverty Ike, bending over him and smiling in his avuncular way. "That *was* your last hope. You see, the Spell of the Entrails showed me everything I need to know tonight. I've taken steps to thwart every move you and your friends have planned to make—magic against magic, you could say. I've used it to shape your future, to give you an opportunity to become the most powerful primo vampire in history.

You'll learn the magic yourself, Mark, and you'll use it to survive, as I myself have done. By the way, I also found out that
your grandmother held something back from you—something
you have a right to know, I think."

Mark stammered, drenched in sweat and tears. "W-what did
she hold back?"

"She'd planned all along to let me get your mother, Rita
Crowe. She'd planned to allow Rita to bear my son—you—and
fully intended for you to end up where you are now."

"I-I don't believe you."

"Believe what you want, son, but this is the truth: Elspeth Carey meant to use you as a weapon against me. For some reason,
she thought you could be persuaded to kill me, that somewhere
you would find the strength to do it." Poverty Ike wagged his
head from side to side, as if the stupidity of witches was beyond
comprehension. "It's irrelevant now, of course. All that matters is
that you're here, and that we're free to get on with our business.
You see, Mark, you're about to become the crown prince of a
brand-new race of humans. They'll each live a thousand years or
more, because they'll be primo vampires. They'll be wise and
well educated, tempered by long life and study. In time they'll
rise naturally to lead this poor world, and they won't need to
hide away in ruined castles and caves any longer. They'll come
out and live openly. The rest of the world will respect them for
their wisdom and power.

"You'll see all this come to pass, Mark, because your life is
just beginning. Mine is nearly over, I'm afraid, but when I die,
I'll have the satisfaction of knowing that I left something worth-
while behind, something I've struggled for hundreds of years to
achieve. I'll leave *you* behind, Mark, and you'll make it to the
promised land, even if I don't."

He reached behind him and pulled Kristen close to the bed.
Mark was naked now and shivering uncontrollably. He saw re-
gret in his sister's face, and pity. But he also saw resignation.
She'd accepted her fate and was ready to do whatever Poverty
Ike wanted.

"Let me offer a little libation before you lovebirds get started,"
said Poverty Ike, motioning Bellona Drumgule forward. The old
witch had been busy lighting candles and placing them around
the room. Now she brought the bowl that contained Skye
Padilla's blood and set it on a bed table. From the folds of her

dress she produced a ladle and three long-stemmed wineglasses. Poverty Ike ladled blood into two glasses and handed one each to Mark and Kristen. "I drank this and regurgitated it myself, so I can vouch for its being properly tainted. Only the best for my kids." He fell silent a moment, as if dredging up some cherished memory. "I became a bartender back in 1940," he went on, smiling in his wrinkled way, "because I was tired of living the lonely life of old Clovis Gestern. I'd staged my death in 1935, as Skip probably told you over dinner, and I figured that staying away five years was long enough for people to forget what I looked like. So I became Poverty Ike and took over an old saloon I'd foreclosed on right after the crash of 'twenty-nine. Nobody in town made the connection between Poverty Ike and old man Gestern, because hardly anyone had even laid eyes on me in the first place."

He ladled a glass of blood for himself. "I've poured a lot of drinks in the past forty-eight years, Mark. I've told a lot of stories and I've seen a lot of people come and go. In all those years of playing the barkeep and storyteller, I've never had greater pleasure in pouring a round of drinks than the pleasure I feel at this moment." He held his glass high, offering a salute.

Mark found he could move his arms now. He found too that the hunger had come alive with a vengeance. The scent of Skye Padilla's blood sweetened his craving with delicious promise. He knew that one sip from this glass would seal his fate forever.

Maybe this fate won't be so bad after all, whispered a silken voice deep inside him. *Long life, study, wisdom.* What more could a historian ask, than to live through the centuries? *Think of the histories you can write. You can become a modern Marcus Aurelius, if you choose—an enlightened scholar-king!*

He put the glass to his lips—and went blind with a vision from hell: *The dead man's one intact eye rotates in its socket and stares at him. The mouth, though burbling with blood, moves: "Root it out, Dr. Lansen." Leo Fobbs says this as casually as a passerby might comment on the weather.*

Mark convulsed and spilled blood onto his bare chest. His lungs froze. He gagged for air, but got none. Another vision exploded in his mind: *The slug engulfs Mark's face, stifling his scream, and presses its warm, wet mouth to his ear: "Root it out, Dr. Lansen. . . ."* God help him, the voice belongs to Tad. *"If you know what's good for you, root it out!"*

Mark knew what was good for him. His lungs relented, and he
hurled the blood into Poverty Ike's face. He crushed the wineglass in his fist and let it fall in a tinkling rain, but he kept one
shard, which he wielded like a scalpel.

"Root it out . . . !"

His free hand shot out and tore away the front of Poverty Ike's
robe, then plunged the shard into the old man's chest. He ripped
downward, just as Poverty Ike had done to poor Skye Padilla,
creating a slit that spurted putrid blood over his hand, his
arm, his shoulder. The slit was big enough to admit Mark's fingers, which were quickly growing talons now, and he tore out a
fist-sized chunk of Poverty Ike's ribcage.

The old vampire yowled with pain, shattering the leaded windows of the suite. His hands flew to Mark's wrists and tried in
vain to push them away. Bellona Drumgule screeched, and
would have leapt onto Mark if Kristen hadn't grabbed her and
hurled her through the window, shattering the medieval trefoils
in a blizzard of wood and lead.

"Kill him, Mark!" Kristen screamed. "For God's sake, *kill*
him!"

Mark heard the whump of Mrs. Drumgule's body on the paving stones in the drive below. *"Root it out . . . !"* Somewhere in
the millennium-old body of Lord Yesterday lived a slug, Mark
knew, and he meant to find it and rip it out by its filthy roots.

iv

Tressa stared up at the second-floor landing where Skip
Gestern stood in his shredded smoking jacket, covered with
blood, his eye hanging out of his head. Smiling grotesquely, he
spread his arms and metamorphosed into a beast similar to that
which Mark Lansen had become on two occasions, a slimy thing
with glaring golden eyes and a cavernous mouth full of enamel
spikes.

"This is not a primo vampire," whispered Father Le Fanu,
holding tight to Tressa's elbow. "This is an underling, an offspring. He means to stop us from ascending the stairs. We can
fight him with magic."

Then insanity erupted. The night came alive with screams the
likes of which Tressa had never heard in her life. She herself

screamed when Brett Omdahl tried to climb up her back in panic. Gretchen's wheelchair hummed as she whirled around and headed for the front foyer. But then Gretchen halted, turned the chair around, and glided back to the foot of the stairs.

"The duel has started," whispered Le Fanu, himself pale in the glow of flashlights. "We must go up there—quickly!"

"But what about—?" Tressa pointed to the second-floor landing, only to see that Skip Gestern was no longer there.

"He has joined the fight," said the priest. "There isn't much time. Brett, you must carry Gretchen in your arms. Leave her chair here."

The four of them quickly thumped up the curving staircase, their flashlight beams dancing across paneled walls and displays of medieval weaponry. Tressa clutched Father Le Fanu's sleeve as she climbed, and Brett toted Gretchen like a favorite stuffed animal.

V

Mark Lansen and Poverty Ike hung from the ceiling, locked in mortal combat, each howling and shrieking like beasts of some alien world. Mark had managed to sink his claw deep into the old monster's body, where he groped and searched among mis-shapen organs for the thing he knew lived there—a slug that was a brother to the one that lived inside himself.

But Lord Yesterday's mental tentacles invaded Mark's head. They tweaked and pinched at his spiritual processes, injected Poverty Ike's will where Mark's will lived. They tore at his values, his principles, his morals. They broadcast living nightmares and lies and hallucinations that sometimes caused Mark's body to twist and gyrate in mad spasms, and occasionally made his heart freeze up and stop beating.

Mark lashed out with teeth and claws. He ripped and swiped at Poverty Ike's fierce golden eyes. He sliced through the banded arteries of Poverty Ike's neck, spraying blood in all directions. He bit strips of flesh from Poverty Ike's back and shoulders, all the time probing and groping with the claw buried deep in the old monster's guts.

Skip Gestern tried to join the fray on his father's side, but Kristen ambushed him from the ceiling and sank her teeth deep into his face. Skip screeched and threw her off, and would have pounced on her if Gautier Le Fanu hadn't swept into the room. The old man grabbed Skip by the forearm and flung him against the stone chimney over the fireplace, where he stuck like a moth smashed against a windshield. Le Fanu raised his boom box and shouted some words in an ancient language, generating another burst of mind-wrenching static. A snake of dazzling green light shot out from the speakers and quickly spun itself around Skip Gestern's body, held him tight against the chimney until detonating in a shower of sparks that left behind nothing of the vampire.

Le Fanu advanced to the center of the room and stood fearlessly beneath the battling Mark Lansen and Lord Yesterday. Mark heard the priest's voice in his head, telling him something he already knew: *Lord Yesterday is winning. He is destroying you with his mind.*

"I *know* that!" Mark roared, shaking loose plaster with his volume. "Feel free to jump right in, Walt! Now is a good time, believe me!"

Lord Yesterday tightened his stranglehold on Mark's reason, and Mark felt himself weakening, his mind choking. Le Fanu set down his boom box and reached high over his head to wrap his fingers around Lord Yesterday's skull. Webs of green light skittered and crawled between his fingers, then spread out to invade Lord Yesterday's golden eyes. Mark felt the stranglehold on his own mind weaken. He felt a writhing in the old vampire's innards, which signaled a disconnection between the slug and its host.

Mark's fingers closed around the foul thing, and he ripped it out, a slippery, undulating creature that looked for all the world like a monstrous garden slug, except for the slitted golden eyes at the ends of its stalks.

vi

Tressa saw the vampire fall from the ceiling and land at the feet of Gautier Le Fanu, who stood bathed in an eerie glow. Lord Yesterday shuddered and convulsed on the blood-soaked carpet, his body ripped and mutilated by Mark's teeth and claws. He reverted gradually to human form, and Tressa recognized him as Poverty Ike—the *late* Poverty Ike, the real Clovis Gestern. His was the face that had appeared in an obituary in the *Oldenburg Clarion*, dated July 31, 1935.

Mark, too, plopped to the floor and reverted slowly to his normal shape. Tressa wanted to run to him, to throw her arms around him, but he still clutched the undulating slug in his left hand. He raised the dripping thing to Le Fanu, his eyes round with wonder and disgust.

"What do we do now?" he whispered.

Father Le Fanu turned slowly to face Tressa, Brett, and Gretchen, who huddled arm in arm in the door of the suite. He gave a gentle smile, then pulled a handkerchief from his pocket and wiped a spot of gore from his wire-rimmed glasses. He walked slowly to where Kristen Lansen crouched near the bed and bent low, touching her pretty blond head lightly with his hand.

"Don't cry, my child," he said. "I will rid you of the abomination inside you." Then he cupped her head in his hands, gazed into her tearful eyes, and wrenched her jaws apart with his bare hands. Before Mark could draw a breath to scream, Le Fanu plunged his hand into the girl's quivering innards and ripped out a squealing, wriggling creature nearly identical to the one Mark held in his own hand. Kristen was dead before her ruined head hit the carpet.

Choking and gagging, Tressa watched as Gautier Le Fanu walked back to stand face to face with Mark. Mark's cheeks were awash with new tears mingled with smeared blood—Lord Yesterday's blood, his own blood, and Skye Padilla's. His sister had died before his eyes, and he was barely able to stand. "Wasn't there some other way?" he asked Le Fanu. "Couldn't you have saved her somehow?"

"There was no other way, my son."

Mark went to his knees, but he still managed to hold the slug up to Le Fanu, as if it were an offering, a precious thing. Le Fanu took it from him. The priest's mouth widened grotesquely, and he shoved first one slug into it, then the other. He chewed them with abominable squishing sounds, and the slugs mewled as they died. When Le Fanu turned around, his eyes were golden.

"Please, God, *nooooooo* . . ." breathed Tressa, her heart weltering. "Don't let this be!"

When Le Fanu smiled, he did so with long, razored teeth.

vii

Using his last calories of strength, Mark reached out with his mind and found entry into Le Fanu's. He knew now why he'd been unable to catch glimpses of the old priest's thoughts—Le Fanu was a primo vampire like himself. Le Fanu could shield his mind as easily as an ordinary person breathes, when he concentrated on it. At this moment, though, Le Fanu saw no reason to shield his mind, and Mark read it like a storybook.

Gautier Le Fanu was a vampire who masqueraded as a vampire hunter, an imaginative and effective ploy that had served him well over the centuries. He was indeed a defrocked priest, whom the Vatican had excommunicated for heresy and witchcraft in 1722. He was also the ancient enemy of Lord Yesterday, whom he considered—

"A fool!" said Le Fanu, turning back to Mark. He'd detected Mark's intrusion. "I considered him a fool, monsieur, because he believed that vampires could one day live openly among normal mortals. He even believed that vampires could involve themselves in public affairs, become political leaders. Worst of all, he intended to create a legion of fertile primo vampires, who would procreate a whole new race."

"Why was this so foolish?" Mark asked.

"Think about it, monsieur. To live openly among mortals is to invite the mortals' fury. Throughout history, whenever a vampire's identity has become known, mobs have formed, burnings have occurred. When humans have failed to kill vampires through conventional means, they have procured the services of genuine hunters and sorcerers, people who know the secrets of killing vampires. If Lord Yesterday had succeeded in founding a race of primo vampires, the reaction of the mortals would have been sweeping and extreme. Every vampire on earth would have been hunted down and killed. This is why I have fought him for so long. This is why I have struggled to foil his schemes throughout the centuries, because his idiocy would have resulted in the extermination of the few remaining vampires on earth."

"Kyleen LeBreaux worked for you, didn't she?"

"Indeed, she did, monsieur. If she had been a competent witch, you would have been dead long ago. As it was, she fell in love with you and put off the necessary action until it was too late. The Blood Star reached its high cycle, and you began to feel the stirrings that every primo vampire feels when he reaches your level of maturity. Kyleen LeBreaux could not have killed you at that stage."

"I suppose you'll kill me now."

"I have no choice, monsieur. You may consider it a favor. You yourself told me that you would rather die than live with the slug inside you. I shall do for you what I did for your sister."

"Then you'll let the others go?"

Le Fanu rendered a wide, toothy smile that was somehow regretful. "Alas, I cannot grant you this, monsieur. For the sake of all other vampires in the world, I must kill them. They know the truth, you see. They know that vampires exist, and one of them may succeed in convincing someone else of that fact. This, of course, could be most detrimental to the vampire community. We live hidden, silent lives. We choose our victims carefully and seldom kill anyone, though I must confess that I took too much of Velma Selvig's blood. We cause sickness, yes, an occasional suicide, but most of us disdain the murderous predation that made our ancestors so infamous."

"But there are other people in Oldenburg who know about this. What about the Baylisses? What about—" He thought of his mother, Marta, and immediately regretted it. She knew that vampires existed, and now Le Fanu knew that she knew, having heard his thoughts. "You can't kill them *all*," blurted Mark, but then he realized that, yes, Le Fanu could indeed kill them all.

"Already dead, I regret to inform you," answered Le Fanu apologetically, "though there is yet one more, a physician named Schell. I will finish him off tonight and be gone back to France by the light of morning."

More grief yawned in Mark's heart, but he couldn't cry, because he needed the energy for one last battle. He knew he couldn't win it, so drained was he from the fight with Lord Yesterday, but he had to try. He had to try to save Tressa, Tad, and the others.

"Very foolish of you, monsieur," said Le Fanu, having heard his intentions. "You will only cause yourself more agony. Why not go quietly?" He reached down and touched Mark's face gently with a talon.

viii

Sam Darkenwald stumbled through the front door of the mansion, holding Bob Gammage's Sig Sauer in one fist, a torch in the other. He'd found the gun on the stone floor outside the dungeon where the female vampire had dropped it after wrenching it out of Gammage's hand. He now meant to use it, if he could only find the proper someone to use it on.

He was angrier than he could ever remember being. He yearned to find the old beast who had killed Skye Padilla, because with his dying breath Bob Gammage had charged him to do this. But he also meant to find that ugly bitch, Mrs. Drumgoo, and do something horrible to *her*.

He saw movement in the driveway beyond the porte cochere, and he stumbled toward it, not believing his good fortune. Mrs. Drumgoo lay in a lake of her own blood, having plunged from the second-story window. She wasn't dead, but her torso was crazily twisted, as if her spine was broken, and she appeared capable only of flopping around on the paving stones.

Sam stood over her, pointing the Sig Sauer at her head, not quite able to squeeze the trigger.

"Go ahead," wheezed Mrs. Drumgoo, her face bloody and bruised. "Kill me. I won't use magic to fight you off, and I won't send a demon after you. Do an old woman a favor, and put her out of her misery."

Sam's finger tightened again on the trigger, but still he couldn't go through with it. He'd killed only once in his life—Kyleen LeBreaux, who herself had been trying to take an innocent life. As much as he craved doing it, he couldn't kill the abominable Mrs. Drumgoo.

"Why do you want to die?" he asked, lowering the gun.

"Because I've nothing more to live for. The man I've loved for more than a century is gone. My dreams are dried blood and broken glass. I want only to take my place in hell."

Sam raised the gun again, pointed it at her face, tried again to pull the trigger.

"You're a coward," hissed Mrs. Drumgoo. "A man who can't kill isn't worth his salt."

"I'll give you the gun, and you can do it yourself."

"My arms are paralyzed, you hulking oaf!" She wriggled around so that her face lay directly between Sam's feet. "If you can't do it on your own, then I'll get inside your head and do it for you!"

·"No!" Sam jumped back a few steps, frightened now. "Nobody gets inside my head! Nobody!"

"Wrong, my darlin', bouncin' boy—somebody already has! Remember that night at Poverty Ike's, when you got into the fight with that drunken lout, Gary Bayliss? Poverty Ike himself was inside your head. He read your fears and your weaknesses. He found out you were scared of the FBI, and he made you think that Gary Bayliss was an agent who was following you!"

Despite the excruciating pain it caused, Bellona Drumgule laughed, causing Sam to cringe. "Poverty Ike wanted to get you and that no-good private detective out of the way," she went on, "so he drugged Mr. Robert Gammage and made you start that fight with Gary. You almost succeeded in getting the detective killed, which would've been oh-so-wonderful indeed. We certainly didn't need Gammage poking around here, snooping after Skye, trying to take her away from us." She laughed again, a whistling wheeze. "So you see, someone already *has* been inside your head—Poverty Ike himself, the noble Lord Yesterday. I can't do it as easily as he could, but I can get inside your head if I want to. I can make you do anything I want."

Sam Darkenwald reeled from this revelation, which he knew now to be true. He did remember feeling something in his head that night in the bar, a strange crawling sensation. He'd felt it when he happened to make eye contact with the barkeep, Poverty Ike. He'd attributed it to the electromagnetic radiation that the FBI was beaming at him, but he understood now that Poverty Ike had been the culprit.

"Kill me!" Bellona Drumgule screamed up at him, her doughy face tinged pink with the light of the Blood Star. "Kill me, you clumsy, lurching lunatic! Kill me, or I'll—"

Sam fired twice, and Mrs. Drumgoo was no more.

He turned to stare up at the dinosaurian bulk of Gestern Hall. *I got one of 'em, anyway,* he said prayerfully under his breath. Bob Gammage had died quietly in his arms, drained of blood. Sam's own clothes were sticky with it. *I've done my best, Mr. Gammage.*

He heard screams that he knew couldn't be human, coming from the broken window through which Mrs. Drumgoo had plunged. Though tempted to run away into the night, he trotted back into the porte cochere, feeling that he had a duty to perform.

50

Slugfest

i

Tressa saw Le Fanu's clawed fingers close around Mark's head and felt a stirring in her heart, a fluttering to life of some precious thing that she'd once thought was gone forever. A potent whirring filled her ears, the whine of wood and wind, the turning of a wondrous wheel. Its power enveloped her, vibrated through every cell in her body, and made her feel warm.

"He's going to kill Mark," hissed Brett Omdahl, who stood next to her with Gretchen in his arms. "He lied to us, that bastard! All his talk about needing our goodness, our spiritual strength—it was all bullshit! He only said those things to make us come quietly. He meant to kill Mark all along, and he means to kill us, too, just like he killed Velma! He's a fucking vampire!"

"He won't kill us," said Gretchen evenly. "He can't. We're too strong for him."

Tressa stared at the girl draped in Brett's arms, at her strangely delicate and pretty face, her calm blue eyes. "You *feel* it, don't you, Gretch," she whispered. "The sound, the warmth. It's in me, too."

"Take me to him," Gretchen said to Brett. "It's time to fight."

Brett hesitated a moment, but then walked resolutely toward the center of the candlelit room, while Gretchen clutched her rosary, her eyes closed in prayer, her lips moving. Tressa walked beside them, knowing that she too had a role in this. The whine of the spinning wheel grew louder, and she knew that it had awakened something good in both Gretchen and herself—the power of love, perhaps, against an old and elemental hatred that insisted on duels and wars and the spilling of blood. This goodness was what made human beings more than animals.

Mark's scream of agony cut through the whirring and turned

Tressa's flesh to ice, but still she moved forward with Brett and Gretchen, a soldier going into battle with her comrades. The atmosphere roiled with electrical turbulence, and all the candles stuttered and died. Moonlight poured through the broken window, tinted pink with the fury of the Blood Star.

They reached Le Fanu, who turned from his murderous work to leer at them, his teeth gleaming in the ambient moonlight, his golden eyes beaming hatred. He transformed himself fully now, and his clothing ripped loudly as his body shifted and bent, as his limbs lengthened. He raised a claw, meaning to dispatch the three of them with one slice, but something lunged onto his back. Something else clawed at his legs.

Tressa heard tiny squeals that could have come from the throats of elves or sea monsters or even tiny chiropractors. Somewhere in the distance she heard the laughter of a little girl named Desdi. . . .

Go get 'em, George! Go get 'em, Elmer!

A four-year-old's imaginary friends. The friends who'd stayed with her to the end and beyond.

Tressa's eyes welled with tears of joy, rage, love. She flung herself on the vampire, knowing that Gretchen Bayliss had seized the thing's mind. Through a tingling telepathic connection she knew that Le Fanu was paralyzed by a vision of Joan of Arc standing over him with her sword held high, her trusty Jean d'Aulon at her elbow, and her power beaming forth like lantern light from a distant midnight canyon. . . .

Tressa tore at the vampire's throat, whether with her own hands or the tiny hands of Elmer and George, she didn't know. She felt gobs of flesh come free. She felt the spray of blood in her face, felt Le Fanu thrash uselessly against the saintly goodness of St. Joan. She heard Father Charlie's voice in her head, cheering her on, telling her that she herself was good and worthy of forgiveness, that the world needed people like her.

She saw Mark Lansen rear up to join the fight, his eyes golden, his hands grown into the claws of a demon. She saw him rip into Le Fanu's chest and grope through the gore, saw him pull out a black and wriggling creature that shrieked hellishly as its stringy umbilicals ruptured. She saw Le Fanu thud to the floor like a puppet whose strings had been cut, quivering and dying at last.

Mark instantly reverted to human form, depleted, naked, and

covered with slime. Someone moved past Tressa in the dark, an old woman with hoary hair and rattle-boned limbs. She went straight to Mark, took the slug from him, and plunged it into the glistening wet bag she carried.

ii

Somewhere far away, a repairman ministered to a power line severed by a lightning strike, and the lights came on again in Oldenburg. The lights also came on in Gestern Hall, just as pistol shots reverberated throughout its upper rooms.

Mark bounded into the next room, where his dead father had taken his son. Sam Darkenwald, of all people, stood over the inert body of the late John Lansen, holding Tad close against his chest. Sam had a gun in his hand, and his eyes were wet, and Tad was sobbing uncontrollably.

"The little guy's okay," Sam breathed as Mark grabbed the boy from him. "He's seen more than any kid should ever see, but he's not hurt. I think he'll live through this."

"Leave the boy!" commanded Elspeth Carey from the doorway, where she stood naked, her flesh proud and bloody and peeling away from her bones in places. She held the bulky sack woven of her own skin, inside which the slug struggled furiously. "Your son will be fine with Sam. Come quickly, because we haven't much time. This bag will confine a slug for a while, but not forever."

"What about *him?*" asked Mark, pointing to the rotting corpse of John Lansen. "He looks dead now, but he—"

"He's dead. The magic that rousted him from the grave is gone, having died with the man who wove it."

"I shot him," explained Sam, pointing to the rotting body of John Lansen, "because he was about to kill your boy, Dr. Lansen. I heard the ruckus up here, and when I came through the door, he had his hands around the kid's neck."

Mark handed Tad back to Sam, and the boy blubbered loudly, having no intention of letting his father leave him again. "You've got to stay here for now, Tad Bear," said Mark, himself naked, slimy, and smeared with blood. "I'll be back soon, I promise. Uncle Sam will take care of you. Everything will be fine, you'll see." He kissed the boy's cheek and dashed into the next room, closing the door so he couldn't hear his son's cries.

He snatched a sheet from the bed and wiped himself of blood and slime, then quickly pulled on his clothes. Elspeth led the four of them down the stairs and out the rear door of the mansion, Mark and Tressa with their arms around each other, shoring each other up, Brett carrying Gretchen.

No one spoke as they plunged into the forest without benefit of flashlights or lanterns. They simply followed the twiggy old woman whose flesh barely clung to her bones for lack of skin. No one asked aloud how she could even be alive, having done this to herself. They simply followed.

She guided them around fallen logs and boulders and patches of holly, somehow kept them from stumbling and colliding with tree trunks, from falling into new brooks generated by the storm. Somehow she brought them to Mesatchie Illihee.

iii

Elspeth limped to the center of the low knoll on which she'd given birth to Mark's mother, and stood still in the pink haze of the Blood Star, holding the bag against her oozing chest. After a silent moment, she beckoned Mark forward, but stopped him before he came too close. "When Lord Yesterday told you that I had held back the truth from you, he was right. I *did* mean for him to take Rita, your mother. And I *did* mean for you to be the vehicle of his destruction."

Mark said nothing. A night bird called from far away, and choirs of insects sang in the thicket. He heard none of these. He heard only Elspeth's voice, the incomprehensible truth.

"I didn't tell you that Poverty Ike was Lord Yesterday, either. I simply thought it was best for you not to know until the final moment, because if you'd known, he would have read it in your mind."

"Did you know who Le Fanu really was?" Mark asked, barely able to speak.

"Yes. In fact, it was I who inspired Father Briggs to contact him. I cast a spell and gave Father Briggs the knowledge of Le Fanu in a dream, made him think that he'd heard of him through a friend in the Vatican. I wanted Father Briggs to summon Le

Fanu, you see, because I knew you couldn't kill Lord Yesterday alone."

"Why did you keep *that* from me? Why didn't you tell me Le Fanu was really a vampire?"

"Because Le Fanu would have read that knowledge in your mind and would have killed you immediately. I needed to make certain that the two of you could work together, don't you see? As for the killing of Le Fanu, I gave you your allies. . . ." She waved a bloody hand, indicating Tressa, Gretchen, and Brett. "Using the magic of the spinning wheel, I *empowered* their minds and souls—do you like that word? *Empowered.* Very popular now—all the politicians are using it." She giggled painfully, and Mark winced. "I drew upon the goodness in each of them," she went on. "Tressa's love for her daughter and her need to atone; Gretchen's piety and devotion to St. Joan. For a brief moment, I gave life and flesh to their noblest dreams and visions, and these were enough to kill Le Fanu—with *your* able assistance, of course."

"Did you do the same for me? Was it a dream or vision that gave me the strength?"

"You must answer that question for yourself, Mark." She tipped her face skyward and gazed at the red gem that hung directly over the knoll, a burning ruby among countless grains of diamond dust. The ancient image of Sahalee Tyee gazed down on them from its perch on a weathered totem pole in the shadow of a hemlock, seemingly alive.

"Surely you know now that you're free," Elspeth said. "Old Clovis Gestern tried mightily to plot your future for you, to bind you to a destiny that *he* wanted for you. But he failed, didn't he? Not even the Spell of the Entrails worked for him. In the end, you chose your own destiny, Mark. You chose that which you knew to be good, despite all the forces arrayed against you."

"But I was still your pawn. I was doing exactly what you wanted me to."

"I manipulated you, yes, but I couldn't decree that you would find the goodness within yourself to do the right thing. You are what you are, Mark, and you are what you've *chosen* to be."

Mark bowed his head, so tired now that he could barely stand. He shivered. "But I have a slug inside me. I'm still a primo vampire."

Elspeth stared at him, and after a moment raised the squirming bag over her head. Droplets of blood oozed from it and spattered her face as she whispered an ancient charm.

The fury of the Blood Star intensified. A ray shot out directly from it and centered on Elspeth Carey, a celestial spotlight. The energy in the air made Mark's skin itch and his ears ring. He glanced back at Tressa, Gretchen, and Brett and saw them huddling on the edge of the clearing, terrified, covering their ears with their hands. When he looked at Elspeth again, he himself flinched, for she'd lowered the sack of skin and was holding it out to him. In it he saw the golden-eyed slug that he'd wrenched from the gullet of Gautier Le Fanu. It appeared to be afraid of *him*.

Elspeth Carey didn't need to tell him that a moment of truth had arrived, that the Blood Star had achieved the zenith of its cycle. This was his one chance to expel the evil that lived inside him. Not for another hundred years would such an opportunity arrive.

"Root it out, Dr. Lansen . . . !"

But he was so tired, so bone-weary. He wanted nothing more than to fall down and simply sleep in a bed of wet devil's club, to dream of Viking conquests and Templars' crusades, to revel in fantasies of bygone ages. He wanted only to rest.

But he couldn't do that.

He felt his jaw unhinge like a boa constrictor's, felt a mass taking shape in his gut. It undulated and twisted, mashing his organs excruciatingly against the walls of his abdomen. He couldn't breathe. He choked and retched, but nothing came out. He clawed at his throat and pounded his gut with his fists. His lungs screamed for air, his brain for oxygen, and the world spun crazily.

Somewhere in the chaos of his being glowed an ember that flared bright and glorious, ignited by Mark's determination to *choose*. He *chose* to make it grow into an inferno, *chose* to make it race through his mind and body, like a wildfire racing through a drought-stricken forest. He willed his body to reject the seed that Clovis Gestern had planted in it.

The slug spewed from his mouth and landed in the bag woven of Elspeth's skin. Elspeth immediately bound the bag up tight and jerked it away.

Mark collapsed as pain shot through his organs and bones. He lay with his cheek against a pillow of wet ferns while his body righted itself, while his jaws reconnected. He forced open his eyes and saw Elspeth holding high the squirming bag, chanting to the heavens, singing in a voice as strong as steel.

The whirring of Elspeth's spinning wheel resonated through the forest, drowning the night songs of birds and bugs, rattling the leaves and limbs of trees. Mark saw the spinning wheel in his mind, standing in the dark corridor of Gestern Hall, turning wildly and shaking the foundation of the mansion with its vibrations. Elspeth called to him, her voice barely audible against the fury: "Don't worry about your son! He is not a primo vampire, and the slug within him will never mature if he never receives the first taste. Your son will live his life as a normal man . . . !"

But he'll have abnormally perfect teeth, thought Mark.

A cloud of red light coalesced and engulfed Elspeth and the bag. Sparks flew up from the knoll of Mesatchie Illihee into the heavens, where bright clouds gathered and swirled to form a supernatural hurricane. The ground rumbled, and a wind rose. Branches bent and snapped with ear-splitting cracks. Thunder cannonaded through the night sky.

"Take care, Mark Lansen!" Elspeth shouted. "You may find this hard to believe, but I love you, just as your mother loves you! We'll *always* love you . . . !"

Trees and bushes heaved back and forth in rushing waves as a globe of embers whirled in the center of the clearing, where it hovered for barely a heartbeat, then exploded with force enough to suck the air from the lungs of the people who cowered nearby. Its remnants swirled into the vortex of the hurricane above, leaving behind no trace of Elspeth. She was gone, her atoms scattered to the cosmos. The slugs too were gone, forever beyond harming another child of the earth.

Silence descended, and within moments the insects of the forest had begun to sing again.

EPILOGUE

Tigard, Oregon

The Tigard Public Library served the presentable Portland suburb of Tigard, Oregon, which lay between the equally presentable suburbs of Beaverton and Lake Oswego. The building boasted clean, contemporary lines and sweeping expanses of glass. It stood on a manicured campus that it shared with the police department, the city manager's office, and a flock of mallards who lived in the pond out back.

On the evening of October 31, 1991, a long Cadillac limousine glided into the circular drive in front of the library and halted. The passenger removed his expensive Serengeti sunglasses and glanced at his watch, which told him that it was a few minutes after seven o'clock. He punched the intercom button and spoke to his chauffeur. "I may be here a while, Morty, so go ahead and have yourself a butt. But do it outside, okay? You know how cigarette smoke affects my sinuses."

"No sweat, Mr. Darkenwald. You won't smell a thing."

While walking to the front door of the library, Sam breathed deeply of the crisp autumn air. He glanced up and saw a thin cloud crawl across the face of a moon that was nearly full. *Perfect Halloween,* he thought, remembering his boyhood. *I wish I could go trick-or-treating again.*

Suddenly he was wading through a knot of jostling children dressed in colorful Halloween costumes and carrying sacks full of candy—witches, clowns, fairy princesses, Batmen, even a pair of ETs, all under the shepherding eye of two young women. One of the women bumped into him and smiled her apology.

"Story night," she said, as if this explained the turmoil. "Special costume party for Halloween. I think every kid in town is here, under the age of six."

Sam grinned and watched her herd some strays out the door. The kids piled into a van and were off to other holiday festivities.

This is good, thought Sam, *but it can't take the place of trick-or-treating. Too bad things have gotten the way they are—razor blades in the caramel apples, strychnine in the cookies. Parents are scared, and Halloweening just isn't like it used to be.*

He went to the checkout desk and approached a pretty, dark-haired woman, who, like the other library staffers, was in costume. She was Little Red Riding Hood, and her basket of goodies sat on the counter. Sam asked her where the children's storyteller did his thing.

"I'm sorry," she answered, "but the party ended a few minutes ago. We do this every Halloween, you know, from five-thirty to seven—stories, goodies, games. Was your child a participant?"

"No, I don't have any kids. I just want to chat with the guy who tells the stories, that's all. He's an old friend of mine."

The young woman directed him to the children's story corner, which was in the rear of the building, where a tall, kindly-looking man with gray hair was packing some notes into a briefcase. Sam approached quietly, his expensive topcoat slung over one arm. The man didn't see him until he was but three feet away.

"Sam!" Mark Lansen reached out, clutched Sam's hand in both of his. "Sam Darkenwald, is that *you?*"

"It's me, doc. Amazing what a good suit of clothes will do for a man, isn't it?"

Mark gazed at him a long moment, grinning, and suggested that they retire to one of the library's study rooms, where they could talk. On the way, he ducked into the library staff room and procured two cups of coffee.

Sam sat at the table in the study room and sipped from his cup. "Well, I won't keep you in suspense," he said. "I won the lottery three years ago—thirteen million dollars. Took it in a lump sum and paid the taxes up front. I'll never work again, and I'll never eat out of a damn Dumpster, either."

"My God, Sam, that's great! That's absolutely wonderful! Congratulations!" Mark lifted his coffee in salute.

"I can't take any credit for it. Old Elspeth Carey, your granny, gave me the winning numbers. She handed me an envelope the night Bob Gammage and I sneaked into Gestern Hall, and—" Sam saw a tight, cringing look spread across Mark's lined face, and he cut himself off. Clearly the mention of Gestern Hall hurt. "Hell, I'm sorry, doc. I didn't mean to dredge up bad memories."

"It's okay, Sam. Finish your story. I can handle it."

"Like I said, old Ellie gave me the winning numbers of the lottery—I figure she got 'em in her scrying mirror, looking into the future. She gave them to me for services rendered, or something like that. To be honest with you, I don't quite recall *why* she gave them to me. Anyway, I played 'em, and here I am, a rich old fart. So how are *you?*"

"I'm fine. Deidre and I have been divorced for over two years now, and Tad's living with her. He just turned twelve, and I see him twice a month. He's growing like a weed. Wants to be a psychiatrist." Mark took a picture out of his wallet and handed it to Sam. Thaddeus Lansen was a lean and handsome kid with an adolescent pimple or two. He had clear hazel eyes and perfect white teeth, just like his father, and an open smile suggested no lingering effects of the ordeal he'd suffered at Gestern Hall.

"Kids are resilient," said Mark, putting the picture away. "They bounce back faster than we old farts, and they do a better job of forgetting. Tad doesn't even have any bad dreams anymore. In fact, I myself don't have more than one or two a week."

"Look, Mark—do you mind if I call you Mark?"

"Sam, I'd be honored if you called me Mark. I don't even care if you get my last name right. You never could."

"I'm on my medication regularly now, and I'm rational as a rabbi. You're Mark *Lan*sen, professor of history."

Former professor of history, Mark corrected.

"Thought you might be interested to know that I don't worry about the FBI anymore," said Sam, "especially now that I'm rich. The feds don't bother rich people these days. Anyway, I'm here because I've heard how tough things were for you after that night when—" He cleared his throat, mulled his choice of words. "That *night*. I know there was a long murder investigation."

"I came out of it okay. There were bodies everywhere, as you well know. But nobody found any real evidence to charge anybody with anything."

"You lost your job at the university."

"They suspended me, pending the outcome of the murder investigations. The suspension became more or less permanent, even though I was never actually indicted."

"And Tressa lost hers, too, right?"

True. Mark explained that she'd eventually found a position with a small community theater in northern California, where she and Gretchen now lived. He visited them whenever he could, and they were doing fine. Brett Omdahl, too, was doing fine—he'd just started his sophomore year at Oregon State. He paused a moment, deep in thought, then ventured the idea that he and Tressa might even hook up as lovers again, after enough time had passed. Something in his eyes, though, said this would never happen.

"Mark, I'm not going to beat around the bush any longer. You need money, right? You've been doing odd jobs, I hear, some tutoring, a little storytelling, nothing that really makes you any money, am I right?"

Mark admitted that he was just barely getting by.

"Then let me help you out. God knows I've got more loot than I can ever use. I'll give you as much as you need to get on your feet again. You can pay it back when you get around to it, or *never* pay it back—I don't care."

"That's good of you, Sam, but—"

Suddenly the door of the study room opened, revealing two figures, a male and a female. Both wore elaborate vampire costumes—white pancake makeup, blackened eye sockets, satin capes and phony fangs that dripped theatrical blood. The male—Sam judged him a high school kid from his voice—asked when the storytelling would begin. Mark explained that the Halloween party had already ended. Five-thirty to seven, every year.

"That's a bummer, man. We heard the guy's really good, you know? We heard his stories aren't just for little kids."

Mark advised them to keep an eye on the library bulletin board. The storyteller often helped out when the children's librarian had trouble filling her events calendar. The "vampires" thanked him and backed out the door, leaving a strangely uncomfortable silence in their wake.

"What about it?" pressed Sam, getting back to the matter at hand. "You're entitled to a little happiness, aren't you? Wouldn't you like to travel, maybe go to Europe and visit some of the castles you used to lecture about . . . ?"

"I'm happy the way I am, Sam. Oh, my hair is prematurely gray, and I've got the wrinkles of someone over fifty, but I have a modest little house not far from here, and I'm comfortable in it. I've made some friends. Life is quiet, but it's good. I'll be fine."

Sam sat silent a moment, then stood. "Well, I tried. Your life is your own, obviously. If you ever decide to start living it again, give me a call." He took a card from the breast pocket of his expensive suit and laid it on the table. "Don't get up. I know the way out. Stay happy, okay, Mark?" He opened the door and put one foot over the threshold, but turned back again. Mark smiled at him in his kindly, wrinkled way and thanked him. "Promise me you'll call if you decide to start living again."

"I promise," Mark said.

Sam pulled the door shut behind him, and felt a little sad. Without knowing precisely why, he understood that he'd just seen the last of Dr. Mark Lansen. On his way out of the library, he stopped and stared a moment at a hand-lettered sign tacked to the bulletin board. In bold orange-and-black letters it called on kids of all ages to attend the Tigard Public Library's annual Halloween party. Special treat this year, it promised—a story told by Tigard's favorite storyteller, Poverty Mark.

Sam shook his head and went out into the crisp autumn night.

In the tradition of Stephen King and Clive Barker...

JOHN GIDEON

__GREELY'S COVE   0-515-10508-2/$5.99

The first miracle in Greely's Cove was a joyful one—the
sudden cure of a young autistic boy. The other miracles
were different, stranger and darker. Now every man and
woman in Greely's Cove is terrified by evidence of human
sacrifice...and resurrection.

*Don't miss John Gideon's newest
spellbinding novel of mortal sins,
immortal secrets, and unearthly seduction...*

__GOLDEN EYES   0-425-14287-6/$5.99

Portland University professor Mark Lansen is researching
the history of his hometown of Oldenberg. But what Dr.
Lansen discovers is an evil connected to Oldenberg's
Gestern Hall—an ancient house that was transported stone
by stone from Europe...and that is transforming the
residents of Oldenberg into vampires.

Payable in U.S. funds. No cash orders accepted. Postage & handling: $1.75 for one book, 75¢
for each additional. Maximum postage $5.50. Prices, postage and handling charges may
change without notice. Visa, Amex, MasterCard call 1-800-788-6262, ext. 1, refer to ad # 508

Or, check above books and send this order form to: The Berkley Publishing Group 390 Murray Hill Pkwy., Dept. B East Rutherford, NJ 07073 Please allow 6 weeks for delivery.	Bill my: ☐ Visa ☐ MasterCard ☐ Amex _____ (expires) Card#_____ ($15 minimum) Signature_____ Or enclosed is my: ☐ check ☐ money order
Name_____	Book Total $_____
Address_____	Postage & Handling $_____
City_____	Applicable Sales Tax $_____ (NY, NJ, PA, CA, GST Can.)
State/ZIP_____	Total Amount Due $_____

Author of the #1
New York Times Bestseller

DRAGON TEARS
and
MR. MURDER

Dean Koontz

___	MR. MURDER	0-425-14442-9/$6.99
___	THE FUNHOUSE	0-425-14248-5/$6.99
___	DRAGON TEARS	0-425-14003-2/$6.99
___	SHADOWFIRES	0-425-13698-1/$6.99
___	HIDEAWAY	0-425-13525-X/$6.99
___	THE HOUSE OF THUNDER	0-425-13295-1/$6.99
___	COLD FIRE	0-425-13071-1/$6.99
___	WATCHERS	0-425-10746-9/$6.99
___	WHISPERS	0-425-09760-9/$6.99
___	NIGHT CHILLS	0-425-09864-8/$6.99
___	PHANTOMS	0-425-10145-2/$6.99
___	SHATTERED	0-425-09933-4/$6.99
___	DARKFALL	0-425-10434-6/$6.99
___	THE FACE OF FEAR	0-425-11984-X/$6.99
___	THE VISION	0-425-09860-5/$6.99
___	TWILIGHT EYES	0-425-10065-0/$6.99
___	STRANGERS	0-425-11992-0/$6.99
___	THE MASK	0-425-12758-3/$6.99
___	LIGHTNING	0-425-11580-1/$5.99
___	MIDNIGHT	0-425-11870-3/$6.99
___	THE SERVANTS OF TWILIGHT	0-425-12125-9/$6.99
___	THE BAD PLACE	0-425-12434-7/$6.99
___	THE VOICE OF THE NIGHT	0-425-12816-4/$6.99

Payable in U.S. funds. No cash orders accepted. Postage & handling: $1.75 for one book, 75¢ for each additional. Maximum postage $5.50. Prices, postage and handling charges may change without notice. Visa, Amex, MasterCard call 1-800-788-6262, ext. 1, refer to ad # 227c

Or, check above books and send this order form to: The Berkley Publishing Group 390 Murray Hill Pkwy., Dept. B East Rutherford, NJ 07073 Please allow 6 weeks for delivery.	Bill my: ☐ Visa ☐ MasterCard ☐ Amex	(expires)
	Card#_____	
		($15 minimum)
	Signature_____	
	Or enclosed is my: ☐ check ☐ money order	

Name_____ Book Total $_____

Address_____ Postage & Handling $_____

City_____ Applicable Sales Tax $_____
(NY, NJ, PA, CA, GST Can.)

State/ZIP_____ Total Amount Due $_____

THE MOST ACCLAIMED
HORROR DEBUT OF THE YEAR

CURFEW

"A styish novel of the occult...will shake even the most stolid reader."—<u>Publishers Weekly</u>

PHIL RICKMAN

"A powerful book and a thoroughly good horror story...classic stuff."—<u>London Times</u>

A New-Age millionaire thinks that tourists will be drawn to the Welsh town of Crybbe, a former spiritual center, if he restores the standing stones that once surrounded the town. But the people of Crybbe know better. For centuries, their rituals have been keeping an ancient evil at bay. And that dark hunger will not be sated if the stones are replaced.

___ **0-425-14334-1/$5.99**

Payable in U.S. funds. No cash orders accepted. Postage & handling: $1.75 for one book, 75¢ for each additional. Maximum postage $5.50. Prices, postage and handling charges may change without notice. Visa, Amex, MasterCard call 1-800-788-6262, ext. 1, refer to ad #529

Or, check above books and send this order form to: The Berkley Publishing Group 390 Murray Hill Pkwy., Dept. B East Rutherford, NJ 07073 Please allow 6 weeks for delivery.	Bill my: ☐ Visa ☐ MasterCard ☐ Amex Card#_____ (expires) Signature_____ ($15 minimum) Or enclosed is my: ☐ check ☐ money order

Name_____

Address_____

City_____

State/ZIP_____

Book Total $_____

Postage & Handling $_____

Applicable Sales Tax $_____
(NY, NJ, PA, CA, GST Can.)

Total Amount Due $_____